"NO ONE SHALL HEAR HOW WE SPEND THIS NIGHT, MILADY."

"Begone!" Audra cried. "After what you did tonight, you are bold to think I would welcome you into my arms."

She tried to move away, but Lynx's strong hands brought her against his body, which was as unyielding as iron. She averted her face, but his fingers steered her mouth beneath his. She must not want to be with this man who rode with the night to destroy her home, but her body's need to savor his touch silenced all thought. He pressed his mouth against the curve of her throat, and she gasped at the pulse of passion racing through her.

"Have no fear," he murmured.

"I am not frightened of you," she whispered breathlessly. She closed her eyes and brought his mouth to hers.

Harper
Monogram

Ride the
Night Wind

✺ JO ANN FERGUSON ✺

HarperPaperbacks
A Division of HarperCollinsPublishers

HarperPaperbacks   *A Division of* HarperCollins*Publishers*
10 East 53rd Street, New York, N.Y. 10022

Copyright © 1995 by Jo Ann Ferguson
All rights reserved. No part of this book may be used or
reproduced in any manner whatsoever without written
permission of the publisher, except in the case of brief
quotations embodied in critical articles and reviews. For
information address HarperCollins*Publishers,*
10 East 53rd Street, New York, N.Y. 10022.

Cover illustration by Bob Sabin

First printing: February 1995

Printed in the United States of America

HarperPaperbacks, HarperMonogram, and colophon are
trademarks of HarperCollins*Publishers*

❖ 10 9 8 7 6 5 4 3 2 1

*For Jan Hunsicker, Rainy Kirkland,
Janet Kuchler, and Judy Turner,
dear friends, great writers, and fellow veterans of
the good fight. Thanks for listening and believing.
And especially thanks, Rainy, for saying,
"Why don't you try a medieval?"*

Ride the Night Wind

1

"Sister Audra?"

The young woman, who was surrounded by a half-dozen children, paused in the midst of the story she had been telling and smiled at a plump woman who was hurrying toward her with undue haste. Both women were dressed identically in the drab robes of their religious order, but the slender one's blue eyes brightened her appearance.

She looked up the aisle between the pews in the chapel. Why was Sister Margaret disrupting the children's lesson with such a frantic call? It was too lovely a day to hurry. Sunlight flowed through the uneven panes in the mullioned windows to light the last few pews, but was lost in the smoke of a handful of candles on the altar behind the children. Remnants of incense clung to the air, stifling any hint of freshness from beyond the oak door.

"The abbess wishes to see you," Sister Margaret said, nearly out of breath. "She implores you to hurry."

Sister Audra's smile faltered as she stood, her hand resting a moment on the head of one of the children. Sister Margaret never rushed about on a warm day unless something was horribly amiss. She wondered what might be wrong now. Then she relaxed. The abbess was sure to have an explanation to allay this sudden pulse of dread.

"Stay with the children," Sister Audra said. "Tend them carefully so they cause no mischief."

A grim expression on her round face, Sister Margaret nodded. "Go and return as swiftly as possible."

Sister Audra fought not to smile as she left the chapel at a more decorous pace. Although Sister Margaret had skills to coax vegetables and herbs to grow in the most barren ground, she was discomfited by childish laughter. The same sound filled Sister Audra's heart with wordless joy.

Her soft slippers made no sound in the cavernous gallery. Her rosary beads rattled at the waist of her somber tunic that fell to the floor. Around her face, a novice's wimple concealed all but one curl of her ebony hair. She pushed it beneath the unbleached linen as she looked through one of the windows to admire the flower garden.

It was the most glorious spot in the abbey. Unlike the cool gray tint of the stone walls and the pews, the flowers were a tapestry of colors, each blossom a testament to the beauty that touched the abbey so infrequently. Here, she reminded herself, the splendor must come from within, not from ornaments. Yet she could not help delighting in the flowers' pagan exuberance.

Sister Audra pushed such defiant thoughts aside. They had no place in the head of a novice who was soon to take her vows as a sister of this order. Pausing before the abbess's door, she surrendered to a smile. When she first came to Clarendon abbey, the abbess had frightened her. Tall and imposing like one of the stern statues of the saints, the abbess possessed a heart as enormous as her generous soul. She cared for each of the sisters, novices, and children in the abbey as if they had come from her own body.

Sister Audra pushed the recalcitrant lock of hair back beneath her wimple again when she heard the command to enter through the thick door. The abbess never tolerated dishevelment among her novices. Maybe today was the day Sister Audra had waited for—the day when the abbess deemed it proper for her to take her vows. Although Sister Audra had been ready to speak that pledge for more years than her impatient heart wished to recall, the abbess had quietly told her again and again that the time was not yet right.

The door's leather hinges creaked softly as she opened it. Sunlight was banned from the abbess's office. The single window was almost hidden behind the statue of their patron saint. Shadows claimed each corner and darkened the rushes on the stone floor. A single candle burned on the long table in front of a crucifix.

Crossing to where the abbess sat on a low bench, Sister Audra knelt and kissed the ring on the old woman's withered hand. The abbess stroked her head as gently as Sister Audra had the child's.

"Welcome, dear sister," the woman murmured. Her smile creased her wrinkled face anew.

"You sent for me?" Sister Audra asked.

The abbess rose slowly and motioned to her right, where three men stepped out of the shadows. A gasp caught in Sister Audra's abruptly arid throat. On their dusty surcoats, the men wore the colors of the earl of Bredonmere. Years had passed since she last saw the crisscrossed scarlet and dark blue interspersed with gold, but the design was burned into her soul.

The gray-haired man dropped to his knees before her, and the two younger men followed like well-trained dancers. Taking her hem, the gray-haired man pressed it to his forehead. "Milady, I vow my arm and my life to you as I vowed it to your father and your brothers."

A chill pierced her with the force of a broadsword. This could not be true. No one should be pledging fealty to her. Audra was the least daughter, the one no one had minded doing without when she was sent to Clarendon Abbey. She had a half-dozen brothers and nearly as many sisters older than she. If these men were coming to her, calling her by the title she had never expected to hear spoken to her, that meant her family was dead.

All of them.

"No," she choked as she pulled away. "You must be mistaken."

The abbess put her gnarled hands on Sister Audra's shoulders. "'Tis no mistake. Listen to me, my child. Here you have learned a reverence for God and the obligation of service. Now you must accept that God's will is that you serve elsewhere. Your family's retainers have come to you in need. Can you turn your back on them?"

"This is my home," she whispered. This was all wrong! It must be some grievous error.

"Bredonmere Manor will be your home," the abbess said, her voice firm. "Serve these men and the people they represent as you would have served

Clarendon Abbey. Remember the lessons you have been taught. They will guide you."

"You are sending me away?"

"I would send away no one in these dangerous times. If you wish to stay, I would not deny you sanctuary." Holding up her hand to forestall Audra's answer, she added, "Think well before you speak what is in your heart. Think of the reasons that compelled these men to journey so many leagues to you."

Long ago, long before this year of 1350, she had severed all but blood ties with her family and Bredonmere Manor. She could remember little of the manor, which was ruled—which had been ruled—by the earl of Bredonmere. An indistinct image of the room where she had slept with her siblings on pallets wafted into her mind. Not much clearer was the day her mother had told her farewell and sent her to the abbey. She could not picture her mother's face.

Pain clogged her throat. This must be a wicked dream! Surely this was meant to be a test to prove herself worthy of becoming a true sister at the abbey.

She looked at the men who were still kneeling. The gray-haired man's gaze rose to meet hers, and she pressed her hand to the crucifix on her chest. His obvious agony stripped away her foolish hopes. She closed her eyes. No comfort soothed the jagged edges of her tortured soul. Her family . . . all of them dead.

"How?" she whispered. She doubted she could speak louder.

The man answered, "'Twas the Black Death that stalks every manor and cottage. Your father, the earl, bless his eternal soul, was taken only after he buried all his sons. More than half of the manor's people are dead." He took her icy hand in his and held it to his forehead in the ancient pose of obedience. "Milady, I beg you to come home. You are the earl's only surviving child. We need you, for you are of the blood, to lead us against the troubles stalking Bredonmere."

Audra wanted to turn away from his fervent plea. She knew that if these men had had another choice, she would have remained forgotten in Clarendon Abbey. They had no other choice.

Nor did she, for obligations of blood must outweigh the longings in her heart.

"I shall come with you to Bredonmere Manor," she said in a muffled voice. "I shall do my best to lead you."

The men's shoulders sagged with relief, but they remained on their knees. Belatedly Sister Audra recalled they were waiting for her permission to rise. Telling them to do so, she wondered how many months would past before she became accustomed to having others await her orders.

"We must not delay long," the leader said gruffly.

"You are—"

"Crandall, your steward." His eyes appraised her with the same candor as his words. He named the youngest man Fleming and the redheaded man Shaw, the commander of the manor's men-at-arms. "We must not delay," he said again.

"Why?"

He looked at the abbess, who had spoken with uncharacteristic sharpness. "With so many dead, the villeins threaten to claim some of the earl's lands for their own. With one of the blood in the manor, we can prevent that."

"You are wise."

"We have learned through cruel lessons."

Sister Audra struggled to think the simplest

thought. Her whole family dead! When she saw the abbess nod at Crandall's urging to hurry, Sister Audra reached for the door. A gentle order stayed to her hand.

"Not back to the hall of novices, milady," said the abbess.

Audra stared at her. Exchanging her title as "Sister" for another announced the incredible changes ahead of her. She tried to breathe, but her chest felt as heavy as if an ox trod upon it. "I wish only to tell my sisters good-bye. And the children! They must not think that I have abandoned them."

"Long farewells leave deeper wounds. Let the heat of pain deaden your heart-deep grief. The sisters of this abbey are no longer your sisters. You are Lady Audra Travers, countess of Bredonmere and vassal to His Majesty King Edward III." The abbess motioned for her to kneel. Behind her, Audra heard the men do the same. The abbess murmured a prayer over their heads. "God bless you, my dearest child. Do as you know you must, milady, and never allow anyone to convince you not to follow your heart. It will guide you well."

Crandall stood and said, with obvious impatience, "Milady?"

Audra rose, looking down into the abbess's eyes. When she saw the old woman's sorrow and acceptance, she glanced once more around the room, trying to store the memory of each corner in her heart. Nothing would ease the pain of this parting, but her back was straight beneath the weight of her sorrow as she left the only home she could remember.

Crandall led his lady out into the yard where their horses waited. Her fingers on his hand trembled like caged butterflies, but her face was serene.

He smiled. She was just like the earl. This boded well. Lord Travers had never let another be privy to his thoughts. His strong features were softer on his daughter's face, but her eyes were as blue and, he hoped, as all-seeing. The earl of Bredonmere had observed everything around him and used what he had learned to his advantage. If his daughter was to have even the slightest chance of holding Bredonmere now, she must do the same.

He sobered at the grim thought. After a decade of serving as the earl's steward, only he and the earl and his countess had known where the youngest Travers child was. Never had anyone expected he would need to find her. He shivered as he imagined what would have happened if he had been stricken with the scourge as well. It would have been his final responsibility to pass his knowledge to a trusted man who could bring Lady Audra back to govern the fief.

"We should complete our journey in two days if the weather remains pleasant," he said to fill the awkward silence.

When the slight woman looked at him, he nearly staggered as he saw the depths of her anguish. His respect for her doubled. In the manor, hysterical weeping had announced each death, but his new lady, who had lost more than anyone else, had braved the tidings with quiet courage.

"We may delay a few minutes if you wish to—" He did not know what to say. Life behind convent walls was nothing he understood. It was even possible his lady knew how to read and write, skills her father had not possessed.

"It is the abbess's will that I depart immediately."

His heart threatened to splinter anew. Lady

Audra might have her father's face, but her melodious
voice was an echo of Lady Sabina's.

"But you are a countess!" blurted Fleming. "You
can do as you wish."

Crandall scowled at the young pup. Fleming
shifted uneasily, his light brown hair bouncing on the
wool cape tied about his shoulders.

"To you, I may be Lady Audra T-T-Travers." She
winced, but continued in a stronger voice, "In Clarendon Abbey, as a sister, I relinquished my will to the
needs of the abbey."

Crandall said, "That has changed, milady. Your
will is ours now."

"I know," she answered softly.

He wondered if she mourned more for her dead
family or her dead dreams. Mayhap she did not yet
understand the breadth of her legacy. Bredonmere
Manor was the most powerful holding in the heart of
England. King Edward had often called its earl to
court to seek his counsel. William Travers had been
with the king when the plague exploded through Bredonmere. After rushing home, he had arrived in time
to attend the funerals for his wife and eldest son.
Then the earl had sickened and died.

Crandall tried to suppress his misgivings. If he
had remained silent, no one would have suspected
anyone with Travers's blood remained alive. There
had been rumors that King Edward would offer Bredonmere to Gifford deWode. The baron was a distant relative of the Travers family, but his line traced
from an illegitimate union. He would have been the
perfect choice to hold Bredonmere, save for one
thing.

Lady Audra Travers.

Crandall lifted her onto a chestnut horse. Shaw

had been vehement that the new countess must arrive at the keep on her father's mount. Handing her the reins, he turned to his own horse. Then he heard a shriek. He whirled, his hand on the broadsword at his waist. Lady Audra was sitting on the ground, astonishment on her pretty face.

"Milady, forgive me," Crandall murmured as he brushed dirt off her cotehardie. In horror, he pulled his hands away from her dark gown. Never must he forget that she was his countess. "I thought you were well settled in the saddle."

"The beast moved." She winced as she touched her elbow.

"Crandall?" called Fleming softly, and crooked his finger.

Shaw snickered as Fleming described what they had seen. Slowly, Crandall turned to look at his lady. What a witless fool he had been! But how was he to have guessed? Maybe Fleming was wrong.

Crossing the courtyard, Crandall asked, "Milady, do you ride?"

"No." She glared at the horse, which dipped its head to the soft grasses near the wall.

"Milady," he continued, despising the desperate tone that crept into his words, "you must ride. I did not have the foresight to guess you might not be capable of handling a horse." He did not add that her brothers and sisters had been comfortable on their mounts before their fifth birthdays. His lady's new life might be far more difficult than any of them had guessed.

Lady Audra sighed. "I shall do my best to stay atop the beast."

He snapped a leading strap on her horse's halter. When he glowered at Shaw, the redhaired man lowered his eyes, which were crinkled with amusement. Listening to Shaw had been his first mistake. He should have insisted that they bring Lady Sabina's gentle mount.

When he turned the horse to where Lady Audra stood, wide-eyed with dismay, he said, "All you need do is hold on." He hesitated before asking, "Do you think you can do that?"

A flurry of emotions swept across her face. Sickness clawed at his stomach. If this was a portent of what awaited them at Bredonmere, coming to retrieve Lady Audra might prove to be his greatest error.

"I shall do my best to stay atop the beast," Lady Audra repeated quietly.

Crandall nodded. He could ask no more of her. Again he lifted his slender lady to the saddle. Only when he was sure she was balanced on the flat seat did he release her. As he instructed, she gripped the waist-high board at the front of the saddle. Tassels bounced against her legs as he led the horse toward his own.

He looked over his shoulder as he mounted and signaled the others to follow through the abbey's stone gate. He sighed. It was too late to turn back . . . even now. Lady Audra must succeed at holding Bredonmere, or every promise Crandall had made by his lord's deathbed would be broken.

Audra's head hurt. Her hips hurt. Her feet were tired from dangling by the horse's side. An itch in the middle of her back hinted that she might not have had the bed at the inn to herself last night.

As the night breeze lashed her, she drew the cape Crandall had purchased closer to her face and wished for the spring warmth of that afternoon. These clothes were thinner than the robes she had worn at Clarendon Abbey. She guessed Crandall paid dearly for these rags, but she understood his concern at having his lady arrive at her ancestral home in the garb of a novice.

How much farther could it be to Bredonmere Manor? An hour had passed since Crandall informed her they had arrived on the lands belonging to her family . . . belonging to her. The steward had increased their speed, not hiding his impatience to reach the manor before dark.

They would have been at Bredonmere Manor by now if Shaw's horse had not picked up a stone at midday. Halting to tend to the beast before it went lame, the men had worked to calm the horse while Shaw extracted the small pebble.

Rubbing her hip, Audra smiled grimly. Two days of being perched on this horse had left her sore, although she had learned to hold her seat without Crandall twittering over her. How she wished she would wake up and discover this was a nightmare! She would be back in the safe womb of Clarendon Abbey. She had not appreciated the serenity of the abbey until she was thrust into the world beyond its walls.

Grief twisted through her as she remembered passing deserted villages. "Plague towns" Crandall had called them. Every person in them had died from the blight sweeping across England, snuffing out life as readily and carelessly as a servant smothered a lamp with the coming of dawn.

As trees sucked them into a false night, they rode from shadow to the last faint smoke of twilight. The men's hands rested on the hilts of their swords. Audra gripped her saddle as she searched the horizon for the manor. Its high walls should be visible soon. Then they would be safe.

Crandall had hinted that no one knew they had gone to Clarendon Abbey to bring her to claim her heritage, but secrets seldom stayed secret long in the small world of manor or abbey.

She listened to the sounds around them. They were comfortingly familiar. Birds called good night, their songs interspersed with the hoot of a distant owl. Overhead, whirling bats danced after sleeping the day away in abandoned byres. A creek trickled near the road. The damp, green smell of bushes fading into dewy sleep was muted by hints of smoke from a hidden cottage. Sights and smells and sounds Audra had known all her life.

Her horse slowed. Crandall motioned for them to stop. Not that she had a choice, because he continued to hold the leading rein of her horse. She peered through the dark and saw something in the narrow road. A stump or a pile of rocks.

She scanned the woods. Nothing but shadows. "Ride around it." Her voice sounded too loud.

Crandall nodded. "Shaw, lead the way. Fleming, stay behind us. Milady, if you will come with me . . ."

"Go." This was no time to waste on protocol.

"Go quietly." Crandall shortened the leading rein so his knees brushed Audra's. He held out something that glistened in the faint light. "My knife. Do me the honor of using it as your own."

"I do not know how to wield a blade."

"I pray you shall have no need to. Take it."

She obeyed, astonished how heavy the blade was.

Suddenly a laugh splintered the night. Audra choked back a scream as shadows appeared from the

mist like demons out of the depths of hell. Terror
clamped its talons around her throat, strangling her.

"Hold tight, milady!" Crandall shouted over the
rasp of his broadsword escaping its scabbard.

Audra slapped her feet against the horse. "Go!"
she cried.

More laughter sounded as the dark congealed
into a company of riders. She hid the knife in the
folds of her skirt and stiffened. Let these brigands
laugh at her! They would find nothing amusing about
this knife cutting out their black hearts.

Shock buffeted her. That was an unworthy
thought for a sister of Clarendon Abbey, but she had
left that world behind. She was the countess of Bredonmere and must be ready to protect her manor.

For an eternal second, no one moved. Then one
man edged away from the silent predators. Audra
stared at the rider, who was draped in shadow. A
black cape whipped back from his wide shoulders like
a raven's wings. She guessed he would top even
Shaw's height. When she saw a dull flash, she bit her
lip to silence her fear. He was carrying his weapon
bare before him.

Her steward raised his sword. "Begone, knave!"

"Knave?" The shadowed man chuckled. He came
closer, and his smile was visible. When he paused the
length of a sword from Crandall, Audra saw cloth
swathed the upper portion of his face. "You speak
brave words for a man who rides through my lands
without permission."

"Your lands?" Crandall slashed at the night
rider. He swore as the man in black met steel with
steel.

Audra cringed at the screeching sound. Crandall's sword flew out of his hand. "No!" she shouted

as the night rider's blade sliced into Crandall's surcoat. "Spare him!"

The black-cloaked man chuckled as the steward stoically waited for death. "Then whom would you wish me to kill?"

"Begone from here." She was astounded by her temerity.

"By whose authority do you give that order? The earl is dead. All his get are dead. No one holds Bredonmere."

"I do." Audra raised her chin in defiance. "You have been warned once, knave. Begone."

His smile vanished as he moved his horse between hers and Crandall's. The steward snarled a curse, but one of the night rider's men held the tip of a sword to his throat. Metal rang behind her, and she twisted to see Fleming facedown on the ground.

"Do not scream," came a soft order in the night rider's velvety voice, which was as dark and deep and mysterious as the night. "I have no interest in slitting your throat or the throats of your companions, wench, unless you make it necessary."

"He is—"

"Not dead, but he shall be more prudent before he disobeys my orders again."

Audra breathed a prayer of thanksgiving when Fleming stirred. She had no chance to see more before her face was grasped in a gloved hand and her body turned sharply until she almost fell. She gripped the saddle as she stared at the night rider.

The shadows had not misled her eyes. Even concealed beneath his cape, his shoulders were as broad as a smith's. As he tilted her head back, she stared up into his eyes. Hooded by the dim light and edged by his mask, they offered no clue to his thoughts. It did not matter, for his sword spoke his opinions boldly.

"Who are you?" he demanded. "You risk much by daring to claim what belongs to Lynx."

"Lynx?"

"'Tis what I am called, wench. I await the courtesy of your name."

Trying to keep her voice as steady as his ebony gaze, she answered, "I am Lady Audra Travers, countess of Bredonmere. *You* risk much by claiming what is mine."

"Countess? The earl's family is dead."

"All but me." She tightened her grip on the knife. "I will tell you but one more time to begone, sirrah!"

His men found her insult amusing. Beneath their laughter, he murmured, "Although you cannot be of the earl's legitimate get, you should be, wench. Did your mother play the whore for the old earl so her bastard could try to win Bredonmere?" His fingers softened along her face as his thumb traced her cheekbone. "For whom do you play the whore, pretty one?"

Audra's elbow struck him between the ribs. His breath burst from him in a curse. Pulling back, she slashed with the knife. It tangled in his cloak. She heard Crandall shout to flee. She groped for the reins, but Lynx's arm blocked her. She raised the knife again.

He pinched her wrist between his fingers and wrenched the knife from her numb hand. She stared at him in horror, then screamed when he jumped from his horse, dragging her down to stand next to him. Pain shot through her left ankle when she landed. She ignored it when he turned the flat of her blade to tip her chin up. Twisting her arm behind her, he pulled her to his hard chest.

"Release her!" shouted Crandall. "Lynx, take our lives, but, if you have a hint of honor, leave Lady Audra alive."

"Silence!" His growl became a low purr as Lynx smiled coldly. "My words are for this woman. If you were a man, pretty one, I would kill you. Because you are a woman, I give you this warning. Do not make me slay you."

"I care nothing for your clemency. You have ambushed us. You have insulted us. You have shown your ignorance in many ways." When she heard the sharp intake of breath from the men around her, she did not hesitate. She would not end her life begging for mercy from a thief who dared not show his face. She had not aspired to govern Bredonmere, but the task was hers, and she would not neglect it. "We have suffered enough of your attentions for one night. Begone back to whatever demon spawned you."

"Milady, pray do not infuriate him! You have no idea what damage he has done in the past pair of fortnights," Fleming said as he took a step toward them. He halted before a barricade of cold steel.

Lynx lowered the knife. "You are brave to speak so plainly, pretty one. Not wise, perhaps, but very brave." He ripped her hood from her head. Clasping a handful of her hair through her wimple, he tilted her face back so he could see it in the weak starlight. "You have the looks of the earl." Reluctance seeped into his voice.

Her resolve not to let him see her suffering kept tears of pain from cascading along her cheeks. Slowly he loosened his grip on her hair. She rubbed her aching elbow as she stared up at him, her bravado saving her from collapsing in terror. At any hint of fear, any sign that she was ready to surrender, he would destroy her like the beast he was.

"Mayhap because the earl was my sire," she said with the sparse dignity she had remaining.

"The Travers family lies dead from the Black Death."

She swallowed roughly at his crude reminder that none of her family would be at Bredonmere Manor to welcome her. "All but me."

"Who are you?"

"I told you. I am Lady Audra—"

"I know what you call yourself. Names mean nothing. Where have you been while the others sickened and died?"

"Clarendon Abbey."

Amusement glittered in his eyes. "A nun? They think a *nun* can hold Bredonmere Manor?"

"Better a nun than an outlaw who is loath to show his face!" she shot back.

He shoved her toward Crandall. "Go. Take up the reins of the manor. Try to prove to those who reside there that a woman can hold. This countryside has mourned too long. It is time for laughter. What better way to amuse the peasants than a countess from a convent trying to hold Bredonmere Manor?"

Crandall muttered, "If you have hurt milady, I—"

"Shall do nothing. We have had enough of her playing the tomfool." Lynx motioned to Fleming with his sword. "You, if you have nothing to do but cluck like a nervous chicken, help your cloistered lady onto her horse. I do not envy you your task of proving to the manor that she is of the earl's get."

Audra ignored the aches in her back as she settled into the saddle with Fleming's assistance. She lifted her hood into place and continued to watch Lynx.

Concealing her trembling hands in her skirt, she said, "In farewell, I give you a warning, you who call yourself Lynx. Discard your dreams of possessing Bredonmere Manor. I will hold. The blood of earls flows through me. They have held this fief in the name of the king. So shall I."

She urged her horse forward, but it balked. Her hands clenched the reins. She must not let Lynx see her incompetence on horseback. Slapping her feet against it, she screamed when the horse reared, pawing the air. She pulled on the reins. The horse sped past the night riders, scattering them like milkweed spores.

"Stop!" she shrieked. The horse was racing toward the stones piled in the road.

An arm snaked around her waist. She was plucked from the saddle and slammed into a hard body. Her horse tried to clear the rocks. Horror strangled her when its hind feet struck a stone. Crashing to the ground, it screamed louder than she had.

She pressed her face to her rescuer's chest to block out the sound. The familiar smell of wool comforted her. Beneath her ear, a heart slowed to a steady beat. Strong arms cradled her as she shuddered when the horse cried out again in agony.

A sharp order echoed through the chest against her cheek. In horror, she looked up at a black mask. Lynx's arm tightened around her, keeping her from pulling away. His smile was colder than the starlight.

"You fool!" he snapped, then shouted his terse command again.

"Kill the horse?" she repeated. "But—?"

Lynx's dark eyes offered her no mercy. "Would you have the beast agonize longer? Its legs must be broken after such a fall."

She gasped when he tilted her head back so he could capture her with his dark gaze. A fingertip grazed her cheek as he murmured, "You shall need a harder heart if you wish to hold, milady."

She stared at him, amazed. By calling her "milady," he acknowledged her claim to Bredonmere Manor. Was this another of his brutal jests? She could not tell when he disguised his thoughts as thoroughly as his face.

"Beware, milady," he continued, "for there will be others even less willing to accept you than I."

"You accept my claim? Then you shall leave Bredonmere?"

His lips parted in an ironic smile. "I shall leave when I choose. You have yet to demonstrate that you can convince anyone other than a doddering old man and two feeble-minded simpletons that you are the daughter of the earl of Bredonmere."

"I shall prove it."

"Will you? How?" His hand rose along her back, pulling her even closer to him.

The intimacy of his touch overwhelmed her. Beneath her, his muscular legs brushed hers as the horse stirred. Her breasts pressed against the rigid wall of his chest with each breath. Slowly his hand slid along her back, slipping beneath her wimple to loosen her thick hair. He ran his fingers through its silken strands. She shivered as strange sensations roiled within her. Not fear, but something as potent and as consuming in its sweet flame. His face lowered toward hers, his breath cool against her suddenly hot cheeks.

"You should have stayed in your convent," he whispered, "where you need never have learned the lure of temptation."

Audra had no chance to answer, for Lynx set his horse to a brisk trot. He dropped her across Crandall's knees. When the steward asked if she was unharmed, she nodded. She was not hurt, but the odd feeling still taunted her when she looked at Lynx's challenging smile.

"Here is your countess, old man," the night rider said. "She will have to ride pillion to Bredonmere. Let all those within the manor see exactly whom they are about to swear allegiance to."

"You bastard!" Fleming cried. He reached for his broadsword.

"Touch it, fool," Lynx replied with a cold smile as he yanked his sword out of its scabbard, "and her blood will stain the road."

Audra leaned away, but the sword followed her. Lynx's eyes burned with fury. Finally the weapon lowered. She released the breath burning in her chest, but the next stuck in her throat as Lynx clasped her chin in his wide hand.

"Enjoy your manor while you can, pretty one." His smile broadened. "Bright eyes and soft lips may make men flock to your side, but only a strong arm and a wily wit can hold Bredonmere."

She wrenched her head away. "We shall see who is the victor. It is written that the meek shall inherit the earth."

He laughed as he slid his sword back into its sheath. "You have inherited the earth, milady, but who shall hold it for you?" He signaled to his men, then saluted her. "Until we meet again, milady . . . as we shall!"

With a shout, he and his men raced away into the darkness. Behind her, she heard Shaw's soft curse. She seconded the sentiment in her heart.

She and Lynx would meet again. He would make sure of that. Next time, she feared, she would not be allowed to escape so unscathed.

2

"I should have sliced his bragging tongue from his head," Fleming grumbled.

"You?" Shaw's snide laugh was as insulting as the night rider's. "You acted like a scared suckling."

"You did nothing!"

"Enough," Crandall said. "Milady, allow me to be the first to welcome you to Bredonmere Manor."

She nodded. Since the confrontation with Lynx, she had said nothing. The masked brigand possessed an undeniable ability to cause terror in his foes, and she had not been immune to that strength of will. His effortless command of his men warned her that he was no ordinary thief. The manor's men-at-arms had been unable to halt him, so she would have to. But how could she stop him when she could not stop herself from thinking of the warmth of his shockingly gentle fingers and the trill of delight that had soared through her at his touch?

Audra shook away the thoughts. Lynx was a common thief. He would be stopped. Then he would pay for his crimes.

As she crossed the drawbridge connecting the keep with the world beyond and rode into the inner bailey, she stared up through the thickening fog at the stone walls. For more than three centuries, they had repelled invaders, keeping the Travers line safe. Only a rampaging pestilence had breached these lofty walls. Now she must halt this new assault.

Fleming refused to go unheard. "That damnable bandit is getting too sure of himself. To threaten our lady is—"

"Do not fall prey to Lynx's tricks," Crandall ordered sharply. "Take a lesson from our lady. She remains unmoved by his threats."

Audra almost laughed, but the old man was serious. He had misjudged her stifling fear for quiet serenity. Brushing dust from her robe after Crandall helped her from the saddle, she said, "We are within Bredonmere. We are unharmed, save for our pride. For that, we should be thankful."

When Fleming mumbled, she knew he wished to repay Lynx for the insulting coup. To the young soldier, his pride was as important as his sword arm. Telling him and Shaw to rest, she went with Crandall across the well-trod ground of the courtyard toward the keep.

No memory stirred in her when she saw the high tower at the far corner, but she was not surprised. Neither the wooden drawbridge nor the iron portcullis had disinterred her buried memories. Nothing told her that this once had been home.

Entering the keep through the double doors that were ajar to welcome warmth to banish winter's chill, she edged around sleeping forms nestled on the stone floor. Tapestries hung on the walls, but darkness obscured their patterns. Mayhap, with the light of dawn, she would discover one of them held the key to unlock memories of the life she once had lived . . . and must live again from this night forward.

Crandall stopped. With his toe, he roused two lads sleeping near a closed door. They mumbled but tugged on the arched planks, which were held together with thick strips of iron.

Four steps led up to the great hall. In the entryway that ran the width of the room, Audra saw racks where warriors could store their weapons, but she could not tell if they were full or empty. She put her foot on the first stone riser and winced. Her left ankle had twisted when Lynx pulled her from her horse.

Murky smoke filled the hall, which was twice the size of the abbey's refectory. A fire burned on the central hearth beneath the roof, which was laced with blackened rafters. Windows, set near the peak thirty feet above, splashed starlight across the uneven floor. The panes were covered with latticework in the Bredonmere crest. It was grand and completely unfamiliar.

As Crandall's iron-soled boots struck the floor, sleepers stirred on the benches by the tables. He started to wake one man, but Audra shook her head.

"Milady," he argued, "the sooner your people know you are here, the sooner you can—"

"I can do nothing tonight when I think only of bed."

Crandall started to retort, then nodded reluctantly. "Your comfort is of primary importance."

She guessed he had wanted to introduce her with the most extravagant formality, but she needed to be more certain of herself before she endured such a ceremony. Following him through the hall, she rubbed her back. Her body ached in creases she had not known existed. After days of riding, the bandit's ambush had been a final insult.

Damn Lynx! She started at the unworthy thought. Too easily she was setting aside years of training in humility and charity. She had forgotten those lessons when confronted by a masked fool who dared to try and steal her family's fief.

With care, Audra gauged each step to the doors at the opposite end of the hall. Her feet seemed too far from her throbbing head. Pain twinged in her left ankle, and she leaned against the wall. When Crandall offered his arm, she accepted it gratefully.

"Milady, I do not presume to tell you what to do—"

She stopped, forcing him to do the same. "Crandall, I cannot hold Bredonmere if you will not be honest with me."

"As you wish, milady. I will endeavor to be forthright." When he refused to meet her gaze, she knew he was accustomed to receiving orders, not suggesting alternatives. He must change as she must. She could not find her way through the labyrinth of this new life alone.

As they climbed the narrow stairs to the upper floors, he listed the tasks awaiting her in the morning. She kept one hand against the cold stones of the wall. No rope was set on the other side of the risers. A single misstep could send her to her death.

The third-floor corridor was silent in the darkness, which was broken by a pair of torches set in the wall. Rushes rustled beneath her feet as she struggled to match Crandall's pace. The odor of mildew burst from them. On the morrow, she would take an inventory of the household and give the staff orders to bring the keep up to the standards set by the abbess at Clarendon Abbey.

Tomorrow, she promised herself with a tired sigh. Tonight she wanted only to sleep and forget about the transformation in her life . . . and Lynx.

Her hands clenched. Letting the bandit invade her thoughts was foolish. She must rid the manor of his predators. Then she could turn her attention to other things and forget the tantalizing caress of his hands and his bewitching ebony eyes.

Crandall pulled a heavy iron ring from his belt, which held a single key. Putting it in the lock, he opened the door. He took a brand and led the way into the room.

As he lit candles on the tables and started a fire, she looked around. The room was large, nearly as large as the abbess's office. A narrow window allowed in enough wind to make the candles flicker. An arched doorway would lead to other rooms. Benches edged a long table in the center of the floor, and blankets were piled in a corner. She wondered where the servants who should sleep there were. With a shiver, she realized they might all be dead.

Audra walked to the window. Drawing the glass panes closed, she turned to find Crandall watching her with sorrow in his eyes.

"Are these my parents' rooms?" she whispered.

"Your rooms, milady, as the countess. If you wish other rooms . . ."

For a moment, she was tempted to say yes. She could not imagine herself overseeing this manor house and the lands beyond it. She touched the bench where her father might have sat at the end of a day of training with his men or dealing with matters of law. As she stroked the wood, which was smoothed by years of use, strength flowed through her. The earl of Bredonmere's line would not be shamed by its final member.

"Of course, I will use these rooms," Audra answered. "I shall use this one for audiences. The ones beyond I will keep for my private use."

For the first time, she saw Crandall smile. "As your father used them. If I may suggest—"

"Crandall," she warned, fatigue honing her voice.

"If you prefer honesty, milady, I shall tell you I think you should rest." He dropped to one knee and bowed over her hand before leaving her alone with uncertain memories and ghosts she could not name.

Taking a candle, Audra went into the next room. It was an antechamber where she could spend time with the ladies and servants of her bedchamber, if any remained alive. More benches were shoved against the wall beneath the window slit.

She gasped as she opened the door to the next room. Instead of rushes, a wool rug lay on the floor. An intricate tapestry hung opposite the door. To her right, a huge fireplace commanded one wall. Facing it, a large window wore diamond-shaped mullions. Benches and chests cluttered the room, but her gaze went to the wide bed. In an alcove beyond the fireplace, it sat on a raised platform with steps broad enough to use as seats on a cold night.

Memory seared her as if she had been struck by an ember. She had been. Lifting her left hand, she touched the puckered skin on her smallest finger. She could hear childish screams and adult shouts. No one had known how she had scrambled onto the hearth without anyone noticing or how her sleeve had caught fire. She closed her eyes as she recalled someone holding her and comforting her through a long night of pain.

Was this memory of her mother? Or had a maid comforted her? The teasing of half-formed thoughts taunted her as cruelly as Lynx had.

A tentative knock startled her. When it sounded again, so quiet she could not have heard it if the inner bailey had been full, she opened the door.

A thin woman dipped in a deep obeisance. "I am Shirley, milady. I have been sent to attend you. I assisted your lady mother's chambermaid before both were taken by the Death."

"Oh . . ." To think of such intimate service was almost impossible. Nobody at the abbey, not even the abbess, had the luxury of a body servant.

"If I do not please you, milady," the gray-haired woman gulped, "you need only say so. I shall find another—"

"No, no," Audra said hastily. With a sigh, she pointed to a bench. "Please sit."

The gaunt woman moved a half step, then hesitated. Instantly Audra understood. To sit while her lady remained on her feet must be inconceivable to Shirley. Audra sat on the raised hearth and pointed again toward the bench. With an exhausted sigh, Shirley obeyed.

Audra smiled. "You may find many of my ways strange, Shirley. I have much to learn."

"Is it true you were to be a nun?" Then she flushed. "I mean no insult."

"Nonsense. If you always say what you mean, you will be doing me a great service. I have asked

Crandall to be honest with me. I hope you shall be the same."

Shirley bent forward. "Milady, there are those who do not wish a woman to hold. Even though you have a legitimate claim, this manor has never been held by a woman."

"I realize that. However, for now, I wish to sleep. Would you bring me water so I can clean the dirt from the road off my hands and face? If you see that I remain undisturbed until cock crow, I would be very grateful." She rose and went to the window. Something bright flared in the distance, and she asked, "Shirley, what is that?"

The woman choked. "That must be the byre at Vinson's farm." She cursed under her breath. "Lynx rides again with the night to destroy what he soon will learn he cannot have."

Audra's hands fisted on the wide sill as she stared at the distant flames. This challenge she could not ignore. She would find some way to defeat Lynx before he undermined her hold on Bredonmere Manor. Then he would be sorry he had not listened to her warning to leave.

Sunlight crept along the floor. Inch by inch, it crawled over the carpet, up a carved chest, and to the oak bed. Oozing through the thick, velvet curtains draping the bed in scarlet and navy, it toyed with the gold tassels before tickling the eyes of the woman curled up there.

Half-awake, Audra opened her eyes. She glanced around in confusion. This was not the abbey.

Bredonmere Manor!

She slid off the bed, and onto the thick carpet.

She had never seen a tapestry on the floor, but she thought it an excellent idea. On her way back from the privy chamber, she peered into the bathing room. The bath, which was cut into the floor, was surrounded by tiles. She considered ordering a bath, but that would have to wait until the end of the day.

Audra opened the tall window in her bedchamber to let in the scents of spring and the thicker odors from the stables. She folded her arms on the sill. Looking at the undulating hills rolling to the horizon, she could not believe this was hers.

Shirley entered with a cheery greeting. Reluctantly, Audra turned from the window. Crandall had not come to Clarendon Abbey to grant her a life of ease. This morning, she must take up the tasks ahead of her.

The maid bustled about the room, chattering. Audra recognized only the names of Crandall and his men. The rest was gibberish. She tried to sort some sense from the jumble.

Shirley laughed. "You are being very kind."

Pushing her head through the green kirtle the maid held for her, Audra asked, "Kind?"

"You are allowing me to babble, milady." Shirley quickly closed the long row of buttons along the front of the garment.

"What you say helps me to learn about Bredonmere Manor." She shrugged a loose cotehardie over her kirtle and slipped her arms through the gown's slits. Shaking it to settle it over her skirts, she stepped into her soft, leather shoes. She did not ask Shirley where the clothes had been obtained. With so many dead, the storage chests must be filled with unused clothing.

She loosened her black hair to cascade along her back in a mass of unruly curls. Relentlessly, she forced a comb through them, thinking of how she had been anticipating the moment when they would be shorn as she took her vows. Now that would never happen.

When she heard a sob, she spun to see Shirley hiding her face in her wheat-colored apron. Audra put her hands on the maid's arm. "What is wrong?"

Wiping her eyes, she whispered, "'Tis your hair, milady." She touched one tendril. "Like your father's. No one but a Travers could have such black hair and blue eyes. You know, don't you, that Bredonmere was named for just that? Hair as black as a Breton's, eyes as blue as the sea, a legacy that belongs to the Travers family." Her smile returned. "Listen to me babbling again. You must be hungry, milady. Shall I have breakfast brought?"

"I think I should make an appearance in the hall." As Shirley assisted her in arranging a silken gorget over her hair and around her face, she added, "The cock must crow very late at Bredonmere Manor."

"Usually he crows before the sun touches the eastern horizon, milady, but this morn I held the creature's beak closed."

"Thank you." She squeezed Shirley's hand before she went to the door.

Crandall was waiting in the outer room. Audra wondered if he had gone to bed at all, because he wore the same dusty tunic. He inquired about how she had slept, but she doubted if he listened to her answers as they went down the stairs and into the great hall. Like hers, his mind must be focused on what lay ahead. If her father's household would not accept her as his daughter . . . She must not even think of that.

Nearly two dozen people were clumped by a table set above the others. When Crandall murmured these were the manor's residents, Audra stared at him in horror. This keep must have housed many times more before the Death's arrival. She was beginning to understand the breadth of the catastrophe.

"May I announce you, milady?" he asked.

Audra nodded, apprehension squeezing words from her throat. She clasped her hands behind her and kept her spine straight as the abbess had taught her. When she heard the rumble of disbelief in the wake of Crandall's proclamation, she was glad her trembling hands were hidden.

"Lady Audra?" repeated one woman. "Who is Lady Audra?"

A man shouldered past the woman and snarled, "The family is dead, Crandall. Bredonmere is no more."

Another man shouted, "What good does a pretender do? The king will send his chosen lord to hold. Do we fight him as well as Lynx?"

Audra saw Crandall tense at the mention of the night rider, but his voice remained serene. "The promise I made to the earl of Bredonmere on his deathbed is fulfilled. He asked me to bring his youngest child back to Bredonmere before anyone not of Travers blood could claim this manor."

The first man's lips twisted. "Bring back? From where?"

Audra answered quietly, "Clarendon Abbey."

Her answer was ignored by the angry man. "You told us they all are dead, Crandall! Now you want us to believe this woman is of the earl's siring?"

She glanced at Crandall, but the steward did not seem perturbed. With a soft apology, he lifted the veil from her hair to reveal her face and coloring as he said, "Lady Audra Travers, countess of Bredonmere, we wait to serve you." He sank to his knees.

The others stared at her, their mouths gaping, then slowly they knelt. Audra wished she could recall her father's face which must have been so much like her own. When she urged them to rise, Crandall allowed her retainers no chance to ask questions. He gave them orders, including bringing food for their lady. Curious looks were aimed at her as the steward led her to the raised table.

She heard squeaking and saw rats scurrying along the wall. "Why have no cats been set to hunting these rats?"

"All the cats are in the stables," said Crandall as he gestured toward an ornate chair at the very center of the table. "They caused your father to sneeze, so he banished them."

"Bring them back. I shall not suffer vermin underfoot."

He nodded, although he clearly was not interested in so mundane a matter. "Milady, the plague has left us many men short on the tofts. We must get the planting underway."

"What do you suggest?"

"I have no suggestions."

Audra was shocked. She had thought Crandall would know exactly what should be done and only wanted her approval. "Who serves as reeve?" The man who oversaw the manor's farms might have ways of righting the problem.

"Our reeve is dead, as well as his assistant."

She waited while dark bread and porridge were

set in front of her, then asked, "Do you have someone who could serve well?"

"Possibly."

"Bring any men you think are good candidates to the great hall this afternoon. Together we shall deem which is the best."

His face flushed. "Milady, this is of utmost importance. To delay when the crops need to be sowed is foolish."

"This afternoon will be soon enough. This morning I wish to reacquaint myself with the manor."

"Not beyond the walls!"

"I think I shall have plenty to explore within the baileys." She did not want to let him see her smile. Her steward was determined that nothing should happen to the last of the Travers family, but she would not let him stifle her. If she did, she would never be able to hold.

When her breakfast was finished, sunshine drew Audra into the inner bailey, which was nearly empty. From her left, the scent of the stables and the privies in the keep drifted on an indolent breeze. Smiling, she turned in the opposite direction.

A well was set near an octagonal buttress on the smooth wall of the keep. She was pleased to see the shingled roof of the kitchen had been replaced with stone. One of her earliest memories of the abbey was the night the kitchen roof had caught fire.

A garden had been turned near the kitchen. Basil, sage, and marjoram, all essential for cooking, as well as lavender would grow there. She would love to spend time there as she had in the gardens of the abbey, but there was another place she must visit first.

Only a cross carved over the door and a bell set

above it identified the chapel. Making sure her hair
was well hidden beneath her gorget, she entered. A
wave of homesickness washed over her. She took a
deep breath of the incense lingering from past masses.
From beyond the opened windows, she heard the
coo of doves in the cote as they sang their sweet
hymn.

She walked between the stone pews. The only
candles lit were memorial ones, but that did not surprise her. Crandall had told her the priests were
among the first to perish when the Death gripped the
manor.

Familiar devotions eased her aching heart. What
she had learned at the abbey was not lost, for she carried its memory. Closing her eyes, she heard the children singing, their high-pitched voices innocent as
they spoke the Latin words they could not understand.

Her knees threatened to betray her as she walked
to the crypts. This was all that remained of the
Travers family, save for her. She touched the brass
effigy of her father's face. It was as if she looked into
a discolored mirror, for she recognized his features as
her own. So young he looked!

She put her fingers on his over the brass copy of
his ceremonial sword and surrendered to memories.
She recalled his broad hands stretched out to her as
she raced with childish abandon across a wide floor.
Those hands had heaved her into the air and caught
her to the sound of her giggles and the rumble that
had been her father's laugh.

Crandall had hinted the earl had wanted everyone to forget about her. The Death must not have
been the first threat to the manor. Nor would it be
its last. She pressed her hand to her mouth to hold

back questions. Asking her father what she should do was useless, because he never again would catch her before she fell.

Audra turned to her mother's brass. Putting her fingers on the hands clasped as if in prayer, she waited for tears, but they did not come. An utter emptiness ached within her. She should feel something. She felt nothing. These were her parents, the ones who had given her life, but they were strangers.

Her fingers stroked the raised names of her siblings and their children who lay in one mass grave. Euell, the oldest, the heir. Yardley, next. Seeing a woman's name beside his, Audra knew he had wed. When she found both a son's and a daughter's name beneath his, she realized she had lost more than she had known she possessed. The names blurred as she leaned her face against the cold metal of her mother's robes. She needed to speak to them, just once more.

"What are you doing there? Get away!"

Whirling, she saw a tall man standing by the first pew. His crucifix identified him as a priest.

"Father," she murmured, "I came only to see my parents' grave."

"You are Lady Audra?" The dark slash of his eyebrows arched as he regarded her in a manner she found disturbingly familiar. Whom did this priest bring to mind? Not Father Martin. The priest at the abbey was short and plump. She could imagine this priest wrestling the Dark Angel for his soul and winning.

When he gestured toward a pew, he waited until she sat before saying, "Forgive my words, milady." Taking her hand, he bowed over it. "I am Father Jerome."

Shocked that he would show an obeisance to her, she stuttered, "It—it—'tis my pleasure, Father Jerome."

He smiled. "You shall find many things different here from your abbey. I will tell you that I, too, was baffled when I left the seminary. Quickly I learned most people are more concerned about their next meal than their eternal soul."

She returned his smile. "You sound cynical."

"Not at all. I have learned I must be inventive. As you must be to solve the problems facing you."

Leaning back against the damp caress of the pew, she said, "Crandall expects miracles to leap from my fingers. I know only the ways of the abbey, Father. Fortunately, I have proven to be a quick learner."

"That is good, for you will have little time. The planting is overdue, and the villeins are restive. With Hock Day approaching, they are unsure if they should pay their rents."

She recognized the term for the second Tuesday after Easter. It was the half-year day, along with Michaelmas, when the tenants came to the manor to offer the lord his share of their farms' production in exchange for his protection. "Do you think they will accept me in my father's stead?"

When he hesitated, Audra was not insulted. She needed an honest answer. Slowly, he said, "I think they might, but only when you have shown that you can hold."

"How?"

"That I can give you no answer to," he said with a regretful smile. "Be fair, and use the teachings you learned at the abbey. These people are anxious for a strong leader who can assure them that the plague will not return to steal their loved ones."

"I cannot do that! Who lives and who dies is God's will."

"I realize that, milady, but what you can do is reassure them that the manor will be defended against any usurper who would steal it."

She lowered her voice. "What do you know of Lynx?"

"What any man knows," he answered as softly. "He arrived here not more than two fortnights ago, after the earl was laid to rest. He has done nothing irreparable. Mostly broken fences, fired a byre, or set livestock free to wander through the leas."

"More troublesome than dangerous?"

His lips tightened as he shook his head, squashing her hopes. "The man called Lynx could be very, very dangerous."

"I shall not surrender my fief to a coward who fears to reveal his face."

Father Jerome put his hand on her shoulder. "Lynx is no coward. Do not do something foolish to rile him."

Rising, she said, "That I intend to keep what is mine riles him."

"He is not the only one eager to grasp power from the hands left lifeless by the Death sweeping through England." He stood and again put his hand on her shoulder.

She looked up at his black eyes. "May I come back to speak to you?" she asked. "I know you are so very busy, Father, but . . ."

"Never too busy for you, milady. Your words tell me that we share a common vision. Alone, neither of us can achieve peace and prosperity for the villeins. Come to me whenever you need an objective ear."

"Thank you," she whispered.

With a nod, Father Jerome walked away. Envy pinched Audra as she went back out into the sunshine. Having a sanctuary from her troubles would be wondrous.

Shouts ripped through the air, followed by laughter. The sound of merriment, which she had not heard since returning to the manor, drew her to it. Rounding a corner, she saw young men jabbing with quarterstaffs. She sighed. Several were lads, and their skills, even to her untrained eyes, were poor. If this was what was left of the men-at-arms, she understood why Lynx roamed the countryside without fear of reprisal.

She heard another shout. A tall man with black hair strode awkwardly among the lads. His muscular arms were bare, and he wore a short tunic. Each staccato action drew her eyes to his left leg which moved with the stiffness of an injury that had not healed well. He stopped two youngsters and took a staff, which he twirled as easily as a child would an empty milk bucket.

Audra's eyes widened as the dark-haired man abruptly halted the staff and met the attack of a man who leapt at him from the stable. Wood struck wood with a crash that resonated through her bones. Again and again and again, they parried with the poles, hitting with one end, butting with the center, always in motion. The dark-haired man did not let his weak leg hinder him. The youngsters cheered.

Fascinated, Audra walked closer. She winced when the dark-haired man swung the pole in a skull-splitting blow, but the other man leapt away.

Raising his hand to call for the mock battle to

cease, the dark-haired man said, "That is how you deal with surprise."

The boys shouted. Turning faster than Audra thought any hobbled man could move, the dark-haired man met the renewed attack. Her eyes could not follow the lightning motion that tripped up his attacker, but suddenly the dark-haired man was pressing the other man to the ground, the staff at his opponent's throat.

Audra applauded. When the lads stared at her, she stopped, her smile fading.

The dark-haired man tossed his quarterstaff to the man he had bested. "Show them that ploy. I want them to have it perfect before midday." Walking toward her, he rubbed his hands on his stained, brown tunic.

"I did not mean to intrude," Audra said.

"'Twas no intrusion." He smiled. His voice was as resonant as the clashing staffs, but its warmth matched his friendly expression.

"You're French!" she cried, noting his accent.

"Not French." His smile wavered. "From Gascony. I am the king's man." Wiping his arm against his forehead, he left a streak of dirt nearly as black as his eyebrows. His face was strongly sculpted. The sun's rays made his hair glisten with sweat and his skin reflect a deep bronze color. His eyes, which she guessed would intimidate any halfhearted student, sparkled with mirth. "Do you enjoy watching the men train?" he asked.

Although she was astonished he did not bow as the others had, she replied, "Men? They look to be no more than lads."

"They will live to be men if they learn to fight." His grin broadened as his walnut brown eyes looked her over, lathering her with the sun's heat. "My name is Bourne. Are you new in the manor? I do not recall meeting you, and I'm sure I would have remembered a lovely lass like you."

Audra hesitated. He could not know he was speaking to the countess of Bredonmere. If she told him the truth, she would embarrass him before his students. She doubted if he would take such humiliation well.

"You need not be shy," Bourne continued. "I am new here as well."

"You are?"

"My predecessor succumbed to the Death as did the knight I once squired for. Bredonmere needs my talents, and I need a home. It seems the perfect match." He shouted to one of his students. Correcting the chastised lad with the same enthusiastic roar, he turned back to her. "Excuse me, but I want them to learn to protect their necks."

Audra fought her embarrassment. The best thing would be to end this. "I apologize for interrupting your class."

"I was ready for a break." His grin broadened. "'Tis tiring for the teacher, too."

Looking away, so he would not see how he disquieted her, she said, "Harsh lessons are necessary, so they do not learn them when it could cost them their lives."

He stepped closer. His tunic was unlaced to reveal the breadth of his chest. Never had she been this close to such raw virility. That was a lie. Just last night, Lynx had held her and she had sensed the power of his arms, which could be so cruel or so gentle.

Begone, she cried out silently, not sure if she was speaking to Lynx or Bourne or both.

When Bourne put his hand on her arm, she flinched, but he stroked it gently. He murmured, "You are welcome to visit me in the armory if you have a free hour. No doubt our new lady will keep us busy as she tries to prove she is better than any man at holding Bredonmere."

She flushed. His outrageous words might be overheard. She did not want to think of what might happen. Backing away, she bumped into a low wall. There was no escape. Why had she not told him the truth at once?

He closed the distance between them again as his gaze swept boldly over her again. "Why do you not come to the armory tonight? No one will disturb us but the light of the stars. What say you?"

Audra was saved from answering by a shout. Crandall rushed toward them. Bourne's curse heated her face anew as the steward pushed past him.

Crandall puffed, "Milady, if you would—"

"'Milady'?" demanded Bourne in a venomous voice.

"Have you gone blind that you fail to recognize the countess of Bredonmere?" the steward returned as sharply.

"Countess?" Bourne's eyes darkened with accusation for a brief moment. Then he dropped to his knees. "If I said anything disrespectful, milady, I beg your pardon."

"Nonsense!" she retorted more harshly than she had intended. She should apologize, but not when Crandall was listening. "Please rise." To Crandall, she added, "Is something wrong?"

"I have gathered candidates for the reeve's position, milady."

Audra bit back her frustration as she wondered if

Crandall would gainsay all her orders. With a silent sigh, she relented. Spending the rest of the day selecting a reeve would keep her from getting into more trouble. "I will join you when I have finished with Bourne."

"Very well." He dipped his head in a cursory bow. As he walked away, he glanced over his shoulder, curiosity on his weathered face.

Audra faltered, then said, "Bourne, I should—"

"Milady, say no more." He dropped to his knees again with an ease she had not guessed his crooked leg possessed and pressed his fingers to his forelock. "I should have been aware that you are the lady of Bredonmere."

Putting her hands on his shoulders, she gently pushed back. "I ask you not to kneel to me." When he looked up, puzzled, she forced a smile. "I dislike talking to the top of people's heads."

He chuckled and stood. "If you wish a tour of the armory, milady, I would be glad to offer it." His lopsided grin gave him a roguish charm. "Of course, I expect you to ignore my other invitation."

"You speak plainly." Her face was suddenly icy as she recalled Lynx saying the same to her.

"Milady, is something wrong?"

She shook her head to dislodge the image of the enigmatic night rider. "I will visit the armory soon, Bourne. I am anxious to learn all I can of Bredonmere."

"I anticipate that time eagerly."

As he lifted her fingers to his lips with manners which would have graced the king's court, she jerked them back. He regarded her with astonishment. She could not explain that she was so much a prisoner to the thought of another man's touch that she could not trust herself to let this man touch her in even so commonplace a manner.

Forcing her steps to be slow, she walked toward the keep. She did not glance back to see if Bourne was watching her. She knew she must escape before . . . She did not know why she was scared of a thief's bold caress.

And that was what frightened her most.

3

"Milady! I must speak with Lady Audra!"

Exasperated at yet another interruption, Audra continued to read the petition in front of her. A freeman wished to marry a bondwoman and begged permission of the countess of Bredonmere to buy his woman's freedom. It was important because, if the freeman died before his wife did—in this time of plague, death haunted each person's thoughts—his wife and any issue of the marriage would revert to chattel status.

She had tried without success to finish the bottomless mound of petitions on the table in her audience room, but even after a month at Bredonmere, the stack was no smaller. Each day began with good intentions and ended with trying to stave off another disaster. The fears and frustrations since her family had taken ill and died were bursting forth from the tenants of the manor in a flood of questions and demands.

"I *must* speak with Lady Audra!"

At the insistent shout, she saw an unkempt man reeling into her audience room. "No!" she ordered when Crandall stepped forward to block him. "Let him speak."

The blond man rushed to her. "Milady—" He gawked at her as if she were a phantom. Although she had grown accustomed to the stares from those who were meeting her for the first time, she still felt uncomfortable, for she had searched the brass effigy over her father's body and found little that was familiar.

"Show respect to Lady Audra, Ludlow," Crandall snapped.

Kneeling, the man said, "Milady, you must help us. We can fight him no more alone."

"Him?"

Audra ignored Crandall's sharp question. She had no need to inquire about the obvious. "What damage has Lynx inflicted on your toft?" she asked as she motioned for Ludlow to come to his feet.

"The byre is gone. The walls caved in."

"What of your animals?"

"Those bastards—" He gulped and whispered, "Forgive me, milady."

"Speak what you have come to say," she ordered. "There is no time to waste on pretty words."

Respect glowed in Ludlow's eyes as he nodded. "They freed the animals. I chanced to find the cow in the garden. Half-ruined the seedlings, milady. Our lambs strayed nearly to the woods between my toft and the manor, but we rescued them before they could end up in a wolf's belly."

"'Twas decent of Lynx to let the animals go before he fired the byre." Sarcasm scored her voice as her hands became taut fists on the table.

Damn Lynx! How many times had she thought thusly in the past month? His nightly forays left destruction in their wake, and the report was always the same. A tumbledown byre or a shed burned. Gardens trampled. Fences broken. No animals killed, no irreparable destruction, just a malicious disruption of the planting.

Walking around the long table, she stopped in front of the painfully thin man. She wondered if it had been the Death that left Ludlow's ribs poking through his tunic. "I wish to see this for myself."

"Milady, if you do not believe—"

"I do not question your story. Mayhap if I see the damage, I shall be able to find a way to stop Lynx from his next raid."

Ludlow gave an evil grin. "He will make good raven's meat for the executioner."

Audra moved past him, not wanting him to see her disgust. Lynx was a bandit and deserved to die, but she had been taught that vengeance should not be hers. Squaring her shoulders, she reminded herself that a fief had laws. Those who flouted them must be punished as a warning to others.

"Milady?"

At Crandall's low whisper, Audra said, "Please have this petition put where it shall not be damaged. I shall sign it upon my return."

"Milady, you must let me ride with you."

Audra resisted snapping the retort burning on her tongue. Crandall followed her about like a troublesome shadow. He questioned every decision she made, although he seldom openly disagreed with her.

"No," she answered. "I would not want the king's messenger to arrive to find both of us gone."

The steward yielded, but she wondered if he noticed the uneasiness underlying her voice each time she spoke of the king. Audra had sent a letter to her distant cousin King Edward III, to inform him of her claim as the countess of Bredonmere. He had not acknowledged it. Knowing it might take her courier weeks to reach the court and return with an answer, she was growing anxious. She had thought the king would be eager to have the matter of Bredonmere Manor completed. To complete it would mean finding a husband for the new countess. She tried not to think of that often, for the very thought unsettled her.

Audra sent for Shaw to accompany her, telling him to bring a pair of men he trusted. As she crossed the inner bailey, her hands began to quiver. Crandall had attempted to teach her to ride, but the lessons had gone poorly as she tried his patience with her incompetence in the saddle. She could manage a horse on her own now as long as the beast was of a docile nature.

Shaw helped her mount. Gripping the reins, she urged the horse to follow his, praying she would not be unseated in view of Bourne and his students, who were practicing on the far side of the stable.

When they had left the manor walls behind them, Shaw rode next to her along the dusty path leading toward the toft Lynx had attacked. The silent man's lips pursed when she explained what she hoped to uncover.

"An answer?" He gave a short laugh. "Others have had little success in unraveling this puzzle, milady."

"No one knows much of Lynx."

"What do we need to know other than he must meet his end within a noose?"

"Have you no curiosity why he picked Bredonmere for his target?"

"Not in the least."

Hearing the other men snicker, Audra swallowed her fury. She would have preferred to ask Fleming to accompany her, but Shaw was the commander of her men-at-arms. He had not changed his mind since her arrival but waited daily, with avid anticipation, for her to fail. Yet she needed him, as she needed every man she could call to her side. Lynx was not the only threat, although he was the most immediate.

The burned byre, as she had expected, was one that had been in poor shape. A better barn sat, untouched, within a few yards of the charred building. As she walked past the scorched timbers, Audra choked on the stench of water-soaked wood. She avoided looking at Shaw, who wore his superior smile, gloating that she could not decipher a single fact from the disaster.

Mayhap Shaw was not curious, but she was. Why had Lynx suddenly emerged from the night to prey on Bredonmere Manor? Other, less well protected fiefs were within a day's ride and would have been easier targets.

She sighed. No one had curtailed Lynx's mischief at Bredonmere, so he need have had no concern about retaliation. After their one meeting, he might believe she was too frightened to fulfill her vow to see him banished from her lands. Fear had not been what she endured in his strong arms, although the sweet pleasure had been frighteningly potent.

Audra pushed those treacherous thoughts from her head as she spoke with Ludlow while his

wife and four daughters served them a meal of
bread spread with honey and mugs of milk. She
told them she would offer what protection the
manor could.

"No need, milady," the farmer replied. "Lynx is
like lightning. He never strikes the same toft twice.
You would be wise to watch over the south farms.
They have been untouched."

"I will send them warning."

"They need men to protect them."

Shaw laughed. "Ludlow, the only way we are
going to get men to guard those tofts is if you grow
them in your fields."

"The manor will protect you," Audra repeated,
flashing a furious glance at her red-haired commander.
How dare he thwart her efforts with his pessimism!

She waited until they were about to mount
before she added, "Shaw, you would be wise to keep
the present strength of the Bredonmere men-at-arms
to yourself."

"Lying will gain us nothing." His snide smile
returned. "I thought nuns always told the truth."

"They do." Regarding him steadily, she asserted,
"And so do I. The south tofts and the families on
them shall be shielded from Lynx's harassment.
Bourne's students soon will be able to—"

"Bourne?" His laugh chilled her. "Milady, you
shall be undone before you start if you heed him and
Crandall. A lame man and an old toady. Fools! They
see you as the resurrection of the earl! We need no
more of their mewling. We need someone to lead this
fief."

"As I shall."

"A man, milady. A man like your cousin."

"Lord deWode?" She knew nothing of him

save for what Crandall had told her. Gifford deWode's claim on Bredonmere was weak because his father had been a bastard. Although the baron had gained himself lands and prestige through his bravery on behalf of the king, his illegitimacy had prevented him from taking Bredonmere. "Do you know him?"

His eyes twinkled. "All know of him, milady. Mayhap you shall know him better than I if the king sends him to Bredonmere to take you as his wife."

Audra did not answer, because Shaw's words made sense. A man who had gained so much might be a boon to Bredonmere. A shiver passed through her at the thought of welcoming a stranger as her husband.

She accepted Shaw's help onto her horse only because she had no choice. He continued to chuckle to himself as they rode. Ignoring him, she concentrated on staying on her horse. As the sun sank behind them, their shadows reached toward the forest.

Coolness clung beneath the trees. Squirrels skittered away, and Audra saw a tawny doe peeking at them. She smiled. The Black Death had not completely consumed Bredonmere Manor. Life remained. If nurtured, they could rebuild what the scourge had tried to destroy.

They had gone only a mile into the woods when Shaw called for a stop. When she started to question him, he grasped her reins and drew her horse up a steep knoll into the shadows.

"What is it?" Audra asked as she slid from her saddle when he did. Her feet hit the ground too hard, setting her teeth on edge.

He motioned toward where his companions were disappearing into the bushes. "We always pause here on the way back to the manor. Are you so curious about our habits, milady? I thought you cared only for exposing Lynx."

Fire burned Audra's face. When Shaw grinned, she turned away. His laughter remained after he followed his men. At the unmistakable sounds from the other side of the bushes, she wrapped her arms around herself. Father Jerome had been correct. Every day, she was discovering how much she had yet to learn about life in the manor.

The babble of a rivulet tempted her to wash the dust from her face. Edging beneath the trees thick with new leaves, she knelt by the creek. The thick odor of decaying vegetation rose around her as she rinsed her face, delighting in the water's cold caress. She sat back on her heels and dried her hands on her cotehardie. A twinge along her leg reminded her of the fall she had taken while riding with Crandall two days before.

Her gown caught on a bush as she walked back to the horses. When a button was plucked off her sleeve, she gave a soft cry of dismay. She could not see where it landed, for the thickening twilight obscured the ground. She dropped down to feel the ground for it.

Audra hated to admit defeat, but hearing the horses' impatient hoofbeats, she knew how hopeless her search was. Tonight, while she was dealing with the manor's business, Shirley would have to repair her dress.

She pushed aside the bushes to discover the clearing was empty. There was no sign of Shaw or his men or the horses, but she recognized the slash where lightning had neatly bisected an ancient oak long before her birth. Kneeling, she touched the spots where the iron horseshoes had branded the moss. She shouted Shaw's name as she stood, but heard nothing but the echo of her voice.

Where were they?

Fury smothered her. She should have guessed Shaw would do something to repay her for contradicting him at Ludlow's toft. He was more of a fool than she had realized. She had made no changes in her father's appointments, but she had to have men she could trust. Stripping Shaw of his privileged position would show him the cost of his mistake.

"Are you lost?"

Audra whirled around. As she pushed her gorget back from her face, all color drained from her cheeks. She stared at the man who held her manor in a bondage of fear.

"Lynx!" she whispered in horror.

His smile was dazzling beneath the black cloth that covered most of his face. As he moved closer to her, his steps as light as the beast whose name he shared, he murmured, "You need not fear me, milady."

"No?" She backed away, trying to maintain the space between them. "The last time I had the ill fortune to meet you, you held a sword to my breast and vowed to steal my birthright."

"You continue to speak plainly." His gaze, which was darker than the fabric around his head, moved along her. "You are far from plain otherwise."

Unsettled anew by the intriguing warmth she felt, Audra whispered, "Step aside, so I may return to the manor."

"That would be unwise, milady."

"Unwise? What do you know of wisdom? You are nothing but a common thief who preys on those weaker than you!" She took another step back as rage flared in his eyes. When she bumped into a tree, her breath exploded from her in a sharp gasp. Gripping the narrow trunk, she waited for him to run her through for her bold words.

Each slow step he took toward her was another torment. His eyes refused to let hers evade them. Bark cut through her veil as she tilted her head back. He paused when he was so close that a broadsword could not have passed between them. He did not touch her, but every inch of her skin was aware of him.

Softly he asked, "Milady, how do you come to be alone so far from your manor house?"

"My habits need be none of your concern."

"No?" His fingers stroked the hilt of his sword in an unspoken threat. "I ask you again, milady, what errand brings you here?"

Audra swallowed. She knew so little of him. Would he kill her for not answering? She would not give him the satisfaction of goading her into death. Softly she said, "I was riding to see the damage inflicted by you on my innocent tenants."

"You were *riding*?" He chuckled. "Perchance your mount ran away again?"

Pricked by his derision, she retorted, "I have asked you to leave my lands. Still you bring misery here. Have these people not suffered enough? Begone, and take your demonic mischief with you."

"I regret I cannot do as you wish, pretty one."

Audra tensed, recalling how he had called her that when he held her in his arms. Where was Shaw? She would forgive him anything, if he would save her from this man whose heart must be as ebony as his cloak.

"Then I shall end this," she said as she edged to the right.

"Not yet, milady." His hand settled on the tree inches from her head. "*I* shall decide when this is to be ended."

Terror ricocheted through her. He was playing with her as a cat toyed with a mouse before killing it. Was that what he meant to do to her? When his fingers teased the curve of her jaw, she knew, if he intended to slay her, it would not be immediately.

"You cannot leave when you have not satisfied me," he murmured.

She choked and shook her head. His finger beneath her chin forced her to look up at him.

"So satisfy me, milady, by first telling me what you are doing in this wood alone."

Audra was shocked anew. If she told him the truth, would he release her? She saw the malevolent glitter in his dark eyes, and that faint hope faded. This was his way of taunting her.

Yet every minute he delayed slaying her was another chance to escape. Quietly she told him how Shaw and his men had left without her. She watched Lynx's face, but she could not guess what he was thinking. His hooded eyes concealed more than the black cloth.

"So they left you to die?" he asked.

"No!"

"Few want a woman to succeed in holding Bredonmere, milady. Your man tired of waiting for you to give up."

"You're lying!" she cried, although he merely said what she had been thinking. "Shaw came to Clarendon Abbey to get me."

With the chuckle that had so irritated her on their first meeting, he drawled, "Clarendon Abbey. Was that what you wanted? To trade your life as Lady

Audra Travers to become a nun? Never to know a man's loving touch?"

"I had my duty to the abbey then. Now my duty is to Bredonmere Manor." Her chin jutted with pride as she fought fear to keep her voice steady. "Tell all who will heed you, Lynx, that I shall hold. No one, not you nor any other, will keep me from my obligation to my family and tenants."

"A brave speech, but there are those in the manor who wish to see you dead, for you stand in their way of gaining the power you have not yet learned you possess."

"How is it that you, an outsider, have knowledge that has eluded the lady of the manor?"

"Nothing you do is private. You have many enemies, milady. Think of the younger sons throughout England who would be eager to win Bredonmere."

"Better that they should wrest it from me by the king's command than you by deceit."

"You are a fool, pretty one." He pulled a small dagger from his belt and clamped his hand over her mouth before she could scream. Pressing her head against the tree, he raised the knife. "There is only one way, pretty one, to save you from your own folly. This shall not hurt long."

She closed her eyes as she waited for death. Something struck her skull. As Lynx had promised, the agony lasted but a second before every thought vanished into oblivion.

Audra's eyes opened to nothing. Lost in pain, she wondered if she was dead. Slowly her mind untangled itself from webs of confusion. Beneath her was damp soil. She could smell its pungent odor and feel it caked against her cool cheek. But she was alive. Her head ached. Her heart beat. Her toes wiggled in her slippers. Around her was darkness that was so absolute she feared she was blind.

She moaned. The darkness clung to her, suffocating her in its weight. She must escape it. She could not stay here! She would smother. She must escape.

Straw crackled as she rolled onto her side. Its miniature spears pierced her clothes. One stabbed her hand, and she moaned again as she put her cut hand against her mouth.

Rising to her knees, Audra sat back while her head spun. Gently she cradled it in her filthy hands. A dozen smiths hammered against her skull, wiping away the panic she always suffered in close, dark places. Her lips tightened. Lynx must have struck her with the haft of his knife instead of its blade.

For what reason did he wish to leave her alive? She could not fathom the depths of his criminal thoughts. Demanding ransom might be another man's scheme, but Lynx's plot was sure to be less conventional. She was his prisoner. Did he intend to trade her for what he wanted?

Icy terror sped through her once more. Bredonmere! She would die before she ceded her birthright to him.

"Never!" she said aloud. The empty sound of her voice mocked her, but it told her this dark hole was not the cramped tomb she had feared.

Carefully Audra rose. As her head swam, her fingers found a moldering earthen wall. It crumbled as she leaned against it, struggling to breathe slowly. She could move. She would silence her hysteria and find a way to flee.

Clenching her teeth, she tried to envision Lynx as her prisoner, begging for his life as she presided at his trial when she invoked *infangthief*, her right to mete out justice to a thief caught on her lands. She would see him humiliated before handing him to the royal courts to be tried for abduction. It was impossible to imagine. The proud man was as uncatchable as the night wind.

Lynx must have some weakness. She would find it and defeat him. But first she must discover a way out of this black hell.

Lurching across the dirt floor, Audra encountered the opposite wall in only five paces. Her prison was more meager than she had suspected. Where was she? She suspected she was within a league of Bredonmere. Lynx would need a hiding place close to the manor, and it must be small enough to conceal easily. The man made no mistakes!

"Until he met me," she murmured, although she could not ignore how uncertain her situation was. He had not killed her, but that could change at any moment.

She found the door by bumping into it. Mud chinking fell off in her hands, but the wall of timber and wattle was thick. Searching for a latch, she scraped her knuckles on the rusty iron holding the planks together.

"Damn you, Lynx!" She ripped a piece of linen from her gorget and wrapped it around her bloody hand. "You shall be sorry for this."

When her fingers settled on the iron latch, she jerked it upward and shoved the door with her shoulder. Pain seared a sharp line down her back, but the door refused to budge.

"No!" she screamed, pounding on the door. "Let me out! Someone let me out!"

Nobody answered. Frustration flooded her. There *had* to be something she could do to escape.

But there was nothing.

Audra shuddered. Dropping to the damp earth, she huddled against the door. If only she had stayed at Clarendon Abbey. . . . She halted the thought. Her duty was to Bredonmere Manor, and she would see Lynx with his neck in the hangman's noose before she surrendered to him.

A sound came through the door. Hoofbeats! Leaping to her feet, Audra opened her mouth to scream. Then she thought better of it. If Lynx was on the other side of the door, let him think she still was senseless. Edging away, she pressed against the wall and held her breath.

The heavy clunk of a bar being lifted told her why she had been unable to open the door. She tensed as moonlight trickled into her prison. Clenching her hands, she watched the door open. A bit more . . . a bit more . . . then . . . Now!

Audra gathered her feet under her, leaped forward, and struck the door with her outstretched hands. A man stumbled backward. Ignoring his curse, she ran out into the night. A hand grasped at her, but she eluded the fingers. Bunching her long skirts in her hands, she raced toward trees edging a cliff of stone and shrieked. Some woodsman might hear her desperation.

Her arm was grabbed. She screamed. A leather glove clamped over her mouth. An arm encircled her waist. She would not be Lynx's prisoner again! She kicked him, but her heavy skirt interfered. Hearing a cold laugh, she flung her fists backward.

He grunted with pain. He was vulnerable! She hit him a second time. She moaned against his gloved palm when he doubled over. She fell to the ground but scrambled to her feet and fled.

Another pair of hands caught her. Her wrists were gripped and jerked behind her back. Then a hand covered her mouth as she took a deep breath to screech out her defiance. Two of them! How could she fight Lynx *and* his ally?

"Are you hurt, my friend?" came an amused voice from behind her. She closed her eyes and sagged in defeat. How pleasant this voice would be on her ear in other circumstances, but now it warned her that Lynx controlled her again.

"She fights well for a woman raised in a nunnery." There was grudging admiration in the other man's voice. He lurched toward them, his arm over his stomach.

Audra stared at him. His chin and mouth were dimly visible in the moonlight filtering through the treetops, but a material wrapped around his head obscured the rest of his face. Blond hair glistened on his shoulders. His stockings were tattered and covered with cinders.

He laughed. "Beware, Lynx. She might scratch out your eyes."

"I can handle our lady." When she growled against his hand, Lynx tightened his hold on her wrists. Pain burned along her arms. She cursed him in impotent silence as he went on. "Tend to your duties. I want to know what is being said on the tofts."

"The usual place?"

"Yes. By then, I shall have gotten what I wished from our lovely lady Audra."

Fear twisted her heart as the other man nodded and vanished among the trees. She screamed against

Lynx's gloved hand. He must not leave her with this beast.

Lynx chuckled. "You shall never give up, will you? If you had been a son, your father would have had no worries about you holding Bredonmere. Unfortunately, for him and for you, you are female." His voice softened as he breathed against her ear. "Unfortunately for you, but fortunately for me."

She shivered. His words confirmed her worst fears. He planned to rape her before he murdered her. When his fingers stroked her side, she flinched away from the flame they seared into her skin. She closed her eyes and whispered a prayer.

Audra gasped when he pushed her through the open door of her prison. She fell to her knees, then jumped to her feet and whirled around. The door slammed in her face.

"Damn you, Lynx!" she cried, her hands fisting by her sides. "I hope you rot in hell!"

"Such an unforgiving attitude for a woman who vowed to be a nun."

The voice was in the room with her. Flattening herself against the wall, she scanned the darkness. Where was he?

"Go away!" she whispered.

"I thought you might have been lonely here, so I have come to keep you company."

At his mocking, she squared her shoulders. She would not curse him again, for that would give him more satisfaction. Quietly she said, "Not that lonely."

Once more he chuckled. "Please be seated, milady. I have had a very busy night and wish to rest a while."

"I am sure you would."

His broad hand found her shoulder as impatience scored his voice. "I asked you to sit."

Could Lynx see through the darkness with the ease of his namesake? No, he was no more than a man. She need fear nothing from him but what she would fear from any man. That fear pinched her heart as his fingers toyed with the dirty linen of her veil. If he forced her to submit to him, she knew she could not fight his strength.

She was tempted to protest, but making him angry would be foolish. She dropped only to her knees, so she could bound to her feet if she had another chance to flee. As long as he stood between her and the door, she was his prisoner. If he moved . . . She had to be ready.

Before her, the shadows became the silhouette she knew too well. As if he was a lord and this pit his manor, Lynx mused, "I regret I have nothing to offer you to break your fast."

"I am not hungry."

"Odd, for I am."

"Perhaps because you have spent the night wrecking my tenants' fences so their beasts can feast in the newly planted fields."

She could imagine his indifferent shrug as he said, "You give *hayebote* to your tenants. The wood in your forests will repair their fences."

"If you would halt your pranks, they would not need to ask for the old rights."

She heard his boots scrape the floor. When she felt his warm breath on her face, she leaned away. He must be sitting only inches from her. On her knees, her fingers clenched. He would not be defeated as easily as his companion.

"Your people," he continued, "think little of such matters. They are seeking you diligently. What lamenting there is that you may have suffered a horrible death in the woods!" His sarcasm lashed her. "How difficult it must be for your enemies not to exult over defeating you so easily."

"Stop it!" She put her hands over her ears. "I shall not listen."

Lynx drew her hands away. She tried to jerk her fingers out of his, but he tightened his grip. As his rough skin brushed hers, she realized he had taken off the black gloves that matched the rest of his midnight disguise.

If only she could see . . .

A gasp of horror escaped her as his arm slipped around her waist. One sharp tug brought her against him. When she tried to pull away, his arm contracted, cutting off her breath.

"Please, no!" she begged, hating him more for forcing her to plead.

"I asked for your cooperation, milady."

Her head grew light, and she sagged against his hard chest. When her fingers touched wool, she realized he had released her hands. The painful tightness around her center vanished, and she leaned her head over his heart. It beat much more slowly than hers, but quickened when he stroked her back with shocking tenderness. He drew aside the veil which was tangled around her shoulders, then tilted her chin back, freeing her hair to flow across his arm.

"You must stop this," she whispered.

"Must I?"

She could not answer as his mouth covered hers. A pulse raced through her, hot as summer lightning. Frightened, she tried to push him away, but he slowly, thoroughly explored her lips. His tongue teased the corners before outlining them with liquid flame. Her fingers gripped his tunic as he left scintillating sparks along her throat. She trembled in his arms, for nothing had prepared her for the potent sensations surging through her with each touch.

A low moan emerged from her, and she heard his satisfied laugh in the moment before he captured her mouth again. As his arms gentled into an embrace, she softened against the hard angles of his body. Teasing, lilting kisses ignited pleasure on her eyelids, the curve of her cheek, the tip of her nose.

Her fingers moved hesitantly along his chest. When his heartbeat throbbed beneath them, his lips traced the half circle of her ear. Fierce waves of delight swirled through her. Nothing had ever been like this sweet, mind-emptying caress.

He leaned her back on his muscular arm and delved into her mouth, allowing no luscious secret to remain hidden. When he urged her to be as bold, his breath caught against her.

The material of his mask brushed Audra's face. Like a slap, it freed her from the intoxicating enchantment of his lips. This man was her enemy . . . and Bredonmere's. She stroked his shoulder as she tried to fight the rapture coiling more tightly within her as his tongue caressed the curve of her neck. It was madness to surrender to his seduction when he was only using his captivating magic to steal her father's legacy. When he murmured her name against her skin, she reached for the knot binding his mask in place.

Lynx laughed coldly as he caught her hand. He thrust her back onto the straw and leaned over her. "You dare much, my lovely lady."

"So do you!" she snapped through clenched teeth. How could she have allowed herself to become spellbound by this thief? "If my men-at-arms were to discover you holding me like this, they would castrate you before you could beg for mercy."

"Then perhaps I should enjoy you while I can." When she gasped with horror, he laughed again. "Not yet, milady, but our time shall come soon."

He released her and stood. She started to roll away, but he caught her and brought her to her feet. When she twisted away, he let her go. Her surprise faded when she realized he had no worry about her escaping. Lynx would free her only if he chose.

She took a step back and nearly slipped on the straw. Clasping her fingers in front of her, she whispered, "You are mistaken. The only time I shall have for you is when I sit in judgment at your trial."

"You or your husband?"

"That decision is the king's will."

"So you would wed a man whom you do not know?"

"I shall wed a man chosen by our king for the betterment of Bredonmere, a man who needs the prestige of my title while he can bring men to defend Bredonmere. A fair bargain for everyone."

"Is it?" His low voice could have belonged to the night itself. "Is that what you wish, milady? Perhaps the fools in Bredonmere believe that, but I see the truth you hide. You may act the sweet, gentle lady of the manor, but you intend to hold on to Bredonmere like a pup with a meaty bone. You will cede it to no one."

She whirled away, wishing her eyes could pierce the darkness to discover if he was laughing at her. Terror thickened her voice as she whispered, "Who are you that you see into the depths of my soul?"

"You know me now only as Lynx, the night rider, but I vow that someday I shall be more to you."

He gripped her arms and pulled her against the wall of his chest. He laughed as she averted her face. With one strong hand, he forced her mouth beneath his again. As his lips touched hers, she knew she could not fight his untamed passion. Her arms arched up his back as his hands swept along her, pressing her to the firm lines of his body.

Audra was unsure if she heard regret in his sigh as he lifted his mouth from hers. He stroked her swollen lips, then released her. Suddenly she saw him against the moonlight in the doorway. She took one step forward, but froze when the door closed.

The bar dropped with a crash. Hearing laughter on the far side of the door, she cried, "Do not leave me here!"

The only answer was the dim sound of fading hoofbeats.

Turning away, Audra sat on the straw. Amazement filled her. She had been sure Lynx intended to force her to relinquish control of Bredonmere. Instead she had given him her lips.

She locked her hands around her knees and leaned her cheek on them. Her perfidious body ached for his mouth branding her with sensual fire and the caress of him against her. She was mad! How could she crave the touch of the one man who would destroy everything she was trying to save?

The echo of his laugh ridiculed her. Suddenly she feared she understood his cruel bewitchment all too well. He had made her his captive, not with ferocious threats, but with wild kisses she wanted to sample again. She had to battle not only him, but her own cravings.

"Help me," she whispered as she hid her face in her hands. "Someone help me."

Sinking to the ground, she finally found escape in sleep hours later. Fear tainted her dreams, for when she woke, she might be in her enemy's control—and his arms—once more.

4

"Awake, milady."

"What hour is it?" Lady Audra whispered.

"Nearly dawn."

"Allow me to sleep an hour longer, Shirley. I suffered nightmares all night."

Sitting on his heels, Lynx smiled coolly. He gazed down at Lady Audra's face, which was softened to the innocence that had graced it before she was wrenched away from the abbey. Innocent she must be to let slumber overtake her now.

But he must never allow himself to think she was as witless as some of those she called her allies. Lady Audra Travers was no fool. The strength glowing in her cobalt eyes dared any man to dismiss her at his own peril.

Lightly he smoothed her tangled hair back from her forehead as he thought of her eager response to his kisses. That had been unexpected . . . for both of them. His smile broadened. No maiden, raised in the close restrictions of a convent, would have knowledge of the pleasure they could savor. He had heard the self-loathing in her voice when she decried his seduction as being beastly.

Fool! He was the fool for forgetting, even for a moment, the reason he had come to Bredonmere lands. He had not traveled leagues to bed its lady. A surge of desire, more powerful than the strongest ale, throbbed through him as his gaze caressed the curves of her slender body as eagerly as his fingers itched to do. No one could gainsay him if he were to keep this woman here until she satisfied him.

Fool! Taking her on this straw-strewn floor would ruin all his carefully made plans for Bredonmere. Not even for lovely, passionate Audra Travers could he set aside his most precious vow. He had waited too long, worked too hard, dared too much, to let her come between him and what he must do.

Sainted Mary, this was the greatest irony he could imagine. Under other circumstances, when he was not Lynx and she was not the last of her family, he could have courted her into his arms. Now she would fight fervently for what she claimed as hers.

If he had known of her existence . . . He shook his head at the thoughts that threatened to weaken his resolve. No woman could hold Bredonmere alone. She would be sent a husband, and he suspected he knew exactly whom King Edward would select. Nothing had changed, save that Lynx would never be unaware of Lady Audra Travers again.

He allowed himself a low chuckle. "Nightmares"? Had she suffered the same sensual torment that plagued him while he imagined spending the night with Bredonmere's lady? From the moment his gaze first touched hers, he had known he must alter his plans to fit her into them. She would be no man's willing puppet, but she would help him whether she wished it or not.

With a smile as savage as his namesake, Lynx slipped an arm beneath her shoulders. Her body shifted under him, and he fought the yearning to throw caution aside and succumb to desire. When her lips parted, he pressed his mouth to their gentle warmth. Her breath pulsed into him, and he pulled her closer, wanting to feel every inch of her while he could.

Audra's dreams solidified as strong arms held her against the unyielding planes of a hard body. Lost in the nether world between sleep and waking, she was unsure what was real. Lips burned against hers, demanding lips that would be satisfied with nothing less than her surrender. A faint sigh of pleasure brushed her ears. Only slowly, as lips swept across her face to caress the sensitive skin along her neck, did she realize the sound had come from her. It was a luscious dream, filled with dangerous longings and potent pleasures. She did not wish to wake.

Then harsh skin, unshaven and rough with windburn, rubbed against her face, and the tip of a tongue teased the curves of her ear. A shiver coursed through her. Her fingers swept along coarse wool to wide shoulders that dared her to explore them. The shoulders were as broad as those of—

Audra stiffened, and her eyes opened. "Lynx!" she cried, as she stared up at the black material that was visible in the faint light oozing beneath her prison's door.

"Good morning, milady," he answered with a slight bow of his head.

She cringed, not that she could fault him for

being amused at her foolishness in welcoming him into her arms. She had been asleep when he invaded her dreams and . . . She halted the damning thought. Even to herself, she could not admit that he had given life to those nebulous dreams.

Putting her hands against his chest, Audra tried to push him away from her. She could not move him.

"Are you going to fail to give me the courtesy of wishing a good morning in return, milady?" he asked, his voice as taunting as the twist of his lips.

She turned away from his victorious smile. When he bent to brush his lips against her ear again, she struggled to escape. His bold laugh warned her that this black-hearted beast was enjoying holding her as his prisoner. She started to snarl an answer to him but froze when she saw the truth in his ebony eyes. What he was enjoying was the motion of her body against his. She moaned in horror. If she did not fight him, he would use her as he wished. If she did fight him, she was playing a part in the torturous games he was inflicting upon her.

Closing her eyes, praying for strength to endure what awaited her, she realized that he alone set his lawless rules. She must do as he commanded as long as no more than her pride was endangered. "Good morning," she whispered as compliantly as a novice at matins.

He sat down but leaned over her to keep her from doing the same. "'Tis nearly sunrise, milady. I fear the time for you to enjoy my hospitality has come to an end."

"You are letting me go?"

"For now." Behind his mask, his eyes twinkled with malicious delight. "Although they shall, no doubt, hide their evil thoughts well, your enemies in the manor house will be disturbed when they discover you have survived the night. Mayhap, having learned that you are not the fool they consider you to be, they will be less willing to devise such blatant attempts on your life again."

She wiggled from beneath his arm and rose to her knees. With her eyes level with his, she nearly spat out the words. "You lie! My enemy is you!"

Regret deepened his voice. "That is where you are mistaken. I pray you shall know the truth before your enemies end your short hold on Bredonmere."

"If you would begone, I could—"

"Die." His answer lashed into her with the fury of a summer tempest. "If you don't believe that after I have saved your life by keeping you from your enemies on the night they would have slain you, I doubt I can persuade you to heed my warning today." He reached beneath his long cape and withdrew a strip of material. "Turn around, milady."

"What are you going to do?"

"If you choose to cooperate, I shall take you to a place from where you can find your way to Bredonmere Manor. If you choose not to cooperate . . ." As before, there was no need for him to finish his threat.

Audra loathed the circumstances that forced her to obey him, but she did as he ordered. She would have her revenge when he was *her* prisoner, as he would be. She vowed that. Lynx would pay for this humiliation with his freedom.

He swathed her face in stinking wool. When her hair caught beneath the thick knot, she stifled a moan. She would give him no more pleasure at her pain.

"It is for no more than a few minutes, milady." His hateful chuckle rumbled, warning her that he hid his thoughts far better than she could. "You are an earl's daughter. Prove your father's line proud by withstanding a bit of discomfort for the sake of your life and your manor."

"I shall see you dead!"

"Mayhap, but not today."

Audra struggled to stay on her feet as she was herded from her prison. Smells of a fresh morning struck her along with the warmth of the rising sun. Beneath her feet, the soft earth was damp with dew. She sought any clue to tell her where she was amidst the greenwood that surrounded Bredonmere. The muted whisper of a rivulet, the sharp slope of the ground, the cry of a hawk, she heeded them all.

Strong arms raised her up and tipped her over a brawny shoulder. She opened her mouth to scream, but the sound became a groan as she was flung over a horse. Her nose struck the saddle, blinding her with agony. She tried to touch it, praying it was not broken, but her hand was caught in a vicious vise. When the saddle shifted beneath her, a squeak of leather warned her that Lynx was climbing into the saddle.

Something heavy was draped over her, and she guessed he was using his black cloak to conceal her from anyone who might chance to see them. He pressed her hand against her back to keep her from moving.

The steady rhythm of the horse's bones beneath her stomach ground through her skin and threatened to leave her weak with nausea. She refused to sicken before her enemy. If she showed any sign of frailty, he would use it to his advantage. Audra almost laughed at the thought. All advantage was his now.

Sooner than she expected, Lynx stopped the horse. He dropped quickly to the ground and lifted her off with the gentleness she continued to find astonishing. Then he set her on her feet.

His low laugh was her only warning before he pulled her against him. His mouth claimed hers, scorching her with the tempting fire that implored her to forget he was her nemesis. As her breasts pressed against his strong chest, she could not keep her hands from slipping up his back. She hated him, but she could not resist this madness he invited her to share.

Audra swayed as he released her. Trying to see through the thick wool still blinding her, she gasped when he lifted her hand and placed something small on her palm. He closed her fingers over it.

"What is this?" she asked.

"Such curiosity is indeed charming, but it shall be your undoing if you do not take care. Until next time, milady," he murmured.

"No!" she cried. "There can be no next time!"

When he did not answer, she struggled with the knots in the material wrapped around her head, wincing as she pulled free the hair snarled in the cloth. When she undid the last twist, she pulled the blindfold off to see what she had guessed, although she had heard no sound of hoofbeats.

She stood in the middle of a deserted road.

Alone.

Audra paused at a fork in the road. Most likely, Lynx was laughing at her even now. He had left her, as she had suspected, less than a league from the manor house. Looking along the road to the left, she could see Bredonmere's highest towers over the trees. She should continue along that road, but her gaze was caught by a small cottage to the right. It clung to the shadows under the trees, but its fence was unbroken and a wisp of smoke told her the house had not been emptied by the Death.

She staggered toward the cottage. She would seek help to send a message to Bredonmere. Although she was not far from its walls, she feared she could walk no farther. Somewhere, while riding prone over Lynx's horse, she had lost her right shoe, and her head resounded with pain from sleeping on the damp ground.

The gate squealed like a piglet as she pushed it open. A light brown dog watched her closely but did not rise from its spot by the door. She called a greeting, not wanting to think what she would do if it was not answered.

A woman peered out of the stone cottage. As Audra walked closer, she saw the woman was well past middle age. The coarse material of her wimple matched the apron she wore over a shapeless wool kirtle. Her hair was as white as bleached linen, making a wispy aura around her wrinkled face, which creased with a smile.

Holding out a veined hand, the old woman cried, "Milady! Praise the Lord for bringing you back to us safely."

"Yes, praise the Lord," she whispered, although it was the devil that had spawned Lynx and afflicted her lands with his trickery. "Do you have someone to deliver a message to the manor?"

"My dear lad should be coming from the manor soon." Her smile broadened as she added, "He visits me each day with the tidings. Today I shall surprise him with the glad news of your reappearance."

"He is of the manor house?" Although she had denied Lynx's assertion that someone in the manor wanted her dead, she could not ignore the suspicions he had planted in her mind. She yearned to disregard the tales told by a thief, but they mocked her. Shaw *had* abandoned her. Had there been more to that than his hope of embarrassing her before her retainers and villeins?

"Come," the old woman said, stepping aside. "We can speak more easily within. May I offer you something to break your fast?"

"Yes."

The old woman chuckled at her immediate reply. "Good. I have a porridge bubbling over the hearth now. That and a bit of fresh milk will fill your belly while we wait."

"Thank you." She tried to smile but failed. "What is your name?"

"Ida. Step up, milady."

Although the old woman appeared fragile, she was strong enough to assist Audra into the cottage. The warm fragrance of food and the herbs hanging from the rafters drew Audra toward the table and pair of benches in the middle of the floor. Against one wall, a closet bed could be seen through an uneven door. Beneath her feet, the dirt was as hard as a tiled floor, for it had been smoothed by many feet.

"Sit, milady," Ida said as she paused by the time-worn table.

Audra obeyed and stared into the flames, too tired to move, too frightened to think.

"What is it that you are carrying, milady?"

Slowly Audra opened her fingers to discover she still clutched what Lynx had given her. It was the gold button she had lost by the brook. Lynx had found it and returned it to her. Why? She could not even guess what thoughts flowed through his head.

She shuddered and dropped the button to the table as she pressed her hands to her face, surrendering to the fear she could fight no longer. She had not escaped from Lynx. His wicked shadow darkened every thought and had crept into her soul after he tempted her with the wiles of a demon. Last night had served to show her how powerless she was against him. She must continue to battle him, although she had no idea how.

"Oh, milady," Ida moaned. "'Twill be all right. I swear by all the saints 'twill be all right."

Meeting the old woman's brown eyes, Audra whispered, "I would pray that you are right. Forgive me. I should not burden you."

"Nonsense." She set a wooden spoon by the gold button. "Eat, milady. 'Twill do you good."

Audra's hand trembled as she dipped the spoon in the bowl of porridge Ida had put in front of her. She was unsure if she could swallow a single bite, but once she had taken the first spoonful, she realized how hungry she was. She drained a mug of warm milk eagerly, and Ida refilled it.

Guilt suffused her. She was greedily eating this old woman's food. Such a small toft would provide little. As soon as she returned to the manor, she would have Crandall send Ida more than enough food to replace what she was eating.

"Good morning!" called a deep voice in a familiar accent.

Audra looked over her shoulder, astonished to see Bourne. There had been no reason for her to guess that the man who worked in the armory and trained the lads on the mock battlefield was the man Ida awaited. That was not what surprised her. She was astounded by the intense joy she felt at seeing someone from Bredonmere. Someone she hoped she could trust.

She scowled at Lynx's warning that resounded through her head. Was this another of his ploys to undo her? If he convinced her to have faith in none of her retainers, he could undermine her hold on Bredonmere even more quickly.

Bourne came forward, dropped to his knees, and pressed her hand to his forehead. "Milady."

"Rise, my friend," she murmured, suspecting he had misread her expression. Her frustration was not with him, but with the man who rode the night. "You do me much honor when I intrude on your home to seek the sanctuary of . . ." She hesitated, realizing she was not sure of the relationship between Bourne and Ida. "Your mother's company?"

"Not my mother, milady." He smiled at the old woman, who was pressing her apron to her lips. "Ida served as a nurse to the mother of my late knight. Like his mother, Ida is of this country."

"That is true," Ida murmured, turning back to the hearth to stir one of the pots.

Bourne stood, towering over her so that she had to tilt her head at an uncomfortable angle to see his face.

Her breath caught. Bourne and Lynx were nearly of a height, and she had become closely acquainted with the breadth of Lynx's shoulders, which were as wide as the armorer's. Dark hair, dark eyes . . . Could they be one and the same? No, she thought, chiding herself for her silly hopes. Lynx was no ally, and his voice was deeper than Bourne's. And . . . She forced herself not to look at his leg, which twisted on every step.

Be thankful, she told herself. She needed Bourne

as her ally. His training of the youngsters might be the sole way to protect Bredonmere if the manor came into contention.

"You are sorely missed, milady," he said, sounding as out of breath as if he had raced from Bredonmere to this toft. "Crandall has had us seeking you everywhere since sundown last night. Yet I find you here only a half mile from the manor. Where have you been?"

Ida said quickly, "Give Lady Audra a chance to finish her breakfast."

Accepting another cup of milk, Audra took a sip. She saw how her hands trembled as memories forced her back into the captivity she had despaired of ever escaping. She berated herself. She *was* falling prey to Lynx's artifice. She must not let him convince her to see perfidy where there was none.

"I have been Lynx's unwilling guest," she answered.

"Lynx?" An iron kettle fell from Ida's fingers to crash on the dirt floor. Her face was gray as she whispered, "He abducted you?"

"He found me." Honesty compelled her to add, "Shaw left me in the forest."

"Shaw?" Bourne asked tightly.

Audra nodded, lowering her gaze away from his rage. She understood it too well but was grateful to see it on Bourne's face. Unless he had the skills of a mummer, this was a surprise to him. Her hands tightened on the cup. First Shaw must pay for betraying her, then Lynx.

Bourne went on, "Did Lynx hurt you, milady?"

Unsure how to answer, she stared at the cup. She must never speak of the pleasure she had found in her enemy's kisses. She put her fingers to the tender spot on the back of her head. "I have been hurt worse falling off my horse."

Gulping the milk Ida had handed him, Bourne gently brought Audra to her feet. "Come, milady. I will take you back to the manor. It is time to let the glad tidings of your safety be known."

Audra thanked Ida again. The old woman waved aside her gratitude, but Audra could tell that she was disturbed to learn her lady had been Lynx's captive. That sentiment would be shared by the rest of Bredonmere. If the anger swelled enough to urge them to hunt down Lynx, she would support them. More than ever, she wanted to see him brought to justice. She must stop him. If he continued to roam the night freely, he could solidify his hold on her fief as he worked his bewitchment on her.

She winced as she put her weight on her right foot. Before she could take another step, Bourne scooped her up into his arms. She stared at him, shocked he would treat her with as little regard as a piece of armor.

"You are clearly hurt," he said in the same taut voice. "I shall not let you take another step and risk endangering yourself more. My horse waits outside, and I will take you directly to your chambers." His anger lessened as he added, "With your permission."

"I am glad for your assistance, which will save me from looking the fool before my household."

"No one in Bredonmere would mistake you for a fool, milady."

Audra glanced at him, startled by his unexpected words. He was looking past her as he bid Ida farewell. With a sigh, she rested her head against his shoulder as he limped slowly out the door. She was tired of fighting—of fighting those who did not believe a woman could hold Bredonmere, of fighting Lynx, of fighting herself. It had to come to an end, but she feared what the ending might bring.

5

Shouts preceded them as Bourne led his horse with Audra on it into the inner bailey. Children swarmed around the horse's legs, and he shooed them away.

Audra remained silent, staring up at the walls rising up to the sky, and the crucifix-shaped slits through which bowmen could fire upon anyone reckless enough to dare the might of Bredonmere. More than ever, she knew she could not admit defeat. This manor had become home. These were her people, who depended on her to give them protection from the enemies who were not hers alone.

The children's cries must have alerted their elders, for others surged from the keep. Bourne stopped to help Audra down. She put her hands on his shoulders, hoping she could depend on this faithful man. Again she forced the poisonous thoughts from her head. Lynx sought only to besmirch the loyalty within the keep. She would listen to his nonsense no longer.

She sensed rage within Bourne. If that was aimed at Lynx, it might be the proof she sought that Bourne was truly her ally.

When she slid from the saddle, she was shocked that he cradled her in his arms once more. "I thank you for your help," she said, not wanting to insult him, "but I can walk alone."

"No, milady," he said with a smile. "I told you I would carry you to your room before I let you wound your tender feet more. That is what I shall do, unless you say nay."

She relaxed and nodded. Since their first meeting, he had kept a respectful distance, offering her the deference he would have given her father. Still, there was something wondrously comforting about his brawny arms holding her as if she were no more than a babe.

"I shall not say nay to your kindness," she whispered.

"I thought not."

When he shifted her in his arms, she found her head resting again against his shoulder as he hobbled toward the keep. Ignoring the sounds of questions from the crowd, she closed her eyes. For the first time since leaving Clarendon Abbey, she felt safe. Bourne was her ally. He would protect her, always defending her and Bredonmere from what waited in the darkest shadows. Just now, she wanted nothing but to feel safe.

He quickly brought them from the heat of the morning sun into the keep's cool dankness. Again and again, he repeated, "Lady Audra is unhurt. Please step aside. She needs to rest."

She added nothing to his orders. Letting the others think she was asleep, she kept her eyes closed while they crossed the great hall and went to the staircase on its far side. She heard the whisper of gossip. Each person they passed must still be wondering what had kept Lady Audra from the manor house all night.

Carefully Bourne shifted her in his arms as he prepared to climb the steep, twisting stairs. "You need take me no farther," she said, hoping he would disagree.

He chuckled. "Do not be offended when I say that you are easier to carry than some of the weapons I deal with daily."

"Bourne—" she began, then was interrupted by a shout from below.

The voice echoed up the stairwell, punctuated by heavy footsteps. Bourne paused and turned so she could see Crandall rushing toward them. At the choleric color of her steward's face, she warned him to slow. He ignored her, running up the last few steps.

Leaning his arm on the wall, he put his hand to his side as he wheezed, "Milady, you are safe?"

"Which you shall not be if you race about like a page doing errands!"

"Where did you find her?" he asked Bourne.

"I suspect milady would appreciate a chance to rest before we scrutinize all the facts of her escapade."

Audra halted any protest from Crandall by lifting her hand from around Bourne's shoulders. When she wobbled in his strong arms, he held her fast. Bourne would not let her come to injury.

"Pray let everything wait," she whispered. "Before I unravel the events of the past day, Crandall, I wish to clean the filth from me."

Although the steward clearly wanted to argue, he nodded and followed them. More than once, he cautioned Bourne to watch his step or to move more steadily so he did not risk their lady.

Audra hid her smile against Bourne's hard shoulder. How shocked Crandall would be to discover she found his concern humorous, for he acted as nervous as a cat with a single kit. Then her smile faded. She was the last of the Travers brood, and he was wise to be anxious when she had vanished without explanation. To allow the manor to come into contention among landless younger sons could mean its destruction.

When they entered her rooms, Shirley pushed the other maids aside and ordered Bourne to carry Audra into the innermost chamber, not waiting to see if he obeyed.

Bourne carefully set Audra on the carpet in her bedchamber. Shirley waved him away, and he grinned. Let the woman have a chance to flutter around her lady. The tears staining the thin woman's face now were of joy.

He opened the window wide to let in the morning air. Across the courtyard, clusters of people pocked the bailey. All eyes were fixed on the spot where he stood, and he knew every tongue was wagging about Lady Audra. And well they should. Never in memory of even the oldest had one of Bredonmere's ladies disappeared so mysteriously.

In Bourne's mind, though, there was no mystery other than why Shaw had deserted his lady in the woods. He suspected the answer to that puzzle would be forthcoming as soon as Lady Audra turned her attention to Shaw. Her anger would not be as gentle as her kind heart might suggest.

He went back to Lady Audra, who was wobbling on her feet as Crandall tried to pry answers from her, and put his hands on her shoulders to brace her. "If you would recall, Crandall, milady has said she would prefer a chance to rest before she discusses this."

The steward's face paled in shock. Shirley gasped aloud and clutched her folded hands to her chest. No peasant gave orders in the bedchamber of the countess of Bredonmere.

"Bourne is correct," Lady Audra whispered. "Crandall, pray give me some time to set my head aright. Have Shaw in my audience room at midday. I shall wish to speak to him before I do anything else."

"Come," Shirley said, putting her hand on her lady's elbow to steer her past the large bed. "Your bath should be ready. I have had water heating on the hearth all night."

Again Audra nodded slowly, her head weighted with fatigue. Bourne understood. No one had slept last night.

He was astonished when she turned and placed her slender hands on his arm. "Good friend, I thank you for all you have done for me this morning."

"I have done little for you this morning."

"There are times when a little means more than the grandest boon." Her smile was fleeting. "Stay, if you will. It would please me to have you here during the discussion we must have."

He knelt and brought both of her hands to his

forehead. "Trust me, milady, when I say all I can do for you is my greatest pleasure."

He raised his gaze to look past her hands and saw bafflement in her eyes. That he understood, too. A man she had trusted had betrayed her. Now she questioned each person who claimed fealty to her. He would ask questions of his own in his own time to find his own answers. That much he owed his lady as she battled her enemies.

Sunshine tickled Audra's face, luring her out of sleep. She was startled to see sunlight halfway across the floor. Fighting the cobwebs in her mind, she tried to recall why she was so late abed. Memory returned with the ferocity of the haft of Lynx's dagger against her skull.

"Milady, how do you fare?"

Audra smiled as she saw Shirley rising from the bench by the hearth. This friend was one she knew was trustworthy. Shirley and Crandall would stand by her no matter what came to pass in Bredonmere. And Fleming. The young man had made no secret of his eagerness to bring Bredonmere back to the glory of her father's reign. And Bourne? Today had proven that he was truly her friend.

But as for the others, she had no answers. Shaw must be sure of himself if he had acted with such boldness. If he had turned her men-at-arms against her, she must counteract at once. She was a Travers. It was her duty and honor to hold Bredonmere. Those who doubted her skills must be shown how mistaken they were.

Yet what punishment could she give Shaw? Bourne would wish her commander put to death for his subterfuge. Mayhap he was right, but she could not condemn Shaw to death for this. So many times, the Abbess had insisted on seeking a merciful course. There must be a way to let Shaw feel her displeasure and still be merciful.

Banishment? No, she would be unwise to seek that path. If Shaw was so brash, he must have the support of others. By keeping him in the manor, she might be able to discover his allies and put a halt to their attempts to undermine her authority.

"I shall be fine," she answered, hoping no sign of her thoughts were visible. Sitting up, she saw the sunlight glowing across the stone floor. "What hour is it?"

"Just past midday."

She nodded. That explained why only the roughest edges of her fatigue had been sanded away, for she had slept but a few hours. She had no time to waste on slumber now.

As Audra stood, Shirley rushed forward with a tan kirtle. Slipping her arms into its sleeves, Audra asked, "Have the others had a chance to rest and eat?"

"Yes, milady," she answered with a smile. Getting a brush from a nearby table, she began to unsnarl Audra's curls, which remained damp from her bath. As she braided it into a series of plaits to encircle Audra's face, she added, "They wanted to wait for you in the outer chamber, but I told them you would rather they were well rested also."

"Call them now."

"Yes, milady."

Audra said nothing when she walked through the antechamber and into her audience room a few minutes later. She looked from Shirley's face, which was drawn with fatigue, to Crandall's barely suppressed fury. Behind them stood Bourne and Father Jerome. She hid her dismay at seeing the priest. He reminded her of the lie she held in her heart. No one must know of the illicit passion she had discovered in the arms of a masked outlaw.

"Shaw awaits your pleasure, milady," said Crandall.

"Then let us deal with this at once."

The steward went to door while she sat on the wooden bench in the center of the room. The rest of the furniture had been carried to the walls, making it clear that everything of import would happen from where she sat. She brushed her fingers against the smooth wood, wishing she might find the wisdom of her father. When Crandall opened the door, she was not surprised to see Fleming guarding Shaw, so he would not flee her judgment.

Shaw dashed across the room. Bourne stepped forward, his hand on the blade in his belt, but paused when Shaw fell to the floor and pressed his head to the hem of her robe. "Milady, condemn me to death. Banish me from Bredonmere. Sell me into bondage. I cannot beg your forgiveness for what happened yesterday. Punish me as you see fit."

Overwhelmed, Audra drew her kirtle away. "Do not tempt me to do things I have already considered."

"I beg your compassion. I was a fool to play such a prank on you, milady."

"A prank?" she asked coldly.

"I thought if you were lost in your own greenwood—"

"I would be confirmed to be unsuitable to see to the welfare of Bredonmere and its inmates," she finished in the same frigid tone. "Is this a test each one who claims Bredonmere must endure, Shaw?"

When the man did not answer, Audra looked at the others in the room. She could read their thoughts as if they were her own. Crandall and Fleming would have her order Shaw's death. Shirley would applaud such a decision, although Father Jerome would counsel against such vengeance. And Bourne . . . She hesitated. She had no idea what he was thinking. His gaze was focused on Shaw, but his face held no more expression than the stones in the wall. She wondered how an outlander would view English justice. Her justice.

The decision was hers. She clasped her hands in her lap. Quietly she said, "Shaw, I owe you a debt of thanks."

"Thanks?" he choked.

Crandall began, "Milady—"

"Heed *all* I have to say," Audra said, raising her hand to warn that she expected silence. "Shaw, your bungling has proven the loyalty of my retainers and your ineptitude. You are relieved of your duties and hereafter will assist the gong farmers who are digging new pits for the privies in the south tower." She turned away, not wanting to see his fury at the degrading punishment. "Fleming, you shall assume the duties of the commander of the men-at-arms. Bourne will assist you as you deem necessary."

Fleming colored nearly as red as Shaw's hair as he grinned with boyish pride. Dropping to his knees, he whispered, "Thank you, milady. May I fulfill the trust you have put in me."

"I trust that you shall. Your first duty is to see that Shaw begins his new duties." She kept her head high while Fleming jumped to his feet and motioned for Shaw to precede him out the door.

As soon as the door closed behind them, Crandall muttered, "That is one dirty job that shall not be needing other volunteers coerced into doing it."

"He should deem himself lucky that he was not given the task of digging his own grave," Bourne growled.

"Now, now," said Father Jerome. "No need to be so grim. Our lady is returned to us, well and unharmed."

Audra closed her eyes and sighed. She could not order Shaw's death for such a misjudgment. The abbess had taught that each person must be forgiven for his mistakes. If Shaw refused to accept his punishment, he could leave Bredonmere. Exile was not the horror it had been before the Black Death. Every fief was eager for another man who could wield weapons with skill.

She was about to stand and halt Crandall's jokes at Shaw's expense. She gasped as the sound of familiar laughter filled her ears and Lynx's face filled her mind. Lynx? Here?

She jumped to her feet and turned to discover Father Jerome laughing with uninhibited delight. As the priest went to speak to Bourne, she stared at him. She wanted to deny what her eyes were revealing to her, but it was impossible.

Father Jerome's coloring matched Lynx's, for his eyes were ebony dark as was his hair. If it was covered by a swathe of black cloth, his tonsure would be invisible. His height was the equal of the night rider's and his voice undeniably similar with its deep, spontaneous rumble.

Could Father Jerome be the guise Lynx assumed in the daylight? No one would suspect a priest of trying to wrest the rightful authority of the countess of

Bredonmere from her. Sickness twisted her stomach as she realized that the man who had kissed her with such unfettered passion, and pledged to return to do so again, could be a priest.

Or was Father Jerome actually not a priest? He could have disguised himself in churchly raiment to take over the chapel when all the churchmen in the manor were struck by the plague. Suddenly Audra wished she was far from Bredonmere and the intricate plots twisting her heart until she was no longer sure what she should do.

She must decide—and decide with haste—or Bredonmere and everything she hoped to save would be destroyed.

Audra pressed the signet ring that had been her father's into the wax beneath her name on the long document. The heavy ring was not comfortable on her hand, so she kept it in a velvet pouch in the rosewood box that held her writing materials. Letting the parchment roll up, she handed it to Crandall.

The steward wore a bilious expression, but she paid it no more mind than the rain splattering beyond the window. She knew he was displeased that she did not have to depend on him to read to her and act the scribe for every document she sent forth from Bredonmere. So infernally slow was his tortured writing that she had lost her patience and taken over the task herself.

"It fills my heart with hope to see two more payments of merchet," Audra said with a smile. "With each marriage, there is a new beginning for Bredonmere."

"'Tis not the sixpence the wenches pay to the

manor when they are wed that will bring a new beginning, milady, but the announcement that *you* have decided to take a husband."

She closed the small bottle of ink and set the quill aside, keeping her eyes from meeting Crandall's. "I have yet to hear from my cousin the king on this matter. The message I dispatched to him, informing him of my claim on Bredonmere and trusting my future and Bredonmere's future to his wisdom, was received as you well know. He will decree when and whom I should wed."

"This delay concerns me."

"Everything concerns you, Crandall." She tried to smile again but failed. "The king is busy with troubles throughout his kingdom, for the Death has been even more unstinting in London than here in the country. He will turn his attention to Bredonmere when he deems the time right."

Crandall slipped the parchment into a pouch on his belt and began to pace in front of the table. His shadow wavered on the wall as the single candle danced in the cool breeze blowing around the window. "Milady, mayhap he waits for you to approach him in person. Your lord father was often in the king's company."

"I cannot leave Bredonmere now." Going to the window, she looked out at the gray day that was fading into a gray night. "The planting is going well, but I must remain to oversee the manor."

"The planting goes well since Lynx has vanished."

"There have been no more reports of night mischief?"

Crandall shook his head. "Not for longer than two fortnights, milady. I dare to believe the scoundrel has been convinced that, with one of Travers blood holding Bredonmere, he has nothing to gain but a hangman's noose about his neck."

"I had not guessed him to admit defeat so easily."

"Easily?" the steward exploded, his hands clenched into fists at his sides. "How many byres have been lost? How much more mischief would you wish him to inflict upon us?"

Audra did not answer but turned back to stare out into the twilight. Had Lynx left Bredonmere lands? She could not believe it. Her heart cramped as she realized she did not want him to be gone forever. His antics, yes, she wished those would never return, but she had spent too many nights dreaming of his arms about her and his mouth pressed to hers.

Her hands fisted on the wide sill. How much more Crandall would sputter if he learned of her traitorous thoughts! She whirled away from the window, yet she could not escape the truth that pulsed through her with every breath. Lynx had not been successful in invading her lands, but he had invaded her heart. She could not rid her thoughts of his challenging eyes and bold caresses.

"I have," Audra said with the quiet authority she had copied from the abbess, "too many matters that require my consideration to trouble myself with the king's delay in finding me a suitable husband to serve as the earl of Bredonmere. We must let the future unfold as it may. King Edward will not forget Bredonmere."

"I am certain of that, milady," Crandall answered hastily. His face was drawn with anxiety, and she was accustomed by now to his attempts to atone for his outbursts. Not that she faulted him, for his loyalty was first and always to her and to Bredonmere. "The king will send you a strong, wise husband to relieve you of the burden of overseeing this fief."

She waited for the proper words to come into her head, but none formed. She could not say that she had no wish to be relieved of what Crandall named a burden. For her, it would be too soon that a man was found for the countess of Bredonmere. Then everything she hoped for might come to an end.

She must never give voice to that thought, nor could she speak of how she feared no man would stir her heart as Lynx did. That would be the greatest mistake she could make.

Audra closed the door from the great hall behind her and released a sigh of pent-up frustration. Tonight during the late meal, Crandall had spoken of nothing but the husband the king would be sending to her. He acted more like an anxious bride than she did.

With a shudder, although the night air was gently warm in the wake of the remnants of the storm, she thought of the many ideas she had for Bredonmere and how she wished to try each of them. They might be for naught if the man chosen for her by the king refused to let her involve herself with matters beyond the hall. Frustrated, she slapped at the ring of keys at her waist. It was the badge of honor for any lady, but she yearned to see the fields put to better use and to find a way for her tenants to have better lives.

The inner bailey was nearly forsaken. Along the top of the walls, she could see the faint glimmer of light from the guardhouses. One sentinel called to another, their words lost in the distance, but their light voices proclaimed that all was well along the walls. The serenity of the night was broken only by the disquiet within her.

She glanced at the chapel. How could she go to Father Jerome with her dilemma when he would be the first to remind her of her duty to marry as the king commanded? And if he actually was Lynx . . .

She wandered across the rough stones. She wanted to talk to someone but no longer knew whom to trust. She had never felt such confusion in the abbey.

Audra paused by a thick wall and realized she was standing in front of the armory. In spite of Bourne's invitation, she had never visited it. Suddenly she decided to view the weapons that would foil any attack from beyond the walls of Bredonmere.

The heavy door nearly daunted her, but she put her shoulder to the thick oak and pushed it open. Feeble light from a brand on the wall by the door welcomed her into the room. The ceiling reached almost to the top of the inner bailey's wall, and a collection of broad tables was scattered about the room. The stench of wood smoke filled each breath she took, but the hearths were quiescent.

She wandered among the pieces of mail and stared at the ferocious weapons of death on the tables. These were only some of the ways Bredonmere could repel an invasion, because she knew the walls themselves had been built with traps for any man foolish enough to test them. With a frown, she stared at a staff in the center of one table. What was its purpose?

She was about to call Bourne's name to ask him to come and explain, but the words evaporated in a heated pulse of dismay as she saw a familiar figure moving within the shadows of the armory.

Lynx! He had not left her lands after all!

How dare he lurk in the heart of Bredonmere Manor as if it were his domain! She would prove to him—once and for all to know—that *she* and she alone held Bredonmere.

Holding her breath, she lifted a sword off the table. Its tip scraped across the wood. She tensed. Her breath eased past her lips when Lynx did not turn. Whatever mischief he was up to must be engrossing him. Seeing mire clinging to his clothes, she wondered what he had intended to do this night. It mattered little now, for *she* intended to halt it.

She eased around the half suit of armor and raised the sword. When she saw him reaching for the knot holding the material in place over his face, she froze. *This* was the moment she had hoped for. Now she would discover the man behind the mask.

She inched forward so she could see past a suit of mail. A board creaked. Lynx whirled around. She held the tip of the sword to his chest.

"You are my prisoner, Lynx," she said with satisfaction.

"That appears to be the truth." He spoke calmly.

"How did you get in here without the watch seeing you?"

He smiled.

"Lift your hands away from your sword," she ordered when he did not answer.

He slowly raised them, his smile never wavering.

Audra hesitated. Should she march him across the bailey to the hall where her allies could share the moment of revelation, or should she demand that he unmask here?

He took a step toward her. With a startled gasp, she moved back. Was he mad? His low chuckle slid over her. She flinched at its sarcasm. *She* held the sword. He was *her* captive!

"What do you wish, oh, master of my fate?" Lynx asked, with another laugh. "Or should I say 'mistress of my fate'?"

"I wish you to begone."

"Do you?" He moved closer.

She put both hands on the hilt to hold the sword steady. "None of your tricks, Lynx. Your reign of terror is over. I want you gone from Bredonmere lands."

"And never to return?" When she opened her mouth to retort, he added, "Never to hold you again in my arms as your breath strains to mingle with mine? Never to have you lie against me as I taste the fragrant flavors of your skin? Never—"

"Be silent!" she cried. She must listen to no more of his enticing, enthralling words. The tremor of desire flowing along her warned that she could be betrayed once more by her body that yearned for his touch.

"As you wish, milady." He put his fingers to his forehead as he bowed toward her.

"Lynx, I—" She shrieked as, with a lightning fast motion, his cape tangled with the sword and he wrenched it out of her hands. In terror, she cried, "Bourne! Help me!"

As the sword clattered across the floor, she groped for the table. There must be another blade on it. Where was Bourne? She did not want to battle Lynx alone, but she would not flee like a frightened serf. She would not cede Bredonmere to his treachery. She would—

Fear strangled every thought as he gripped her chin in his hand. She stared up at him, trying to read his expression, but it was impossible. His eyes betrayed none of his thoughts.

"Milady," he whispered, "a sword is not your weapon. Let your warriors use that while you use the skills you possess."

"I will not allow your words to twist the truth to your own ends."

"You think you have no skills?"

"I have many." She pulled her chin from his grasp and held it high. "*I* am the chatelaine of this manor."

"So it would seem."

"Then, if you acknowledge that simple fact, obey my command to begone."

"Why would I wish to leave when we can enjoy this?"

She should have known by the eager edge in his voice. She should have been forewarned by the suspicion of a smile on his lips. She should have run in the opposite direction, but when his arm curved around her waist, she could not keep him from pulling her to him as his mouth found hers with the memory of their last kiss.

She fought her craving to succumb to the sweet temptation he offered. It was nigh to futile. Her heart beat with the yearning he brought to life, and her fingers tingled with the need to touch him. As he pressed her to the wall, his hands stroking her waist and his mouth on hers, his firm body held her in the sweetest imprisonment she could imagine.

"Why are you here at this hour?" he whispered against her ear.

He had to repeat the question before the words penetrated the golden haze in her brain. Blinking, she gazed up at him. "I was walking."

His broad fingers framed her face, seeking beneath her gorget to coil through her hair. Kisses, hot and swift, swept over her face as he murmured, "Why?"

"I wanted to think."

"And of what did you think?"

Audra shook herself. To speak the truth—that she feared what would happen when the king sent a husband for her and that she wondered if that man would excite her as Lynx did—would be foolish. When his finger grazed the curve of her ear, she shivered again, but with the longings she was struggling to ignore.

"Did you," he asked as his lips brushed her ear, "think of me, milady?"

"I think of you often."

"Do you?"

"I think of all my problems often," she retorted.

"You do not think of this?" He teased her ear with his tongue.

"No."

"Or of this?" His mouth moved along her neck, tracing an effervescent flame into her skin.

"No." Her voice trembled as she clutched his arms.

"Then perchance do you think of this?"

Her gasp of astonishment was lost beneath his mouth as his fingers curved up along her breast. Not even the layers of wool between her skin and his could lessen the flutter of ecstasy erupting through her. When his leg brushed hers in an invitation to even more intimacy, she slid her hands up his arms to encircle his neck.

"I think of this," he murmured as his fingers roved to the very tip of her breast. Chasing pleasure along her jaw with gentle nibbles, he laughed. "I think of *this* often. It is—" He cursed under his breath.

Audra watched his mouth harden into a straight line. Then she heard what he had. Footsteps, furtive footsteps, coming toward them. Before she could speak, his hand clapped over her mouth. He tugged her down into the shadows, his cloak enveloping both of them.

"Say nothing," he hissed.

She would have retorted if she could, but then she heard the creak of a foot on one of the boards. Bourne? Was rescue so close? She fought the arm pinning her against Lynx's body.

He growled under his breath and clamped his arm tighter around her. Unable to breathe, she could not fight him. Blackness gnawed at her, but slowly vanished as he lightened his grip.

No voices betrayed the others in the armory. When she heard the clank of steel, she tried to see past Lynx's broad shoulders. His cape, which made them one with the deepest shadows, hid the rest of the room from her.

Audra was unsure how long they crouched there. Her legs grew cramped, but Lynx allowed her no room to shift. The room became silent save for her swift breathing and the rhythm of his heartbeat so close to her ear. Suddenly all light vanished.

"Say nothing," he whispered as he had before.

Only when the sound of the door closing echoed through the high-ceilinged room did he stand. He held out his hand to her. Grateful for his assistance, she let him bring her to her feet. She winced as needles pricked her right foot.

"Next time you hide from your enemies," she snapped, "you need not—"

"Not my enemies, milady. Yours."

"How can you say that?"

He lit a single brand. "Look." He pointed with it to the table.

Audra pressed her fingers to her lips to silence her moan of despair. Every weapon that had been set on top of the table had vanished. Stolen!

She started to speak, but Lynx motioned toward the door. "Return to the safety of your keep, milady, and do not leave it again tonight."

"Lynx—"

"Go!"

She stared at him, wondering how this stern tyrant could be the same man who had sent delight soaring through her. Backing away from him, she followed the maze through the pieces of armor toward the door. She shoved the door open, then turned to look back.

The armory was empty! How had Lynx slipped away without coming this way? She silenced the fearful awe by telling herself there must be another door. Even so, she ran to the keep as if her feet had wings.

She staggered through the double doors and to the steps leading into the great hall, then dropped down on them. Her legs would take her no farther.

A shadow slipped over her. Horror paralyzed her as she looked up, then she closed her eyes in relief. 'Twas Bourne. His lips tilted into a smile as he leaned on the wall next to her. Although she wished to chide him for not being in the armory when she needed him, she was too glad to see him to think of anything but that she was safe.

"Milady, why are you sitting here?" Amusement

drifted into his voice. "Are you waiting for me to take you on a tour of the armory?"

In spite of herself, she smiled at his ironic reminder of their first meeting. She squared her shoulders and sat straighter. All was not lost as long as she had allies like Bourne, unless he . . .

Audra glanced at his pointed-toed shoes. Dust was caked on them. Her stomach twisted. What better way to hide the damp mire on his shoes than to cover them with the dust from the inner bailey? Was the unthinkable possible—could her loyal Bourne be riding the night as Lynx?

"I am just returned from the armory," she said slowly.

His forehead creased in bafflement. She could not tell if it was feigned or genuine. "At this hour?"

"It was a most interesting tour."

"Milady, I would have been more than delighted to show you about, if you had asked."

She gave a sigh. If she let Lynx unsettle her so much that she believed any man within the keep could be the night rider, she would lose what little control she had on her father's lands. Bourne could not be Lynx. He had none of the dangerous lure of the night rider. His voice, his stance, even his smile, which was hesitant, was different from the man whose kisses filled her dreams.

Softly she said, "I had another guide."

"Who?"

"Lynx." She watched his face closely as she spoke the name.

His eyebrows arched. "He is a bold one."

Audra had not expected such an answer but plunged ahead. "He is not as bold as the ones who have plundered the armory of every weapon."

All humor vanished from Bourne's face. "If this is a jest, milady—"

"'Tis no jest. Everything is gone."

"Gone? Are you sure?"

"Do you question what I saw with my own eyes, Bourne?"

Without asking her permission to retire, he pushed past her and raced out of the keep. She heard him yell to the watch. More shouts answered his.

Audra struggled to her feet as Fleming rushed from the great hall. He nearly knocked her to the floor. Pausing to apologize, he did not wait to hear her answer before he sped out the door.

"This way, milady." Crandall's voice reached her through the din.

She followed him back into the great hall and quickly answered his questions, leaving out—as she had before—how she had let Lynx lure her into his arms. Crandall's sharp orders set the great hall to life.

As he was about to stride away, Audra grasped his arm. "Crandall, did you see Bourne here tonight?"

He irritably replied, "Yes, he has been here all evening."

"All evening?"

"Why do you insist on disbelieving me?"

She shook her head as she murmured, "I had had the thought he might know why Lynx was waiting in the armory tonight."

The old man made a low sound that might have been laughter or vexation. "Why are you filling your head with worry about the whereabouts of your allies when you should be thinking of the whereabouts of your enemies? Tonight we are nearly defenseless against them. If they choose to attack us now . . ."

He did not finish. He did not need to, for Audra knew the truth as well as he. Tonight Bredonmere was easy prey to any of her enemies, and she was beginning to realize how many she had.

6

Something oozed by Audra's legs, brushing her dress. She looked down at the silver gray cat that had claimed her bedchamber as its private sanctuary. The cat's stomach was distended from the success of its recent hunt.

Audra scratched the cat's ears. Since the cats had been welcomed back into the keep, they had put a quick end to the patter of rats.

"I wish I had your claws to deal with my enemies as swiftly," she said, yawning.

She had found no sleep for the past two nights. During the day, she had visited the armory on every excuse. Bourne and his men were keeping the hearths alive with ceaseless fire and the cacophony of hammers on steel as they shaped new weapons. Even with her inexperienced eye, she could tell it would take more than a fortnight to fashion enough to replace the stolen ones.

Audra heard shouts as she came down the stairs and entered the great hall. Fleming raced in from the inner bailey, waving a slip of parchment in his hand. Before Audra could ask what was amiss now, he knelt before her and held the square of paper out to her.

"Milady, Father Jerome asked me to bring this to you with all due haste."

She took it and turned the page over to see words written with the bright juice of red berries. The message was short:

> To Lady Audra,
> Greetings. I return to you what you have lost.
> Until we meet again . . .

It was signed, Lynx.

"Where did you get this?" she asked, as her hands clenched in the russet folds of her cotehardie.

"Father Jerome—"

"You said that," interrupted Crandall, who had followed at a slower pace. "Who gave it to him?"

Fleming bounced to his feet at Audra's motion. "Father Jerome told me to tell you that these were the words given to him by Lynx's messenger."

"Did Lynx write this?" she asked.

"Father Jerome must have written it." He laughed sharply. "Lynx? How would a low-bred bastard like him learn to write?"

"I don't know. I . . ." She did not finish the explanation, because she did not want to see the disbelief in Fleming's eyes when she said that she was unsure if Lynx was the low-bred bandit he portrayed. Something about his voice, the way he expressed himself, suggested he might be a banished knight or even the outlawed younger son of a dissolute baron.

"He is nothing but a cur," snapped Fleming. He looked over his shoulder and grinned when the priest entered the great hall.

Audra suspected she had forgotten how to breathe as she watched the tall, dark-haired man walk toward them. With a mask over his face . . . No, she would not make the mistake of accusing Father Jerome of being Lynx until she was sure.

The priest's forehead was lined with fatigue, and Audra urged him to sit. "No time," he said. "Did Fleming tell you the amazing thing that has happened? God bless Lynx for his help."

"Why should we thank God for *him?*" Crandall grumbled.

Ignoring her steward, Audra asked, "Father, what does this note mean?"

"I wanted you to know posthaste that the weapons missing from the armory are waiting just beyond the drawbridge."

She glanced at Crandall, who was regarding her with skepticism. "Am I to believe that *Lynx* arranged for our stolen weapons to be returned?"

Father Jerome nodded. "He sent his messenger—"

"A blond lad?" she asked faintly.

"Yes." The priest's eyes narrowed. "Are you acquainted with this messenger, milady?"

"Only barely." She rubbed her knuckles with her palm as she recalled the young man she met the night of her captivity, then sighed. "So Lynx sent his messenger with our weapons to the gate?"

"Yes."

She took a deep breath and released it slowly. "It appears I am now in the unfortunate position of being in debt to my enemy."

"Mayhap he wishes to atone for all he has done," Fleming said. He hurried to add as Crandall fired a glower in his direction, "Anything is possible."

"Aye," Audra said. "Anything is possible. And that is what we must prepare ourselves for if we hope to best Lynx and our other enemies at their cruel escapades."

"If they are not one and the same," Crandall muttered. He folded his arms over his brown tunic. "Have you given no mind to how readily that night rider rounded up what had been stolen? How better to do so than gather them from his allies?"

Father Jerome frowned. "Are you suggesting, Crandall, that Lynx stole the weapons, then returned them only to throw us off guard?"

"What other reason would he have had for being in the armory when he was nearly caught by Lady Audra?"

Audra had no response for him nor did any of the others, but she knew she must try to find answers soon.

"You look as if you need some assistance, milady."

Audra clutched her horse's reins to be sure it did not bolt but turned to see Bourne coming toward her, leading a pale brown horse. She stepped from the mounting block and smiled. "This horse and I continually battle to determine which is the master." She laughed. "I fear the foolish beast may be the victor."

He patted her horse on the nose and whispered something. She watched as it nuzzled Bourne's arm, which was bare beneath the short sleeves of his frayed earth-colored tunic. For such a strong man, Bourne had a rare gentleness that had been welcome over and over. Yet he never flinched from a task. She had been pleased when Fleming appointed Bourne to be in charge of the defense of the outer walls.

"I would offer my company during your ride," he said as he ran his hand along the horse's neck.

"I would enjoy that." She let him help her into the saddle. As he mounted with an ease that startled her and which, she had to admit, she despaired of ever emulating, she added, "I planned only to go to Newman's toft to view the three babes that were born to his good wife. Father Jerome says this is a sign of God's favor being returned upon Bredonmere."

He chuckled. "The good father looks for any omen of good fortune to ease the fears of a return of the Death. Rather he should thank Newman's interest in his wife for such a generous birth."

"You have little faith, Bourne?" she asked as they rode through the gate and onto the road leading toward the toft by the river. She noted how well he settled in the saddle and wondered how many leagues he had ridden by his knight's side as they fought for the king. Bourne had been at the battle against the French at Crécy, Crandall had told her when Fleming spoke of how Bourne was working to help the young men hone their skills with their crossbows, which the English had used to rout the French that day.

"I have much faith, milady, but not in a man's determination of what God's favor might be. I respect Father Jerome's learning, yet no one has brought the promised peace to this ravaged land." His dark brows rose. "Do you cry heresy on such plain speech?"

"I was taught in Clarendon Abbey that God helps those who help themselves."

Again he laughed. "And there are many who are helping themselves to the ruined tofts and fiefs, milady."

As they rode, dust clung to her murrey cotehardie, turning it a grimy gray, but sunshine filtered through her linen wimple. It was a lovely day, and the fields were a lush green. Cows grew fat on the new grass, and many more chickens were scratching in front of the cottages they passed.

She spent little time at the toft, for she saw the young mother was spent from the attention and caring for three babes as well as the two youngsters hiding behind her skirt. With a toothless grin, Newman accepted the bottle of wine that Audra had brought and vowed to drink a toast to her and Bredonmere. She was glad to leave the dank darkness of the cottage and return to the sunlight.

Bourne kept his horse's gait slow as they turned back to the manor. "If you would, milady, there is another toft that awaits your visit."

"Another?"

"Ida asks often of you."

Audra smiled. She had not had a chance to thank the old woman in person for her hospitality the morning Lynx released her from captivity. Urging Bourne to lead the way to the small cottage, she set her horse to follow.

Ida's broad smile creased her wrinkled face as she came out of her cottage to greet them. "I thank *you*, milady," she said when Audra apologized for not visiting sooner, "for your generosity when it was my honor to offer you succor that day."

"Will you not ask Lady Audra in?" Bourne asked with a smile.

"I—" Ida glanced over her shoulder as she backed into the doorway. Tension sharpened her voice. "Of course. Forgive me for my lack of hospitality."

Curious at the woman's behavior, Audra looked into every corner as she entered, but could see nothing amiss. It was as it had been before, save that the doors to the cupboard bed were closed. That was usual during the day. If Ida was distressed at the simplicity of her cottage, Audra must assure her that no person on Bredonmere's lands was judged by their surroundings.

Before she could speak, Bourne launched into the tale of how the weapons had been returned to Bredonmere. Audra sat on a bench and listened as he entertained the elderly woman with a light-hearted version of the traumatic days and fearful nights.

"And if Lynx had not returned the weapons, I swear we would have worked for—"

Audra jumped up as a crash came from the cupboard bed. Seeing Bourne exchange a glance with Ida, whose face was ashen, she whispered, "What was that?"

Ida started to answer, but Bourne interrupted her with a chuckle. "You cannot hide the truth forever." He walked to the cupboard bed and threw open one door. With a shout that rang Audra's ears, he called, "Good day, Granny. You are late rising this day." He turned and said in a normal voice, "'Tis Ida's mother. She is as deaf as a stump."

Audra let the tension flow out of her shoulders. Allowing every sound to frighten her would betray her to those who would see her fail. She went to the bed and spoke a greeting but got no reply from the form that was huddled under the blankets. The woman's pale hair spoke of many years.

Bourne smiled. "She says little, and what she says makes less sense than a baby's babbling, but Ida tends to her as I shall tend to Ida when she grows as aged and decrepit." He winked at the old woman and chuckled.

A sudden void ached within Audra. While she

busied herself with all the demands of Bredonmere, she could forget that she was the only one of her family left. The line behind her was broken with nobody to speak to her of family traditions. Beyond her, there was nothing . . . yet, for it would be her duty to give Bredonmere an heir.

She was glad when Bourne suggested that they could not linger. Riding by his side back to Bredonmere, she yearned for the family she had lost even before the Death took them. She wondered how the sisters at Clarendon Abbey fared. She had given them scant thought in the past fortnights. What had they thought when the abbess spoke of her hasty departure? And had the children forgiven her?

Bourne's voice jolted her out of her self-pity as he said with a chuckle, "You prove the gossipers right when they say you shall be a benevolent lady of the manor."

"Gossip?" She knew there must be much talk of a woman who dared claim her family's fief. "What else do they say?"

"They are curious if you shall be greeting your husband soon."

"Mayhap."

"Mayhap?"

Audra smiled as they slowed by a stone bridge. "I cannot know until the king sends me word. Until such tidings arrive, I must continue as I have."

"Foolishly."

Her smile faded at the sharpness in his voice. She had thought Bourne her ally. Now he sounded like Shaw, who continued to mutter about the idiocy of having a woman hold Bredonmere. "I find your answer bothersome."

"You should." He leaned toward her but swung out his arm to encompass the fields. "Milady, if I had not chanced upon you, would you have ridden out by yourself?"

"Crandall is impatient with my lack of skill in handling my mount, and Fleming is so busy that—"

She was shocked anew when he interrupted. "So you would have gone forth alone."

"We are but a short distance from Bredonmere's walls."

His dark eyes drilled her, seeking any chinks in her confidence. Then they narrowed. "You dare much when there are many outlaws who are eager to prey on the unwary."

Audra slapped the reins on her horse's neck, then gasped as Bourne gripped the bridle, stopping her. He leapt from the saddle and slowly led both horses to the side of the road. Looping the reins over a bush, he turned and held up his hands to help her down.

When she did not put her hands on his shoulders, he said tautly, "It will be easier to teach you to defend yourself than to change your stubborn mind, but I can give you no lessons while you perch on that horse."

"*You* dare much with your coarse words," she fired back.

"No more than you dare by risking Bredonmere with your antics. If you are killed or abducted, milady, then your father's manor could come to ruin."

"I know, but I cannot huddle behind the walls of Bredonmere. My people need me."

The fury in his eyes lessened. "They need you alive, milady."

"Then do as you suggest and instruct me as you do the youngsters."

Audra set her hands on his shoulders. Easily he lifted her from the saddle, but he lowered her only until their eyes were even, her mouth a spare inch from his, her legs brushing his. She said nothing as she saw the storm of emotions in his gaze. It spun through her, alerting her to a danger she had not anticipated. She breathed a sigh of relief when he set her on her feet. Surely she had mistaken his courteous behavior for something else.

"You risk bringing Crandall's fury on you when he learns of this," Bourne said, and she hoped he had not noticed how her hands trembled as she clasped them behind her. He went in his oddly rolling step around the horse, but his voice remained as sharp as the sword in the scabbard by his saddle. "He argues no woman should have to defend herself; that is the duty of your men-at-arms."

"How will my steward learn of this if I say nothing and you say nothing of this day's lessons? Even Crandall must admit that I would have been well-served to have known how to wield a knife when Lynx chanced upon me in the forest."

Bourne rested an arm on his horse's rump but did not return her smile. "Do not think to confront your enemies with the sparse knowledge you may gain today. It would take you years to learn how to turn any battle in your favor."

"Teach me what you can."

He drew his long sword from the scabbard on his saddle and rested it across his palm. The blade was as wide as his large hand. Turning it so the hilt faced her, he offered it to her.

Audra faltered as she looked from his face to the weapon, which glinted malevolently in the sunshine. When he had spoken of her learning to defend herself, she had guessed he would teach her to use the short knife he wore in his belt. The only other time she had touched such a tool of death had been in the armory when Lynx showed her how inept she was.

He smiled. "If you wish to refrain, milady, no one would call you a coward."

"Save for myself." Taking the sword, she gasped as the blade struck the ground with a dull ring.

"Here." Bourne took it from her. Holding it easily, he slashed the air as if he sought to bring an invisible enemy to defeat. "See, milady? Always keep it high, and strike when your attacker does. It is not so difficult."

"Assuredly, when you battle nothing but motes of dust."

"Then I shall give you the opportunity to face a foe." He returned the sword to her and pulled his short dagger. "Unarm me, if you can, milady."

"When you have only that small blade?"

"If you are afraid . . ."

His laugh stung her. She raised the heavy sword, determined to prove that the last of the earl of Bredonmere's children was as brave as the first. Putting both hands on the hilt, she faced Bourne. He held the dagger loosely in his hand and bent as he prepared for her attack.

"Milady, if we are chanced upon by others, I hope you will assure them that this is no more than a lesson." His eyes twinkled merrily. "It would do little good for my reputation if it was to be suggested that a woman of your size and lack of experience had disarmed me."

Poking the long blade experimentally in his direction, she gritted her teeth. "But think how it would enhance mine."

When he laughed, Audra swung the sword. She would back him to the trees, then order him to lay down his knife. That was what she planned, but, before she could react, the sword was spinning in the dust at her feet and Bourne's arm was about her waist. At her throat, the flat of his dagger rested on the collar of her kirtle. She stared up at him, wide-eyed, and he laughed again.

"Surrender, milady?"

"Surrender?" she gasped, as she saw something more than amusement flash in his eyes. She had no chance to guess what as he bent her head back with the knife.

"Surrender your foolish assumption that you can protect yourself. You need a trained man at your side whenever you leave the walls of Bredonmere."

"I do accede to your greater wisdom on this matter," she whispered.

When he released her, Audra rubbed her stinging fingers. He bent to retrieve his broadsword. "You will be pleased to know, milady, that all the lads are learning this trick to disarm an opponent. Your men-at-arms may be few in number, but we shall stand ready to repel anyone who tries to steal Bredonmere from its rightful lady."

"I am glad to know I shall not have to stand alone."

"You are never alone. You have many who would follow you willingly into death to defend the manor."

Audra dared to look into his face, which was as somber as his words. "If you are as quick against any invaders as you are against me, you will have our enemies capitulating before they can draw their weapons." She kneaded her aching wrist.

"Did I hurt you?" he asked with sudden concern. He touched her hand and gently probed the skin. "'Twas not my intent."

She winced. "'Tis nothing but the cost of facing my own foolishness. The lesson is well learned, Bourne."

"Forgive me, but I have learned a lesson today as well. I shall never again forget you are not accustomed to the rough life of a warrior."

"But I must learn."

"I would teach you whatever you wish, milady," he whispered.

His fingers slowly closed over her wrist. She put her hand over his. She wanted his friendship. She needed his fealty. This one man asked nothing from her but what she wanted to give. He was as different from Lynx as any man could be. Or mayhap not, for Lynx demanded of her what she wanted to give as well. She had given him her lips and welcomed him into her dreams.

"No!" she murmured, pulling away. Damn Lynx for infecting her with the passion she yearned to savor once more. *Begone,* she ordered as she had so many times, but his image listened to her no more now than the real man had.

Bourne flinched, then dropped to his knees. "Forgive me for whatever I said that has injured you, milady."

"No," Audra said yet again, but with sadness. "You have said nothing for which you need to apologize. 'Tis I who have offended you wrongly by becoming lost in my thoughts. Bear with me, my friend, for I need your strong arm and your steady head and your allegiance."

"I would offer you my very life to be certain that no one usurps your hold on Bredonmere."

"I hope I never have to ask for it." She sighed as he went to gather the weapons. As she went back to her horse, she wondered how much longer she could live a lie of saying how she wished to defeat Lynx while she longed to be in his arms again. To discover that could bring disaster for Bredonmere and its lady.

7

The great hall was nearly vacant. In the distance, the sound of voices, as thin as a wisp of smoke, drifted from the kitchen. Two dogs snarled over a bone by the hearth in the center of the floor, but Audra ignored them as she tried to decipher the tiny numbers in Crandall's handwriting. His accounts from the tofts and mills were always filled with detail. She could call him to explain, but she was glad of the chance to read without him peering over her shoulder.

At the noise of footsteps, she glanced up. The heavy door crashed open. "What is this?" she cried, jumping to her feet.

Fleming did not answer as he tried to keep a group of shouting men from entering, but they swarmed past him. She recognized the villeins, but not the rage on their faces as they surged toward her. Fleming called for help, and three men-at-arms scurried to his side. He sent one racing out the door, then ran with the other two to stand between the intruders and Audra.

"We want to speak to our lady," bellowed one villein.

Audra did not answer as she met their angry glares steadily. When she spoke no greeting or curse at their insolence but remained as unmoving as the brass effigy of her father, the men looked at each other, uneasy. Slowly one, then another, then all of them knelt before her.

A shout heralded Crandall's arrival, but he stopped in the door when he saw the men on their knees. He edged around them to come to where Audra stood at the raised table, dismay still on his face.

She followed his gaze to the new reeve, who knelt among the others. "Halstead, rise." When the man climbed off his bony knees, she asked, "Are you part of this delegation, or have you come to aid Fleming in halting them?"

The reeve, whose sallow cheeks were dented with pox marks, hung his head and twisted his felt cap. Swallowing so harshly the sound reverberated through the high rafters, he said, "With them, milady."

"Then your comrades are welcome to come to their feet also. I know any allies of yours will bring me no trouble."

Scrambling to stand, the dozen men exchanged more guilty looks. One elbowed Halstead, but the reeve remained silent.

"Which one of you wishes to speak for his comrades?" Audra asked as she came around the table to stand on the edge of the raised platform. She must show she had no reason to fear them, although each man wore a blade.

"I speak for them," said Halstead with more assurance. "Milady, 'tis that damnable Lynx. He and his men got into the pinfold and let out all the stray beasts."

"Lynx?" Audra's face grew cold. "Are you sure Lynx is the culprit?"

"Aye. 'Twas his sort of mischief. The strays tramped right through John atte Water's fields." He pointed to a balding man who was nodding vigorously. "Ate out of Ludlow's corn bin. Ludlow's wife saw the bastard in his black cape riding along the road, laughing like the prince of evil himself. He must be stopped."

She took a deep breath and nodded. Nobody must suspect that she feared she was lying when she said, "I promise you his work will come to an end. Until he is apprehended, you must bring the stray beasts within the walls of the manor. He may be daring, but he knows better than to strike against the armed men of Bredonmere." When they smiled, pleased with her quick solution, she added, "Which among you has sheep?"

Although the reeve seemed as startled as the other men by her query, he answered, "Most all keep a few about the yard for wool and mutton."

"Good." She smoothed her sweaty palms against her gown. The future of Bredonmere, if Crandall's numbers spoke the truth and she knew they did, might depend on this. "You must stop killing the sheep for meat."

"Milady—"

Audra ignored Crandall's shock. "Go to your tofts and find the best ewes and the strongest rams. Look for the ones with the finest wool. Breed them, and do not slaughter the lambs. The price of wool is rising. If we turn this to our advantage, we can restore this manor to the prestige it had before the Death."

John atte Water stepped forward, a nervous tic pulling at his left eye. "Milady, we'll be without food for us and our stock if we think only of sheep."

"I would not ask that of you." When she held out her hand, Fleming helped her down to stand amidst the men. "Our fields must yield food and flax for linen. There are few of us to harrow the leas. Sheep require little attention, save to protect them from raiders and beasts."

"And Lynx," grumbled Crandall.

Again she pretended not to note her steward's words. "I think of Bredonmere. The week-work you owe the manor shall be with sheep. Think how wise it would be to raise your own flocks at the same time. Are you with me?"

The men nodded slowly, but she saw greed glistening in their eyes and knew they were hoping to raise enough money by selling wool that they would be able to pay her instead of working the demesne's fields. That time would be far in the future, but hope could be the fuel necessary to set their dreams afire.

When they began to launch questions at her, she told them to do as she had asked. Once it was ascertained how many sheep were set for breeding, they would begin.

"Milady?" came a soft voice at her side.

"Not now," Audra said impatiently. Louder, she called, "Crandall, have tankards brought, so these men might have some ale to dampen their throats before their walk home."

"Milady?" repeated the maidservant beneath the grateful cheers from the villeins.

Spinning, she demanded, "What is it? Can you not see that—?" Audra's voice faded away as she saw the man behind the serving woman. The distinctive

badge closing his dusty cape on his shoulder told her
that he had traveled to Bredonmere at the command
of King Edward III.

The man knelt. "Milady, I bring you the greetings
and salutations of our king."

"Rise," she whispered.

He withdrew a rolled page from a worn leather
pouch hooked to his belt. "Do you wish me to read it
to you?"

"No." She held out her hand, for she doubted if
the man could read the message he had memorized.
Pride filled her when she kept her fingers from trembling. "I shall read it."

"Milady, it would be my honor to impart its message to you," the messenger said.

"I would read it myself."

"As you wish, milady." He placed the small scroll
in her hand.

Audra turned away, hoping that Crandall was so
busy that he would fail to notice this messenger until
she learned the message's contents. A deep breath
steadied her, but nothing could slow the fierce throbbing of her heart. As she climbed the steps to the
raised table, she hastily read the letter.

She sat in the first chair and reread the intricate
writing again. King Edward sent greetings to his
beloved cousin the countess of Bredonmere and
prayed that she enjoyed good health and a fine planting season. Her heart halted in midbeat as she read
that the king enjoined her to welcome Gifford, Lord
deWode, to Bredonmere, so that she might decide if
she would choose to wed her cousin.

Her brow knit with puzzlement. This was not the
edict she had anticipated, for the king was offering
her the privilege of making the decision herself. Never

had she heard of such magnanimity. A shudder ached across her tense shoulders as she wondered why she was being allowed to choose.

"Good tidings from the king, milady? Does he name your husband?"

Audra turned to Crandall. "We shall speak of this alone."

His brows arched at her cool words, but he nodded. "As you wish."

"Order food and drink for this messenger, then attend me in my private chambers."

Audra evaded her household as she climbed the stairs to her rooms. The outer chambers were crowded, and she looked about for Shirley. Finding her, she had Shirley take her servants away from the antechamber. Only when she was alone did she unroll the parchment and read it. Nothing had changed, and nothing was explained.

When her door opened, she saw Crandall was not alone. She smiled gratefully when Father Jerome entered the room.

"Forgive my boldness, milady," he said, "but your marriage is a matter that concerns me greatly."

"As it does me." She tapped the message. "Lord deWode is being sent here for my approval."

"Approval?" Crandall repeated. "I fail to understand."

"King Edward has granted me the rare privilege to make the decision if I wish to marry the baron or not."

Father Jerome lifted the parchment and muttered a prayer under his breath. When Audra looked at him, he let the scroll slowly close. "I do not like this, milady. The future of Bredonmere is too important to hinge on a whim."

"I assure you I shall give the matter great thought."

He sighed. "You know quite well I mean you no insult. This just makes me uneasy."

Crandall sat heavily on a bench. "I share your disquiet."

Clasping her hands, Audra looked from one man to the other. "The king has requested me to consider the baron. I cannot disregard our sovereign's command. Lord deWode is to be made welcome upon his arrival."

"And then?" asked Father Jerome tightly.

She shook her head. "I have no idea."

Her advisers stayed to discuss the unusual message until there was nothing else to say. Audra urged them to speak to no one else of the matter until she could find the proper way to announce the tidings. Leaving the two men debating, she went down the stairs. She had left Crandall's accounts in the great hall and must retrieve them. She could have sent a servant for them but wanted time alone to sort out her confusion.

Collecting the papers, she took them to Crandall's small office near the back of the keep. She smiled as she recalled how amiable the villeins had been to the idea of raising sheep. Would Lord deWode agree with her plan?

Coldness crept through her as she walked along the twisting passage. In the past months, she had become accustomed to guiding Bredonmere's future. She wished for a partner to rule with her, not for a man to take her place.

"So glum?"

Audra froze as she recognized the low voice. Lynx! How dare he invade Bredonmere in the middle of the day! She started to turn, but the sharp point of a blade against her nape halted her.

"Do not move. We must not waste time," came the velvety voice that haunted her dreams, "for I can linger but a moment, milady."

"Before you go to fire another byre?"

His laugh caressed her as his fingers stroked her arm. She longed to succumb to their beguiling invitation, but straightened her back and raised her chin.

"It was being said," he answered, "that Lynx had admitted defeat. That is not true, as you can see."

"I can see nothing but that you shall pay for this daring."

"And who shall make me pay?" His breath teased her skin as his fingers swept aside her gorget. "Not you, for soon you shall be no more than the manor's lady, tending the sick, giving your husband pleasure and an heir to *his* manor."

Audra gasped, "How do you know?"

"Of your impending visitor?" He chuckled. "When will you learn that nothing you do is secret, milady?"

"What do you care for Bredonmere?"

He grasped her arm and spun her to face his black tunic. She stared up at his half-hidden face. "Be wary, milady. You are about to involve yourself in dangers you know nothing of. The goodness you have tried to instill in this manor will come to naught when Lord deWode arrives."

"Lord deWode will see the end of your reign of terror."

"Will he? And will he see the end of this as well?" He captured her lips as his arms encircled her.

Every thought of pushing him away vanished into the vortex of longing as his tongue enticed hers into a wild dance. As she touched the rough wool of his sable cape, his hands slipped along her kirtle and beneath the wide opening of her cotehardie. When his fingers swept along her breast, she pressed closer, wanting, needing to feel every inch of him. He seared kisses into her neck. Heat roiled within her, melting her to him. When he gently nibbled on her earlobe, she whispered his name.

Audra opened her eyes, startled, when he drew away. The mocking smile tilted his lips, but she heard sincerity in his voice when he whispered, "Be wary of Lord deWode, milady, or you shall lose more than this pleasure."

She reached for him, but he eluded her fingers, bowed his head to her, then turned and raced toward the end of the passage.

Staring after him, wishing she knew how to call him back, she stiffened. How had Lynx known the king was sending Lord deWode to Bredonmere? Only Crandall and Father Jerome knew of the contents of the message from King Edward. She closed her eyes as old suspicions burst to life. Lynx . . . Father Jerome . . . Could they be the same man? Somehow she must learn the truth.

"Be wary," Lynx had told her. He was correct, but what she needed to be most wary of was her heart, which threatened to entrap her in an outlaw's game.

Audra reined in her horse at the call of her name. In the six weeks since she had urged her villeins to increase their flocks, she had spent each day visiting tofts, teaching the men what she had learned at the abbey. Bourne always rode by her side. When she saw a cloud of dust rising from the road, she recognized the rider in front of it as Fleming. She drew in her horse and waved to her commander of the guard.

"Milady!" he shouted as he neared. "He is coming."

"He?" she asked in confusion.

At the same time, Bourne demanded, "Is it the baron?"

Fleming wiped dirt from his sweaty face. "A messenger has just reached the manor house to inform us that Lord deWode and his men shall be arriving at Bredonmere with the sunset."

As if her voice belonged to someone else, Audra heard herself say, "Return posthaste and arrange a welcome for the baron. Have Shirley prepare my finest gown. I shall follow at the best pace I can."

"Milady, there can be no delay." Fleming's face turned down in an anxious frown. "If the baron reaches Bredonmere before you, he shall take insult."

"I shall—"

An arm around her waist lifted her from the saddle. Before she could react, Bourne set her behind him on his horse. She wrapped her arms around his waist as he grasped the reins of her horse and said, "I shall have our lady there before the baron crosses the river. Ride, Fleming, and do Lady Audra's bidding."

"Aye, the men shall be ready, milady."

Audra noted Fleming's uneasy expression as he pulled on his reins to turn his horse. Slapping his feet against its side, he sped along the twisting road. How well she knew Fleming's troubled thoughts, for Lord deWode's appearance could herald a new future for Bredonmere.

Bourne said, "Hold tightly, milady. We must ride on Fleming's heels."

"Yes, go at the best speed you can."

Her disquiet must have seeped into her voice because he said, "I have heard that you can decide if you wish to marry your next-of-kin. While it would surely please King Edward to have the matter taken care of, there are many others who would be glad to take you to wife."

"But will the king have patience with me if I fail to do as he wishes?"

"I cannot answer that."

"Nor can I." She shivered as he set the horse to an easy gallop. "Mayhap the decision shall be easy. Lord deWode must be a courageous and able man to have advanced so far in the king's favor."

"'Tis your favor he must win now, if he hopes to claim Bredonmere and its lady's bed."

Audra was glad his back was to her as heat rose along her face. She had avoided thinking of the intimacy she must share with her husband. A quiver coursed down her as she recalled Lynx's amusement at her intentions of becoming a nun. When he had kissed her, stirring her into a tempestuous torment, she had wanted what he offered. That could never be.

"Milady?"

Flinching, she broke free of her daydream. When Bourne glanced back, his brows were knitted with emotions she did not want to decipher. "Make haste, Bourne. We can waste no time."

He slapped the reins on the horse's neck. Tightening her arms around him as they raced toward the manor, she leaned against his firm back. She must be smiling when she entered Bredonmere. No one must know that she mourned for the loss of a man who did not exist. She longed to have a man with Bourne's gentleness, Father Jerome's compassion, and Lynx's

powerful enchantment that had made her his captive
the first time he had kissed her.

Audra waved away her servants so she could undress.
Anxiety made her fingers clumsy on the tabs and buttons holding her clothes closed. She listened for the
trumpeting welcome that would announce Lord
deWode's arrival. She would need to be ready to greet
him with every formality. Anything less would shame
Bredonmere.

"Your burgundy robe and gold cotehardie are
waiting, milady," Shirley said.

"Bredonmere's colors?"

"I thought you would wish to impress the baron."

Audra almost laughed, but she had never felt less
like laughing. By the time Lord deWode reached the
keep, he would have seen the fields where the crops
grew in the summer sun. He would have counted the
tofts and noted the plump animals. Her appearance
would be of little concern to a man who wished to
claim her father's title and fief.

As Shirley tied her hair in an ornate pattern
across her head, Audra contemplated the mystery of
Gifford deWode. That he was much in favor with
both the king and his son spoke well of his strength
on the field of battle, but she would have preferred
learning he had been innovative in introducing new
crops on his fief.

She drew her cotehardie over her kirtle. Across
the bodice, silk threads were embroidered with
small buttons in a zigzag pattern. Needlework at her
wrists gave the appearance that she wore tight
bracelets decorated with small gems. Over it, Shirley
draped the burgundy robe. As Audra slipped her

arms through the slits, the maid adjusted it on her shoulders.

Shirley set Audra's gorget in place. It left most of Audra's raven hair visible, allowing it to assume a ruddy glow in the setting sun. Lastly she picked up a long gold cape and draped it across Audra's shoulders.

Audra stroked the fox fur along the edge of the cape and thought of her mother, who must have worn this. She owed her family a duty to see that their line did not end with her. She would be the last Travers by name, but their blood would flow in the bodies of her children.

Crandall, dressed in a clean tunic and unpatched chausses, was waiting in the antechamber. His greeting was interrupted by a horn blast from the wall. He stepped back to allow her to lead the way to the great hall but offered his withered hand. She placed her fingers on it, not looking at him. Somehow she must keep her most loyal retainers from discerning her fear.

"We are with you, milady," Crandall said in a low tone, which would not carry past her ears.

Gratitude filled Audra. She should know she could trust her steward to offer her respect and honor. That would not change, even when she wed, for Crandall would be loyal first to the Travers line.

On the steps leading into the keep she waited for Lord deWode's party to enter the inner bailey. As her retainers surrounded her, Fleming arranged his men. Her hands tightened into fists. Nothing could make the pitifully few men appear a stronger force, not even with Bourne and the youngsters who stood beyond them.

Her eyes were caught by Bourne's. No amount of

distance could hide the intensity in their dark depths. Hastily she broke away. For those like him who were so unquestioningly loyal, she must think now only of Bredonmere.

Another shrill blare of a trumpet was muted by horseshoes on the drawbridge. Audra hid her amazement at the number in Lord deWode's party. There must be more than two score. The gestum for so many men would strain the larders of the manor. She would have to ask Crandall to arrange for more kegs of ale and mead to be brought from the cellars, although she was sure he was making such plans already.

The men were heavily armed and rode with lances in their hands. They were not battle lances, for banners hung from the staffs that were nearly twice as tall as a man. Every horse wore bards, and she was certain that on this warm day the beasts suffered beneath the light armor as she did in her heavy robes.

The lead man dismounted. Handing his sword to a page who ran forward, he walked to Audra. The last rays of the sun glistened with golden fire off his hair. His gaze moved along her with candid interest, and she resisted the desire to conceal herself. That he was regarding her with eager desire was no insult, for this handsome man must be the one the king had chosen for her.

Dropping to his knees, he said, "My lovely lady, Gifford, Lord deWode, pledges his life and honor to you."

"Please rise, Lord deWode," she murmured, not trusting her voice to speak louder. "You do Bredonmere Manor honor with this visit."

As he climbed the steps, she realized he was as tall as Father Jerome. He smiled broadly. "May I say you are far more beautiful than even the lauds of the poets had led me to believe?"

"Thank you." When a maidenly flush climbed her cheeks, she lowered her gaze. Not because of his effusive compliment, for he must be well acquainted with courtly talk, but because of the candid lust in his eyes. She felt as if he was removing her clothing layer by layer. The thought twisted through her stomach.

He snapped his fingers, and his page ran forward. Her people craned their necks to see what the youngster carried. Taking the small casket, Lord deWode offered it to her. "A token of the affection I pray shall grow between us."

She tilted the box from one side to the other but could not determine how it opened. With a smile, he undid the latch. She drew back the top and gasped. On a bed of grass-green velvet lay a ring of twisted gold and precious stones that sparkled with blue and red fire.

Boldly, he took her left hand and slipped the ring on her fourth finger. Stroking her skin, he smiled. "It is a bit too big. I had heard how dainty you are, milady. Grant me leave to tell you how pleased I am to see the truth with my own eyes. I rejoice in my good fortune."

She clenched her fingers to keep the valuable ring from slipping off. This was no simple gift. He meant this to be her betrothal ring. The baron possessed a pleasing appearance and was warrior hardened, but she found his arrogance distasteful. He presumed she would be eager to become his wife. Warning herself that she must not make too hasty a judgment, she motioned toward the hall. "Lord deWode, you are welcome to quench your thirst after your long journey."

He held out his hand. Although it was no more than a polite gesture, she felt as if it was a command. He did not hide that he intended to assume his place as the earl of Bredonmere immediately. As she raised her fingers to place them on top of his, she saw Shaw watching them. A chill ran through her. Not once had he spoken to her since she stripped him of his title and prestige.

She looked up to see the baron following her gaze and smiling tightly. Astonished, she glanced back at Shaw, but the red-haired man had vanished among the others.

"The day is hot," Lord deWode said. "I would appreciate that taste of ale."

Audra gave him no answer other than to lead the way into the keep. She banished Shaw from her mind. He was no longer in a position to cause trouble for her or her guests.

Beneath the banners attached to the roof timbers, deWode's men eagerly surrounded the lasses carrying mugs of ale. Musicians began to play from the gallery, but the three-stringed rebec could barely be heard over the conversation. She saw Fleming move surreptitiously among the guests. His men were doing the same. She guessed he had ordered her men-at-arms to ensure no untoward behavior happened the first night of the baron's visit to Bredonmere.

"You have a wondrous fief," said deWode as he led her to the raised platform and the table atop it. "Rumors reached my ears that you were plagued by night riders, but I saw no sign of trouble."

She sat. When his blue eyes narrowed, she realized he was surprised she had claimed her father's chair as her own. Raising her chin, she said, "I hold Bredonmere against any intruders, milord."

"You are as wise as you are beautiful," he said with a return of his smile. As he sat beside her, she realized his position was unenviable, for he must wait upon her decision. She doubted if he ever had expected to have his fate hanging on what he would consider the caprices of a woman. Halting a servant, she took a mug of cooled ale from a tray.

"Milord?" she asked as she handed it to him.

Taking a deep draught, he wiped his pale mustache and mouth with the back of his hand. "I pray you might find it comfortable to call me Gifford."

"Thank you." She did not offer him the same intimacy, and again she saw his lips tighten with frustration. Rank was the only weapon she had to combat his eager eyes.

She presented Crandall and Fleming and watched their reactions. If they could not serve the baron wholeheartedly, she would have no choice but to reject his suit. She learned little, for they kept their faces and words guarded. Later she would speak to them and to Bourne.

She hoped they would feel better about the matter than she did and would come to convince her that Gifford deWode was the manor's salvation, or she feared more trouble awaited Bredonmere.

8

Gifford deWode was the most amusing guest Audra could have hoped for. He was amusing to everyone but her. Although he offered her pretty poems and listened when she spoke of her plans to raise sheep, she soon discovered that he heeded little of what she said. He was more concerned with wooing the favor of her people. Each day, he insisted she ride with him about the fief as he met her tenants.

Surprisingly Crandall was the first to be won over by the man who might be his next lord. When he deferred to the baron during a discussion about the upcoming harvest, Audra tried to hide her dismay. This was as it should be, but she continued to delay granting Gifford leave to ask her to marry him.

Her steward was enthusiastic when Gifford told her that the baron had arranged for her to ride with him and Crandall out to the northern tofts. "Halstead is anxious to show Lord deWode the sheep he has selected to breed," Crandall reminded her.

"Do come with us," Gifford urged. Taking her hands in his, he stroked the ring he had given her. "I have so much yet to learn from you about selling Bredonmere's wool throughout England. Your voice as you speak of such matters—that few ladies would trouble their heads about—is a joy upon my ears."

She slipped her fingers out of his and stood. "I am honored by your invitation, but there are matters which require my attention within the keep today. I must—"

When he put his hands on her shoulders, his smile was warmer than his eyes, which warned her he was unaccustomed to having his requests denied. "Milady, I wish to discuss things other than the villeins' needs and the defense of the walls. Allow me this chance to learn more of *you*. Grant me the opportunity to show you how I can help you with this onus of responsibility you have shouldered so unceasingly."

"Gifford, today I am so busy. I—"

His hands tightened as he drew her closer and lightly touched her face. "Our king is eager for the match of your line with mine. Do you dare flout the will of Edward?"

Audra looked past him and saw Crandall's rare smile. If her steward trusted Gifford, she must make an effort to do so as well. "Very well. Let me send for Fleming."

"What need do we have of him? My sword arm will protect you from any foes," Gifford said as he brushed dust from his tawny tunic. "And Crandall is coming with us." He chuckled as he clapped the older man on the shoulder. "He will protect you from any thoughts I should not have."

The two men laughed, and she guessed neither of them noticed she did not join in. Knowing that the only way she would have a chance to finish her work was to take the morning to ride with them, she did not protest again as their mounts were brought.

In spite of herself, she glanced across the inner bailey toward the armory. She had missed her rides with Bourne more than she expected. When Gifford assisted her into the saddle, she realized she had not spoken with the armorer since the baron's arrival. She wondered if Bourne would leave Bredonmere if she wed Gifford. Bredonmere needed Bourne's skills, and she needed his friendship and willing ear as she spoke of her dreams for the manor. She had not considered that she would lose Bourne, too, the day she agreed to Gifford's suit.

As they rode from the manor house, Audra tried to enjoy the sunshine, but her mood was too grim. Beside her, Gifford and Crandall spoke with the intimacy of master and steward. She was not included in their conversation. This, she knew, was what her life would be like when she wed.

Be wary of Lord deWode, milady, or you shall lose more than this pleasure. Lynx's warning rang through her ears, refusing to be ignored. Everything she loved about her life at Bredonmere could come to an end once she accepted Gifford as her husband. Each day, she was reminded of that.

When the two men drew in their horses, she stopped hers. "Is something amiss?" she asked.

Gifford patted her gloved hand. "Do not fret so, milady. Crandall was only telling me of the spring among these trees."

"It never weakens," the steward said, "even in

midsummer. Its waters remain as cold as a wintry morn."

"Perfect to wash the dust from my throat." Gifford leaped to the road. "May I bring you a drink, milady?"

"I have nothing to carry water in."

"Then may I bring you to get a drink?"

She let him lift her from her horse. Holding her skirts out of the dirt, she crossed the yard. Tufts of grass grew among the broken wheels that had been left behind when the farm was deserted by those fleeing the Death. To Crandall, she said, "That oldest lad of atte Water's has proven to be industrious, has he not?"

"This toft would take an industrious man to bring it back." He stepped around the edge of the tumbledown byre. "A fitting match, milady. Do you agree, milord?"

Again Audra had to bite her tongue to keep from retorting that, until she wed the baron, the decision was hers alone. She remained silent while Gifford sat her on a hummock and went with Crandall to clear leaves away from the cool waters of the spring. She wrapped her arms around her knees and listened to the sweet song of a lark.

Angry voices frightened away the bird. She stood as she heard her steward curse at the baron. Rushing to where Crandall stood, his hands balled into fists, she looked from one furious man to the other.

"Crandall," she said, startled at his sudden anger, "you disgrace Bredonmere by using such language to our guest."

"No more than *our guest*"—Crandall spat the words like another curse, "disgraces Bredonmere when he tries to bribe me to leave you alone with him.

If his intentions were honorable, milady, he would not suggest such a thing."

She glanced at Gifford, whose face was twisted with rage. "There must have been a misunderstanding."

"His words were plain," Crandall retorted. "He tires of waiting upon you."

"You insult me, old man!" The baron pulled a fallen branch from the ground.

Audra screamed as he swung it into Crandall. Her steward reeled backward, then collapsed. Blood flowed from a wound on his head and stained the leaves underneath.

Gifford seized her elbow to keep her from going to Crandall. When she tried to push past him, his arm snaked around her waist. He tugged her to the far side of the spring and into his arms.

"Release me!" she cried. "I must see to Crandall. Such a blow could kill him."

"And well rid of him I shall be."

"He is *my* steward! He is my concern."

With a rough laugh, he murmured, "Your only concern at the moment, milady, is to please me." He bent to place his mouth against the curve of her neck.

"Gifford, are you demented?" She could not break his hold.

He ripped the gorget from her head and tossed it aside. Laughing again, he twisted his fingers in her hair and sent it tumbling along her back. "How lovely," he whispered. "You should wear your hair loose, milady . . . Audra."

"Stop this!"

When he pressed on her shoulders, she could not fight him. She fell to her knees.

"Let us see who is the true master here," he said with a triumphant smile as he kept her from scrambling away. "I have waited too long for you to give me what should already be mine."

Her cries were smothered beneath his mouth. He held her head in a tight grip. When he tried to slip his tongue between her tight lips, she refused him that intimacy. He growled as he forced her back onto the green blanket of grass. Catching her flailing fists in one hand, he pressed them to the ground. His smile broadened as he placed a brawny leg over her thrashing ones.

"A wench should be tumbled before the contracts for marriage are drawn up," he murmured. "Otherwise, how can I be sure if you will bring me pleasure?"

"Pleasure?" She spat out the words. "What care you for pleasure? All you want is Bredonmere!"

"Not true." His free hand fondled her eagerly. She moaned and cringed from his touch. "I want you, Audra, for you are ripe for a man's loving. I shall prove to the king that I am man enough to hold Bredonmere when you are round with my child before we stand by the church door."

"I shall not wed you!"

"But you shall!" He reached for the ribbons holding her cotehardie closed.

As she struggled to escape him, she realized her motions were inciting him. In horror, she feared he wanted her to fight him, so he could savor subduing her. He cared nothing for her feelings. All he wanted was to foist his bastard on her, so she would have no choice but to marry him.

A twig cracked. Audra stiffened. Again the baron chuckled, and she knew he had not heard what she had. Lost in his lust, he thought only of having her. She moaned in disgust.

A shadow crept along the ground and over her face. Horror and joy entwined within her as she stared at the dark eyes above Gifford. Surrounded by his black mask, Lynx's eyes hardened into fury as the baron forced his knee between her legs. Lynx put the tip of his broadsword against deWode's nape.

The baron froze. "Crandall, you old bastard—"

"Not Crandall, milord," Lynx said. "'Tis another who would not wish you to treat Lady Audra so coarsely."

Looking from Gifford's angry face to Lynx's cold smile, Audra tensed. She did not know what Lynx intended. Nor could she guess what the baron would do.

DeWode glanced over his shoulder. His eyes widened as he stared at the man in a black tunic and chausses. "Lynx!"

"You know me, Lord deWode? I should be honored." He motioned with the sword. "Mayhap I shall be honored enough not to run you through if you release Lady Audra. You will find, milord, we do not treat our women thus in Bredonmere." A smile tightened his lips.

The baron rolled away, followed by Lynx's sword. Audra was unsure if she could stand. She smoothed her robe back into place and stared up at the man whose black cape barely moved in the light breeze. Looking from his low boots along his strong legs to the tunic, which was as black as Gifford's heart, a sweet warmth flowed through her.

Lynx held his hand out to her without moving the tip of his broadsword from deWode's chest. She let his wide fingers envelop hers and bring her to her feet. Clutching his arm, she stepped closer, caught anew in the bewitching web he spun with no more than a smile.

"Who are you?"

Gifford's question cut through her, and she backed away from Lynx. Had she lost her mind to be so close to Lynx when Gifford deWode was a witness?

Lynx's arm kept her close as he said, "Men call me Lynx."

"That I know." He gave a derisive laugh. "You may have frightened this woman and her weaklings, but give me my sword, and I shall show you which of us deserves to rule this fief."

Lynx's smile broadened. "Whether you or I are the victor, proves nothing today. Lady Audra Travers holds Bredonmere."

Audra stared at Lynx. His alliance with her might bode well for her and the fief, or it might mean disaster.

"Speak, milady," Lynx added, drawing her deeper within the arc of his arm. "Speak your will, and I shall reveal to you the faithless blood in the veins of this bastard."

"No!" she whispered. "Do not kill him, Lynx."

He smiled so coldly that she shivered. "Why do you beg mercy for this man? Do you bear an affection for him?"

"No," she whispered as his fingers moved along her arm.

"So you do not love him?"

"Would any woman love a man who treats her so?"

He chuckled at her vehemence. "Milady, even I, as a loyal subject of our king, must say Edward was mistaken to inflict this cur upon you and your household. I laud your patience with this fool." His voice deepened. "And I laud you."

When his lips covered hers, she did not resist. They were both mad, mad with a desire that would not be denied, even though it was wrong. As she gasped for breath, his tongue tasted her mouth, probing, taunting, bold, and assured of a welcome. Her fingers gripped his tunic, for her knees were weakened by his searing touch. His hand swept down her back, enfolding her even closer to his body that could not hide his desire for her.

When he lifted his mouth from hers, she clung to him, raising her gaze to find his was focused on deWode. Even while Lynx held her, he clearly never once forgot the vile man lying on the earth. He would not give Lord deWode a chance to attack. She did not want the magic to end. Then the doubts would torment her once more while she tried to persuade herself that she would never surrender to him again.

"My sweet lady," he murmured so low only her ears could hear, "how I wish I could touch you as I did before. My hands crave the chance to learn every inch of your softness."

"Lynx—"

"There is no need for you to tell me no when I cannot have what I wish today." His tongue teased her ear, and she gasped. "What we both wish."

She could not deny the truth. She wanted to touch him; she wanted him to touch her. Her fingers slid along his shoulder to the line of his jaw.

"Be wary, milady," he said with sudden coldness as he caught her hand in a ruthless grip. "This mask protects you as well as me now. Do not risk yourself more."

"I did not mean to draw it aside," she whispered. She could not speak of her fear that if the mask was brushed aside, she might be looking into the face of a man she knew as Father Jerome.

Slowly, without speaking, he released her fingers.

When her fingertips grazed his cheek, he smiled before he claimed her lips once more. She knew he understood that he needed no force to convince her to stay in his embrace. There was no place else she wanted to be.

"Slut!" snarled Gifford.

When Audra gasped and drew away from Lynx, Gifford repeated the epithet. He bit back his next insult as the sword pricked his nose.

"You insult the countess of Bredonmere," Lynx snapped.

"She kisses you with the eagerness of a tavern slut!"

Lynx chuckled. "And she fights you because you wish to tumble her like one."

"You think I still want to—"

"Yes, Lord deWode, you want Lady Audra, her title, and the wealth Bredonmere's flocks can bring you. The fact that she values her life . . . and yours enough to surrender to me makes her no less appealing to you."

Astonishment swept over Audra. When Lynx had put his arm around her, she had had no fear for her life, only for her sanity, which he tore asunder with his eager touch. His dark eyes captured hers from the shadows of his mask. Lynx was her ally today. Confusion imprisoned her as his arms had moments before. Why did he wish to help her now? She recalled the many times he had insisted he was her ally. Mayhap he had been honest.

"Knave, give me a chance at my sword," said Gifford. "I shall show Lady Audra which of us is the better man."

"Never let it be said that I did not give you a chance to prove yourself a total ass." Lynx smiled as he took a step backward and put the tip of his heavy sword to the ground.

Lord deWode came to his feet and reached for Audra's arm. He swore as Lynx twisted her behind him. "Release her, cur!"

"This is between us, Lord deWode," Lynx answered smoothly. "Lady Audra need not dirty her hands with teaching you a few manners."

"Then she shall see you bleed to death."

"First you must wound me." He chuckled as he pointed toward the horses. "For that, you need more than your bare hands. I give you to the count of five." He smiled. "Can you count that high, milord?"

The baron spat an incoherent threat.

Lynx's voice never wavered from serenity. "You test the limits of my patience. If you continue, you may give me no choice but to slay you outright in front of this lady who has asked me to spare your life. As I told you before. To the count of five. One—"

"I will not be intimidated by your games! You are nothing but a—" Lord deWode choked on his invective when he heard the solemn count of "two."

Audra noted how Lynx's eyes glistened in malicious anticipation as the baron rushed to pull his sword from his saddle. Circling so he remained between her and the baron, Lynx motioned for her to stand aside. She nodded and backed toward a nearby tree. Lynx must not think of her while he fought the baron. All his thoughts must be focused on defeating Lord deWode.

The two men held their naked blades before them as they moved closer, circling, falsely parrying as each challenged the other to strike first. When they came together with a crash of steel, Audra clenched her hands. Was *this* the price she would pay for holding Bredonmere? To see Lynx's blood spilled?

She quickly saw how outmatched Gifford deWode was. Lynx met every thrust with ease. Pressing her hands to her mouth, she silenced a cry when the baron leaped forward to slash at Lynx. The blow went wide. With a triumphant laugh, Lynx sliced through the top of the baron's left ear.

"Mayhap now you shall hear better the next time a lady tells you she wants no more of your pawing," he said.

"Who are you?" the baron cried.

"For you, I am a messenger from hell who calls you to account for your sins." He drove Lord deWode toward the spring.

The baron's foot slipped at the edge. Lynx's laugh rang through the trees as he struck the baron's backsides with the flat of his sword. The blow sent Lord deWode into the pool.

"I anoint you, deWode!" Turning to Audra, he smiled. "What do you think of my way of cooling your admirer's ardor, milady?"

Audra's answering smile vanished as she saw deWode leap from the pool. "Look out, Lynx!"

Lynx whirled to face the baron. He ducked and, with a twist of his shoulder, sent the baron flying to the ground. The baron groaned once and was silent.

Holding his hand in front of the baron's bloody lips, Lynx said, with a hint of regret, "He lives."

"Thank God!" She whispered a quick prayer. She looked up into Lynx's eyes. "Will you let him live?"

Lynx stroked her loosened hair and said softly, "Only because I do not wish you to suffer seeing his end. Go before he wakes, pretty one. He is sure to be in a fouler temper than normal."

"Crandall—"

"What about him?" Lynx asked sharply.

"Gifford left him senseless over there." She pointed to the trees on the far end of the spring.

His inky eyes slitted with a rage she hoped would never be aimed at her. "He downed Crandall so he could rape you?"

"Do not speak of it," she whispered. She pressed her face to his black wool tunic. Not caring who he was or what, she wanted only the comfort of his strength. When his arms surrounded her, they did not hold her captive.

Too soon, he took her face in his hands and tilted it so he could see her eyes. "Return to your keep, milady. I shall tend your man."

"Lynx, do nothing to hurt him."

Sadly, he stroked her cheek. "Neither you nor Crandall have done anything that warrants my vengeance."

"Then why are you here on Bredonmere lands?"

"Do not ask me questions I can give you no answer to." He shoved her away. "Go, milady. I cannot always be here to protect you from your eager suitor."

She reached for his arm. "Will I see you again?"

"You are wasting time with foolish questions, milady. There is unfinished business between us." His eyes shimmered. "Pleasurable business. I vow to you it shall be soon."

9

Bourne was not surprised that Lady Audra had surrounded herself with the retainers she trusted most. Yet a priest and her maid would offer little help if Lord deWode used more force to persuade the countess of Bredonmere to wed him. As he stood in the far corner of her audience chamber, Bourne watched how stiffly Lady Audra lowered herself onto the bench in the middle of the room as she prepared for this meeting. Lord deWode had hurt her body but had been unable to punish her spirit, which had not flagged in its determination to hold Bredonmere.

He looked at Father Jerome as the priest sat next to Shirley on a pair of stools near the hearth. An ungodly fury burned in the priest's dark eyes, and Bourne knew Father Jerome was far from ready to forgive the baron for abusing their lady. Shirley's face was drawn with the tears she had wept when her lady returned to the manor house, bruised and filthy.

Bourne smiled when Fleming entered to stand by the door, his fingers only inches from the hilt of his sword. This was good. At the least provocation, nothing less than Lady Audra's direct order would stay his hand.

Only Crandall was absent. Bourne rubbed the knuckles of his right hand against his left palm. His fingers itched to repay deWode for the pain the steward suffered.

His gaze returned to the lady who sat with such silent dignity. Lady Audra was dressed in the outfit she had worn to greet the baron little more than a sevenday ago. About her shoulders, the rich cape edged with fox fur could not hide her shudders. More than he wished to avenge the attack on Crandall, Bourne yearned to beg Lady Audra to forgive him for failing her. Others might have been blind to deWode's treachery, but he was not. He should have been watching the baron more closely.

By all the saints, he was the greatest fool of them all! He had allowed Lady Audra to ride into danger, simply because he had lulled himself into believing that deWode would do nothing to risk this betrothal and his chance to claim Bredonmere.

Bourne straightened and placed his hand on the sword he wore on his hip, as Lady Audra signaled for Fleming to usher in the baron. She did not rise when deWode entered. Bandaging covered the baron's torn ear, and one eye was blackened.

The slightest flick of Lady Audra's fingers brought Father Jerome forward with the box Lord deWode had given her upon his arrival. "Take back your gift, Lord deWode," she said. "I would not want you to leave it behind when you depart today." Her icy words warned she would accept no argument.

"We of Bredonmere thank you for your visit. You may be sure I shall be contacting our king with my decision."

DeWode snatched the casket from Father Jerome but did not open it as he swaggered toward her. Fleming took a single step forward, and the baron halted. Gladly Bourne would have run the baron through, but that pleasure was denied him unless Lady Audra commanded it. He was pleased to note that she was revealing none of her thoughts. DeWode's face was not so devoid of emotion, though. He still intended to have Lady Audra and the manor. DeWode wanted the manor's wealth, and he wanted to punish its lady for making him look the fool he was.

Lady Audra must be careful. Gifford deWode had the ear of the Black Prince and through him to his father the king. He could inflict much trouble on Bredonmere.

"Farewell, Lord deWode," Lady Audra continued. "I wish you a peaceful and easy journey."

"I will await your decision at the king's court."

Bourne tensed at the threat. DeWode would petition the king to command that Bredonmere's lady become his wife. Again he glanced at Father Jerome and saw dismay in the priest's eyes. They must confer on how best to battle deWode. He cursed under his breath. What could the manor's priest and its armorer do to save Bredonmere and its lady?

Fleming followed the baron out. Bredonmere's men-at-arms would be certain that the baron and his men did not forget for a single breath that their welcome was at an end.

"So what now, milady?" asked Bourne.

Audra rose and accepted a glass of wine. After taking a sip, she said, "I must be sure how much I am willing to imperil Bredonmere if I win the king's disfavor."

"He did seem eager for you to wed deWode," said Father Jerome. He poured another glass of wine and took it to Shirley, who gave him a grateful smile.

"Yet he offered me the choice."

"Mayhap as a lark," Bourne answered. "I am doubtful he will offer you such an opportunity again. The next man sent to Bredonmere will come as your betrothed."

Frustration fired her voice. "I did not sleep last night as I debated that very issue."

"Mayhap," Shirley said with a weak smile, "the king will send you a man you can welcome with open arms."

"I must have a lord who can stir fervor in our men-at-arms. Lord deWode is an accomplished warrior." Her fingers tightened around the stem of her goblet.

"But Lynx bested him," interjected the priest. "If he can be beaten by a common criminal, can he be counted upon to lead our men if they are called to safeguard Bredonmere?"

"Lynx is not—" She clamped her lips closed and turned away, but not before Bourne saw the conflicting emotions on her wan face.

He went to where she stood by the window. He rubbed his aching leg and swore again silently. Damn this leg! What would he do if he needed speed to save Lady Audra? Over her head, he watched dust rise behind deWode and his retinue as they rode away. The baron would not accept defeat easily. Putting his hand on the wall near her dusky hair, he whispered, "What is Lynx not, milady?"

"He is not what he appears to be," she answered

in a low voice. She did not look at him, but he heard her despair.

"I agree. He is no demon with a cloven hoof, sent to take us into hell."

She faced him and flinched when she saw how near he stood. He backed away, lowering his eyes. Her voice trembled. "Lynx is not of the neifty. No man born to serfdom would act as he does. He speaks with the words of a learned man. His skills could not have been learned on a toft."

"A renegade knight mayhap?"

"I think not. He is neither a renegade knight nor an enemy."

Again he pounced on her words. "Do you mean you see him as an ally, milady?"

"Ask me no more, Bourne, for I can tell no one the truth I suspect."

"You believe you know who hides behind the mask?"

Looking away, she whispered, "I asked you to ask me no more."

"We all shall know the truth when you apprehend him."

Although her shoulders stiffened, she said only, "My friends, I must ask you to excuse me. It behooves me to begin immediately the correspondence I must have with King Edward."

"May we help?" Father Jerome offered.

"I would that you could, but this onerous task is mine alone." A sad smile matched the resignation in her eyes. "It was my decision to banish the baron, so I must be the one to present the king with a satisfactory explanation. I must not delay."

Shirley murmured, "Milady, you need to tend to that matter in the kitchen."

"It must wait."

"Milady, they are quite unsettled."

Irritation crept into Audra's voice. "Very well, but it must be tended to quickly. I do not wish to wait a moment longer to write to the king."

"Very wise," Father Jerome said.

Bourne caught the priest's gaze as they walked out of the chamber. When the door was closed behind them, Bourne said, "I would talk with you, Father."

"As I would with you, but first tell me, as a man with a knowledge of the intricacies of battle, can she best deWode alone?"

Bourne shook his head. "Unlikely, for you know as I do that he is more powerful than our lady suspects. His men bragged ceaselessly of his association with the younger Edward. That warns he has amassed favors beyond what his title suggests. He wants Bredonmere."

"And its lady."

"Most definitely he wants Lady Audra." Bourne's face became grim as they descended the narrow stairs, edging around a child playing with a top on the lowest step. Again he rubbed his hobbled leg. "And he would have had her, if he could have controlled his lust long enough to get her consent to the marriage."

Father Jerome stroked his chin. "We must be sure she does not falter in her determination not to marry deWode."

He snorted ungraciously. "How? Lady Audra will do what she deems right, and no man alive shall convince her otherwise."

"Even Lynx?"

Bourne's eyes narrowed as they entered the great hall. The room was oddly empty, and he suspected the household was huddling in distant corners as they gossiped about the baron's expulsion. "I doubt if even he could change our lady's mind on this."

"I disagree with you on that." Father Jerome chuckled softly, and Bourne regarded him with astonishment. "You cannot be blind. Can you not see, as I can, the influence he is having on her thoughts and plans for Bredonmere? She has been changed by her meetings with the night rider."

With a smile, which felt uncomfortable on his tense face, he urged, "If there have been changes, pray for a change in fortune. Too much evil has taken place in Bredonmere. It is due good fortune."

"As a priest, I should tell you that there is no such thing as good fortune, only God's will. But I shall pray God's will keeps deWode far from Bredonmere. As you must."

"As we all must." Bourne sighed. "You may not believe in luck, Father, but it may be Bredonmere's only salvation now."

Twilight was surrendering to the darkness that blanketed the countryside. Tendrils of fog came out from beneath the trees to swathe the ground in cool whiteness, slithering over every knoll and filling every hollow with its dim glow. Over the tops of the trees, which were motionless in the stillness, clouds had erased any hint of starlight from the sky. A storm was coming and the world waited, silent, expectant, fearful.

He heard the muffled sound of hooves on the moist soil. Whirling, he put his hand to the hilt of his sword. Few friends rode the night.

"Lynx?"

He did not relax at the whisper, but drew his hand away from the sword. "Here, Eatton."

The lad pushed through the bushes surrounding the forest clearing and paused only long enough to lash his horse to one of the low shrubs. Running to where the taller man stood, he said, "There's trouble."

"Aye, but there is always trouble."

"Not like this."

Lynx motioned for the lad to sit and squatted beside him. "What is amiss?"

"Everything." The single word came out in a deep sigh. "I cannot believe so much could go wrong in just the two days you have been away, Lynx."

He noted that his young friend did not hesitate over his name as he had when they first arrived on Bredonmere lands. It came as naturally from his lips as it did from their enemies'. Sainted Mary, this had gone on for too long with nothing to show for it but a vow that remained unfulfilled and a bewildered woman who had a hold on too many of his thoughts.

"Unburden yourself, Eatton," he said, hoping the account of the latest dilemma would sweep thoughts of Lady Audra from his head, "and mayhap you will see that the situation is not as fearsome as you suspect."

Again the lad sighed, running his hand back through his blond hair that drifted over his shoulders and tugging anxiously at the material hiding his face. "I wish you were right, but there is a horrible sickness in Bredonmere."

Lynx cursed viciously. "The Death?"

"I do not know. A guard stands at the draw-bridge and turns away anyone who would enter. On orders from Lady Audra, he says."

"She lives then?"

"Aye, so it would seem." A smile tugged at his lips. "Be wary, Lynx, or you shall betray yourself to more than me. Your sympathy for the lady's determination to hold Bredonmere has caught the interest of those who would see her fail."

"Of which there are too many." He stood and folded his arms over his chest. Scanning the night, he heard a muted laugh from the ground.

Let Eatton enjoy his jest! The lad had been curious about how Lynx had managed to rout deWode from Bredonmere lands a fortnight before, but Lynx had not satisfied his curiosity. No doubt, the tale coming out of the manor house had been embellished many times over by Crandall. That old fool had been half crazed with fright and outrage to discover that he owed his life to a man he reviled. Audra had been outwardly composed during deWode's banishment, so he suspected she had said nothing of the matter, leaving Crandall and the gossip-mongers to their babble.

Audra . . . She was a damnable complication he had not needed. Yet, he had to admit—if only to himself—he longed to feel her soft lips beneath his mouth and her enchanting curves pressed against him. Seducing her would be so easy and such a pleasure, but having the daughter of the earl of Bredonmere as his lover would add to the complexity of his task here. He should forget her and concentrate on doing what he had come to Bredonmere to do. Yet her alluring blue eyes haunted the few hours of sleep he managed to snatch each day.

"What is this sickness?" he asked, turning to look at the lad.

Eatton scrambled to his feet. "As I said, they will say nothing."

"Every entrance to the manor is guarded?"

"The drawbridge is."

His smile was as menacing as the rumble of thunder in the distance. "Eatton, you know that is only one way of getting into the manor. Those with an imagination can find a way in anywhere, even the formidable Bredonmere Manor."

"Aye, I am sure you can manage that with ease by now." He rocked from one foot to the other. "But what if their words are lies? What if the Death has returned to Bredonmere?"

Lynx did not hesitate. "Take the others home, for there is no need to endanger all of us, then return with all haste. Leave word as usual of your return."

"As usual?"

"Do you think I can convince *that* ally to flee?"

Eatton smiled swiftly, but his frown returned. "If Lady Audra is dead—"

"Do not call disaster upon our heads with your fretting." He slapped the lad on the shoulder and laughed, but his voice was serious as he said, "Lady Audra must not die until I have gotten what I came here for."

"And then?"

Lynx did not answer as he drew his mount from beneath the trees. He did not want to divulge that he had made no plans past that time for Bredonmere Manor or its lovely lady. For now, he must think only of what had brought him to this manor.

He must not fail.

Audra tipped another pot of water into the garden. When it washed over her slippers, she sighed. Shirley was sure to grumble at the mess. With a sigh, she recalled that her body servant was slowly recovering in the makeshift infirmary in the room behind the great hall. Shirley had been one of the first to take ill. Now the room was crowded with nearly a score of feverish patients.

Kilting her skirts, Audra carefully made her way through the puddles back toward the kitchen. With so many ill, every hand was needed at the hearth, even in the middle of the night. Others prepared the broth while she toted water to the sickroom. Her fingers ached from wringing out cloths to put on fevered brows.

Her foot slipped in a deep puddle, and she muttered an oath under her breath. A hushed laugh drifted to her. She whirled, splashing her skirt more.

Lynx stepped from the shadows near the well and held out his hand. "Do you need some help, milady?"

Delight mixed with dread as she stared at the man who might be her greatest enemy or most loyal ally. She wished she knew which. "I did not expect to see you here, Lynx," she said with every bit of calmness she could muster.

He took her fingers and steered her around the pockets of water. Again she wondered if he had the sight of his namesake. He smiled as he sat on a ledge by the well where the dim light from the kitchen brushed his black tunic before being swallowed by his cape. Tossing her a strip of cloth, he said nothing as she dabbed at the mud that clung to her slippers as tightly as his mask to his face. He drew up one foot and clasped his hands about his knee, looking as if he were a welcome guest in her manor.

"I had heard there was trouble within Bredonmere, so I thought to see firsthand," he said.

"If you mean Lord deWode, he is gone." She

hesitated, then added, "I owe you a debt of appreciation for your assistance in that matter."

His smile broadened. "It was my pleasure to
teach your erstwhile suitor a lesson he well deserved.
You were wise to expel him as you did, for you
offered him meager grounds to complain to the king."

Audra did not ask how he could be privy to the
conversation that should not have been spoken of
beyond these rooms. If Lynx and Father Jerome were
one and the same . . . She did not want to finish that
thought. Mayhap if she ignored what might be the
truth, she could make it be otherwise. Then her heart
would not be urging her to give free rein to her desire
for a priest.

"I trust," he continued, "you have sent King
Edward a listing of your reasons for not accepting
deWode's troth."

"I intend to do so as soon as this emergency
passes."

"You have not done so yet?"

"I had planned to, but what I thought was nothing more than a small emergency in the kitchen
became this illness. I have had no time to do anything
but help the ill." She closed her eyes in exhaustion.
"No one knows the importance of that letter more
than I, but I could not let these people suffer when I
have the skills to nurse them."

"Fool!" he snapped, his indifferent pose vanishing. "If you allow deWode to get the king's notice—"

"You presume much for a night rider!" she
retorted. "Why should I heed the counsel of a man
who will not show his face?"

When he stood, she refused to be intimidated.
She turned to leave, but his arm blocked her way. His
fingers clamped on her elbow. Knowing she should

resist, she could not halt her feet from bringing her closer to him. The scents of the night drifted from him, cool, damp, and mysterious.

"Fool," he repeated, but with less heat. "Why do you trouble yourself about something as meaningless as my mask when you and this manor you love may be lost even now through your procrastination? After you were so wise to give the baron his dismissal from Bredonmere, I had not thought you would delay contacting the king."

"I told you. I have had no time to write to the king."

"Let Crandall—"

"He is no scribe! It would take him longer than I, even if he were not sick."

His eyes narrowed. "So it is true. There is sickness within these walls. Has the plague returned?"

She twisted her arm out of his hold. "Many are sick, but it is not the Death." She shuddered as she whispered, "Crandall made it a priority to acquaint me with every symptom of the Death, so I am reassured *this* is not that horror. Many have sickened, but all are growing well, albeit slowly. They suffer no more than a fever that weakens them and confines them to their pallets."

"And you, milady, do you ail?"

Foolishly she raised her gaze to his. Caught by the ebony intensity of his eyes, she could not look away. Not taking his gaze from hers, he slipped his hand beneath her loosened gorget and slid it off her hair. As her hair streamed down her back, his fingers followed, brushing her nape, her shoulders, the sensitive length of her back. Reaching her waist, his palm curved along her to bring her closer.

His lips brushed her forehead. "No sign of fever here."

She closed her eyes as his mouth slid in a sinuous path along her cheek and throat. Her bare legs discovered the rough texture of his clothes, the sensation sweet and dangerous and enticing.

"A bit warmer," he murmured, his breath caressing her skin, "but no fever."

Her fingers clutched his sleeves when he tasted the skin above the neckline of her kirtle. His tongue laved her skin with liquid fire, and she quivered, longing to cede herself to this rapture, knowing she must not.

"Warmer yet, but not with fever," he whispered, then, with a groan, he captured her mouth as his arms surrounded her, enclosing her against his intriguing strength.

She answered his kiss with all her longing that could not be concealed when she was two night's short of sleep. Every defense she had against his sensual assault fell.

Suddenly he released her. The sound of a footfall on the stones, coming from the direction of the kitchen, warned her what he had heard. She glanced toward the kitchen door and saw someone lurching toward them. Guessing it was one of the kitchen maids carrying a heavy pot, she turned to tell Lynx to flee.

"Write to the king before another day passes," he whispered.

"I shall try." She looked back toward the kitchen again. "You must go."

"Do not dally another day. Otherwise we both shall be sorry."

"Both of us? Lynx, are you—"

"Ask no questions now." He pressed his mouth to hers again, then quickly drew away. As he eased back into the shadows, he whispered, "Be as willing to listen to my advice as you are to come into my arms. You must do as I implore you before it is too late for anyone to save you and Bredonmere."

He was gone before she could ask him to explain what he meant. Her stomach cramped as she realized she already knew. Gifford deWode would be even more determined to claim Bredonmere now that she had dishonored him with her rejection. He would use any means to claim the manor and her.

And he would be resolved that no one would stop him this time.

10

Dear cousin,

I trust this missive shall find you in excellent health and peace of mind. We continue to do well here at Bredonmere, for the summer rains have been benevolent. Hope drifts on the air and touches each of my household, a blessing that we pray wafts to you as well.

May I take this opportunity, cousin, to express my gratitude for your continual interest in this vassal and the lands she holds upon your pleasure? You have been generous with your interest in us, which is why it grieves me to have to write you this letter. The recent visit by Lord deWode did not come to the ending any of us might have wished. Lord deWode was unable to obtain the support among my men-at-arms, which is necessary to hold

*Bredonmere. I do not doubt that he has
explained this matter to you already at length,
and I hope . . .*

Audra stared at what she had written, grimaced,
and threw the page onto the fire in the hearth. Shirley
looked up from her sewing in shock.

"Mayhap you should give yourself some relief
from trying to write to his majesty," Shirley said. Her
voice still trembled from weakness after her sickness.

"Why won't the right words come? I cannot
delay sending my message to King Edward much
longer. After all, it's been three days since—" She
swallowed the truth that would have betrayed her.

Audra went to the window and opened it to let
air into her bedchamber. An afternoon thunderstorm
had done nothing to ease the thick air. As she ran her
hand across her damp nape, she heard Shirley come
to stand behind her.

"Since?" her maid asked gently.

"Since I said I would have the letter completed."
That much was the truth, although she could not tell
her faithful servant that the pledge had been made to
Lynx. She sat on the wide sill and sighed. "This is so
important I fear that a single wrong word will convince the king to listen to the lies Lord deWode may
be telling him even now to poison his mind against
me and Bredonmere."

Shirley smiled with sorrow. "You are straining
too hard for the truth that should come easily from
your heart."

"The future of Bredonmere hinges on this."

"Write to the king of what you wish for Bredonmere. He will heed the wisdom of your aspirations."

Audra smiled wryly. "And if they are not wise?"

Wagging her finger like a mother with a trouble-some child, Shirley said, "You are listening too much to Crandall. That curmudgeon sees darkness on a sunny day. You need to spend some time thinking of the pursuits of a young woman. You should be listening to music in the great hall and laughing."

"I know." Slipping down from the sill, she patted Shirley's arm. "You are right. I should set my mind to thinking of other matters. Then the words shall come to me."

"I am sure they will."

Audra suspected Shirley's confidence was misplaced. She spent more hours struggling for the right words to put in her petition to the king but remained unsatisfied. Finally she wrote the best letter she could devise. Rereading it, she decided to have Crandall review it before she sent it. She feared what new troubles her words might unleash.

She found Crandall sitting in the great hall as the bright melody of pipes filled the room. He was deep in conversation with Bourne. Rolling the letter, she slipped it into the sash at her waist. She was unsure why she did not want Bourne to see it but decided to listen to the small voice of caution in her head.

"Good evening." She paused in front of where they sat. "Were you speaking of the good news of a set of triplets born to a ewe on atte Water's toft? This is a wondrous beginning."

Crandall rubbed the healing wound on the back of his head. As thunder rumbled overhead, muted by the thick walls and the merry music, he said, "Take each day as it comes, milady. You are sure to be disappointed if you make too many plans."

She was glad when Bourne laughed and said, "Crandall, you think only of disappointment."

"'Tis difficult to think of anything else after what we have suffered in the past year."

"The past year is past," Audra retorted. She did not want to hear his gloomy tales tonight. "This is the time for daring to dream that good fortune will smile upon us."

"Father Jerome would caution you," Bourne said, "that you are foolish to put your trust solely in good fortune."

Audra looked about the hall as Crandall rose and stomped away. One face was missing among the many gathered around the central hearth. "Where is Father Jerome tonight?"

"Perhaps at his devotions." Bourne leaned toward her. "Your interest in Father Jerome intrigues me."

"There is nothing intriguing about it," she answered, but avoided his eyes, which might discern the truth.

"There is when you have made every effort to avoid him since you banished Lord deWode."

Audra hesitated, longing to give voice to the intuition in her heart. "I am unsure how to say this."

"Speak honestly, milady. The truth always is our best servant."

She faced him. The music and noise vanished as she stared into his dark eyes. If he thought her mad . . . She took a deep breath. "I fear Father Jerome may be involved in business that has nothing to do with the church."

"Such as?"

"I think he is—" She halted, unable to speak her suspicions.

"He is what, milady?"

She tried to swallow past the lump in her throat, but it was impossible. The truth would remain silent no longer. "I fear he may be Lynx."

"Father Jerome?" he asked slowly. She was pleased he did not laugh outright as Crandall would have. His brow furrowed in thought. "He is of a size and coloring to match the description of the night rider, but so are many others." He grinned. "Including me, if you wish me to be honest."

Her hands clenched in her lap. She wished she had never broached this subject, but she could not turn back now. "Father Jerome wanders about the fief freely. Who else could take to the night with such ease?"

"Have you spoken of this to anyone else, milady?"

"No. Who would believe me? I see doubts in your eyes."

"I need time to rearrange my thoughts to fit your supposition." He put his hands over hers. "I vow to you, milady, that no one shall hear of this from my lips."

"Father Jerome could be endangered if the household learned the course of my thoughts."

"And you have no wish for Lynx to come to harm?" he asked as he bent even closer until she could see nothing past his broad shoulders.

"I have no wish for an innocent man to come to harm," Audra answered, knowing she could not reveal even to Bourne, whom she trusted more than any other, the darkest secret in her soul. How he would despise her if she spoke of how wondrous Lynx's kisses were!

"The good father will come to no harm from me. You have my vow that—" He looked past her as her name was shouted.

Fleming ran to her. "Milady!"

"What is it?" Audra asked as she stood.

"Come, milady." He hurried her toward the door to the inner bailey. The music wobbled to a cacophonous end as they rushed through the hall. In the silence, his voice pealed like doom. "A rider has been sighted riding at top speed toward Bredonmere. By now, he must be—"

A woman screamed. Audra's heart caught in the middle of a beat. Was Gifford coming to claim Bredonmere by force? She forgot the baron when a man stumbled toward her. Smoke stains darkened his face and clothes, concealing his identity until he was a few paces from her.

"Shaw!" she cried.

He fell to his knees. Gagging for breath, he choked out, "Lynx . . . south tofts . . . afire."

Audra risked a glance at Bourne. His face was taut, for he might know, as she did, that Father Jerome had planned to travel in that direction this week. Urging Shaw to stand, she ordered, "Fleming, send help, then bring any families without shelter here."

"And Lynx?" the young man asked.

She hid her pain as she wondered how the man who had urged her to write to the king to safeguard Bredonmere could now be trying to destroy her manor. Her voice grew cold. "Take your best trackers. No one shall rule us through fear."

Even before Fleming had raced out of the hall, Audra was calling orders to have the chests emptied of blankets, which would have to serve as beds for the homeless villeins. *Damn you, Lynx!* He was no better than Lord deWode. She had been an idiot to have faith in any man when they all wanted to seize control of Bredonmere.

A broad hand settled on her wrist, halting her. Astonishment filled her anew as she looked at Bourne, who said softly, "This was not the work of Lynx, milady."

"Not Lynx? Who else could it be?"

"I have no answer for that," he snapped, "but Lynx has done nothing like this before. He has burned an abandoned byre, yet he has done no major damage."

Anger consumed her as she pulled away. "Mayhap he tires of childish pranks. Why do you defend him?"

"I simply wish, as you do, milady, not to see an innocent man brought to harm."

"Lynx innocent?" She laughed tersely. "Save your jests for another time."

As she walked past him, he grabbed her arm and twisted her to face him. He gave her no time to protest his unexpected vehemence before he snarled, "'Tis not a jest that you may have a second, more deadly enemy."

"No!"

"Yes, milady, that may be true."

Audra backed away, knowing that shock was emblazoned across her face. She used the question from one of the servants as an excuse to leave Bourne staring after her. Although she tried to put his words from her head, she found it impossible when Father Jerome, smelling of smoke, arrived with the first villeins.

She sent the injured to the sickroom where her household waited with salves and bandaging. Fury flashed through her when Bourne drew the priest aside. If he was warning Father Jerome of her apprehensions, then Bourne was not the man she had guessed him to be.

Not that she should trust any of them any longer.

Each man sought to use her in his own way. Even Crandall, who was trying to mold her into the image of her father. Hadn't Lynx told her to trust no one? *Fool.* He had called her that on more than one occasion. Was he laughing at her naïveté now?

When Father Jerome spoke to her, she wanted to believe his smile was sincere. "Thank the good Lord, no one is dead, milady. However, the corn on more than five tofts is ash."

"He knows our most vulnerable point." Bitterness slipped into her words.

"He?"

Audra flinched when Bourne answered, "It is Lady Audra's opinion that Lynx is responsible." She had not seen him come toward them.

Father Jerome shook his head vehemently. "Impossible! No one man could have started so many blazes at one time."

Audra said quietly, "He had a half-dozen men with him when I met him on my way to Bredonmere."

"No less than a score of men would have been needed tonight. I doubt Lynx has that many hidden on the manor."

In frustration, she turned away. They both believed Lynx was blameless. She wished she could be as sure. Bourne had spoken of another enemy. That was nonsense.

It must be Lynx . . . but how could it be? She had dared to trust her heart, which told her to believe him when he said he was not her enemy. If she surrendered to Lynx by accepting what might be nothing but lies, she risked Bredonmere. That she could not do, even though a pang ached through her as she realized the only way to stop the man who delighted her with fired kisses was to send him to his death.

The choice was Bredonmere or Lynx.

The answer was simple. She must choose Bredonmere.

The watch was calling the hour past midnight when Audra left the great hall. Food and wine had been brought for those who had lost their homes. Sated, they slept on the floor.

Hearing footfalls, she turned, half-expecting to see Crandall, then recalling he slept in his favorite chair. Bourne stood behind her with a frown on his face.

"Milady," he said softly, so as not to wake anyone, "'tis said that you will ride tomorrow to the south tofts. Allow me to go with you."

"I wish you to stay here to train the lads." She shivered as if a wintry wind blew through the passage. "If what you assert is true, we may have need of their skills sooner than either of us expected."

He stepped to block her way, putting his weak leg on the riser in front of her. "You must not ride alone. Do you have no thoughts of the danger waiting out there for you?"

"Bourne," she whispered, "please trust me. I need someone to trust me to do what I must to safeguard Bredonmere. If I am to hold, you must trust me to do as my father would."

"But he was a man."

"And I am not?" She laughed coldly. "I had not thought that you, of all I have met since I left Clarendon Abbey, would use that truth to throw insult in my face." Raising her chin, she said, "I shall prove wrong all of you who disbelieve my assertion that I can hold."

"Milady, I—"

"Say no more, for I wish to hear no more false-hoods tonight." She whirled and raced up the steep stairs.

Audra did not slow as she entered her rooms. They were oddly quiet. She saw mounds, which she knew were her chamber servants sleeping on the floor.

Shirley looked up, groggily. "Milady?"

Audra did not answer as she went into her bed-chamber and closed the heavy door. By all that was holy, she had thought she could depend on Bourne. He had been the single constant through this mad-ness. Bourne . . . and Lynx. She pressed her hands to her head. Yes, madness was sweeping Bredonmere as completely as the Death, and it had infected her if she could name the armorer and the night rider in a single thought.

A knock sounded on her door. "Yes?" she called.

Shirley peeked into the room. "Bourne wishes to speak to you, milady."

"Tell him to wait until morning."

"He anticipated you saying that." She yawned widely. "Excuse me, milady. Bourne asks for only a few moments of your time."

Audra shook her head. She could not speak to him when she was so confused. "Shirley, I will speak to him in the morning. Not before. Tell him to rise early if he wishes to see me before I leave for the south tofts." The maid started to answer, but another yawn interrupted her. Audra added, "Tell him, then seek your bed."

Shirley nodded and closed the door.

As Audra crossed the carpeted floor, she drew her gorget off her hair and tossed it onto a bench. She pulled the letter she had written to the king from her sash and shredded it. Tomorrow she must write another. Tonight had shown her she needed a strong lord to govern Bredonmere. A man as strong and single-minded as . . . as Lynx.

With a shiver, she knew why she had been unable to write the truth to the king. The man she wanted to help her govern Bredonmere rode the night in his ebony mask. But never again must she allow herself to forget that, if everyone, save Bourne, was right in their assertions, Lynx was her enemy.

Audra woke to footsteps. Wishing Shirley had not come to be sure she was asleep, she shifted on the rumpled covers. The night was too hot for sleeping. She glanced toward the windows. They were open to catch any breath of air. Nestling into the rushes, she closed her eyes.

Iron struck stone. She sat up and scanned the darkness, her heart pounding like warhorses' hooves on a hard road. She whispered, "Shirley?"

A hand clamped over her mouth. Terror strangled her as she heard a voice emerge from her dreams to murmur, "Speak not, milady."

Lynx! What was he doing here?

He drew his hand from her mouth. Again he warned her to be silent. She saw the flash of the small blade he carried unsheathed in his hands as he closed the windows. Clenching the blanket in her hand, she tried not to think how he had managed to slip into her private rooms. She had heard no sound of broadswords, but he could not have entered the keep without being noted.

When he dropped the bar on the door to the outer

chambers, she gasped. That sound should have alerted
Shirley. She slid off the bed and took but a single step
before his blade flashed before her eyes again. He said
nothing as he herded her back to her bed.

"Sit, milady." When she obeyed, his smile glistened in the moonlight.

"What are you doing *here?*" Her eyes widened as
he reached for the pin holding his cape about his
shoulders. As he released it, the blackness flew to the
floor like a dying bird.

"I told you there was unfinished business we
must deal with. That time is now."

Her gaze rose from the discarded cape to his
face, which was still swathed in the concealing cloth.
When she realized he was undoing the sword belt, she
opened her mouth to scream.

He chuckled with satisfaction. "Cry out as you
wish. There is nobody to hear you."

"You did not—" She choked on the appalling
thought.

"As much as I want you, I would not slay your
companions to have you. No, I chose a far more civi-
lized way than deWode, who tried to separate Crandall from his soul. I simply arranged for a sleeping
potion to be slipped into the cask of wine in the great
hall. All of Bredonmere sleeps, save you and me." He
grasped her shoulders and pulled her to her knees on
the bed. "No one shall hear how we spend this night,
milady."

"Begone!" she cried. "After what you did on the
south tofts tonight, you are bold to think I would welcome you into my arms."

"You know I did not do that, pretty one." He
held up his full sleeve. "Do you smell smoke from
me?"

"Your orders could have fired the tofts."

He stroked her bare shoulder, and she shivered with the longing she did not want to feel. "Believe what you wish, but I did not come here to speak of such things. I came to satisfy the longings we share."

"No!" When she tried to scramble away, his strong hands brought her against his body, which was as unyielding as iron. She averted her face, but his fingers twisted in her hair as he steered her mouth beneath his. As each time he had held her, she found she was fighting herself instead of him while his lips wooed her.

She must not want to be in the arms of this man who aimed to destroy Bredonmere, but her body's need to savor his touch silenced all thought. When her hands slid up his brawny arms, he opened the collar of her thin smock to press his mouth against the curve of her throat. She gasped at the pulse of passion racing through her.

The aromas of heated wool and musky sweat surrounded her. With a gasp, she pulled away and looked at the window. "You climbed in that way?"

He laughed as his mouth brushed her ear, sending a new flurry of uncontrollable fire along her. "A prize's worth is determined by how difficult it is to obtain. You, milady, demanded every bit of my skill to devise this way to be here with you tonight."

Her breath caught in her throat as he knelt on the bed next to her. His hands encircled her face, tilting it back so he could view her features in the dim light secreting between the mullions.

"Have no fear," he murmured.

"I am not frightened of you."

He smiled at her breathy response. Moving closer so each accelerated breath stroked her breasts against him, he urged, "Think not of the past or future. Think only of now."

"When you should not be with me." Her assertion was weak as his fierce kisses left her flushed with a desire she could not control.

"On that matter, you are very, very wrong." He chuckled when she gasped as his fingers moved along the soft curve of her breast.

She closed her eyes as she swayed. Gently, so gently she was sure a butterfly would touch her no more lightly, his fingers sought the dulcet, swiftly building desire along her breast. A single fingertip roved into the hollow between them, then brushed the other until ripples of pleasure flooded her, sweeping all thought from her head. As if her smock did not remain between them, she could feel the flame of his skin against her. She brought his mouth to hers, wanting to share the delight before it overwhelmed her.

As he leaned her back on the bed, he drew the curtains around them. She was startled by the sudden darkness and smothering heat. When she reached to open the velvet drapes, he caught her wrist.

"Do not touch the curtains while I am with you, milady." His low tone could not soften the threat.

He slowly lowered her wrist to the pillow as his mouth came down over hers. Leaning across her, he pinned her to the rushes. The strength of his body surrounded her, entreating her to touch him.

When material brushed her face, she gasped against his mouth. He was removing the fabric which hid his face. Heart-stopping horror choked her. If she saw his face, she would discover who he really was— friend or foe. Instantly her heart negated the panic.

Whether friend or foe, tonight he would be her lover. For one, magic night, she wanted him and what he alone could give her.

When he took her hand and drew it over his shoulder, he bent to place his mouth in the dusky valley between her breasts. Again it was as if her thin smock had vanished, for the heat of his mouth burned it away. Her back arched as she ceded herself to the yearning. Against her, his pleased laughter was as melodious as the song of the wind.

She laughed when his tongue flicked playfully against her ear. The sound became a deep moan when his breath along its crescent sent shivers to the depths of her bones.

Bringing his mouth back to hers, for she hungered for its caress against her lips, she ran her fingertips across his chest. The brawny muscles quivered, and his breath quickened until it surged into her mouth like a fierce storm.

When he drew back, she whispered, "Lynx?"

"Fear not, pretty one," he said with a ragged laugh. "I shall not leave you all night." Taking her hands, he drew her up to sit before him. He knelt next to her as he ordered, "Undress for me, milady. Let me see all of your beauty."

She hesitated, holding her collar closed.

He lifted her hair aside and whispered, "Audra, you are no longer a nun. Of all the decisions your father made, that was the most absurd. You were not made to be a nun."

"I would have been a good nun."

"But you shall be even more wondrous here, my pretty one." He ran a fingertip along her collar and pulled her fingers away. "Such a life is not for a woman who scintillates with the heat of the sun and dares me to share her fire. You need not shut your passions away ever again."

"I must," she argued, but faintly as his finger slowly loosened the laces along the front of her smock.

With a laugh, he said, "My dear one-time Sister Audra, let me prove to you how impossible that is for you."

He gripped her thick hair and brought her lips to his. No gentle kiss courted her now, for his mouth burned like red embers on an open hearth. When she gasped, his tongue surged into her mouth, caressing the smooth moistness within. As he urged her tongue to move as intimately against him, his hand led hers to the sash holding his tunic in place.

Pulling his mouth away so slightly that his lips brushed hers on every word, he whispered, "I shall help you, and you will disrobe me, milady."

"Lynx—"

He silenced her beneath another crest of passion as he pushed aside her smock to reveal her to his eager eyes. His arm encircled her waist as the brush of his tongue against her breast sent into oblivion any thought of refusing him—and herself—what they both wanted. Her body strained, wanting more, wanting to touch him with every inch of her. The abrasive caress of his rough cheeks burnished her as, teasing and taunting, his tongue laved her skin.

When the wool of his tunic drooped against her, she untied the sashes holding it in place. She slid it off his shoulders and down along his arms. As his naked chest touched her, she clenched the material. He pressed her into the bed, and she moaned with the unrestrainable craving to delight in what his kisses promised.

He drew his tunic off and kicked it aside. When

he brought her fingers to the waist of his chausses, she knelt again. She leaned against him, the curling hair on his chest caressing her. Into her hair, he whispered her name.

Her rapid breath tightened in her chest. The strange shapes of his male body were revealed against her fingers, then against her body as she lowered the chausses along his legs. When she tossed them into the darkness at the end of the bed, he caught her shoulders and brought her atop him as he reclined back into the bed where she had slept alone for so long.

She moaned softly as the warmth of his body burned against her skin to introduce her to his craving. His mouth against hers moved with a rhythm that resonated through her whole body. When her fingers traced a lazy path along his chest, he groaned. Growing more bold, she let them slip farther down. The textures of his body fascinated her, the rough skin of his chest, the silky hardness that she longed to have deep within her.

"Vixen," he growled as he twisted beneath her, rolling her onto her back.

She discovered his body over hers was what she had craved without knowing what she wanted. His swift kisses left her gasping for breath before his mouth moved along her body in a slow exploration. Even as he teased her with his tongue, his fingers were slipping along her legs, daring to caress her as she had never guessed a man would.

She did not need him to urge her to touch him. She wanted to explore him as she was engulfed by the heat of his hands. When his fingers slid upward to explore her most sensitive warmth, she moaned against his mouth. He sought within her for the passions he had promised they would share.

Her fingers swept through his hair as she pressed against him, wanting a release from the rapture that threatened to rip her from him and all the world. His lips took hers as he brought them together.

The pulse of his body against hers eclipsed all ecstasy she had known. When he moved, she followed the rhythm his lips had taught her. Shivers of desire rippled through her, strong, sweet, unstoppable. She gasped into his mouth as she dissolved into the molten ecstasy racing through her. As the fire exploded outward, she held on to him, for she did not want to lose the perfection that should never have been.

Gentle, teasing kisses brought Audra back to herself. A hard form moved near her, keeping her pinned between it and the rushes. When she opened her eyes, she could see little, but sight was unnecessary. As she stroked the strong shoulder beneath her cheek, she savored the rapture she had discovered in Lynx's arms.

At the thought of his name, she stiffened. She *was* mad!

Lynx drew her into the arc of his arm. "Audra," he whispered as he kissed the top of her head, "it is too late for second thoughts."

She reached to tilt his face toward her. His fingers grasped her wrist, forcing her hand back. Betrayal erupted within her. Nothing had changed between them, save that he had bedded her. When she tried to pull away, his arm became a prison. She spat a curse at him, and he chuckled.

"Such language from you, milady!"

"You are a—"

He interrupted with another laugh. "Undoubtedly,

but to hear such a word on your saintly lips is astonishing, proving yet again that you should not have become the nun your family wished you to be."

"Why did you come here tonight?" she whispered, hurt anew by his jesting when she wanted him to be the tender lover he had been moments before.

He stroked her hair, which was lying across his chest. "There are many reasons, but the most important is that I have wanted you since I first saw you. You faced me squarely and demanded that I leave your lands."

"Which you did not do."

"Nay, for the work I have to do here is far from done."

Frustration sharpened her voice. "Do you aim to destroy my home as you have my honor?"

Pressing her deeper into the mattress, he snapped, "I do you no dishonor by showing my desire for your loveliness. Fear not, milady, for as I have told you before, neither you nor your manor is my target."

"Then why—?"

His finger over her lips silenced her. "Speak no more of the hatred beyond your bed. Use your sweet lips instead to thrill me."

Shaking her head, she reached for her smock. Before she could grasp it, his hands caught her shoulders and pulled her back against his sleek length. "No, Lynx," she whispered.

"You have no yearning for me?" His hand swept along her breast. When she trembled, he laughed. "Do not deny the truth. Your place is in my arms. My place is deep within you."

"Lynx—" Her voice vanished into a sigh as his lips found the most sensitive spot along her neck.

In the seconds before his lips touched hers,

which ached for his kiss, he whispered, "Tonight is ours, and you are mine."

She knew he was right. The night was theirs. On the morrow, she would have to face the insanity of her desire for Lynx. But, as she exulted in his touch, she knew she would pay any price to have this pleasure . . . just one more time.

11

He woke, tensing. Darkness surrounded him, softness cradled him. This was all wrong! He had trained himself not to sleep at night. No comfortable bed should be beneath him while moonlight shone through heavy curtains. War had dragged him from such luxury, first the king's war, now his private one.

A murmur close to his ear brought a smile. Shifting, he gazed down at the woman sleeping with her cheek against his shoulder. Strands of dusky hair caressed his bare chest and concealed the luscious curves of her naked body that was curled against him as she dreamed of longings she alone could know.

He resisted chuckling. During the sweet hours of the night, he had learned of many of Lady Audra's longings. The passions he had seen in her eyes had been released when he held her here.

But now morning was coming, and he must face

what awaited him. DeWode was gone from Bredonmere, but that banishment would not last long if the baron could gain the king's favor on his claim of the manor. DeWode must never claim Bredonmere, for the faithless cur needed no more honors heaped upon his unscrupulous head.

Again his thoughts were interrupted as Audra stirred in her sleep. He watched a smile flit across her lips like a butterfly sampling the nectar in a field of fragrant blossoms. A craving to capture her mouth beneath his surged over him. With a groan, he sat up and turned away from sweet temptation. The hour of dawn was too close. He must be gone before the sun roused the keep.

His smile returned as he reached for his chausses. Sainted Mary, how could he have been such a fool? The solution to all he wanted was as simple as convincing King Edward that a better man than deWode could be found for Bredonmere's lady. The right words would persuade the king not to give Bredonmere and Audra to the baron.

As he dressed swiftly he resolved to convince the king of that himself, once he was certain Bredonmere could stand alone while Lynx did not ride through the night.

He slid open the curtain, pulling it aside silently as he saw the first hints of gray light flow through the window. Time to go. Looking back at the bed, he reminded himself that if all went as he wished, there would be many other nights for him in this bed with Bredonmere's lady. Other nights that would be all the more gratifying because deWode would have lost everything he had hoped to gain.

*   *   *

Staring at the charred ruins of a byre, Audra listened to the mournful song of the breeze in the leafless, scorched trees. Everything green had been eaten by the fire, which had razed the toft and the fields surrounding it. Exactly as the other farms had been. Nothing offered a clue to name the man who had ordered this damage inflicted on the villeins of Bredonmere.

She walked around the cottage, which was rubble. The voices of her companions were muted. She coughed as soot rose on each step. Seeing the glow of embers nearly hidden among the ashes, she backed away.

She had heard whispers that the fires had been started by lightning from last evening's storm. If it had been but a single fire on a single toft, she might have accepted that, for it was easier to endure than the brutality of an enemy who was able to strike so viciously, then vanish.

Audra mounted her horse and turned it toward the road. She held her gorget over her nose, so she could breathe more easily. Blinking, she tried to keep the cinders from searing her eyes. Behind her, she heard other hoofbeats but no voices. Fleming and Halstead, the reeve, had become as silent as the death around them when they came upon the remnants of the first burned toft.

She edged her horse around the blackened timbers, which were heaped like castoff twigs in a wood pile. The damp smell of the rain, which had done little to contain the fires, stank.

"Be careful, milady," Fleming urged. He pointed to the broken foundation directly in front of her. "If you chance to ride into the root cellar, you could be hurt badly."

"What do you make of this?" she asked, ignoring his warning, which she had not needed. She was very aware of the dangers awaiting them amid the ruins.

"'Twas no accident."

"That I know! You are the commander of my guard. I need you to give me answers to questions I cannot answer myself."

"Milady, forgive me, but I have none for you." He hung his head.

Shame ached inside her empty heart. She could not blame Fleming for her peculiar feelings today. Last night had seemed a dream when she woke alone in her bed this morning. If she had not found her clothes jumbled at the foot of the bed and her door still barred from the inside, she might have believed the delicious memories of a forbidden love were nothing but a dream.

They were not. As she had bathed and dressed to ride out with Fleming, her skin recalled the sensation of Lynx's strong hands against her. Her body remembered his touch, refusing to let her forget the ecstasy she had found in his arms when he made them one in their desperate need to seek satiation. How fiercely his mouth had incited her passions! How easily she had given herself to him, knowing that their love was doomed.

In the first light of morning, she had to acknowledge that she had betrayed everything she once held dear to have this man. The woman who had been Sister Audra was now Lynx's lover. The woman who had vowed to hold off any foe to Bredonmere had surrendered to an outlaw. Yet, not even in the unforgiving blush of dawn, could she regret the choice she had made. She loved Lynx, although she realized, with growing dismay, she could not guess if he felt anything more than a lustful desire to share her bed.

Audra sighed as she put her hand on Fleming's arm. "Forgive me, my friend. I did not sleep well last night." She flushed, for that was the truth. Lynx had granted her little time for slumber. His eager caresses had drawn her to him again and again to sample the power of their merged passions.

"Nor did I."

"You did not sleep well?"

He regarded her with puzzlement. "How can you think I would find rest when *this* awaited us?"

Pretending to be interested in something on the far side of the blackened lea, she avoided Fleming's eyes. She did not want him to see her shock. Lynx had asserted that the wine had drugged everyone in the keep. "I beg your forgiveness again."

"Nay, for I beg yours." Vehemence returned to his voice. "We both shall be able to find a good night's sleep only when I determine a way to capture Lynx and his treacherous allies."

"This is not Lynx's handiwork."

Halstead whirled from where he was kicking a blackened door that had somehow retained its shape. Surprise appeared on the reeve's soot-etched face. "Not Lynx? Last night, when we came to the manor, you seemed convinced of his part in this treachery."

"And I admit to having been wrong." She backed her horse onto the road. "Father Jerome told me many men would be needed to set fire to these tofts. I can see now that he was correct."

"Father Jerome is wise," the reeve agreed, albeit grudgingly. He leaped into the saddle.

"I shall heed his counsel more fully next time." She did not add that the priest was not the one who had persuaded her of Lynx's innocence. If she divulged that she believed the assertions of the man who had shared her bed during the night, she would see the fealty in their eyes turn to loathing.

"Then who did this?" asked Fleming as he jumped his horse over a log to catch up with her. He grimaced and batted at the shower of cinders cascading over him at his unthinking action.

"I had hoped to find some hint here to tell me who dares to risk the ire of Bredonmere, but there is nothing."

Fleming lowered his voice. "Mayhap we should look farther afield. These tofts border the lands of Lord Norwell."

"Lord Norwell?" She gripped the reins more tightly. "Is he in residence on his fief?"

"I am unsure, for he travels often to London, milady."

She frowned at the hills rolling away into the distance. Her neighbor should have given her the courtesy of a welcome upon her arrival at Bredonmere. When no one came to the manor house, she had guessed all her neighbors were dead or awaiting the pleasure of the king at his court. "What do you know of him?"

"Little, milady." Fleming scratched the back of his neck and shifted in the saddle. "I have seen him but once, from a distance. A tall man with hair the shade of a raven's wing. Strongly built, if I recall aright. As I said, he remains close to the king's court."

Audra faltered. The description would fit Lynx! What more perfect disguise for a night rider than a neighboring baron? Certainly Lord Norwell would be the first to profit if Bredonmere was put into contention. He could claim the lands bordering his before another man could arrive. "Mayhap I would be wise to send a summons to Lord Norwell, requesting that he present himself at Bredonmere so I may know him better."

"You suspect he would do this?" Although his words had suggested it, Fleming clearly found the very idea of a lord preying on his lady disgusting.

"Rather we should think of the meeting as a chance for two allies to determine if together they might have the information to end this destruction."

The young man grinned. "And at the same time, you shall try to learn if he has, indeed, played a role in this."

"Be assured, my friend, I shall suspect everyone until I find the outlaw who dares to put the torch to the tofts belonging to Bredonmere."

"Which you must, milady, if you wish to save Bredonmere from a curse worse than the Death itself."

Audra wished she could share Fleming's assumption that she would soon expose the man who had ordered the fires set. As they rode over the drawbridge and beneath the mighty portcullis in Bredonmere's inner gate, she had no more answers than when she departed at dawn. The massive manor house might be impenetrable, but they would starve if every field was fired before harvest. Somehow she must find an answer before the destruction was complete.

As Audra entered the hall, a cry went up. She could not comprehend the words, for the sound was blurred by the many voices and the distorting echo of the timbered roof.

Shirley raced up to grasp her hands. "Milady, you are unhurt."

"Of course, I am well. What—?"

Crandall rushed forward, halting behind her maid. His voice puffed over her as he pressed his hand to his side and wheezed, "What foolish thought did you take into your head that you should sneak out of the keep? When will you learn, milady, that you are the target for Lynx's crimes?"

"I am well aware of the dangers beyond these walls. That is why I took Fleming and Halstead with me."

The steward ran his hands through his hair, and she suspected he would have enjoyed jabbing a finger at her as he did when he admonished the servants. Taking a deep breath, he asked in a taut voice, "Where in the name of the good Lord have you been, milady?"

"I rode to see the burned tofts. Certainly you recall me telling you of my plans last night."

"You told me nothing of it."

"I recall it well. You were sitting at the raised table by my chair and . . ." She remembered that Crandall had been one of the first asleep last night. He must have consumed a generous serving of the drugged wine. Uneasily she added, "Mayhap your thoughts were busy with the disaster last night."

He shot an accusing glower at Shirley, who was wringing her hands together. "As must have been yours."

"I—Forgive me, milady," the maid rushed to say. "I was so sleepy last night, my mind was only on seeking my pallet."

"When she reported you missing," Crandall

continued fiercely, "what was I to think but that you had come to harm again?"

Loosening her gorget, which was dusty from her travels, Audra dropped to a bench, exhausted. The ride alone would have been enough to tire her even if she had had a full night's sleep. Feeling a flush on her cheeks anew, she prayed her dear friends would not guess the course of her dangerous thoughts.

"I rose while you still slept, Shirley," she said. "I had no wish to disturb you."

"You left without waking me? I always listen for you, milady."

Audra bit back her answer. No one must be privy to the fact that Lynx had drugged the wine in the hall—and in her room as well, she realized with a start, for her maids had been busy there all evening. He must have an ally within the keep, unless he was one of her household.

She gave them a counterfeit smile and said, "I saw no reason to wake you."

"What did you find on the burned tofts, milady?" Crandall asked.

Her hands clenched. "Nothing granted me a clue to the culprits, but enough to convince me it was not Lynx."

"How can you be so sure?"

"You must trust me on this, Crandall."

"Milady—"

"It was not Lynx." She rose and added, "I would like to retire for a while, so I can clear my mind. Crandall, be certain that all those who need food are fed. Where is Bourne?"

"On the training field."

"Send for him. I have delayed too long speaking with him."

"Oh!" gasped Shirley. "Amid the excitement, I nearly forgot. He left word before he went out onto the field that he asks your forgiveness for his fervor. He wants you to know that the message he sent with me to you last night was only to ask you for that forgiveness."

Audra frowned. Was that all it had been? Bourne had been so insistent. She was foolish to give the matter another thought when he was no longer distressed. She did not need another puzzle in her life. Feigning a yawn, she hid her face behind her hand. She must have her thoughts in order before she spoke to anyone else.

Audra left them watching her as she crossed the hall. Other stares followed her, too, but she ignored the curious villeins. Until the man who had destroyed their homes was raven's meat, she had nothing to say to them. She wanted to sleep, to lose her anxieties in the dreams that had been interrupted last night.

As she entered her bedchamber, she realized how naïve her hopes were. Those dreams had been of Lynx, and he had come to her to make them real. She closed her eyes as she touched the upright of her wide bed. Leaning her head against the carved wood, she recalled how wondrous and enchanted the night had seemed. In the glaring light of day, she knew it was but a fleeting dream she had been lucky to grasp once. Lynx had left without saying he would return.

He would be a fool to risk coming to her again. Once he had managed to slip past her guards. A second time . . . He would be gambling his life as she endangered her father's—*her* fief by giving herself to a night rider.

She stared at the gray stone walls surrounding her. She loved Bredonmere, and she loved Lynx. She could not have them both.

Nothing had changed.

At the window, Audra folded her arms on the broad sill and gazed south. Whoever had attacked the tofts still rode free to continue wreaking malicious damage on her tenants. She must not let Bredonmere fall before intruders.

Not to Lynx, not to any other.

The door opened, and she turned to see Crandall striding toward her. His face was as grim as a winter morning. "This was delivered for you, milady."

She took the rolled paper he held out and opened it. Her hopes that this letter brought salvation for Bredonmere faded when she saw the unbroken seal on it. It came from King Edward. Guilt stung her as she looked at the remnants of parchment still on her table. She had forgotten to write a new letter to the king this morning before she rode south.

Dismay dropped to the very pit of her stomach as she read what had been sent from the king's court. Lynx had warned her. How had he known?

"Good tidings, milady?" the steward asked hopefully.

"Yes, yes," she managed to answer. Struggling to smile, she added, "I must respond to this at once, Crandall. I trust the courier remains in the hall."

"He does, although he appears highly agitated. He urged me to inform you that he has been told to return with your answer as soon as humanly possible."

"Go, and be certain that he is well rewarded with food and drink for his efforts. I shall endeavor to have him on his way before nightfall."

Audra ignored the curiosity in Crandall's eyes. When he left to do as she had asked, she opened the scroll again. She hoped she had misread it the first time, but the words were unchanged. Lady Audra Travers, countess of Bredonmere, was commanded by His Royal Majesty King Edward III to betroth herself to Lord Gifford deWode and arrange for their marriage to be celebrated with all due haste.

That could not be! She would not allow deWode to take Bredonmere away from her. He cared nothing for the fief save the prestige it could bring him. Trembling as she thought of his heavy hands pawing at her, she drew out the box that held ink and precious paper. She began to write, the words falling from her fingers like notes from a minstrel's lyre.

No sound but the scratch of the quill against the rough paper intruded on her. When, an hour later, Audra sat straighter, she read what she had written. She ignored the formal greeting to the king and her polite queries to his health and the health of his family. She was interested solely in what came after.

The words were simple but from the heart. Bredonmere needed a strong lord to help her combat the dark minds who wished to see the fief come to ruin. Lord deWode, although a proven warrior, had not gained the respect of her household or her men. If he came to claim Bredonmere, it was sure to lead to more trouble. Therefore, she implored the king to find her another, more suitable lord, who could come to Bredonmere posthaste. There must be no delay, for she was eager to obey the dictates of her king and welcome the best lord possible to help her oversee Bredonmere.

She lowered the page to the table, stood, and walked to the window. She looked out into the green fields beyond the walls. Somewhere Lynx hid behind his daylight garb. If only he could have been chosen by the king to be her husband, she would gladly have taken him as her partner in ruling the fief and in her bed.

With a shiver, she turned from the window. Lynx was the one man, among the many looking with lustful eyes on the manor, who acknowledged her skills at holding Bredonmere. Yet he had overmastered her every protest when he came to her bed last night. Mayhap he would be no different if he had the chance to hold Bredonmere as its lord.

Audra whirled back to the table. Her fingers faltered as she reached into the box for her father's signet ring. She must be certain the letter would gain the king's attention and sympathy. As she had last night, she wondered if another set of eyes might discern some misused word she could not see. But whose?

The answer was obvious, but it opened her to more danger. Asking Father Jerome to read her letter might be the greatest mistake she could make, for if he truly rode the night as Lynx, she could be creating more difficulty for Bredonmere. Yet, she guessed he was the only other in the manor house, save Crandall, who could read. Her steward would give her no help with the letter. Crandall would be furious that she did not denounce the baron openly to King Edward.

When she went out into the courtyard, the summer heat ground down into her shoulders and sent sweat bubbling along her forehead. Hearing shouts, she hoped Bourne would realize that if the lads sickened from training too long in the sun, they would be little help in a crisis.

The chapel was hushed and welcomingly cool. Beneath her cloth slippers, the stones were free of rushes. The quiet was a balm for her uneasy spirit and a condemnation. This circle of prayers and devotions was the life she had assumed would be hers.

Lynx's laugh echoed in her head as she recalled his touch. Those memories swept aside her yearning to belong to this sacred world once more. Yet, as Lynx had told her—as she had discovered on her own—her proper place was as the lady of Bredonmere.

It was time she acted that way.

"By all the saints!"

Shirley looked up at her lady's surprising outburst and asked, "Would you like me to help you search?"

Audra shook her head as she upended the box that contained her writing materials onto the table. She was sure she had put the small velvet pouch holding her father's signet ring back into the rosewood box after its last use. Now she could not find it among the pieces of parchment and pointed quills.

"Mayhap I left it with Crandall," she said.

"I can check with him, if you wish."

"No need to disturb him now." She paused as she heard the watch call the hour at the middle of the night. "The king's messenger shall not start back before sunup."

Shirley dampened her lips, then whispered, "Is it as I have heard? Has His Majesty given Bredonmere to Lord deWode?"

Again Audra was amazed at how little of her business was kept a secret. No doubt the messenger had babbled once his lips were loosened with ale. She should have known better than to leave him in Crandall's care.

Carefully setting the materials back into the box, she said, "I hold Bredonmere until the day I give it to my husband."

"But—"

"We have plenty of time to discuss this on the morrow, Shirley."

Her maid frowned at the scold, but said little as she helped Audra get ready for bed. Bidding her lady a good-night's rest, she went out into the antechamber to seek her own sleep.

Audra selected a sheet of parchment and sat at her table. With ease, the words flowed from her fingers. All the questions about Lynx and the few clues she had about him. And the circumstances that could prove he was of Bredonmere. She listed everything, but when she was done and she read what she had written, she saw she had nothing.

Lynx and Father Jerome had come to Bredonmere at about the same time, but so had Bourne and many others who had been left without homes by the Death. Lynx was tall and dark haired. So were Father Jerome and dozens of others. More than half of the men in the manor had brown eyes.

This was leading nowhere. She rose and prowled her room, unable to loosen the chains of anxiety wrapped around her. As a lone candle sprayed light along the wall, she paced, looking for an answer to even one of the problems haunting her.

Hearing the watch call the passage of yet another hour past the middle of the night, Audra knew she must accept what she had tried to ignore. Lynx was not returning. She wrapped her arms around herself and rubbed her bare skin. The night was hot, but she suffered an icy grief.

Audra could tolerate the silence no longer. Going into the antechamber, she hoped to find someone awake. All the maids slept, enjoying their simple dreams. With a sigh, she turned back into the private chamber. She shut the door, her fingers faltering on the bar. There was no need to lock out the world when she was alone.

"You are late abed, milady."

Audra spun around. From the shadows by her bed emerged the form she knew better in darkness than her own. Lynx did not speak again as his hand settled over hers. Slowly he guided her hand to slide the bar into place.

"Forgive me for leaving you alone so long," he whispered as he brushed her hair back from her face. "I would have come to you sooner if I could."

The faint scent of ashes billowed over her. With a gasp, she pulled away. "You smell of smoke!"

From behind his mask, his eyes burned with malevolence. "I, too, wish to capture the man who does such wickedness in my name. A ride to the south tofts gave me no answers and delayed my arrival at your side tonight."

"You found nothing?"

"No more than you, milady." His hand curved along her cheek. "But of such unpleasant matters I have no interest when I see you before me. You left the window open for me, Audra. Did you hope I would return to you tonight?"

"I had not known if you should return." She could not imagine lying to him. "You risk your life coming here."

He persisted, as always, in chasing her like his namesake hunting across the leas. "But you wished for me to come back to you tonight?"

"Yes."

His throaty chuckle sank through her, stripping her bare of all pretense. Pulling her tight to him, he whispered, "You learn quickly, my pretty Audra, of the truth I told you last night. From the moment your eyes touched mine, you belonged to me."

Although she knew she should not cede herself to the temptation of his love, she could not halt her soft moan of longing. When he drew her to the bed and leaned her back on the soft covers, she brought him with her. She did not think of the sin of coveting her enemy when he drew away her smock to place heated kisses along her neck. All she knew was that she wanted him as she had no other. If she must feel regret in the dawn light, she cared nothing about that as he reached for the curtains of the bed to swath them in the loving darkness once more.

Audra was roughly routed from sleep by shouts from her antechamber. She heard Shirley caution someone to silence, but a fist pounded on her door.

She gasped, "Lynx, you must leave! If—"

Opening her eyes, she realized she was alone in her bed. The drawn curtains and her smock, crumpled on the bed, were again the sole clues that the glorious night had not been a dream. She threw her smock over her head and pulled a blanket off the bed to wrap around her shoulders in the moment before the door crashed open.

Again she was shocked. She had barred the door. Why had Lynx removed the bar to slip away before the gray light of dawn could light her room? She had no time to find an answer as men flooded into the room.

Fleming halted, a blush climbing his cheeks as he stared at the blanket about her shoulders. He gulped, then said, "Milady, the urgency of this message would not allow me to wait upon your arrival in the hall this morning."

Looking past him, she saw fear on Crandall's face and fury on Bourne's. "What is it, Fleming?"

"Another attack on the tofts. These farther south along Lord Norwell's borders. Among those who survived—"

"There are dead?" she choked, clutching the blanket to her chin as renewed cold sliced into her.

"Nearly a score, milady," Bourne said tautly, his accent almost obliterating his words as he spat each one through clenched teeth. "There may be more as daylight reveals the bodies in the ruined cottages."

Audra swallowed the bile climbing her throat. She could not be ill now, not when the villeins would be looking to her to put an end to this dark scourge that had grown as deadly as the Death. "Have my horse readied, Fleming. I must see this myself. Perhaps this tragedy will bring us the answer to our enemy's name."

"There is no need to search for the culprit's identity," Fleming said as he fisted his hand on the table. "The leader has been named by one who barely lives."

"Name the knave! We shall see him brought to justice for this outrage!"

Fleming said derisively, "There is no doubt any longer, milady. It was Lynx."

12

"It could not have been Lynx!" Audra struggled to keep from turning toward the window that gaped open. She did not want to think that Lynx had climbed through it after spending the twilight setting fires that had killed innocent people. Surely he had been honest when he said the scent of smoke on his clothes came from his exploration of the tofts that had been fired the night before.

Fleming's fingers clasped the haft of his blade. "The witness left no doubt. Not only did the leader have Lynx's bearing, but the witness heard the other night riders call him Lynx as his men set the fires that destroyed the byres and the fields."

She groped for the table. When a hand steadied her arm, she looked up at Bourne. His lips were twisted with rage, and she feared much of it was aimed at her. And why not? He had every reason to despise

her. She was defending a man who was the embodi-
ment of everything Bourne hated.

A man who had lied to her over and over, yet she
welcomed him into her arms and her bed.

"Thank you," she murmured as she sat by the
table. In a stronger voice, she added, "There is something amiss with this. Why would Lynx's men use his
name, knowing that it could betray him and them?"

Crandall rumbled, "Mayhap they no longer fear
reprisal, milady."

"Lynx saved your life! Why do you believe this
tale?"

"He tries to wrest Bredonmere from you," the steward shot back. "Why do you seek to vindicate him?"

Bourne said quietly, "She only seeks the truth,
Crandall."

"The truth is Lynx must be stopped before he can
kill again."

Audra did not listen as Crandall continued his
tirade. She yearned to believe Lynx had played no
part in the night's tragedy, but she could not keep
from recalling how his tunic and cape had smelled of
smoke. Mayhap she was the fool Crandall named her.
If she had let Lynx's sweet seduction blind her, she
was no longer worthy of claiming the fief.

Something must be done to halt the violence
against the villeins of Bredonmere. She wished she
knew what it should be.

The colored threads on the altar cloth Audra was
embroidering blurred in front of her tired eyes. Puffs
of heat from beyond the walls rolled over her in a
thick, oily caress. In the fields, the villeins, who still
had crops to harvest, must be suffering from the

sweltering day. For the past four days since she had retrieved her father's signet ring from Crandall and sealed the message the king's courier had carried from Bredonmere, even the manor house had offered no refuge from the summer heat.

The floor beneath her feet remained cool. She doubted if it ever lost its chill. When winter settled on them, the keep would be as uncomfortable as the draughtiest cottage. Then she would miss the warmth of summer.

The clatter of hoofbeats beyond her window did not disturb her, for the sound heralded only a pair of horses. If Gifford deWode returned to collect her and the fief he longed to possess, he would arrive with the grandest show of strength. Then he would make her and all of Bredonmere pay for the way she had shamed him.

A sharp rap on the door to the antechamber brought her head up. She glanced to where Shirley sat by the hearth. Audra ordered, "Send whoever it is away. I have no wish to be disturbed now."

"Of course, milady." She rushed to the door. Opening it, she repeated Audra's message.

"I shall see Lady Audra," came back the reply in a gruff voice. "She has commanded me to call, and call I have. Step aside, woman, or I shall be forced to walk over you."

In amazement, Audra stood to watch a tall man lurch into her rooms. The cut of his forest-green tunic and the sheen of the wool, which was decorated with brass and gold, told her this was no boorish villein. The jaunty feather in his beaver hat on his ebony hair bounced on each assertive step.

"You presume much, milord," she said, "with such words to my maid."

"As do you, milady," he replied in the same brusque tone. "Even your father—may God bless his eternal soul—had the decency to *invite* a man to attend him. We of the baronage are not cloistered sisters to wait upon your command."

"May I assume, by your words, that you are Lord Norwell?"

"Knox Norwell, milady, of Ashdowne Hall." He gave her a curt bow and nearly tumbled onto his nose.

Audra bit her lip to restrain her amusement. It served the pompous man right to have his underpinnings collapse, but she must not let him see her reaction. Motioning to a bench, she said, "Pray be seated. I shall send for something to ease the dryness of your journey."

"Ale, milady, stout, English ale." His aristocratic nose wrinkled as he reeled past her maids, who scurried aside. "I would suffer none of that weak wine which comes from across the channel." He dropped to the bench so quickly he almost upended it.

"Ale for Lord Norwell," Audra said to Shirley, glad to be able to turn and hide her smile. The man was a dolt! That she had considered, after hearing Fleming describe the baron, this man might be the alter ego for Lynx now seemed ludicrous. Even though they were of a height, the baron's nose was longer than Lynx's and his chin was not molded to the strong line her fingers knew so well.

While Shirley conveyed her order to one of the maids, Audra sat down on the bench facing the baron. "I am pleased that you have deigned to travel to Bredonmere on my *invitation*, milord." When he glowered, she knew she would gain nothing by baiting him. "There are grave matters I wish to discuss with you."

"The night rider?" He chuckled without humor. "You need not look so surprised. The fires on your tofts have been visible from my walls. It takes but a few questions to uncover the truth."

"Which is?"

"A foul band of outlaws is taking advantage of the fact that no strong hand holds Bredonmere."

Her fingers tightened until her knuckles ached, but she kept her voice steady. "You do me grievous dishonor with your words. Bredonmere is under siege, I admit, but we have not surrendered."

"A womanly sentiment, I am afraid. You have lost both men and the crops in your fields. How long can you survive when you have no villeins to till your fields and nothing to feed those who survive?"

"You need have no worry on my behalf, milord."

He fisted his hands on the knees of his dark brown chausses. "We all need to worry if this violence spills from Bredonmere onto other fiefs."

"Then I assume I can count on your assistance to suppress it."

"You assume mistakenly. My men guard my lands, milady. If you need assistance in tending to your own, you should petition the king for aid."

Coolly, she answered, "I need to seek no help from the king. I thought only to join forces with my neighbors to bring this to a close more swiftly. However, you need not bestir yourself, milord. Steps are already underway to end this matter to my satisfaction." She let a smile tease the corners of her lips. "I thought that you would wish to share the glory in bringing this heinous outlaw to justice."

When his dark brows arched with curiosity, Audra did nothing to appease it. Let the arrogant man think what he wished. She would disclose nothing of the plans that still remained unformed in her mind.

"I trust your fief does well," she continued as a maid returned with a flask of ale for the baron and wine for Audra.

"We expect to enjoy a good harvest." He drank deeply, then wiped foam from his mouth onto his sleeve. "I am but recently returned from the king's court. Although the parliament was disbanded because of the plague, I remained in London to serve our king as an impromptu minister."

"The plague arrived nearly a year ago. You are only now returning to your estate?"

She was surprised when his smile became a hint warmer. "I travel often between Ashdowne Hall and London. You should know well by now how much personal attention is required to keep the villeins at their tasks when they would prefer to spend each day idle."

"That's odd, for I have not had to confront that problem here. My people are grateful to be alive and eager to reap the harvest which will see us through another winter."

He laughed and drained the rest of the ale from the flask in a single gulp. "Travers always kept a firm hand on his people. How long do you think they will recall the fear he inspired in them when they look at his daughter?" Putting the empty glass on the table, he stood. "I beg your leave to depart, milady. Ashdowne Hall is still a good half-day's ride. My wife will be most distressed if I do not arrive before sunset."

"On your next visit, you must bring your lady with you."

"Lady Beverley is with child, so she travels little." Masculine pride jutted his chin. "This shall be our eighth."

"Extend to your lady my hopes for an easy and healthy birth."

"We shall send you the tidings in due course. Should be next month or the one after, so it is unlikely she will be in attendance at your wedding."

Audra gasped. "My wedding?"

"Surely the king has informed you of his wish for you to wed deWode."

"I have received the message," she answered, regaining her composure, "but, as you can see, Lord deWode is not here."

"A surprise." He rubbed his narrow chin. "As hastily as he hied out of London when the king gave him his leave, I had been sure he would be at your side by this time."

"Mayhap other matters required his attention." She hid her hands in the folds of her cotehardie. If he saw how tightly they were clenched, he was certain to inform Gifford of her distaste at the advent of his arrival.

Lord Norwell's laugh vexed her. "I can imagine nothing more important than coming to collect this manor. DeWode shows himself to be a fool to leave you unattended, milady. He would be wise to take this manor out of your feminine hands."

"Which have kept it from ruin for the past months, milord."

"I mean you no discourtesy, milady," he said with a smile that told her his words were courteous lies. "However, even you must admit that this fief needs a lord to rule it."

Audra recognized the futility of arguing with

Lord Norwell, who clearly, if he was not Gifford deWode's ally, was certainly not hers. "Thank you for taking the time to visit Bredonmere. I look forward to the tidings of the healthy arrival of your new child."

"Just pray the babe will be a boy. I have four daughters already. I need no more." He lumbered to the door, nearly tripping again over the threshold. "Good day, milady."

When the door had closed behind him, Audra grasped the goblet from the table and flung it at the hearth. Two maids leaped aside as glass shattered on the stone. Gentle hands settled on her shoulder, but she shrugged off Shirley's sympathy. She did not want to be soothed. She wanted to remain furious at a world that insisted she could not hold Bredonmere as well as any man.

"Better than Lord Norwell could," she muttered under her breath.

"Milady, this anger serves nothing," Shirley said. "He sought to infuriate you with his mockery, hoping you would show him a fiery temper."

"Which he could then claim would be Bredonmere's undoing." She wiped her hands on her gown and raised her chin. "He is a fool. I shall prove to all of the baronage that Travers blood, be it within a male or female body, will hold this fief."

The thin woman's eyes grew round. "Milady, think before you set yourself upon a rash course."

Audra's lips drew back in a smile as feral as Lynx's. "'Tis nothing rash, but if I succeed, not a man in Edward's kingdom shall dare cry me unfit."

The gate tower rose high above the rough stones of the outer wall. From within its chamber on the top of the wall, a guard could enjoy a view of the main road leading north and south. The steps up its curving side were steep, but very wide, so many men could race up to defend the manor house at once.

As Audra climbed the stairs, she kept one hand against the uneven wall. Such heights unnerved her, but she must speak with Fleming without delay. Lord Norwell's assertion that Gifford deWode was on his way to Bredonmere warned her that they must take the offensive if she wished to halt deWode's plans to possess both her and her fief.

The men within the round room in the tower leaped to their feet when her shadow crossed the open door. Exchanging uneasy looks, they dropped to their knees as Fleming came forward to greet her, sweeping aside his dark wool cape that clung to him with the heat.

"Milady, you honor us with your presence here."

"I would speak with you privately."

He motioned for the other men to leave, and after they complied, he gestured for Audra to enter.

The room was thick with odors, although a half-dozen arrow slits allowed for air to swirl through it. In the ceiling high above, the squeak of birds apprised her that she must be cautious not to be caught in the droppings that littered the stone floor and the rough table and benches. She smiled when she saw the few chessmen left on the board in the center of the table. Clearly she had interrupted a game just as one of the players was about to close in for the kill.

"Your game?" she asked.

"It will be my victory." Fleming unbent enough to smile with boyish humor. "Walton must learn that foolish daring must be backed with cool resolve and the strength of a complete army. A single piece cannot rout the rest of the board."

"Better he learns it here."

He nodded, his face growing stern again. "You shall find that Bourne and I have prepared your men well to repel any attack."

"Even attacks by the night riders?" When he did not answer, she pointed to the door. "Walk with me along the parapets while we speak. I wish no one to overhear what I must say to you."

Audra was grateful that the lanky young man walked between her and the sharp drop within the wall. The machicolations that opened beneath the parapets were black cancers in the gray wall. Stains spoke of fire and blood that had been mixed on these stones in protection of Bredonmere. She must not let that happen again. As weak as their defenses were, they would be as easy to overcome as a pawn on the chessboard.

"Lord Norwell came from Ashdowne Hall to present himself to me," she said quietly as she looked toward the training field where Bourne was drilling the youngsters. Closer to the wall, a flash of red hair told her Shaw was tending to his new duties. Mayhap she should reconsider his punishment in light of his work to help the villeins who had been burned out of their cottages. They needed every trained man.

"I took note of his arrival, milady."

She smiled and patted his arm, which was as stiff as his answer. "I meant no rebuke. I wished only to let you know if you had not been informed."

Pausing, he leaned his elbow on one of the merlons on the battlement. "You seem to have garnered no pleasure from his visit, milady. Did he not have the answers we seek?"

"Not only does he have no answers, he is unwilling to assist us in halting the night riders unless their malicious deeds are perpetrated on his fief." She folded her arms on the sun-heated stone and gazed across the peaceful countryside that hid too much from her. "To be honest, I think he knows no more than what whispered rumors he has heard. He has been seldom at Ashdowne Hall, and he thinks more of his prestige at court than the protection of his villeins." She laughed. "One thing I did learn. He could be Lynx no more than you or I. The man cannot walk across a room without striking a bench or nearly tumbling to the floor."

"So we have no clue where to begin."

"One."

He straightened, a smile of anticipation pulling at his lips. "Speak of it, milady, and I shall turn my attention to it before the sun touches the western hills."

"It must be *after* the sun touches the western hills," Audra answered with a smile of her own. In retrospect, the solution seemed so obvious she had to wonder why she never considered it before. "Tonight we must seek Lynx in his own lair."

His smile faded. "Impossible!"

"Perhaps not as impossible as Lynx would wish us to think. Do not forget, Fleming, that I have been there."

"I try never to remember that, for I fear I will be unable to halt myself from tracking that beast to earth and cutting out his heart while it still beats."

"No," she cautioned, putting her hands on his clenched fists, "that is not the way."

Fleming stamped along the battlement. His russet cape flared out around him as he faced her, but she saw only his anger. "Milady, I commend your generous heart, but the truth remains that Lynx knows our greatest vulnerabilities and attacks us there. Can we allow him to roam the night and destroy everything you have struggled to build?"

"The fires on the south tofts were not Lynx's work."

"You cannot be certain of that."

"I am certain of that."

His blue eyes narrowed. "I would like proof of that, milady."

"That is what I hope to obtain for both of us when we ride out tonight at sunset."

"Sunset?" His voice rose to squeak on the single word. Then he swallowed and added more calmly, "As commander of your guard, milady, I am forsworn to protect you."

"And to obey me." She put her hand on his arm again. "Fleming, I trust you and your loyalty to Bredonmere completely. That is why I have asked you to accompany me."

"As you wish, milady, but I must have someone take my place with the guard. How like Lynx to discover we are abroad tonight while he turns his attention to the manor house."

"Tell one man only that I require your presence tonight. Say nothing else."

He nodded, then began to smile. "I look forward to the chance to rout the beast from his den. After tonight, he shall haunt us no more."

Audra pulled her ebony cloak tighter around her as she led Fleming up a short hill. She had no landmarks to guide her once they passed the spot where

Lynx had left her in the middle of the road to the keep. She needed none, because she recalled every moment of that horrifying ride, not knowing then that Lynx had been truthful when he said he wished her no harm.

"Just beyond this rise," she whispered.

Fleming nodded. He carried his broadsword unsheathed in one hand, while his other hand rested on his knife.

Holding her breath while she pushed through brambles, she almost wished she had let him persuade her that this was madness. She had considered waiting until Lynx came to her, but she feared, when he stood in her private chamber, his eyes glittering with desire, she would think only of rapture. Here, with Fleming by her side, she would be able to think solely of Bredonmere. Or, so she hoped.

The hushed sounds of the forest murmured a threat in the thickening darkness. On every step, the odor of rot rose from decaying leaves. A branch rattled, and she looked up, frightened. She released her breath when she saw an owl fly away into the night.

At the top of the knoll, she knelt behind a boulder. Fleming squatted next to her. When his sword clanged against the stone, he cursed under his breath. "We must leave this place, milady. If your father could know of this, he would rise from his grave to chasten you."

"There!" she whispered, disregarding him. She pointed into a small clearing. "That door in the hill leads to Lynx's hiding place. I recognize it well."

"I have marked it in my mind. Once you are safely returned to Bredonmere, I shall bring a company to—"

*I*f you
have a passion
for great
historical
romance,
here's an offer
you'll love...

4 FREE NOVELS

SEE INSIDE.

Introducing
The Timeless Romance

Passion rising from the ashes of the Civil War...

Love blossoming against the harsh landscape of the primitive Australian outback...

Romance melting the cold walls of an 18th-century English castle —— and the heart of the handsome Earl who lives there...

Since the beginning of time, great love has held the power to change the course of history. And in Harper Monogram historical novels, you can experience that power again and again.

Free introductory offer. To introduce you to this exclusive new service, we'd like to send you the four newest Harper Monogram titles absolutely free. They're yours to keep without obligation, no matter what you decide.

Free 10-day previews. Enjoy automatic free delivery of four new titles each month —— up to four weeks before they appear in bookstores. You're never obligated to keep a book you don't want, and you can return any book, for a full credit.

Save up to 32% off the publisher's price on any shipment you choose to keep.

Don't pass up this opportunity to enjoy great romance as you have never experienced before.

Reader Service.

Yes! I want to join the Timeless Romance Reader Service. Please send me my 4 FREE HarperMonogram historical romances. Then each month send me 4 new historical romances to preview without obligation for 10 days. I'll pay the low subscription price of $4.00 for every book I choose to keep--a total savings of at least $2.00 each month--and home delivery is free! I understand that I may return any title within 10 days and receive a full credit. I may cancel this subscription at any time without obligation by simply writing "Canceled" on any invoice and mailing it to Timeless Romance. There is no minimum number of books to purchase.

NAME

ADDRESS

CITY   STATE   ZIP

TELEPHONE

SIGNATURE

She shook her head. "We must confront him now."

"Milady, you cannot think to fight this man!"

"I shall not challenge him to a show of arms. I wish to speak with him, to put an end to the misery he has brought, and," she added, watching Fleming's eyes widen with disbelief, "to obtain his help in fighting those who have destroyed the south tofts."

"You hope to have Lynx help *you?*"

"Let us petition anyone who might be willing to lend his arm to this battle, whether they be friend or foe."

Audra did not wait to hear Fleming's answer. She could not divulge the truth of Lynx's vow to do nothing to harm Bredonmere or the fact that Lynx had spoken it when he held her in bed. Fleming was right to think she was deranged.

Slipping through the damp leaves, she winced when her toe struck a rock hidden beneath them. She limped across the clearing and raised her fist to pound on the door. In the sparse moonlight, Fleming's shadow crept over her, seemingly as high as the ancient trees around them.

No voice answered her frantic knocking.

"Milady, the beast is not in his lair. We must go back to the keep with every bit of haste. I shudder to think what he might be doing right now."

"I must speak with him."

"Another night."

"I—"

Fleming shouted and, grabbing Audra's arm, jerked her aside. A knife struck the door, burying deep into the wood, inches from where her head had been.

She ran when he tugged on her arm. A man leaped from behind a tree. When his sword crashed against Fleming's, Audra screamed. The man wore clothes as swarthy as the night, but no mask hid his face.

Fleming drove his sword into the man's stomach and jumped aside as blood spurted outward. "Run!"

She stared in horror as blood flowed from him and he gurgled with his last breath. She had never seen a man die.

"Run!" Fleming shouted, shoving her forward.

She tried to keep pace with him as he followed his own command. Branches caught at her cloak, trying to slow her as they raced along the wall of rock at the edge of the clearing. She could not see the ground, which was lost in shadows. She watched Fleming's cape that flapped only inches in front of her.

A hand seized her arm. She shrieked and flung out her hands to strike her captor. Pain exploded in her skull when a fist struck her cheek. Collapsing to the damp ground, she looked up to see a man looming over her. His victorious smile flashed in the moonlight as he reached for her.

Then he choked and fell to the ground beside her, crimson flowing from the hole in his throat. She had no time to react before Fleming grasped her hand and yanked her to her feet.

"Hurry, milady," he ordered.

"Fleming! In back of you!" she cried when more figures emerged from the darkness.

He whirled and met a naked blade with his broadsword. Three men parried at him, and he backed away, pushing Audra behind him. His sword sliced the night, keeping all the men away. Suddenly one darted forward, slashing his blade into Fleming's right shoulder.

The sword fell from Fleming's hand. Audra leaped forward to grasp it, but he shoved her out of reach of their foes' steel. She bumped into the low cliff and moaned. There was no escape here. Fleming pulled his knife with his blood-drenched fingers and thrust it into her hand.

"So you may decide if you wish to follow me into death, milady," he gasped, pain in every word. "Do not let them take us alive."

"I cannot slay you, Fleming," she whispered as the men inched closer. She could not kill her loyal friend.

The men laughed as she raised the knife. Their crude comments sent fire burning across her face, even as she shivered with the cold knowledge that Fleming was right. She must slay both of them before these beasts could torture them.

"You shall not have milady tonight, knaves!"

At the shout, Audra glanced over her shoulder. A shadow stood atop the wall of rock. "Lynx!" she whispered.

Fleming cursed as he tried to push her away from what he saw as a new threat. He jerked the blade from her hand as two of their attackers fell to the ground, knives haft-deep in their backs. The last of the three shouted, and a half-dozen more men appeared from the night.

Lynx scrambled down the rock. Behind him, a slighter form with pale hair followed. Picking up Fleming's broadsword, Lynx tossed it to Fleming. The young man grabbed it, gaping with astonishment, as Lynx and his companion ran to stand beside Audra. Fleming had no time to speak as they were attacked anew.

Audra did not move as she tried to follow the easy slices of Lynx's sword. At his right, his blond confederate battled back the man who had cut into Fleming. Her commander was protecting the left side of the rock. Slowly the three men moved away from the stone, forcing the attackers back toward the trees. Grunts and shrieks of pain combatted the clash of steel.

Suddenly, as swiftly as they had appeared, the attackers vanished back into the shadows. She looked around in amazement, but the forest could have been deserted save for her and her protectors. Releasing the breath she had been holding longer than she thought possible, she choked when Fleming shouted a warning.

Lynx's sword sliced through the night to her right. She recoiled. Was he trying to slay her for daring to come here?

He seized her arm and pulled her to him as he spat, "Touch her, cur, and my blade shall delight in the taste of your lifeblood."

Beyond where she had been standing, Audra saw a man's face, pale as a ghost in the thin light. He tried to turn and run, but his foot caught on a root, and he sprawled to the ground. Before the man could move, Lynx set his foot against his back and shoved him over.

"Who is your master?" Lynx demanded in his coldest voice.

The man shook his head.

Lynx put his sword to the man's throat. "Speak, or you shall not again."

Audra held her hand to her mouth and shuddered as a pinpoint of blood swelled around the tip of the sword and ran along the man's neck. Fleming put his hand on her arm, but she shook it off. She could not surrender to womanish weakness now.

"Speak," Lynx warned again.

The man gurgled, and Lynx drew back the sword only an inch. The captive whispered, "Our master has never told us his name."

"Describe him."

"I have never met him. I take my orders from John Freeman." He choked as he added, "He insists that we call our master Lynx."

"Who is this man who dares to steal my name?"

The man shook his head fearfully. "I know no more of him. He is a stranger to me. He came the week before we burned the first tofts. He pays well. In gold."

Lynx did not move his sword as he looked over his shoulder. "Fleming, do you know of a John Freeman?"

Audra saw her commander flinch at Lynx's easy use of his name. Fleming should have guessed by now, if he had not before, that there were few parts of Bredonmere that Lynx was not privy to.

In a voice rigid with pain, Fleming said, "'Tis a common name. There may be more than five on Bredonmere lands alone. I can have them brought to the manor house tonight, and this man can tell us which is his master."

"So easily you expect to unmask those night riders?" Lynx laughed mirthlessly. "You can be sure John Freeman is not his master's true name."

"No more than Lynx is yours?"

Lynx's cool smile contrasted with his ebony mask. "You make yourself anxious about unimportant matters, Fleming, when your lady's life and your fief are in danger." Turning to the man on the ground, he stepped back a pace and lowered his sword. "Come, knave. You shall become well acquainted with the dungeons of Bredonmere."

The man jumped to his feet and fled. Lynx ran after him but whirled as an arrow sliced through the night. He shoved Audra to the ground, shouting for the others to save themselves.

A scream splintered the night, crawling along Audra like a thousand evil spiders. Hearing Lynx's curse, she gasped. "What is it?"

"Be silent." He raised his head and looked past her. He covered her again with his body as the crash of a horse's hooves reverberated through the forest.

"They are leaving," she whispered.

"Aye." He shifted, and she opened her eyes. His gaze was locked with hers, making her think of all the passion they had shared.

Her hands rose beneath his cape to splay across his back. She yearned to touch every inch of him, to let his enthralling touch wipe her mind clean of the death that had nearly been hers tonight. As his fingers swept along her jaw, she pressed to him.

He sighed with regret when he drew away from her. Standing, he brought her to her feet and put his arm around her shoulders to envelope her in the black wings of his cloak. As she looked at his face, hidden by the ebony cloth, she saw the soft edges of passion harden into fury when his companion went to the downed man.

"Dead," Lynx's blond companion said, although she had not doubted it.

"The price of capture is death, even if the blood of their allies must be on their own hands." Lynx affixed Audra with his cold stare. "You have never been as foolish as you were tonight, milady, to leave the safety of Bredonmere's walls."

"I must halt the night riders."

"By getting killed?" With a terse laugh, he said, "That will halt them, Audra, for then they will have achieved more than they had dared hope for." He turned to Fleming, who was scowling at Lynx's familiar use of her given name. "Despise me for my honesty if you wish, Fleming, but I shall be no less honest when I urge you to return your lady to Bredonmere posthaste."

"Milady, on this I must agree with him."

Audra found it less easy to ignore the distaste in Fleming's voice than his words. Too many questions remained unanswered. She had not jeopardized herself and Bredonmere to obtain nothing.

"Lynx, I came to ask for your help against these men."

"I cannot help you more than I have tonight."

"You have a strong arm, and you have shown you are a match for many times your number."

He pulled her into the dappled shadows beneath the trees. When Fleming's protest was bitten off, she looked back to see Lynx's ally holding his sword to Fleming's chest.

"Fool," snarled Lynx under his breath, but she was unsure which man he spoke of until he added, "I will not harm your lady, Fleming, nor shall you harm him, Eatton. We are strange allies." His smile did not lessen the strain on his lips as he said, "Now you know the name one of us bears, milady."

"And do you have a name other than Lynx?"

His fingers combed up through her hair. "You call me the one you love when I lie next to you."

"Then why will you not fight next to me? You are clearly my ally."

"You know I am ally and more, milady." He looked past her, and she knew he was aware, as she was, of the two men watching them. With a sigh of regret, he released her. "But I can do no more now."

Audra was sure she had mistaken his words. He knew how much Bredonmere mattered to her, and he had vowed to see it never come to harm. *By his own hand,* a small voice reminded her. She hesitated, knowing she dared his awesome temper with her words. "If you reveal yourself to me—"

"I have revealed myself to you before." He laughed with the warm huskiness that fired her blood. "And I shall again."

Audra fought the silken webs of desire he spun with such ease. Closing her eyes, she whispered, "I wish you to reveal your face to me."

"I cannot."

"But you are my ally! Why will you not help me in this time of my greatest need?"

"Look at me." When she raised her eyes to meet his, he murmured, "Audra, your time of greatest need is not yet upon you."

"What horror do you see in my future?"

He ran his finger along her lips, which craved his kisses. "You know as well as I that deWode may be riding toward Bredonmere even now. I would help you, but, until my work at Bredonmere is complete, I cannot grant you this thing that you wish so dearly."

"This work, what is it?"

"It is of an evil I wish you never to know."

His stygian voice sent cold shivers through her. "Lynx," she pleaded, "you must stop whatever it is

that has brought you to Bredonmere before it
destroys all of us."

He grasped her arms. "Nothing shall stop me
from doing as I must. Not you nor anyone else."

13

Fleming was furious as he outlined in detail all he had done to safeguard the manor house against another possible attack by the black-hearted followers of the false Lynx. Crandall was even more outraged when he learned where his lady had been at nightfall. Audra's ears rang as she sat quietly and endured his rebukes.

Only when he paused to take a breath did she say, "Crandall, *I* am the countess of Bredonmere. It is my obligation and my honor to protect those who call its lands home. My hope tonight was to obtain another ally in that battle. Lord Norwell will not help me, and I suspect the rest of the baronage will share his lack of interest in seeing me succeed at holding Bredonmere. To whom else can I turn?"

"To me!" cried Fleming. "Milady, Bourne and I have trained those lads, and they will become the finest army this manor has ever seen."

"Listen to yourself." She rose and smiled sadly. "'They will become,' you said. Fleming, I appreciate everything you and Bourne have accomplished—and what you will accomplish—but we need as much help as we can get *now!* I had thought Lynx and his men might be willing to help."

"Will they?" asked Crandall.

"No."

"So why is he here?"

She turned away to stare out the window at the night. "I wish I knew."

Crandall's scold still resounded through Audra when she rose from the bath that Shirley, who had been silently reproving, had prepared for her. As she wiped the water from her body, she noted bruises that were darkening. They were all she had gained tonight— save the dismay of those who looked to her to save Bredonmere.

Pulling on a robe of a vibrant flame color, she wandered into her bedchamber. What a fool she had been! Although she had told herself that her need required such desperate measures, she had been a fool.

Going to the door to the outer rooms, she slid the bar into place, then dropped into the chair by her table. Everything had been for naught, and for the first time, she had to face the truth that she might not be able to hold Bredonmere alone.

Alone. . . . Would Lynx ever return to her after tonight? She had risked more than she had realized with her daring, and she might have lost everything her heart longed for.

"How can I do this when no one will help me?"

she asked aloud, her frustration too strong for her to remain silent.

"Hush, milady," came the low, warm voice that whispered through her dreams.

Audra stood and turned toward the hearth. "Lynx, are you mad to come here tonight?" she whispered. "Fleming has doubled the watch."

He rose, saying nothing. As he walked to the door and tested the bar she had dropped into place, she waited for him to speak. She suspected he was as irate as Crandall.

"Fleming is a wise man," he said, his voice stiff with rage.

"But you could be caught."

"Not while I am within this chamber. I trust your servants have, by now, informed you of the folly of your ride into the night," he said as he returned to the steps to the hearth and sat again. He held out his hand and added nothing as she put her fingers on it.

She sat beside him, leaning her head against his shoulder. His cape was scented with the damp freshness of the night, the sweet perfume that he brought each time he came to her. "I need your help," she whispered.

"You must depend on those within these walls."

"Fleming and Bourne have done the best they can, but shall it be enough?"

"It must be, as it must be enough for you to wait upon me here."

"Lynx—"

"No, you must never come searching for me again. It could mean your death."

She closed her eyes, not wanting to agree but knowing he was right. "I had hoped that after . . ." She swallowed her embarrassment and plunged on. "I had hoped that after what we have shared, you would want to help me."

"Was that why you welcomed me into your bed, my sweet lady?" he whispered. "Do you offer your body to me in exchange for my arm raised in Bredonmere's cause?"

Fire burned on her cheeks as she drew away. "No," she answered as softly.

His finger turned her face toward him. "Let there be no talk of battles when we are together like this. The time we have is too short to be spent on anything but pleasure."

She flung her arms around his shoulders and met his mouth. His kiss was deep and demanding, stripping her breath away as her heart throbbed to the beat of the craving deep within her. When he slipped his arm beneath her knees and lifted her against his chest, she smiled. Her smile became a gasp of surprise when he placed her on the carpet in the deepest shadows.

"The bed is just over there." She pointed past his shoulder.

His laugh was raw with hunger. "I know very well where your bed is, but I cannot wait even long enough to carry you there to feel you against me, milady."

Her smile vanished as he brushed her lips with his finger. The lush thickness of the carpet nestled her when she brought him over her and let all her questions and fears vanish into the dusky twilight of love.

Over the next fortnight, time passed in a haze for Audra. The needs of the manor demanded her days, and Lynx demanded her nights. She rose when the sun did, for without exception, Lynx vanished in the twilight before dawn. As the preparations were completed for Michaelmas, the most important of the two rent-days on Bredonmere Manor, she was caught up in an ever more rapidly spinning vortex of activity, but she always returned to her bedchamber to be with Lynx.

Fleming brought reports on the progress of the new soldiers that Bourne had trained well enough to join the veteran men-at-arms. From a different part of the fief each day came accounts of the progress of the harvesting. Always by her side, Crandall listed the needs of the manor.

All of their words went into her head, but too frequently, she drifted into a daydream as she stared at the brilliant colors of the windows in the hall and imagined the night to come. Each night, she and Lynx discovered something new and rapturous. Although he made her no promises of faithfulness, he returned every night to share her bed.

"And so, milady, I thought—Milady?"

She focused on Crandall and smiled uneasily. When he huffed with indignation and repeated himself, she tried to concentrate on his words, but she did not want to listen to a lecture about the slow progress on rebuilding the farms when she would rather be thinking about Lynx.

"Put Shaw in charge of that," Audra said, wanting to bring an end to the endless litany of problems Crandall delivered to her each day.

"Shaw?" He seemed to consider the idea, then nodded. "He has shown an interest in resurrecting your good favor upon him."

"If he proves capable of this task, mayhap we might trust him with another. I fear we need every able-bodied man working at the rebuilding rather than digging trenches in the bailey."

Crandall steepled his fingers in front of his nose and frowned. "That brings me to another matter I wish to discuss with you, milady. It is the matter of the precedence among the villeins on rent-day."

Rising, she forced him to do the same. "Crandall, I have heard enough for today. If you will excuse me—"

"Milady—"

"I said, 'If you will excuse me . . .' Good day, Crandall."

The steward did not alter his disapproving glare. "This is of the utmost importance. It cannot be shunted aside while—" A shout from the opposite side of the hall interrupted him.

A lad raced toward them. He dipped to his knees. "A messenger has arrived from King Edward's court. He asks to see you, milady."

She could not keep her voice from trembling as she said, "Escort him to me, Nye."

As the boy ran away, Crandall asked, "You act surprised, milady. Surely you have been expecting this messenger."

"Not so soon."

"Not so soon? You must have been anticipating that the king would send word of a husband to you. Why do you show no curiosity on this most important matter?"

"Because I already know whom I am to marry." She brushed her hands against her saffron robe, which was heavier than the ones she had worn during the heat of summer. To herself, she added, "I pray this message changes that."

He stared at her. "You know whom you are to wed?"

"Crandall, will you please stop repeating everything I say?"

He frowned. "Tell me that what I am thinking is not true, milady."

Audra was spared from having to reply by the arrival of the messenger who was dusted with dirt from his hard trip. When he knelt and handed her the scroll, she knew he had been informed that she would read it herself. She thanked him and sent him to the kitchen to fill his stomach while she determined if any reply was necessary.

Or possible, she thought.

Her faint hopes were dashed when she read the message. Although it was from the king, it mentioned nothing of the letter she had written to him. Edward was congratulating her on her upcoming nuptials to Lord deWode, which he deemed an excellent match, bringing the best possible solution to his cousin's problems.

Crandall's low curse warned Audra he was reading over her shoulder. "This is all wrong! You cannot wed Lord deWode!"

"It is the king's will," she answered as she rolled the parchment again.

"That you wed yourself to a man who would have raped you? You cannot have affection for this man!"

"Crandall, you know affection has nothing to do with marriages among the baronage."

"But you should respect the man you will make your lord."

"It matters little." She handed him the rolled page. "This should be protected. Crandall, I think we can expect Lord deWode's arrival at any moment."

He gripped her hands in his which were as dry and brittle as the paper. Kneeling, he whispered, "I beg you, milady, think of the torment you shall bring upon Bredonmere and yourself with this decision."

"The decision is not mine to make." She drew her hands away.

"The men will not follow Lord deWode."

"They have vowed their fealty to me. When I vow it to Lord deWode, they shall have no choice."

He regained his feet slowly. "No more choice than you, milady?"

"No more."

Audra was not surprised when Bourne and Fleming sought her out. She had been sure Crandall would waste no time revealing the tidings to them. Exasperated by their words, which only repeated what her steward had said, she dismissed them curtly. The betrayal and anger in their faces warned her that more trouble awaited Bredonmere.

Why did they give no mind to the fact that her efforts to persuade the king to rethink his decision had been for naught? She was bound by an oath of allegiance to Edward's will. If she disobeyed, she could be branded an outlaw and Bredonmere made a target of any of the king's loyal men.

Audra sighed as she sat alone at the raised table in the great hall. Was she the only one who had come to sup on time? After all the times that Crandall had chided her, telling her that the lord of the manor—or the lady—should be present at the beginning of each meal, she was surprised he was not here to see her arrive exactly as the church bell chimed.

Mayhap he had been delayed with supervising the plans for cleaning up after the rent-day fair, which had been held in the inner bailey. No one had anticipated the fair with joy. Although no one had mentioned Lord deWode's name to her, his shadow hung over the manor house like a malevolent cloud.

Rubbing her forehead, she sighed again. When Bourne walked toward her, she sat straighter in her chair. She did not wish to be berated again for what she could not change.

Putting his fingers to his forelock, he bowed slightly. He was grinning as he folded his arms on the raised table and looked up at her. "It is wrong for our lovely lady to be sitting alone."

"I await Crandall."

"Eagerly, no doubt, for he would be wise to practice the punctuality he preaches." He glanced to her right, and his smile widened. "And here comes the right man to preach it. Good evening, Father."

"And to you, Bourne." Father Jerome pulled out a heavy chair, the sound as it scraped across the wood grinding into Audra's head. "Do you ail, milady?"

"No," she said, shocked that she could speak a falsehood so easily to the priest. "Nothing more than fatigue."

"A state we all know well in the aftermath of the rent-day fair," Bourne answered, his dark eyes drilling into her. Even so, she was unprepared when he asked, "Did you expect Lord deWode to attend?"

"I don't know."

"I had thought he would have wished to be here for the celebration of the harvest of *his* fields."

Audra flinched at the slight stress on the word,

but said tritely, "I suspect Lord deWode will join us as soon as he is free to do so."

"Join *you*."

A hot flush climbed her cheeks. Hearing Father Jerome mutter something under his breath, she lowered her gaze. She could not blame Bourne for being furious with the king's choice when she shared his distaste for Gifford deWode.

A commotion from the opposite end of the great hall prevented Audra from answering. The door to the bailey burst open, and a ragged man stumbled into the light. Recognizing Shaw, she started to rise. Her knees wobbled as she saw the horror on Shaw's face.

Without awaiting her permission, he staggered up to where she sat, dropped to his knees, and leaned his hands on the floor. Taking thick gasps to slow his breathing, he choked out, "Milady, Crandall is dead."

"Dead?" she repeated in an appalled whisper. As she clutched the table, she heard Father Jerome whisper a prayer. "Shaw, what kind of jest is this?"

"No jest, milady." He tried to stand, but he fell back to the floor, clearly exhausted. "He took a handful of us to investigate Lynx's handiwork."

"Crandall did this without telling me?"

"He said you gave him permission."

Audra searched her mind, but it seemed mired in anguish. "Mayhap I did." She turned to Bourne, but he was staring at Shaw. She could not guess what he hoped to see. "Tell me what has happened."

"We were attacked."

"Attacked by whom?"

"Men with their faces covered in black wool."

Audra ignored a splinter from the table that cut into her palm. No pain was real when the familiar numbness opened up to swallow her. This could not be. Crandall could not be dead. She needed him and his guidance.

"Where did this attack take place?"

At Bourne's sharp question, she forced her gaze in his direction and realized he had come to stand by Shaw. She had not heard him move, although the room was as silent as her father's grave.

"On the road to the south tofts."

"Lynx!" gasped one of the serving lasses.

The name spread out through the room like rippling circles in a pond. Panic swelled into an invisible cloud, smothering Audra in its icy grip. She fought it back. Lynx would not slay her most trusted servant.

Audra clenched her fists by her side. She had been willing to give Lynx her heart. She must be willing to give him her trust as well. He had vowed to hurt nothing of Bredonmere, and Crandall was more a part of Bredonmere than even the stone walls themselves.

Now Crandall was dead. She must discover whose hand had done this heinous deed. Biting her lip, she wished she could ask Lynx for his help, but he had made it clear he would think of nothing but finishing the task that had brought him here.

Taking a deep breath, she braced herself for what she did not want to say. "Shaw, rise and give your full report."

The red-haired man rose to his feet as she regarded him steadily. If he had thought she would crumple into tears, he would learn that the countess of Bredonmere was no hysterical woman. Her pain, when it came, would be too private to share in the great hall.

"We rode on the south road. Near where the main route intersects the road leading to Lord Norwell's fief." Shaw recited the facts as if he was a minstrel embroidering a tale for them. The small party had been riding back toward Bredonmere when—out of nowhere—they had been ambushed. Arrows had been fired from among the trees. Crandall fell as the rest of them fled for safety.

"How could we stay to fight when we wore nothing but short blades?" he asked, his voice trembling.

Audra lowered herself to her chair as Fleming rushed into the hall. When Father Jerome whispered her name, she shook her head. She could not afford to listen to his condolences now. If she allowed herself to feel anything but this numbness, she would shatter.

"You saw their faces?" she asked in a voice that was clear and strong.

Too strong, Bourne thought as he stared at her face, which had no more life than the brass over her father's crypt. Crandall had been the replacement for her father, her mentor in learning the traditions of Bredonmere. Now he had been murdered.

Murdered! His lips twisted in fury. Audra had been warned about unseen enemies. She had encountered them when she dared seek Lynx in his den. Although she would be wise and remain safe behind Bredonmere's walls now, her allies had become the prey of those who wished to repay her for daring to try to hold her father's fief.

"Aye, I saw their faces," said Shaw. "Wh-wh-what could be seen of them." He reached into the pouch on his belt. "This was found on a bush near where Crandall was slain."

Audra put out a trembling hand to take the black material. So often she had seen matching fabric in Lynx's cloak. She dropped it onto the table. "Better you should have captured one of them, Shaw."

Fleming scooped it up and examined it intently. "Black? The color worn by the night rider."

"Many men wear that hue," Audra said.

"Few men murder, milady," he snapped back. "Why do you defend this man who has proven so often that he wishes you disaster?"

"Because Lynx would not kill Crandall!"

"The earl would never have allowed such criminals to take control of his lands like this. He would have routed them out like the beasts they are and hanged them as a warning to other thieves" Shaw said with contempt.

"There has never been a threat to Bredonmere like this."

"How do you know?" asked Father Jerome gently. "Milady, if there was once a time—"

"Never was there such a time. I have learned the history of Bredonmere well. I was taught by—by—" She swallowed her pain, which was gathered into a choking ball in her throat. "Crandall has taught me well of the history of this fief."

"So you will do nothing?" demanded Fleming.

"I will do everything possible to deal with Lynx *and* with this murderer."

"You heard him." Fleming hooked a thumb at Shaw, who looked covetously at the new mug of ale put next to Father Jerome's hand. "Lynx killed Crandall."

"He would not kill him," she said, silently praying her words were true, "because he knows Crandall was my friend."

He laughed shortly. "And isn't that the best reason to slay him if he wants to hurt you?"

"As it cannot be Lynx, it must be someone else. Find out who!"

"Milady—"

She cut Shaw off. "Do as I have told you!" Pushing past the men, she added, "I trust you can enjoy your repast without me. I must see to the plans for Crandall's funeral." Her voice broke. "I must see he is honored in death as I honored him in life."

"Fool," Shaw grumbled as he strode away in the opposite direction.

Bourne silently agreed, although Lady Audra was not as foolish as those who surrounded her. Why had none of them seen the signs of such a tragedy ahead? They must be more alert—*he* must be more alert—or else catastrophe would come again, and the next time Lady Audra might be the target.

14

The moonlight swept across the floor, washing all color out of the rug. The death rattle of the last few leaves rustled in the greenwood beyond the walls. So silent was the night that even that soft sound reached into the manor, twisting through Audra and reminding her that, only an hour past, she had seen the remains of her most trusted servant brought through the main gate.

She wished she could weep, but no sobs relieved the emptiness that had haunted her from the moment she was thrust from Clarendon Abbey into these games where life meant less than power. Had her father cried when he discovered his sons dead? Had tears slipped down Crandall's wrinkled face when he sat by her father's deathbed as the earl breathed his last? She could not know, and she must be stoic now. Not for her was the luxury of the public hysterics Shirley had suffered before Audra sent her to her bed with a glass of drugged wine.

Crandall . . . dead? It did not seem possible.

She sat on the steps by the bed and stared at the fire on the hearth. Fleming would be the right man to succeed Crandall while Bourne could assume responsibility for the men-at-arms. They would never slack in their determination to help her keep Bredonmere strong, but neither would they chide her as Crandall had, nor could they regale her with tales of her family. Her last connection with the family she had known for such a short time before she had been sent to Clarendon Abbey was severed.

Why had Crandall been on an idiot's quest today? Had he been determined to defend her honor—and Bredonmere's—by apprehending Lynx?

"You need not have done that," she whispered. "You served me best as you always did. What shall I do without you now?"

She stared at the unlit hearth. Bredonmere had demanded every sacrifice from her, but she could not turn her back on the obligation she had been given. Soon Lord deWode would return, and this unhappiness would haunt her forever. All the "might have beens" would follow her through each of the endless years of being the wife of a man whom she hated.

Beyond her barred door, she heard the servants readying themselves for bed. Their voices were raised in anger. She wished she could be as angry. Nothing filled her. Nothing. That would change, for grief and dread must come. Without Crandall as a bulwark between her and Lord deWode, she had less chance of maintaining any hold on Bredonmere.

She paced her room, wishing Lynx would come to her. In her heart, she believed him innocent of Crandall's murder, but she must speak to him of the letter from the king. His fury at Edward's decision for her to wed Lord deWode would mute Crandall's, Bourne's, *and* Fleming's gathered altogether. Pain surged through her, for Lynx could never come to her again once she was Gifford's wife.

She returned over and over to the window as the passage of each hour was marked by the watch. The fragrance of the early autumn wind, which was dampened by night, brushed her face. Her hands fisted on the sill as she fought to keep from calling out Lynx's name, sending it on the night wind to drift to his ears and his heart. Fear mocked her, as she wondered if Crandall was the only one to meet death tonight. Because Lynx had made her promise not to go again to his forest hideaway, she knew of no way to contact him.

When a knock sounded on her door, Audra whirled, astonished. Who was calling after midnight?

She went to the door and slid back the bar as quietly as she could. It opened to reveal Shirley's tear-streaked face.

"I thought you were asleep," Audra said.

"A message came for you, milady." Dabbing at her eyes with the corner of her dark brown cotehardie, Shirley said, "Father Jerome begs your indulgence, but asks to speak with you at your convenience."

"At this hour?"

"The message was urgent."

Audra flinched as she wondered if *this* was why Lynx had not come to her. If he and Father Jerome were truly one and the same, then he might be using this excuse to speak with her on a night when the manor house was in turmoil. He could not scale the wall to her window when the inner bailey was filled with people who were unable to sleep in the midst of the dual tragedies of Crandall's death and their lady's impending marriage.

She did not hesitate as she threw on a light cloak. Telling Shirley to return to her bed, she tiptoed past her sleeping servants. She hurried down the stairs and out a side door. Clinging to the shadows, she crossed the inner bailey, not wanting to be stopped by anyone who might ask her questions. Nobody approached her. She knew better than to count on such good fortune to last.

A low sound rumbled from her left, and she recoiled, then realized it was nothing more than a horse stirring in the stalls.

As she reached the door of the chapel, she paused. If she turned around now and returned to her room, no one would know of her suspicions. She shook her head. She must not be afraid of the truth now, when she had nothing left to lose.

She pushed open the door. Drawing her shawl over her head, she entered the chapel. She prayed for the strength she had found here. Tonight, of all nights, she needed to be strong.

Her bare feet made no sound as she walked down the aisle which was cloaked in the dimness. Only the few candles burning behind the altar penetrated it. The hush she had found so comforting when she first arrived now seemed like a gloom. If Lynx and Father Jerome were the same man, she risked more than Bredonmere with her craving for his touch, for her mortal soul could be jeopardized.

Follow your heart. The abbess's voice came to her, and Audra wondered why it spoke so strongly to her on this night. Then she realized that, once again, she faced the destruction of her dearest dreams.

Stopping by a pew halfway to the altar, she dipped to her knees and crossed herself. The rituals of a simpler time offered sparse comfort, but she needed every bit of solace as she faced losing her once unshakable faith.

Rising, she looked for Father Jerome. She froze in disbelief as she saw two forms emerge from the deepest shadows. Both were instantly identifiable by their profiles and their clothes.

Father Jerome *and Lynx!*

How naïve her assumptions had been! Lynx had so often ridiculed her life in the convent, and Father Jerome had never given her any reason to doubt that his faith was sincere.

She must hurry away before she was seen. Although she feared both men would laugh at her for believing Father Jerome hid beneath Lynx's mask, she could not move. Her feet were as heavy as the stones beneath them.

"God be with you, Lynx," Father Jerome said as they paused by her father's grave, "for you traverse a far more dangerous path than ever you have in the past. The costs may be higher than you suspect."

"I cannot stop what I have started. I thought the battle won, but today's tidings change all that. To put an end to it now would be disastrous. If I were to go . . ." Lynx's voice trailed away as he noticed Audra. Even from halfway across the church, she could see his bewitching smile as he added, "Father, I think you have another who seeks your counsel this evening."

Father Jerome's face turned nearly as pale as the stone saints edging the altar. "Milady, I forgot that I had sent for you."

"You sent for her? Tonight?" Recriminations burned in Lynx's eyes.

The priest said sternly, "I had no thought of *you* coming here tonight."

"You should have known better than that." Lynx leaned against a pew, putting his low boot on the seat, but Audra was not fooled by his nonchalance.

Neither was Father Jerome, she realized, when the priest answered, "Mayhap I should have, but many of your ways baffle me, *Lynx*."

Audra was startled by the slight emphasis the priest put on the name. Looking from one man to the other, she wondered what secrets they shared that she was not privy to. Attempting to pry the truth from either would be impossible.

Father Jerome turned to her. "I beg your pardon for putting you into such an uncomfortable situation."

"It is not," Lynx said with a smile, "the first time I have been within Bredonmere, as Lady Audra knows firsthand."

Her face burned as his words brought to life thoughts that should not be in her mind when she stood in the chapel. Raising her head, she held the cloak close to her chin. "No, it is not," she answered coolly, although her heart threatened to shatter, "but I give warning, Lynx. There shall be no welcome for you here in the future." This was not the way she had planned to tell him about her betrothal. In fact she did not know *how* she had intended to reveal the truth to him. She just knew that she did not want it to be tonight when she longed to be in his arms just one more time.

"So I have learned." His eyes narrowed. "Should I say congratulations, milady, on your upcoming nuptials or would you prefer my condolences on that matter as well as on the death of your trusted servant?"

"Lynx," Father Jerome warned under his breath.

"Perhaps Lady Audra would be happier if I granted you some privacy to discuss her quandaries."

"No!" she cried. She reached out a hand toward Lynx, then jerked it back. To touch him when her heart pounded in her ears like the clang of the bell in the tower surely would betray her. She did not want him to leave. Not tonight. Not ever.

But what she wanted mattered little. She must do what was best for Bredonmere, even if that meant giving Gifford deWode free license to destroy her heart's desires.

Trying to calm her voice, she said, "Father Jerome, you obviously are busy. I shall speak to you in the morning."

"It is morning." Lynx smiled. Tipping his head in their direction, he added, "Father, I leave you and the fair lady to your business."

Father Jerome glanced uneasily from Audra to Lynx. "Be careful what you do, Lynx. You have seen the dangers ahead of you if you do not change your ways."

"I will be wary. I have acquainted myself well with the cost of failure." His eyes, which were nearly hidden beneath his mask, twinkled as he added, "Milady, I thank you for allowing me the use of your chapel."

Audra had no time to answer before he whirled away into the shadows. She could not see if he went or lingered. The bereft sensation in her heart, however, told her he was gone.

When a hand cupped her elbow, she allowed Father Jerome to guide her toward his private room behind the altar. He did not speak to her. For that, she was grateful, for she would not have known what to say in return.

He opened the door to the humble chamber and motioned for her to sit on the single stool next to the long table. It did not surprise her that a nearly gutted candle sat on his table, for he must have been meeting with Lynx here where they could speak unobserved. He closed the door, and she wondered if he wished to keep her distress as hidden as Lynx's visit.

She clasped her hands in front of her. She could not let her pain show, for Gifford must hear no word of her despair. His ire would imperil Bredonmere. Now that he had won the lands and its countess, she suspected he would care little for either.

Not like Lynx! The thought came, unbidden. It was the truth. Lynx would never relinquish what he had won, always fighting to hold on to it . . . as he had her heart.

In two steps, Father Jerome crossed the small room and pulled a bottle from within a small chest on the floor. Taking two glasses from a shelf overflowing with a quantity of paper unlike any she had seen since she left the abbey, he poured the wine and offered one goblet to her.

She drained the cool liquid in one gulp. He made no comment as he refilled her glass. This time, she sipped more slowly.

"How do you fare, milady?" Father Jerome asked quietly.

Instead of answering his question, she whispered, "What was Lynx doing here?"

"He would find it difficult to come to confession when I hear it for the residents of Bredonmere." Father Jerome would not meet her eyes.

"Confession?" With a short laugh, she rose and walked about the room. She stared at the wall of shelves where valuable books sat next to icons. "I'm sure he has much to confess to."

Father Jerome gasped. "Milady, you know that is something I cannot discuss with anyone else."

"I did not ask you to reveal what he told you. His sins are, for the most part, public knowledge." She bit her lip as she wondered if Lynx had spoken of his less well known crime of stealing into her room and into her bed. Such a transgression would be difficult for Father Jerome to hide, for his beliefs would have compelled him to confront her with the sin she had not confessed. Turning to face him, she said, "Forgive me. I must admit to being shocked to see Lynx in the chapel of my manor. You do no more than your duty. No sinner, be he miscreant or felon, should be turned away."

Father Jerome lowered his goblet to the table, plucked the glass from her hand, and placed it next to his. When he took her hands between his, he said quietly, "You have not yet asked me why I asked you to come to the chapel at this late hour on a night when you might wish to be alone with your grief."

"My grief is not mine alone."

"It is Bredonmere's." He sighed. "However, you do display a remarkable lack of curiosity at my request."

"I assume you wished to speak to me of the missive from King Edward."

"I have heard tales often of your father. The earl was not a man who accepted another's will easily."

"He would not have challenged the king's order, or he would not have enjoyed the good favor he did."

His dark brows arched, and again the twinge teased her. Such an expression could belong to Lynx, but she knew now how impossible that was.

"Odd, milady, for I have heard how he and Edward disagreed on many matters. The king respected your father's good sense."

"As he might mine?"

He smiled. "My thoughts exactly."

She shook her head. "I sent a letter to Edward. It made no difference in his command to wed Lord deWode."

"Are you certain it was delivered into his hand?"

"I was assured that it was delivered."

"But did you give instructions to have it delivered *into* the king's own hand?"

Audra's eyes widened. "Do you think it was intercepted?"

"I know little of the king's court, but conspiracies are common even here in Bredonmere among the villeins anxious to gain your favor. Think how much more complicated such machinations would be in Edward's household."

"I should write to him again."

He nodded.

Grasping his hands, she said, "Thank you, Father. I am in your debt for such sage advice. Without Crandall by my side, I shall be more in need of your guidance than ever."

"May I beg payment of that debt now?" He smiled at her perplexed frown. "Speak to me, milady, of the other matter that weighs your heart."

"Crandall—"

"Another matter, I fear, for I sensed it before tonight's horrible report."

"Did Lynx—?" She clamped her lips closed. To give voice to the truth was impossible, even to Father Jerome.

"He told me nothing, milady, although I know he remains a dilemma for you. Neither friend nor foe."

Not friend, not foe, but lover. She silenced the thought and forced a smile. "I must handle the problem of Lynx in my own way, Father."

"When you decide to bare your heart to me and God, I shall be here to help you." As she turned to leave, he added, "Milady, if I may offer another word of advice . . ."

"Yes?" she asked as she paused with her hand on the latch.

He stood. "I am no lord to tell you how to run your manor, but I can offer you some counsel on how to deal with Lady Audra. She is a taskmaster who will drive you until you drop from lack of sleep and lose the happiness you once possessed. You must tell Lady Audra to give Audra Travers the time to be the young woman she is. You must tell her this before Audra becomes nothing more than an extension of Bredonmere, as soulless as the walls surrounding the bailey."

Astonished, she nodded. As she whispered good night to him, she knew he was correct, but she wondered if she could alter the path her life had taken. She already was Bredonmere. The only part of her free from her obligations to the manor was the part she shared with Lynx. Mayhap that was what had drawn her to him. His total lack of obligation to anything or anyone but himself appealed to her when she was tied too tightly to responsibilities she could not have imagined a year ago.

Rain struck her face as she emerged from the chapel. She looked skyward in disbelief. When she had come across the courtyard, only a few clouds scudded over the moon. She blinked when a drop struck her eye. As she pulled her cloak more tightly around her, she raced toward the stone keep which was the heart of Bredonmere.

In the outer rooms of her chambers, she tiptoed around her slumbering servants. She smiled when she saw Shirley sitting in a chair, fast asleep. Taking a blanket from the woman's pallet, she settled it over Shirley.

"Sleep well," she whispered, knowing Shirley would be distressed in the morning that she had fallen asleep before Audra returned.

With a yawn, she went to the door to her private chambers. Her fingers quivered as she opened it. Dawn and the time when Lynx vanished into the night were only a few, short hours away.

Tonight could be the first night she would sleep alone since Lynx had first come into her room. As she started to close the door, it was pulled from her hands and shut silently. The familiar black cape brushed her as the bar was slid in place. Its dampness cut across her like the slash of a wet sword, but warm joy flowed through her, melting her lonely fears into sweetness.

"Lynx!" she whispered, raising her hands to touch his cheek. "I did not expect to find you here."

He lifted her wet cape from her shoulders and tossed it aside. With gentle fingers he smoothed her hair, then combed upward through her curls to find her nape. When her head was tilted back, she welcomed the warmth of a hungry mouth against hers. She was lifted from the floor and settled on her bed, but the lips never left hers.

Leaning over her, he murmured, "I had planned to be with you as soon as I finished other business."

"With Father Jerome."

"As you were witness to. And your discussion with the good father, did it go well?" When she did not answer, he whispered, "I trust Father Jerome urged you to petition the king immediately to put an end to any thought of deWode claiming Bredonmere."

"I shall not delay this time."

Twisting a strand of her hair around his finger, he said, "You looked very shocked to see me with Father Jerome. Could it be that you never expected to see me in your chapel, or could it be that you wondered if the good father rides the night as Lynx?"

"How—?"

"You would be wise to hide this."

Audra gasped as she took the small piece of paper he held. She recognized it as the scrap she had used when trying to make sense of her jumbled thoughts. "You stole this from me!"

"You left it out carelessly."

"In my box with my correspondence." Betrayal felt like a sharp knife in her heart. What other places had he searched in her room while she slept, sated from their passion? Pain fired her voice. "How dare you, Lynx? You have no right to paw through my private correspondence."

"I had hoped to help save you from your own folly."

"Then I thank you for acquainting me with it." Her voice was raw with fury. "Do you think that you have succeeded in proving me a fool, unworthy of holding Bredonmere without your wisdom?"

He gripped her elbows and tugged her toward him. "Sarcasm will not help you when deWode arrives to demand a place in your bed."

"At least, he will have no need to sneak in here in order to deceive me." She twisted out of his arms and went to the window that overlooked the road beyond the walls. "He comes with the king's blessing."

"Audra . . ."

At the naked longing in his voice, she could not stop herself from turning. She needed him to hold her, to fill the emptiness with something other than anger. She wanted to speak of love and to hear him pledge his love to her.

"I cannot stay by your side tonight, milady," he said with regret. "I only wished to reassure myself that you shall overcome this horror visited upon your household." He sat on the stairs to the hearth and leaned one shoulder against the bed. Drawing his knife from its sheath, he drove it into the wood. "Take it," he commanded.

"Why?"

"Are you the only one who does not question if I killed Crandall?"

"I know you did not," she whispered.

"Are you so sure?"

Her eyes widened. "Are you trying to persuade me that you murdered my steward?"

"You are the countess of Bredonmere. It is your duty to ask such questions, for you decide justice on these lands." He pointed to the knife. "Take it."

"Lynx, I trust—"

"Take it!"

Biting her lower lip, she pulled the knife out and turned it over in her hand. "It is clean of blood, but that means nothing. A single swipe against a damp cloth will cleanse it of any blood."

"I did not offer it to you to examine. I offered it to you, so that you, as the lady of Bredonmere, could see that justice is done. If you believe me to be a murderer, then you should see my blood spilled in return."

Lynx watched her face turn a ghostly shade in the moonlight. Grief had engraved its memory into it.

She gripped the knife in both hands. "I ask that you affirm to me on what you hold most dear that you did not kill Crandall."

"On the vow that makes me ride the night,

milady, I swear that I did not kill Crandall or any other ally of yours."

When she turned away, he knew he had added to her pain. Sainted Mary, that had not been his intention. He should have listened to those who counseled against involving himself so intimately with Bredonmere's lady.

"My guess," he said softly, "is that those who do their evil in my name slew your man."

Slowly she sank down on the steps beside him. Holding out the knife to him, she whispered, "So this is a warning to me?"

He took it and slid it back into its sheath. "Did you think it would be anything else?"

"No," she said so low he had to strain to hear her, "but I had hoped my enemies had enough honor to face me instead of taking out their rage on an old man."

"Crandall may have been old, but to many beyond these walls, he was your one ally who never faltered in his belief that you can hold." He brushed the back of his hand against her cheek. "You would be wise to warn your other allies that they may be marked for death as well."

"They know."

He smiled. "I am sure they do. I only wished to warn *you* to be on your guard."

"I shall be."

"Against every man who would destroy you?"

"I have already written to the king of this matter with Lord deWode."

"My sweet lady, you must never welcome him here."

"To Bredonmere?"

"Here!" He caught her face in his hands and

gazed down into her clear blue eyes. Never had he wanted her as much as he did now when she had shown her trust of him. He held out his arms, and she moved against him, molding her softness to him. He bent to taste her lips, her succulent lips.

The latch rattled on her door. When the barred door did not open, fists pounded on the thick wood. "Milady!" came a deep voice from its far side.

Audra gasped, "'Tis Fleming!"

"Aye," Lynx growled. "What does he want at this hour?"

"Milady! Let us in! The door is barred! Are you safe?"

"You must go!" she whispered, drawing away from Lynx.

"Audra, we must speak of the matter of deWode. If you think I will allow a man who would have raped you to hold Bredonmere—"

"You must go!" She grasped his sleeve and tried to turn him toward the window. She would have had as much success lifting the chapel over her head, for he was as immovable. "Lynx, if you are found here, you could be killed."

"Milady, there remains much to be spoken of between us."

"But not now!" Another shout came from the outer room, then something struck the door. "Go!" she cried.

He cupped her chin in his palm. "I shall return if I can."

"If?" She ignored a bang against the door as she saw the truth in his eyes. "You are leaving Bredonmere?"

"Is that not what you have asked of me since our first meeting?"

"Yes, but . . ." She sought the words to tell him that, while she knew he must leave, she wanted him to stay.

He smiled gently. "I shall come to you again, milady, but I cannot tell you when."

The door shivered under a renewed assault. Standing on tiptoe, she kissed him swiftly. "Go in peace."

He climbed onto the sill. Regret thickened his voice. "I wish that was possible. My work here is not yet done."

Audra whirled as the door crashed open. Fleming dropped the end of the bench he was holding. His sword rasped as he pulled it. Before he could push past her, Audra ran to him, throwing her arms around him.

"Milady—" There was frustration in Fleming's voice as he strained to look past her.

"He dared to come here!" she moaned.

"Who?"

"Lynx!"

"Lynx?" His lips curled with fury.

She choked back a feigned sob. "You saved me."

"Milady, please . . . Shirley, come to tend to your lady."

When he tried to shift her away from the doorway so he could rush into the room, she clung more tightly to him and sobbed more loudly. He shouted to his men to block Lynx's escape in the bailey as he helped her sit on the bench.

Shirley bustled over to ask if Audra was unhurt. While Fleming hurried into her bedchamber, Audra held her breath. His bitten-off curse tempted her to smile, but even as she realized Lynx must have escaped unharmed, she wondered what a night rider could do to prevent Lord deWode from coming to Bredonmere to make her his wife. She feared challenging the king's edict was a task that would daunt even Lynx and leave her no choice but to marry a man she despised.

15

Father Jerome spoke a final blessing over the open grave and stepped back as two men began to shovel dirt onto Crandall's burial shroud that was spotted with rain. He looked across the scar on the earth, but Lady Audra did not raise her gaze from the grave.

He noted the doubling of the watch on the walls and guessed Fleming would be well pleased when their lady returned to the protection of the keep. No merriment had accompanied the wake and this funeral. In the aftermath of the plague, when death no longer was a constant guest at Bredonmere, those traditions had been revived. He had presided over more than one funeral mass in the past months that was attended by the deceased's friends who were suffering from swallowing too much ale the night before. But not this time.

He sensed the alarm among the household and the tofts. Crandall had been a part of Bredonmere for longer than most had lived. If Crandall could be cut down, there was fear in many hearts that Bredonmere was too vulnerable to stand alone.

He wanted to speak to Lady Audra of that, but she had given him no opportunity. Promising himself that he would soon, he joined the parade of mourners escaping the storm.

Audra took little note of the rain or of the others who were scurrying back into the manor house. Each thud of dirt falling in the grave resounded through the emptiness in her heart. Only when the gravediggers finished their task did she move to kneel and put her hand on top of the mound of dirt.

"Sleep well, dear friend," she whispered. "Know that I shall bring the ones who did this to justice. I vow that to you with all my heart."

"Milady?"

She saw Shirley rocking from one wet foot to the other as she hunched into her wool cloak. Taking pity on her, because Shirley would not return to the keep until she did, Audra stood and said, "Let us leave."

She did not look back.

As each night passed, Audra stood by the window and watched the slim whisker of a moon thicken. As it left behind its crescent shape to become a mound of uncooked dough on the velvet board of the night, she waited for Lynx until sleep betrayed her. Then the moon was as round as the pewter plates in the great hall. When it became a sliver again, hanging in reverse as if her world had been turned inside out, she stopped barring her door. In the darkness of the new moon, she stopped watching for Lynx.

He will come back to you when he can. She

repeated that thought to herself throughout the day, a litany to ease the ache in her heart.

More fires were reported on the tofts, but none did the damage of the last ones. She told Fleming to send Bourne and some of the other men to investigate, although, when she heard nothing from them, she was not surprised. Her enemies—and Lynx's—were too canny to leave behind anything that would reveal their identity.

She went through her days, eating only when Shirley reminded her and seldom leaving her rooms except to go to chapel or the great hall. Until Crandall's death, she had not appreciated the burden of work he had assumed without complaint. She tried to gather the information he had presented to her and arrange it into reports she could share with Bredonmere's next lord. She spoke occasionally to Fleming to hear his accounts of the activity on the walls, but the rest of the manor respected her need to grieve in private.

Even the things that once had brought joy could not break through her empty despair. When she listened to the farmers from the tofts brag about their healthy flocks, she tried to show enthusiasm. She wanted to share their hopes but could not. Her future seemed more and more bleak. Crandall was dead, Lynx was gone, and she had received no reply from her latest letter to King Edward. Although she wanted to believe that was a good sign, she feared he was disregarding her heartfelt plea.

For the first time, she was unsure of what to do or even how to continue the endeavor to keep Bredonmere secure and prosperous. The void that had been an open wound within her when she first arrived at the manor pierced her anew. Yet, as she sat alone

by the hearth in her bedchamber each night when
sleep refused to give her release from her fears, she
vowed that she would persevere. She and those who
were her allies had risked everything for Bredonmere.
She must be sure that their sacrifice—and hers—was
not in vain.

"A visitor, milady," Shirley said as she peered into the
antechamber of Audra's private rooms. "He has
entered the outer bailey and sent word ahead that he
will wait upon you in the hall."

Audra rubbed her hand beneath her gorget and
grimaced at the dampness clinging to her skin. After a
chilly sevenday, the summer's heat had returned the
past two days, even though the days were growing
shorter. Her temper was as heated as the air roiling
through the window slits, for the nights were as
uncomfortable as the days. Sleep was impossible
when she could not keep her ears from listening for
the sound of Lynx's steps on her sill—a sound that
had not come in almost a month.

"Who has arrived?" Her breath caught as she
whispered, "Lord deWode?"

Shirley whispered a prayer of thanksgiving and
crossed herself before answering, "Not Lord deWode,
for the lad would not have failed to tell me that."
When a trumpet heralded the unexpected guest for
the whole manor, Shirley rushed to the window.
"Whoever he is, he rides with nearly a score of
mounted men. I do not recognize the banners under
which they ride."

Audra peered past her maid, her curiosity
quelling the disquiet she felt. The last few riders were
vanishing beneath the gate leading to the inner bailey.

With the thick walls blocking her view, she went into her bedchamber, calling for Shirley to attend her.

This nameless lord must be shown from the onset that Lady Audra Travers was in control of her manor. Sending Shirley for her best clothes, she loosened her hair to let it fall down her back. She avoided looking at her reflection in any mirror as she had for the past two sevendays. She did not want to see how she had been altered since Lynx had left her.

He had vowed to return when he could. She must give him a chance to prove that. Would her barren heart be resurrected when he drew her into his arms and brought their passion to life? She hoped he would return before she had ceded herself to despair.

A maid rushed in as Shirley was putting the finishing touches to Audra's hair. The woman's hands shook as she whispered, "Fleming sends word that the newcomers ride in mail and will speak to no one save you, milady."

"If this is some lord's idea of a way to win Bredonmere's favor, it is a poor one," Audra said as she adjusted the gorget over her hair. "I have neither interest nor time for silly posturings."

Fleming was waiting in the audience room, which did not surprise Audra. Since Crandall's death, he had become ever more protective of his lady. She noted that he wore a neat tunic. With dampness clinging to his light hair, she guessed he wanted to bring no shame to Bredonmere with the workworn clothes he usually wore.

"Not even the offer of ale to quench the dust from the road," he said as he escorted her down the stairs, "would convince them to set aside their helmets. Their odd ways are most bothersome, milady."

"You recognize nothing of their crest?"

"Save for my journey to Clarendon Abbey, milady, I have traveled no farther than the boundaries of Bredonmere." He hung his head as he sighed. "If only Crandall were still alive. He traveled often with your father. He knew so much more than I."

"You serve me well," she said when they reached the bottom of the stairs. "Do not worry your mind with thoughts of what others would do. Now I need your insight and guidance to help me ensure that Bredonmere comes to no harm from any quarter."

His grim smile returned. "Aye, milady."

Despite her calm words, Audra nearly recoiled when she entered the great hall to discover the group of men dressed in mail near the doors to the inner bailey. Little differentiated one from the others, for all twenty wore scarlet surcoats that were devoid of any design. She glanced toward the door to the kitchen. A crowd of her retainers stared at her, waiting for her to name these men allies or foes. She scanned the familiar faces, wishing to see Bourne among them. Then she realized it might be better if he was not here. If trouble came, he could launch an attack to the rear of these strangers.

"Welcome to Bredonmere Manor," she said as she walked to the center of the room. The heat from the central hearth surged around her but could not reach the cold fist of dread in her stomach. Fleming's footfalls told her that he was following close on her heels. She wanted to believe they were overreacting, but they could not be too cautious in these uneasy times. "I am Lady Audra Travers, countess of Bredonmere. How may Bredonmere Manor serve you on your journey?"

One man stepped forward and drew his sword. Her breath caught. She heard gasps. Fleming cursed,

but his half-shouted order faded as the man set the
sword on the weapons' rack by the door. In silence,
she watched as his comrades copied him.

The leader motioned, and a lad rushed forward
and took his mail gauntlets. The squire kept his head
low, his light hair falling forward in his face as he
waited for his master's next command.

"Who do you think they are?" Fleming whispered
with impatience.

Audra did not answer. She would do nothing to
ruin her pose as the serene lady of the manor. She was
glad that half the length of the hall separated her and
Fleming from the strangers, for she did not want anyone to hear her frantic heartbeat.

A man behind the leader drew off his helmet and
carried it under his arm as he came forward a few
steps. Bowing his head, which was thatched with dark
curls, he said, "Lady Audra Travers, countess of Bredonmere, milord Wykemarch entreats you to grant
him and his party the haven of your roof while he
breaks his journey."

"Lord Wykemarch?" she repeated.

He gestured to the man standing apart from the
others, then stepped back among his fellows.

Fleming edged forward to whisper, "That name
is not known to me, milady."

She nodded, then said in a voice loud enough to
carry across the hall, "I would that you identify yourself further."

Again the man who had removed his helmet
took a pace forward. "Lord Wykemarch is the eldest
son of the duke of Exbridge, who enjoys the honor
of being a close confidant of His Majesty King
Edward III."

Audra glanced at Fleming. He bent toward her

and said, "The duke of Exbridge was a name your father mentioned more than once."

"But never his son?"

He shook his head.

By all the saints, this was a dilemma. Audra looked at the man who had been pointed out to her as the duke's heir. "I assume Lord Wykemarch has a tongue of his own to ask for such a boon."

Hearing a rustle of dismay from her servants, she tried to ignore it. Her heart thudded more swiftly against her breast as Lord Wykemarch bent forward to remove his helmet, which was topped by an abundant plume as scarlet as his surcoat. When Fleming muttered something under his breath, she knew his hand was on the hilt of his sword as he prepared for whatever trouble the strangers might be bringing with them. She prayed it was none.

The leader handed his helmet to his squire and shook back his dark hair. As he straightened, he smiled a smile that was shockingly familiar.

"Bourne!" she gasped. No, it could not be the armorer, for the man walked toward her with steps as smooth as a dancer's. Could Bourne have a twin who was of the baronage? Absurd!

"His man gave his name as Lord Wykemarch," whispered Fleming in disbelief. "How is this possible?"

She pulled her gaze from the stranger with a friend's face and glanced at Fleming. He was tensed, his fingers opening and closing above the hilt of his sword. By the raised table, a maid was making the ancient sign against witchcraft.

Audra took a deep breath to steady herself. This was no wicked enchantment, only the work of a man, but she wanted answers. She signaled to the serving lass. "Send to the armory for Bourne," she said quietly. "I wish for him to attend me during this meeting."

"Aye, milady," she whispered, backing away as if the devil himself had entered Bredonmere.

Raising her voice, Audra said, "All visitors are welcome to Bredonmere, milord. Pray come forward and make yourself known to us."

"I am Lord Wykemarch," he said with a dip of his head in her direction. In a voice that held no hint of the armorer's accent, he added, "I am more familiarly known as Robert Bourne."

"Bourne?" She clamped her lips closed when she saw his tilt in a smile as he stopped on the other side of the hearth.

"Robert Bourne, milady."

"So you have said, although you once gave me another name in another voice which I accepted as your own."

He crossed his arms over his unmarked surcoat. With his every motion, the sunlight glittered a new pattern off his mail shirt. "If you will recall, I spoke no falsehood to you on that matter. I told you my name is Bourne, and I stand here to verify that that is the truth."

"Failing to speak all of the truth is no less wicked than giving voice to a lie."

"Then let me beg your forgiveness." Coming around the hearth, he dropped to one knee in front of her and lifted the hem of her cotehardie to his forehead.

The serving lass rushed up to her and whispered, "Bourne is not to be found in the armory, milady."

Audra nodded and longed for Crandall at her side to advise her. *Follow your heart.* Again the abbess's voice filled her head, but every beat of her heart told her what she could not ignore. Bourne— Lord Wykemarch—had played her for a fool with his charade. Now that he had divulged his trick, he must want something else. She would be wise to determine exactly why he had come to her manor in a guise and what he wished now before she banished him from Bredonmere for his betrayal.

"You ask much when you have so much to be forgiven for," she said, unable to keep the strain of anger out of her voice.

He looked up at her. "The breadth of your forgiveness will be a measure of your benevolence, milady."

"The affliction your leg suffered seems to have healed miraculously."

His jesting smile was so familiar her heart ached at the depth of his betrayal. "There were few among us who returned from the war with France unscathed. At one time, that limp was not feigned."

"I congratulate you on your complete recovery."

"Not complete, milady, for it still troubles me when I am on my knees."

"Is that so?" She fought her instinct to ask him to rise. She should have no mercy for a man who had deceived her so hideously.

Walking away, she heard rumbles of dismay from his men that she left him on his knees with no command to rise. She caught Fleming's eyes, and he nodded at her unspoken order as he turned to signal to a lad by the kitchen door. The boy raced away. Soon the few men-at-arms that Bredonmere could claim would arrive and be ready to anticipate her command to clear the great hall.

But not under Bourne's command. A shiver of horror stabbed her. The men had been trained to fight on Bourne's command. Was that why he had come here? To steal the prowess of her men-at-arms by entangling them in a snare of bafflement and lies? Then he could return to . . . She turned away from him. There could be but one reason he had returned. He must wish something of Bredonmere and its lady.

"I am, as you might guess, astonished by your visit, Lord Wykemarch," Audra said as she climbed the raised platform.

"I wished to be honest with you, milady."

Her hand fisted on the carved back of her father's chair as his voice rang through her head. Her memory was pricked. She whirled to stare at him, but her gaze went past him to a man who was entering the great hall.

Father Jerome pushed his way through the crowd, then paused. When he spoke, the niggling taunt within her memory was satisfied, for his voice was as deep and resonant as Bourne's. No, Lord Wykemarch's, she told herself with another pinch of betrayal.

Father Jerome's eyes were wide with shock as he stared at the man on his knees and the others standing by the door. "What do you do here dressed as—?"

"Do you mean to tell me," asked Audra coldly, "that this man is still not what he appears to be?"

The priest took another step forward, then swallowed. "Milady, I would speak of this with fewer ears taking heed of what we say."

"I would wish every ear in Bredonmere to hear me ask *Lord Wykemarch* to remove himself and his men from my lands."

"Milady," the priest said, coming to the table, "you have told me often that you value my advice. I urge you to take it now."

Although she wanted nothing save the opportunity to put an end to this mind-numbing confusion, she nodded. "Speak what you think I should hear, Father."

"Give Lord Wykemarch a chance to talk to you, milady. He deserves the right to explain."

"He deserves nothing." She looked past him and saw that the baron with Bourne's face remained on his knees. His gaze caught hers, and another shiver ached along her shoulders.

He had been her friend and her ally. She had trusted him with the men of her manor and her suspicions about Lynx. All that time, he had been lying to her. How could she have been so foolish?

"Milady," urged Father Jerome, "it will demand nothing but a few moments of your time to listen to what he has to say."

"You know this man to be Lord Wykemarch?"

"Yes."

"From the hour he came to Bredonmere?"

"From before that hour, milady."

She closed her eyes and took a steadying breath. If even Father Jerome had been unfaithful to her and his vow to hold the truth sacred, this must be a nightmare.

"I will speak with you later, Father," she said as she drew out her father's chair and sat.

"And Lord Wykemarch?"

"Send him to me." She looked across the floor again to where the dark-haired man was coming to his feet on the priest's request.

Robert Bourne watched Fleming, a man who once had called him friend, go to stand beside Lady Audra's chair. She sat straight and unmoving as she had the day she banished deWode from Bredonmere.

There was no color on her face, save for her wine-red lips and her eyes that were as cold as winter ice. He doubted that telling her that he had never imagined this moment when he first came to Bredonmere would change anything. Audra Travers was unwaveringly loyal to those who had earned her trust.

Today he had destroyed her trust in him. If she were as wise as she had proven to be in the past months, she would destroy nothing else in the midst of her pain.

Climbing the steps to the raised table, he was silent while she called for drinks to be brought for Bredonmere's guests. His eyes narrowed when they met Fleming's. As much as his lady, Fleming would not forgive what he saw as treachery. Robert took note of Bredonmere's men-at-arms coming into the hall and dismissed them as unimportant. Only on their lady's order would they attack, and Lady Audra would keep her head.

He knelt again in front of her. "I thank you for your granting of this audience, milady."

"You are wasting time on courtesy," she answered in a voice that was as frosty as her last words to deWode, "when the only courtesy I would wish from you is the truth."

Rising, he sat in the chair next to hers. He smiled when a serving lass held out a tankard of ale to him. Her eyes were nearly as round as the chalice. When she had placed a goblet of wine next to her lady's hand and been dismissed by Fleming, who did not lower his guard enough to take a tankard, Bourne looked again at Lady Audra's bleached face.

"I will speak only the truth to you," he said.

She tilted her goblet to her lips. "A welcome change, for you should know that, if I had wished to hear a bard's tale of a misplaced squire who has lost his heroic knight, I would have called for minstrels to entertain me."

"I knew your father well, milady."

"Fleming tells me that my father never mentioned your name."

"In your hearing, Fleming?" he asked.

Reluctance filled Fleming's voice. "That is so."

"I served with your father and your eldest brother during the battles against the king of France. Both of them should be remembered with honor."

"Honoring their memory doesn't explain why you came here in the guise of a knightless squire to take up the tasks of the manor's armorer." Audra took another sip of the wine, wishing it was cooler so it could ease the heat boiling within her as she stared at a man she thought she knew—she thought she could trust.

He tapped his tankard against her goblet and smiled. "I pledge to you that I knew nothing of your existence, milady, for neither your father nor your brother spoke of you being cloistered in Clarendon Abbey. Upon hearing of the tragedy of their deaths, I could only assume that Gifford deWode would be granted Bredonmere as the closest of the blood."

"What does that have to do with you?"

His lips compressed as his eyes burned with fury so strong that Fleming put his hand on her shoulder. She did not shake it off as Lord Wykemarch said, "DeWode should not be granted this manor. A man of his ilk deserves no favors."

"On that we agree, as you know well. However, I

still do not understand. Am I to believe that you came here to undermine his hold on Bredonmere? How? By turning the lads of the manor into men-at-arms for him?" She laughed shortly. "It would seem that you have a most peculiar way of treating a rival."

"You must recall how poorly the lads fought when you first chanced upon their lessons near the armory." He ran a finger around the top of the mug. "It was only when I learned that a legitimate heir of the Travers blood would hold that I began to train them in earnest."

"Why?"

He smiled, the familiar smile she had seen so many times, but it was as if she was staring into the face of a stranger. From beneath his surcoat, he drew a rolled parchment. He held it out to her. "I know you can read this, milady, so I shall not insult you by offering to read it to you."

She recognized the seal. King Edward! Looking at Lord Wykemarch, she waited for him to speak. He said nothing as he raised his tankard to his mouth and took a deep drink. Behind her, Fleming muttered a prayer as he took note of the seal.

She rose and turned, hoping she could gather together the shards of her composure if she did not have to look at the face she had seen so often. *The lying face*, she reminded herself sternly as she broke the wax. She brushed the pieces aside and unrolled the scroll. The ornate writing of the king's scribe had become too uncomfortably familiar. Squinting to read the words, she gasped.

"You seem surprised," Lord Wykemarch said as he stood and took her arm.

Fleming stepped around the chair, his hand on the hilt of his sword. "Milord, you are a stranger to this manor, and milady has not given you her permission to treat her with such familiarity."

"She knows me well."

"Only the lies you have woven, milord."

Audra waved Fleming aside as she drew her arm out of the baron's grasp. Baron! Every thought was a reminder of how gullible she had been to believe his lies. How many had called her fool? Crandall, Father Jerome, the man she had known as Bourne, Lynx. She looked down at the page in her hands so neither man might guess that, even at this intolerable moment, a night rider was beguiling her brain.

She needed Lynx beside her now. His sharp tongue would cut through the web of lies to help her find the truth. He would hold her and wash away her bafflement with a flood of kisses, but she could not guess when he might return. Coming here when a score of mounted knights had sought the shelter of Bredonmere's walls would be too foolhardy even for Lynx, who feared no man.

"Say what you will," she ordered as she faced Lord Wykemarch.

"I would answer any questions you have, milady."

"You may start by telling me that this is simply a jest to complement the one you have played on me since my arrival home in Bredonmere."

"'Tis no jest." He sat on the edge of the table, his motion so reminiscent of the old Bourne that she had to bite her lip again to silence the accusations that would gain her nothing now. "The signature is the king's."

She let it roll closed with a sharp snap. "Then this must be in error if you think I shall believe that Edward wishes me to marry you, m-milord." She struggled not to choke on what she must remember to call him. "I received a message from the king's messenger that I was to consider myself betrothed to Lord deWode."

"You have not read the whole message here."

"I think I have seen enough of this. Good day, milord." Dropping the roll onto the table as if it was of the least import, she raised her chin and gave him the slightest nod. "Bredonmere will be glad to offer you and your companions a meal before you continue on your journey."

"Milady, you should read this in its entirety." He held the parchment out to her. "You know, as well as I, the importance of the king's favor remaining on Bredonmere."

"Do you threaten me?"

"Only with the truth."

"I find it unlikely that you would recognize the truth."

He stood. "I hold the truth paramount, and the truth is that I have heard you speak of how little you wish to wed deWode."

"So you offer yourself in his place?" She fought her fury to speak calmly. "What caused you to think that I would prefer a professed liar to Lord deWode?"

"The choice is yours."

"Choice?"

He opened the parchment and tapped the bottom. "That is what the king offers you. A real choice this time, milady."

"Between you, Lord Wykemarch, and Lord deWode?" She laughed. "That is no choice I wish to make."

"If I had not stepped forward, Edward would have you wed you to DeWode, your nearest relative."

"Then I thank you for your assistance in this

matter, but I do not owe you such a debt that I would give you my birthright."

"You have changed your mind?" He let the parchment roll closed. "You would rather have deWode?"

Audra could not still the quiver that etched her skin at such an abhorrent idea, but she said, "I would rather Bredonmere was left alone to seek its own destiny."

"It shan't be. You have, by your hard work, made it even more valuable to any man who might strive to be its next lord."

"Such as you?"

He cursed. "Is there nothing I can do to convince you to listen to me?"

Audra shook her head. "Nothing."

For a moment, she thought he would argue, but then he nodded. "Very well. However, I ask you the courtesy of the hospitality of Bredonmere for my men and me for tonight."

"You are welcome to stay this one night, milord." She swept past him and threw back over her shoulder, "I trust you all shall be comfortable in the stables."

"My men thank you for your hospitality."

She paused and faced him again. "And you?"

"I shall make myself most comfortable tonight, milady," he said with a smile that sent a chill right through her. "I have learned to sleep in an armory and other places that are less comfortable than the stables."

She wondered what he was intimating with his enigmatic words, but refused to ask. She had suffered from too many of Lord Wykemarch's intrigues. She would suffer no more . . . unless his rival arrived

before he left. Then her worst fears would be given
life, for Bredonmere could become a battleground
between two men who cared more for the manor
than for her.

16

Fleming stormed from one end of the antechamber to the other and back. "You cannot marry him, milady!"

Patting Shirley's shoulder, for the serving woman had succumbed to another bout of tears, Audra said, "I read you the message from King Edward. My only other choice is to name Lord deWode as my husband."

"At least, Lord deWode was open about his treachery."

"I have thought often on that fact in the past hours." Audra went to stand by the open window. Gazing out at the countryside that slept beneath a swath of stars, she thought of the nights when the wind had brought rapture to her. Whichever choice she made would mean the end of any chance to be in Lynx's arms again.

"Speak to Father Jerome of this," Shirley pleaded.

"He has spent most of his life beyond the borders of Bredonmere. He may be able to give you guidance in ways that we know nothing."

She sighed. "Father Jerome has admitted that he knew that the man we knew only as Bourne was of the baronage. Can I trust him?"

Shirley's eyes filled again with tears, and she covered her face with her hands. Rocking back and forth on the bench, she moaned, "Whatever shall we do?"

"What is said among the men-at-arms?" Audra asked, wishing she could surrender to her despair as Shirley had.

Fleming paused in his pacing. "Their confusion is deep, milady."

"What of their loyalty?"

"It is yours, without question." His lips thinned, and she feared she had insulted him with the question, but it was one she had to ask.

"Can they force Lord Wykemarch's men from the manor?"

"The loss of life would be high, for the battle would be fought within the baileys."

She nodded. "That I feared. I must seek another way to deal with this unforeseen turn of events."

"You do not think he will leave on the morrow?"

"I do not know what to think."

"And if he will not leave?" Fleming persisted.

Audra did not answer as she went into her private chamber and threw the window glass aside. The night had grown cool and damp with the setting sun. When she saw a glow flare along the river to the north, her breath caught. Another fire! Hearing a shout from the outer room, she knew Fleming had been alerted.

Closing the window, she wrapped her arms

around herself. Even that was no sign of Lynx, for she could not believe he would have returned to Bredon-mere to continue his mischief without coming to her first. She craved his touch. Surely he wanted hers.

Shirley came into the bedchamber, and Audra let her assist her in getting ready for bed. If she saw more of her maid's tears, she might loosen the fury she could barely keep in. That fury was not aimed at her maid, but Audra was not sure how much longer she could restrain her frustration at the many men who longed to control her life and the loss of the one man she wished to share it with.

Dreams were wondrous things, Audra decided. In a dream, anything was possible. To dance across the sky on a rainbow, to swim to the bottom of the deep-est pond and cavort with the fish, to be in Lynx's arms once again.

Audra's heart pulsated with joy as she dreamed of Lynx slipping into her room once more. Lying in her bed, she would pretend to be asleep. He would tiptoe to her, the whisper of his cloak brushing the bed-curtains as he bent toward her, bringing the aro-mas of the night with him. The fiery pleasure of his lips on hers. Her arms wrapping around his shoul-ders. His low laugh when he drew her beneath him. Each precious image woven together to become joy.

"Lynx," she murmured as the dream started to evaporate into the heat of her longing. She did not want to wake. She did not want it to end, for she yearned to believe, as she once had, that, with enough wishing, dreams could come true.

"Do you call to me, milady?"

Audra's eyes opened wide, straining to see in the

darkness. Strong hands stroked her shoulders. The shadows congealed into the silhouette she knew so well.

"Lynx!"

"Hush, milady. Say nothing to betray us." He smiled as he made sure she obeyed his order by bringing her dream to life with his lips against hers.

With an eager sigh, she sank into the rushes, drawing him with her. Every memory dimmed before the resplendent glow of desire flaring through her as his voracious mouth tasted her skin in a fire storm of kisses. Wanting to be even closer to him, wanting nothing between them but the warmth of their naked bodies, she reached for the pin holding his cloak to his shoulder.

His moan of uncontrolled desire swarmed over her. Sifting her fingers through his thick hair, she quivered when his mouth captured hers. The urgency in his touch as they quickly removed their clothes left her breathless. The pressure of his strong chest against her, the rough warmth of his thighs grazing her legs, the moist demands of his mouth bewitched her and gave life to every fantasy that had taunted her when she feared he would never be with her again.

A gentle shove on his shoulders turned him onto his back. Resting atop him, she listened to his soft groans of pleasure as she tasted the rough skin along his neck and the softer texture of his ear. The salty, warm taste of his skin drew her lips across his chest.

She ran her toes up the inside of his leg and laughed when he whispered, "My vixen, you shall drive me mad with the craving to be part of you."

"We are both mad."

"Mayhap that is so."

"Where have you been?" she whispered.

"Wishing I was with you."

She gasped when he pressed her back into the bed. The gasp became a moan when his mouth began to explore her as intimately as hers had him. He grasped her wrists and secured them to the mattress, holding her with the strength of his body. Nibbles along the pulse in her neck sent a thrilling tremble through her, and she strained against his sweet captivity.

Her nails bit into her palms when his tongue coursed along her breast, setting every inch of her afire. As he traced an ambling path along her abdomen, she could not still the longings of her body. She wanted to touch him. She must touch him.

"Lynx." She could hardly contain her yearning.

"Be patient, my sweet lady, as you have for the too many nights I was far from you. I long to taste every inch of you before the dawn comes."

Her back arched when his mouth found her most private places. Probing and caressing, teasing and tantalizing, his tongue danced across her. His hands released her and slipped beneath her to drift along her legs in slow, easy strokes that became quicker to match the pace of his fevered kisses.

Again she whispered his name. As he rose over her, she brought his lips to hers. The blended scents of their bodies enveloped her as he made them one. Together they moved to the music that came from the depths of their beings. The song became frenzied in the moment before she succumbed to the rapture that erupted through her and him, making him forever a part of her.

*   *   *

"Audra?"

She murmured, not wanting to wake from the half sleep where she could believe Lynx would remain in her life for all time. Burrowing closer to his strong shoulder, she kept her eyes closed.

"Audra, it is time."

"Time?" she whispered.

"To speak of things between us."

"There is nothing between us," she whispered as her fingers lilted over his naked chest.

He chuckled and brought her fingers to his lips. As his tongue brushed the tip of one, she softened against him. So many nights when she had dreamed of this moment!

"I cannot stay longer with you as I am," he whispered.

She glanced at the wall of curtains around the bed. No hint of dawn light sifted past them. "Must you leave?"

"That you must decide."

She sat up, drawing the blanket around her shoulders. "Do you mean that you will stay if I wish?" She laughed like a child freed from the drudgery of chores to flee out into the brilliant warmth of the day. "Of course, I wish you to stay. I love you, Lynx."

"You do not know me, Audra." The odd sound of regret deepened his voice.

"I know you have made me happy and furious and frightened and jubilant." She found his hands in the darkness and held them to her cheeks. "Before I met you, I was empty. You fill my heart with love."

His fingers slipped out of hers and curved along her cheek before drawing away into the shadows. When the bed shifted, she realized he was reaching for his chausses. Confusion buffeted her. This was like none of the other times he had slipped into her room in the darkness. Then he had sneaked away while she slept.

As his hand stroked her face, he whispered, "Audra, you must know the truth."

"The truth?"

"Of the man I truly am."

"Lynx—"

He stood and swept aside the bed-curtains. Only the fire on the hearth lit the room, but the faint glow was enough to outline the stern features that had been hidden beneath his mask . . . and been bare right in front of her since her arrival at Bredonmere.

"Bourne!" she cried as she had in the great hall. She stared at him. She clenched the blanket and shook her head. "No, this is impossible!"

Lynx—Bourne—Lord Wykemarch—She did not know what to call him. He put his finger to her lips, silencing her as he had so many times. She jerked her head away and scrambled off the bed to pull on her kirtle.

"'Tis very possible, Audra."

"Why did you say nothing of this earlier?" Her laugh was hollow. "No need to answer. You wished to play Lynx one more time and seduce me with your lies."

"I thought you must have guessed."

She remembered how his voice had rung an echo in her mind. Only Father Jerome's arrival and his admission of lying to her had put that thought from her head. "Mayhap I am the fool you have called me so often. How you must have laughed after I confessed to you that I believed Father Jerome rode through the night, milord Lynx. Is that what you wish to be called now?"

"Audra, I wished to prove to you that the one precious thing we share was unchanged."

"Until the light of truth revealed your double deception." Going to stand by the hearth, she whispered, "How many more lies shall I endure for your entertainment, milord, before you heed my request and take your leave of Bredonmere?"

His arm curved around her waist, pulling her back to him. "How many must I endure from you, Audra?"

"I have spoken no lies."

"One."

"You are witless!" She struggled to escape, but it was as impossible as when he had played Lynx and held her as his captive. Oh, how could she tolerate her heart when it was breaking at this ultimate betrayal? She had given him every part of her, and she feared he wanted only Bredonmere.

He bent to press his mouth against the curve of her throat. When she shivered, unable to repress the passion he aroused with each touch, he murmured against her skin, "My sweet lady, you do not want me to leave when we can share this."

Audra drew away and stared up at him. Her fingers touched the curve of his jaw. The glow in his eyes grew as heated as the fire on the hearth when her hand followed it as it had each time he had come to her. Slowly her fingers rose to caress his cheek and the strong line of his nose. With a sigh, she walked to the window. Lynx would climb through it no more.

Without looking at him, she said, "Once you accused me of letting you share my bed only so I could have your strong arm for Bredonmere's defense. It would seem, milord, that you seduced me only so you could claim my father's manor."

"You shall prove yourself to be a fool if you believe that."

"Then why did you not come to me when I first arrived and reveal your true name?"

He sat on the steps by the fire. The light from the flames left half his face shadowed in a pain-filled reminder of how he had looked when she knew him only as Lynx. "I could not tell you the truth because I feared you might be forced to reveal it to deWode."

"What does Lord deWode have to do with Lynx?"

"Everything," he said grimly. "He is the reason I am here. I have told you that I never break a vow, Audra. I came to Bredonmere to fulfill a most sacred one."

"To destroy Bredonmere before he could claim it?"

His smile was fleeting. "You are insightful."

"Not insightful, when you have admitted as much earlier today, but I still do not understand why you have lived a dual life as Bourne and as Lynx."

He stood and walked around the bench. When she would have come to her feet, too, he put his hands on her shoulders. He bent and whispered against her hair, "Did deWode never regale you with tales of the sport he enjoyed before the Black Death gave him the opportunity he craved to make Bredonmere his?"

"I have no idea what you speak of." Again she started to rise, but his hands became a weight on her shoulders, holding her in place.

"Then heed the reality of the evil in the man you have considered taking to your marriage bed." Venom lashed through his voice. "DeWode did not find such a welcome in my sister's bed, but he forced himself and his bastard upon her before she retired to a convent where both she and the child died at its birth.

Died unmourned by deWode, who had turned his attention on another woman who offered him a chance to advance himself. I have heard that he left her heavy with child, too, so he could come here to Bredonmere to wed you."

"No!"

He whirled to face her. "You call my story a lie, milady?"

Audra drew his hands off her shoulders and stood. Going again to the window, she stared out at the night. Her fingers clenched on the stone sill as she asked, "So you came here to seek vengeance on your enemy?"

"It was an oath I hold dearer than any other."

She closed her eyes as agony seared her. So much she understood when it was too late. Lord Wyke-march, in both his disguises, had belittled her life in the abbey and had been eager to prove to her that she wanted the earthy delights she would have been denied had she remained cloistered.

"Am I the way you planned to repay him, milord?" she asked, without turning. "It must have seemed to you the perfect solution when you bedded me to avenge yourself for Lord deWode raping your sister."

"Audra—"

"Do not waste your breath on lathering me with lies. As I have told you too many times already, you are granted your leave to take yourself from Bredon-mere on the morrow, milord. You shall find no more tools for your quest for vengeance here."

"You must know the whole truth."

"Truth seems an elusive thing today in Bredon-mere. You have lied to me in all your guises." She smiled wryly. "Even Father Jerome lied to me."

"At my request."

She folded her arms in front of her, keeping her hands from reaching out to him. Her yearning for his touch was the greatest betrayal of all. "Why would he agree to lie for you?"

"He is my youngest brother. As you were, he was chosen by my family to fulfill its obligation to the church."

She sat on the bench and stared at her hands folded in her lap. Once she had suspected Father Jerome of being the night rider. He bore such a strong resemblance to the man she had known only as Lynx. Never had she considered he might be connected to Lynx in another manner.

"He came here to help you in your revenge?" she asked.

"No, he arrived here first. A letter to me, telling me that Bredonmere was certain to be claimed by my greatest enemy, convinced me to ride as Lynx to persuade deWode that Bredonmere was not the prize he envisioned it to be. Jerome did help me find a palatable position as the armorer, although he never has shared my longing for vengeance." He squatted and with his finger beneath her chin brought her face up to his. "Audra—"

She could not let him finish, for he might tempt her to relent. She must not. She would not let him use her any longer. "I bid you godspeed and a fair journey, milord."

His oath struck her ears a second before he seized her shoulders. He held her easily with one hand while he cupped her chin with the other. As he tilted her face up, she could not evade the intensity in his eyes, those ebony, mysterious eyes that had crinkled with Bourne's good humor and had burned with Lynx's desire.

"Then," he said past gritted teeth, "you will wed deWode, who shall beggar your beloved manor to satisfy his lusts." His fingers sifted through her hair as he whispered, "And you shall need to welcome him to your bed as you have me." He kissed her swiftly. "You have tasted his kisses. Do you find them enjoyable?"

"Lynx—Milord—"

"My name is Robert, Audra. I would be pleased to hear my name on your lips."

She closed her eyes as he brushed his lips against her throat. "Robert . . ."

"Will he kiss you like this, or will he think only of you giving him an heir so he can turn his attention to other women?"

"Say no more."

"If you banish me, milady, that is your sole alternative." Again his tone changed as he brought her mouth just beneath his. His lips brushed hers when he murmured, "I fought long with those who would have blocked my words from reaching Edward to ensure you did not have to marry deWode. Will you make my battle for naught?"

"I cannot—" She drew back. When he released her, she almost wished he had not. In his arms, she had to fight only her yearning to cede herself to his splendid caresses. She could forget all else. Going to the bed and pulling a blanket over her shoulders, she whispered, "You lied to me, Robert. Just as he did."

He cursed. "I am not like him."

"Aren't you? In your quest for vengeance, haven't you become the very man you despise?" She met his eyes as she whispered, "The very man I despise? I thought I could trust you when you were Bourne. I thought I could trust you when you were Lynx."

"I am still those men. The only thing changed is my name."

"No, and I fear I cannot trust you again." She scooped up his black clothing and, shoving it into his hands, said, "Farewell, Robert." Her voice broke as she walked to look down at the fire. "Farewell, Lynx."

She did not turn, even when she heard the window open to let in the cool night wind. Lynx was gone, along with all the dreams she knew would never come true.

17

   Misery awaited Audra when she rose from
her bed the next morning. Her head throbbed, and
every step sent a wave of dizziness over her. By all the
saints, she could not be ill now. As she dressed and
splashed cold water on her face, the weakness ebbed.
She was pleased to be able to walk without clutching
her stomach as she left her chambers and went down
the stairs to the great hall to begin her day and face
the changes for Bredonmere.

   She could denounce Lord Wykemarch with the
truth. No one within Bredonmere would pledge fealty
to him if it was known that he had ridden the night as
Lynx, terrorizing the very villeins who would be looking to him for protection. Yet her only choice then
might be to wed Lord deWode. The thought twisted
through her stomach anew.

   Hearing the bell chiming from the church, Audra
did not pause for breakfast. She was not sure she
could have swallowed it, even if she had.

The inner bailey was boiling with activity when Audra crossed it on her way to the stables. Most of the keep's residents were watching and whispering as Lord Wykemarch's men saddled their horses and prepared to leave Bredonmere. Many a gaze turned toward her as she passed, but she kept her serene smile in place while she spoke greetings as if this day was no different from any other.

She found it difficult to believe that Robert would relent with such ease. As Lynx, he had vowed that no one would budge him from Bredonmere until he had obtained vengeance against Lord deWode. Now he was shouting to his men to be ready to ride on his command. Mayhap her head had guided her correctly, for the man who became the next lord of Bredonmere must not capitulate.

When Robert turned in her direction, he glanced at her and then away as if he could not tolerate the sight of her. Why? she wanted to demand. *She* had not betrayed *him* with lies and half truths. She had always been honest with him, especially when she told him she loved him.

Father Jerome waited by the stable wall. He edged forward when she approached. "Milady," he said quietly, "I would speak with you before it is too late."

"I shall return at midday." She motioned for her horse to be brought. "I told Halstead I would ride with him today to see the latest batch of lambs."

"Milady, please rethink your command to banish Lord Wykemarch."

Her self-control cracked a bit as she frowned. "You need not call him anything but 'brother,' Father, for he told me the truth last night." His eyes widened as she added in a whisper, "All of it."

"All of it?" He folded his hands over the crucifix on his chest. "He did not tell me that he planned to—"

"Be honest with me?" she fired back. "It seems time that someone of your family would grant me that courtesy."

"Then you understand his reasons for what he has done. When he rode as . . ." He glanced uneasily around the bailey. "The truth of that matter would not help Bredonmere."

"Or your brother. I have not forgotten that an accusation of murder still hangs over Lynx's head."

Father Jerome's face turned as gray as the stones behind him, but his eyes grew as hard as his brother's. Again she saw the resemblance that had misguided her into believing Father Jerome was the night rider. "He did not slay Crandall. You know that," he said.

"It is not my place to know, but to sit in judgment when the facts are presented." Again her voice broke as she looked to where the men were readying to mount. "I do not want to condemn him to die."

"You love him!"

"Must you make it sound like an accusation?" she asked.

"I implore you again, milady, to reconsider your hasty decision to send Robert far from here."

She shook her head. "I have reconsidered it all night long, and the answer always comes back the same. How can I ask Bredonmere to follow a man who rode the night as . . ." She turned away before she said the words that would betray Robert and her own foolish heart. *Follow your heart* had been the abbess's parting advice, but she could not listen to it now. She must think of the part of her that owed an obligation to this fief.

Settling herself in the saddle on the back of her

favorite steed, Audra urged it forward. Her breath caught over her aching heart as a familiar black steed separated from the group of horses surrounded by Lord Wykemarch's men. Staring at Robert, she clutched the reins more tightly, not wanting to risk her fingers reaching out to brush the firm angles of his face, which had caressed hers in the darkness.

"I thank you for your hospitality, milady," he said as if they were strangers. "As you requested, we take our leave of Bredonmere."

His smile was as savage as the fury in his eyes, so she murmured only, "Farewell, Lord Wykemarch."

"I shall fare better than you, milady."

She dragged her gaze from his. He called an order to his men. They mounted and were gone before she could say words that would have saved her from pain, the words she must keep concealed within her heart forever.

Please stay.

"You are pleased, milady?"

Audra gave Halstead a smile as they rode toward Bredonmere. "How could I not be pleased? Raising sheep seems to be a skill inborn in every villein on Bredonmere lands. They have taken to this plan with the ease of a fish slipping through a brooklet."

"It is true." He hesitated, then cleared his throat. "Will we be continuing with raising sheep?"

"Yes."

"Lord Wykemarch—"

"Has left Bredonmere."

He rubbed his hands against his thighs nervously. She waited for him to speak, but he rode in silence through the shadows dappling the road beneath the bare branches of the trees. She wanted to reassure him but could not find the words.

Halstead put out his arm to slow her as two riders slipped from among the trees and flanked them. Audra did not recognize them, and fear sliced through her. Even though Lynx was gone, she must never forget another man had killed in his name. If these men belonged to the false Lynx, she and Halstead had no way to fight them. Halstead wore no more than a short blade at his side, and she was unarmed.

Bourne's many warnings rang through her head, but it was too late now to admit that he had been the one to unsettle her enough this morning to ride without the small knife she had carried since his lesson with the broadsword.

"Milady?" Halstead asked.

Another pair of taciturn riders emerged from the trees to follow them.

"Say nothing," she warned.

"Milady, if we ride on—"

"Say nothing," she repeated.

When he nodded, Audra held her horse to the same pace as more men appeared from among the trees to surround them. No one spoke in the malevolent parade. She was not surprised to see, as they turned a bend in the road, a lone man astride a warhorse.

Beside her, Halstead drew in his breath sharply, but she continued toward Gifford deWode. She should have guessed she would meet him as soon as this exhibition began. He never did anything without boasting of the men he commanded. How much more trouble could this sevenday bring? Robert Bourne yesterday. Gifford deWode today. The devil himself must be due on the morrow.

She shivered. Mayhap the devil had arrived today. She would never forget Lord deWode's brutality when he was last here. Memories of Crandall, facedown and bleeding by Lord deWode's hand, flashed through her head.

"Greetings, milady," Lord deWode called. "We are well met on this lovely day."

"Bredonmere is honored by your presence, milord," she replied coolly. "However, I am baffled by this unnecessary show of strength between kinsmen."

He edged his horse closer. "I know your foremost thought is always of the security of your fief and your tenants. I thought to show you why the king has granted me leave to wed you." He flung out his hand, and more men rode from the shadows. "Edward knows the men who look to me as their lord are many."

From the corner of her eye, Audra saw Halstead straining to look around them as he counted slowly on his fingers. She did not need to count. A quick scan had told her that the baron had come with the same double score of men he had with him during his last visit to Bredonmere.

"You are welcome always to visit Bredonmere, milord," she said in the same icy tone. "If you will come with my reeve and me, we would be honored to escort you to the manor."

Gifford waved his hand in the air. Before Audra could react, every man around them had drawn his sword. The baron smiled triumphantly at her.

"Milady," whispered Halstead, "what—?"

"Say nothing," she ordered once again. Raising her voice, she said, "As I have already told you, Lord deWode, such a display of strength is not needed between allies and kinsmen. I commend you on the men you have with you. Bredonmere's hospitality is—"

"No longer yours to offer." Gifford moved his horse next to hers. Putting his hand on hers, he slowly squeezed her fingers into the leather reins as he said, "Bredonmere is mine by the king's decree."

"Only if we are wed." She strove not to wince. Keeping her head high, she added, "Bredonmere is mine to hold until the day I marry. Until then . . ."

Gifford leaned toward her, his nose only a bare inch from hers. "Milady, that decision is no longer yours. The king, who is far wiser than a woman raised in a convent, has deemed that you are to be my wife."

"I—"

"*You* have no say, Audra." He pulled her toward him.

Halstead cried, "Release milady!"

"Silence, knave!" said Gifford with a snarl. "You dare to gainsay your rightful lord. Tell him I am your rightful lord."

"You are—" she took a steadying breath, then sat straighter, "you are a guest on my lands, and—" His hand contracted over hers, and she gasped as pain shot up her arm.

"The king has given you an order. You are to marry me."

"Or me!"

Audra looked over her shoulder as a shout rang through the greenwood. Caught in the sunlight, his riding cape flying back from his shoulders in an ebony shadow, was the silhouette that had filled her nightmares and her dreams. Her heart thudded with joy. She wanted to call out, "Lynx!"

But that dream had come to an end last night with the truth of deception and betrayal. What was Robert doing here? He should have left Bredonmere hours ago.

De Wade released her and stared along the road. His eyes widened when Robert rode from the sun's glare.

"Wykemarch?" he asked in disbelief. "What are you doing here on my lands?"

"On Lady Audra's lands, unless you have wed her since she left Bredonmere's manor this morning." Robert glanced at her. Fury strained his face when she cradled her aching hand in her other palm. "I see by your gentle wooing that you have not yet succeeded in convincing her to take you for her husband. I must say that you look much better without the bruises Lynx left on you."

"Bruises? How did you know about—?"

DeWode tensed, his fingers ready to draw his sword as Audra opened her mouth to answer. He relaxed only outwardly when she said, "I can assume you did not have the opportunity to meet Bourne, Bredonmere's armorer, on your last visit to my fief."

Her eyes were cold as she looked at him, and he knew she was no more his ally than when she left the manor house to meet Halstead. As much as his fingers itched to pull his knife and put an end to deWode's cursed life, he longed to pull her into his arms. She would not believe him if he spoke of how he had not intended to let his obsession for revenge hurt her. She had not heeded him last night. She would not now.

DeWode's snarl brought his gaze back to his enemy who was now his rival. "You were here?" He laughed, but Robert heard an undercurrent of unease. "As an armorer? Not the usual life for the son of a duke, is it?" With a curse, he shouted, "Take yourself off my lands."

"Not yours. Not yet," he added when Audra stiffened. "It seems our king has seen the lack of wisdom in the decision to grant you the privilege of marrying Lady Audra, a decision which he finds he cannot recall making."

Audra gasped. "Are you saying Edward did not truly sign the decree requiring me to wed Lord deWode?"

Robert caught her shocked gaze and held it. "Neither I nor our king would dishonor Lord deWode by calling him a liar. The decree exists, but there is a question of how it came to be over the king's signature. Of course, being the fair man he is, Edward will not accuse you, deWode, or your allies of using his name for your own gains. He does, however, trust the countess of Bredonmere to decide between her suitors."

"Her suitors? What suitors?"

Bowing his head, he said, "It would seem you and I are her suitors, deWode."

The baron laughed loudly. "You ask much for an enemy sitting among my loyal men. A single order will put an end to your life."

"Or to yours." Robert whipped back his cape and pointed to the forest.

Audra stared at the tips of arrows sticking out from the trees on both sides of the road. Even her untrained eye could see that they were set on crossbows. Bourne had been exacting when he taught her men-at-arms to use the weapon with skill. His own men would be experts, able to kill with precision.

Not trusting her voice to speak more loudly, she whispered, "Milords, there is nothing to be gained by such tactics. I offer you both the welcome of Bredonmere, but I must remind you that the decision is one that I alone shall make."

"Bah!" Gifford snarled a curse. "What does a woman know of these things?"

"Do you agree, milords?" she asked, ignoring Gifford's question.

Robert bowed his head toward her. "I am delighted at the opportunity to enjoy your hospitality for a while longer, milady." As he raised it, she saw the twinkle in his eyes. He was enjoying this occasion to humiliate his rival.

She looked at Lord deWode. Reluctantly he nodded and motioned for his men to follow him.

"Milord?" she called.

He drew in his horse as he looked back at her. "Yes?"

"You should know that all allies of Bredonmere leave their weapons at the door of the great hall."

She thought he would argue, then he nodded. With a shout, he led his men along the road toward Bredonmere.

Audra put her hand on Halstead's arm. "Thank you, friend."

"I did nothing, milady." His voice continued to shake.

"You did all I asked, and I can ask no more than that." When he looked past her, she knew she could avoid Robert no longer. Turning to him, she said, "I thank you as well, milord, for your unforeseen assistance. It has proven to be good fortune that you traveled so slowly across my lands."

"'Twas not merely good fortune," he said as he lifted her aching hand from the reins. Gently he ran his fingers along hers to check for broken bones. "I knew deWode to be traveling no more than a day behind me. My men watched all roads that could bring him to Bredonmere—" holding her hand in his, he added, "while I kept watch over you and your reeve. Audra, you have seen now that deWode is a beast fit for no lady's bed."

"I know."

"But still you are considering his suit. Why?"

"The king has requested this. I must obey him."

His eyes became dark slits, but his fury slipped through to strike her with its power. "You know as well that deWode lied about the king's favor."

"I have only your word for that." Just moving her hand sent another wave of pain up her arm, but she drew it away.

"My word should be enough."

"Once I believed you, Robert. I believed everything you told me. But no more." She sighed, aware of too many ears heeding every word she spoke. "I must query Edward about this myself. I will not allow Bredonmere to come into contention because I failed to follow the king's orders."

"That will take time."

"To hurry a decision that will affect Bredonmere for all the years of the future would be foolish."

He smiled. "And few have accused you of being foolish, Audra."

"Save you."

"For good reason, if you recall." He signaled to his men. As they rode from the trees, he put his hand against her cheek. The sound of the hoofbeats were muted beneath the pounding of her heart as she delighted in the warmth of his touch.

Audra sat straighter when she realized Robert's men were herding Halstead away at a gallop. "Halt!"

"They will bring no harm to your reeve, but we

must delay here no longer. If deWode was to over-
power Fleming and your men, you could find yourself
unable to get into your own manor house."

When she gripped the reins, she winced.

"We will follow more slowly," he said. "You need
risk yourself no more today." With a smile, he reached
out and snapped a rein to her horse's halter. "This is
not the first time I have rescued you in this wood."

Warmth swept away the aches along her arm as
she thought of the night when Lynx had held her as
his prisoner, when she first dared to believe that he
was her ally and when he first taught her of the passions they could share. She fought the sweet sensations flowing over her. She must not let him seduce
her with words as easily as he had seduced her with
his fiery caresses.

Forcing her voice to harden, she said, "I am
grateful for all your assistance."

"Only grateful?"

"What more do you expect?"

"The truth."

She laughed as sharply as Gifford had. "Odd that
you would wish that when you refused me the same
thing."

"My longing to hold you in my arms is honest,"
he whispered.

His arm circled her waist, enveloping her in his
bewitching touch. As his finger stroked her cheek,
he brought her lips beneath his. She gripped the
front of his surcoat. The mail beneath it was no
harder than his chest. Slowly his mouth lowered
toward hers, offering to bring her lost dreams back
to life. She wanted him. She wanted to be in his
arms, to feel her breath strain with his, to have him
be a part of her.

With a moan, she pulled away. "Do not do this."

"Do not touch you, sweet Audra, when you wish this as much as I?"

She gazed up at him. "Do not use this to persuade me."

"DeWode will use any method he can to persuade you, even breaking your fingers."

A shudder rumbled through her like the resonance of a thunderclap. "Don't you understand? I can fight that wickedness, but I must be certain that any decision I make for Bredonmere is not tainted by my own desires."

"I understand."

"Good." She looked along the now deserted road. "It will be easier if you remain distant until I have heard from the king."

He seized her arm and turned her back to him. "I said I understood, not that I would cease showing you how much I need you and how much you and Bredonmere need me. You will see that, Audra."

"Do you offer that as a threat to me?"

"'Tis only a pledge, milady, but one that I will keep until my last breath."

Again Audra drew away, and he tugged on the leading rein to guide her horse back to the manor house. Robert made no vow lightly. He would not let deWode best him, and his words heralded disaster for Bredonmere. A disaster she feared she could not halt.

18

Autumn clamped its damp hand on Bredon-mere. A steady rain during the night would make travel almost impossible, for the roads were as impassable as a bog. In the keep, the hearths once again blazed with fires to combat the chill, but their warmth reached only a few feet into the cool rooms. The speech between the two lords within Bredon-mere's walls was colder still.

Audra sought her bed early, because she tired of trying to put a halt to the verbal combat between Robert and Gifford. Fleming had been anxious to speak with her, but she had asked him to wait until morning when she would speak to him in her audience room. Nothing must ruin the façade of serenity within the manor house. That might be the only way to keep a catastrophe from erupting.

When she woke the next morning, wishing the past few days had been nothing more than a nightmare, a headache weighed on her brow. She burrowed into her pillow, but even that slight motion was a mistake. A cramping in her stomach added to her misery, and she considered going to Shirley for a posset, but her maid would wish for her to stay in bed until she was well. She had no time for cosseting herself when two men vied to take Bredonmere from her.

Her stomach threatened to revolt when she stood. Pressing one hand on it and clamping her other over her mouth, she fought to keep from being ill. She managed to sit down on the nearest bench.

A knock intruded on her discomfort. "Come in, Shirley." Audra put a hand on the back of the bench as she rose.

"Milady, are you ill?"

She shook her head, sending her stomach into another paroxysm. "Just a stomach ailment."

"Again? You were ailing last week."

"I think I may have eaten something that irritated it." Swallowing harshly, she added, "What is it? You look distressed. Shirley, what is amiss?"

She took a step toward the door, but the motion nearly undid her. Shirley ran forward to keep her from falling. Waving her maid aside, Audra straightened. Pain spasmed through her middle, and she wrapped her arm around herself.

Through clenched teeth, she said, "I shall be fine, Shirley. If this is what I suffered last week, I shall be feeling better soon. I have found that this unease seems to become less as the day progresses." When she heard a choked sound, she glanced at Shirley. Her maid's face was a deathly shade of gray. Again she asked, "What is amiss?"

"Nothing."

"You are as pale as clouds on a sunny day. What is amiss?"

Shirley wrung her hands as she said in a low voice, "You are describing the same discomfort suffered by one of the kitchen lasses."

"What ails her?"

"She thickens with a child, milady."

Audra's fingers clenched on the latch. Forcing her face to remain tranquil, she asked herself why she had not considered what the results could be of her nights of love with the man she had then known only as Lynx. She hastily counted the days and realized she could be in the same condition as the kitchen maid.

She closed her eyes. How many times had Robert denounced her as a fool? There were ways to prevent conception, but she had not spared a moment's thought to anything other than ecstasy. If she truly had conceived a child, she must not let anyone discover the truth.

Her attempt to laugh fell heavily from her lips. "I expect my ailment to pass much quicker than nine months."

"Milady," Shirley said softly, "is this why you allowed Lord Wykemarch to remain here after you ordered him to depart yesterday? Do you delay in ordering his banishment because he sired your babe?"

Audra whirled away, catching a glimpse of her face in the mirror. If possible, it had become a sicker shade of gray. "I have no idea of what you speak."

"You cannot be false with me, although you may fool the others. I am your body servant. I have seen the changes when I help you dress." Her tone gentled as she knelt. "My dear Lady Audra, I also am your ally. Your friend, if I may be so bold. Nothing Lord deWode has or will offer me would induce me to betray you."

"He has tried to bribe you?"

She dampened her lips as she stared at the hem of Audra's burgundy kirtle. "When last he was here, he questioned me and offered me rewards if I would answer with the truth. He questioned all of those within your chambers."

"About?"

"What men you favored." She gripped Audra's robe and pressed it to her forehead. "I vow to you, milady, that we told him nothing. His gold and promises could not buy our hearts, which belong to you and to Bredonmere."

"What could you have told him when there was nothing to say?"

"Milady, you must not delay in marrying." Uneasily glancing over her shoulder, Shirley added, "Bredonmere's heir must have the protection of his father's name."

"Impossible."

"Impossible? The man is dead?" Her hands flew to her mouth. "Crandall?"

Audra might have laughed under other circumstances, but no laughter bubbled through her when everything she had worked for was collapsing around her. "Do not be silly. Crandall was a trusted friend. No more. You are worrying yourself needlessly."

"You are not with child?"

"I was to be a nun," she said, hating the taste of hypocrisy in her mouth. "How can you ask me such a question?"

"Forgive me, milady, but I fear for you."

Shirley did not believe her. Audra wanted to be

honest with this dear friend, yet she knew she could not.

Although her middle ached, Audra hurriedly dressed. She had Shirley bring her writing materials. This message to the king must be written and delivered without procrastination. The words came quickly, and she hoped the answer would come as swiftly.

Giving the rolled parchment to Shirley to deliver to a messenger, Audra went through the outer rooms as fast as her thick robes would allow her to move. She did not slow her pace as she went down the steps. If she could stay ahead of her disquiet, she might be able to ignore the truth.

The smells of the day's first meal threatened to undo her again, so she did not pause in the great hall. Coming out into the inner bailey, she took a deep breath of the rain-washed air.

She heard a shout and saw a rider going at full speed across the drawbridge. Her message was on its way to the king. All she had to do was wait.

Her fingers touched her still flat abdomen. She no longer had as much time as she had hoped.

Fleming wished he was anywhere but Bredonmere. Already this morning, he had had to put a halt to a fight between one of Lord deWode's men and one of Lord Wykemarch's. He had separated them, then knocked their heads together before sending them reeling across the inner bailey with instructions to remember that they were in Bredonmere, not in some low tavern. Minutes later, he had interrupted three more of Lord deWode's men who were pestering one of the kitchen maids. Then there had been the incident with two men, whom he had not bothered to identify, racing their horses through the outer bailey.

If the devil himself came to gather all these unwanted guests and take them to his black pit, Fleming would have offered his assistance with glee. Not only were the barons' men causing trouble, Bredonmere's men-at-arms flinched at any sound. Every nerve was set to detonate, and he must stop that. He was unsure how long he could be successful.

Storming up the stairs to the guard tower along the east wall, he looked skyward. The sun was only a small way above the trees. It would be a long day and a longer night before he could relax again.

He went into the guardroom, then froze as he saw who was standing by the table in its center. "Milord, greetings," he said, keeping his fury from his voice.

Robert smiled. "A most interesting configuration on this board."

"I did not know you were a devotee of chess, milord."

Pretending that he had not noticed the sarcastic edge Fleming put on his title, Robert said, "I enjoy any game which requires guile and skill."

"That is common knowledge when we learned of how you betrayed all of us."

"How have I betrayed you, Fleming?"

Fleming pursed his lips, making him look old beyond his years. "You have deceived milady by taking on another identity, and—"

"How have I betrayed *you*?"

"You . . ." He faltered, then turned away. His shoulders squared before he added, "It matters little what you did to me, milord. It matters greatly to me how you have treated Bredonmere and milady."

Robert sat on the bench and rested his elbow on the table. Scanning the chessboard, he swept a bishop across the board in a flamboyant motion guaranteed to catch Fleming's notice. "You know as well as I that you and the men you had remaining in the wake of the Death could not have prevented deWode from claiming Bredonmere."

"Lady Audra's claim was the only true one."

"That would have meant little if deWode claimed the manor by right of conquest."

Fleming frowned as he sat across from him. Picking up a knight, he leaped it forward to counteract the bishop's attack. He folded his arms on the table. "I must admit that, as Bourne the armorer, you taught me and the others skills even the earl did not know."

"So you could protect Lady Audra and her fief."

"From deWode and that damnable Lynx!"

When Robert brought his queen into play, he said, "Check. Lynx is no longer a problem for Audra."

"He is gone?" Fleming looked up from the board, anticipation in his eyes and his scowl fading. "How do you know, milord?"

"Even an outlaw as dauntless as Lynx would not be imprudent enough to challenge Bredonmere when all these trained men wait behind its walls."

"Confronting us openly has not been his way, as you have seen." His lips twisted. "I would gladly see his neck in a rope for the way he has treated Lady Audra."

Robert leaned back against the bench. "His attacks on her tofts?"

"Not her lands, but her."

"Explain."

"He is a bold bastard, not offering her the consideration a countess deserves. I have seen him act as if she is a wench he would tumble in the nearest bed of straw."

"Your lady is a lovely woman."

"I cannot deny that, but—" He wore a grim smile as he moved his bishop to take Robert's queen from the board. "A woman without protection is doomed."

"My very thought." With a low chuckle, he brought a rook from the far edge of the board. "Check and mate, my friend. Protection can come from unexpected, startling sources."

As Robert stood, Fleming stared up at him. Slowly the younger man came to his feet, too. When Robert held out his hand, Fleming grasped it.

"Never forget," Robert said, "that I have vowed to halt deWode from profiting in any way."

Fleming nodded, started to speak, then hesitated.

"Say what you think, Fleming. You never tempered your words to me before."

He dug the pointed toe of his boot into a crevice in the stone floor. Without looking at Robert, he said, "We agree that deWode must not hold, but you need to know, milord, that I will abide by milady's wishes on her choice of the next earl of Bredonmere."

"Again we agree."

"Do we?"

"We do . . . at least until deWode is gone from here."

"And then?"

"Then we may no longer be allies, my friend."

As Lord Wykemarch strode past him, as assured as the rook he had just moved across the board, Fleming backed away. He had already seen that Lord Wykemarch could be a powerful and valuable ally. He dreaded the day when he might have to consider him an enemy.

Audra smoothed her robes and glanced at the shield on the wall by the door of the bathing room. She still appeared as slim as the day she arrived at Bredonmere. Hurrying out of the room before Shirley could take note of her peculiar motions, she went into her bedchamber.

Cold air buffeted her. Shocked that anyone would have left the window ajar on a chilly evening, she rushed to close it. The night air gnawed at her bare hands and sent a renewed ache across her fingers, which recalled Gifford's abuse.

She went to sit by the hearth as Shirley hurried through the bedchamber and out into the antechamber. Holding out her hands to the fire, she was grateful for the silence. All day, she had been haunted by Gifford's insistence that she take heed of all the reasons why he would make Bredonmere a good lord. She had to admit that, if he was being honest, he was a more capable lord of his own lands than she had guessed. That he could recite numbers about the harvest and his tofts astonished her, although he refused to answer any questions she asked. She was coming to believe he had done no more than memorize the facts his steward had given him to impress her.

When she felt lips pressing against her throat, she gasped. Looking up, she saw amusement and candid desire in Robert's eyes.

"You look as beautiful as the first morn of spring," he murmured in her ear. As he stroked the fine wool of her robe, which was the same blue as her eyes, he adjusted the gold trim on her gorget circling her face.

"How did you get in here?"

He pointed to the window. "I have found that way allows for no questions."

"Are you mad?"

"With desire for you, Audra. To see you throughout the day, to learn that you have been in deWode's company when you should be in my arms, I am becoming quite mad."

He held out his hand to her, and she could not keep from staring. Never had Robert looked so much the son of a duke. The inside of his thigh-length black cloak was the same scarlet as the trim along his dark green tunic. On his shoulder where it hooked onto his tunic, a gold medallion was imprinted with an emblem that was too intricate for her to see without moving closer. That she must not do, for she knew how easily she could be enmeshed in the magic of his touch. She let him bring her to her feet, but withdrew her hand posthaste.

"I had hoped to have this time to speak with you alone before we join deWode in the great hall," Robert said, his voice once again as cool as the night wind that had invaded her room.

"What do you wish to say to me?"

"To be cautious."

"I am."

"Moreso than ever." He cupped her right hand in his. "This torment is only an example of what you might suffer if you fail to acquiesce to good sense."

She dropped her voice to a whisper, "A message is already on its way to the king."

"To question all the missives you have received?"

"Yes."

When he smiled, she was astonished. She had thought he would chide her for contacting the king

about the decision to let her choose between him and
Lord deWode.

"You have learned well the lessons I taught you
when I was here last, pretty one."

"Bourne never—"

"Not Bourne, but another."

"Lynx never—"

His fingertip against her lips silenced her again.
"The lessons were in the answers I did not give you,
for then you had to find them yourself and learn to
hold this manor until I could come to you with the
king's decree to deny deWode his easy victory." He
held out his hand and bowed his head. "Milady, it
would be my honor to bring you into the great hall."

Audra nodded as she set her hand on his. Not
once had she thought of Lynx as her teacher, but as
she thought of their many conversations, she recalled
how his taunting words had goaded her to work harder to make Bredonmere invincible and proud once
more. She should owe him a debt of gratitude, but he
did not hide that he had done this to fulfill his vow to
prevent deWode from claiming the fief.

When Audra arrived at the great hall with
Robert, Gifford deWode rose to his feet at the raised
table. He stormed down from the table to intercept
their path near the central hearth.

"It grieves me, milady," he said furiously, "to see
you enduring this knave's attentions."

"Lord Wykemarch has been gracious," she
answered.

"Tonight he has. You are unfamiliar with the real
man lurking behind his false polish."

Robert gave him a condescending nod. "You
wound me with your words that suggest Lady Audra
fails to see clearly."

"I suggest only that she has been misled by her kind heart." Plucking her hand from Robert's, he bowed over it. "Forgive me if I said anything to distress you."

"You both distress me!" she said, pulling her hand away. "I would rather you speak without these honeyed words that mean nothing. If you think to impress upon me your diplomatic skills, let me assure you that, in these days when every manor is weakened by the Death, there are scant occasions for the insincerity of court protocol."

When Robert chuckled, Gifford frowned and said, "If you wish me to speak plainly, milady, let me tell you that I have no yearning to listen to more of the brayings of this ass. You banished him from Bredonmere, but he did not obey you. I would be proud if you would ask me to remind him of that order."

Audra was tempted to throw her hands up in the air and let the two men argue. As she was about to say that, Robert stepped forward to stand between her and Gifford.

"There is but one way to decide this." He smiled at his rival. "Of course, it would require both skill and bravery, so you must ask yourself if you can play any part in it."

DeWode bristled. "You insult me, Wykemarch."

"No, I suspect I give you credit where you deserve none." Holding up his hands to silence the baron's bluster, he said, "I propose a way to settle this whole matter of which of us shall be the next lord of Bredonmere in a chivalrous way that should satisfy both the needs of Bredonmere and our king."

"Have I no say in this?" demanded Audra.

"Speak," ordered deWode, ignoring her.

Robert resisted acknowledging Audra's frustration. He was tempted to soothe her pain, but he must put an end to her suffering. Allowing this decision to linger unresolved even a moment longer could destroy everything she had sought to bring to Bredonmere.

"It has reached my ears that you have been boasting all day about your prowess in the lists," he answered, pulling his knife and rocking it back and forth in front of him.

"'Twas no boast. Only the truth."

"A rare quality here of late," Audra said. "Milords, I implore you to recall that the king has given *me* the right to make the decision about the next lord of Bredonmere."

DeWode chuckled as he rested his hand on a table at his side. "A task of which you are incapable."

Before Audra could voice the fury burning in her eyes, Robert drew back his knife and threw it. The blade drove into the table a finger's breadth from deWode's hand. The baron jerked away and stared at him.

"A challenge," Robert said with a smile. "I challenge you, Lord deWode, to a joust. The winner is the one who holds his seat longest. The prize? Bredonmere and Lady Audra, of course."

DeWode reached for the blade, but Audra was fast. She tugged it from the table and dropped it to the floor. "Have you lost your wits?" she demanded. "So many have perished from the Death, and you suggest risking your lives needlessly."

"Nay, 'tis not needlessly. 'Tis for a fair prize," said deWode. "I accept your challenge, Wykemarch. Name the date and place."

"One week from today. Here at Bredonmere.

That will give both of us a chance to train on the field chosen for the joust."

"Will neither of you listen to me? In spite of your assumptions, I remain the lady of Bredonmere."

"One sevenday from today," deWode answered. "It shall be my greatest pleasure to watch you fall from your mount, Wykemarch."

As he called for wine to seal the agreement as if he was already Bredonmere's lord, Audra turned and walked toward the door. Her rage blinded her, and she refused to hearken to the call of her name. She was halfway up the stairs when her arm was grasped. Trying to shake off the familiar grip, she was surprised when Robert released her.

"Audra, you must listen to me. We have only a few seconds while deWode busies himself ordering a cask of your father's best wine for his men. Then he will take note of my absence and yours."

"Why should I listen to you? You do not listen to me when I urge you to be sensible."

"I made the challenge to deWode to protect this manor."

She paused on the stairs and faced him. His eyes were level with hers, and she saw honesty within them. "Why?" she whispered. "So you can ensure it will suffer no damage when you claim it as the next earl of Bredonmere?"

"Because you care so much for these people and the legacy left you by your father."

"Which you wish to take from me."

He took her hand and drew her up the steps and along the hall to her audience chamber. "Audra, you know you will never be allowed to hold alone. Turn deWode and me away, and another will be sent to you." He frowned. "Or deWode will come back with the king's true blessing next time. You should know that your neighbor Norwell is much in favor of deWode holding Bredonmere."

"Norwell is an imbecile."

"He commands much respect among the king's court." Closing the door behind them, he said, "I need to speak with you alone while I can."

Her heart stopped in midbeat. His words suggested he feared what the joust might bring. But if he thought Gifford could defeat him, why had he challenged him? She dared not think of the reasons. Instead she had Shirley clear the room. She took a seat on the bench where she dispensed justice for the manor. He sat next to her and, taking her hand, turned it over and pressed his mouth to her palm.

"There is much you need to know," he murmured, "but I would prefer to relish the sweet flavors of your skin."

His hand caressed her shoulder. If he was killed, never again would she feel this exquisite touch. As his warm breath touched her skin, she let him draw her back against him.

"I needed an excuse to remain at Bredonmere as well as one that would keep deWode here, too."

"Keep him here? I thought you wanted him gone!" She turned enough to see the fury in his eyes.

"A murder was committed in my name, and I shall find the one who did this deed and if it was done at deWode's command."

"You must not!" She glanced toward the door, but it remained closed. "If it was to become known that you and Lynx are one, Gifford would use that to his advantage. He would gladly see you pay for Crandall's murder."

"Lynx is accused of that murder, but Robert

Bourne is not. That is one of the reasons I returned as I did. That is why I asked for a week's delay before the joust."

Her fingers rose along his clean-shaven cheek before drifting through his hair. When she guided his lips toward her face, his mouth greedily claimed hers. Her breath was frayed when he drew away and stood.

"Do not tempt me with your sweetness," he murmured, "when bitterness consumes me. I am so close to my goal."

"Vengeance?" She rose and shook her head. "What will that gain you, Robert?"

"I don't know, but I do know I owe Crandall the obligation of finding his murderer as I owe my sister the duty of seeing deWode pay for his crimes against her." He framed her face with his hands. "I know you think I have little honor, Audra, and what I possess is tarnished. I will not be stopped from seeing justice done to those who deserve to suffer its punishment."

"Even if you must die for it?"

"Yes."

19

Robert dumped a bucket of water over his head and shivered. The water streamed down the back of his leather tunic that had sealed itself to his back with sweat. This morning's practice runs in the cool, fresh air had been satisfying. He had left deWode there to continue his practice. His rival needed every moment of work to improve. The end of the sevenday was only two days from today, and Robert would be glad to send deWode spinning into the dirt.

A malicious smile crossed his face as he wiped water from his eyes and looked at the mud on the earthen floor of the stable. If all went for the best, rain would fall the morning of the joust, and the field would be as muddy as this floor. What a splash deWode would make when he landed in a puddle!

Taking a piece of the cloth used to brush down the horses, he rubbed his own head as he walked out into the early morning sunshine. He whistled lightly under his breath. Although he had never expected his vengeance against deWode to unfold in this way, he could not complain.

A lyrical laugh drifted across the inner bailey, seizing his attention as powerfully as he gripped his jousting lance. He looked to his right and smiled.

Audra was walking with two small girls. She held their hands, swinging them in tempo with their steps. As he admired the way her gown flowed along with each step, she led the children to the sheepfold that had been set not far from the stable. Wrapping the cloth around his neck, he followed.

He said nothing to disturb her as she bent to lean on the low fence. The children chattered with excitement as she pointed out a pair of newborn lambs. They started to reach over the fence, but she gently drew their hands back.

"You must not disturb the lambs until they are a few hours older," he heard her say, her scold as kind as her smile. "The ewes do not like the scent of us on their lambs, and it confuses them, for they seek their own babes with the help of scent."

"So cute!" cried one little girl, clapping her hands.

"So cute!" echoed the other.

At a deep laugh, Audra looked up, startled. She wondered how long Robert had been standing there. She had thought she never could be unaware of him, even when she was lost in the delight of childish company. Her stomach fluttered when she saw the water in his hair and the way his tunic clung to his strong body. She took a single step toward him, wanting to be enfolded in his strong arms. Then terror clamped its hold on her as she realized why his clothes were damp.

By all the saints, why would neither man heed her request to put an end to this joust before tragedy struck Bredonmere anew? Both were determined to prove the other the lesser man. She had learned it was useless to waste her breath remonstrating with them.

"Milord, you are welcome to view the sheep, if you wish," she said.

Her words must have been colder than she intended, for the little girls grabbed her hands as they stared up at the man who was whispered about throughout the manor house.

"Good morning, milady." He bowed his head toward her, then smiled. "And to you, young ladies. May I say that this is a charming tableau?"

"The lambs are adorable, aren't they?"

"I thought rather of the sight of you with these pretty lasses."

The little girls giggled, then ran back toward the kitchen.

Robert's brows arched with surprise. "Did I frighten them?"

She laughed. "They were overwhelmed with your compliment. You must learn more about children, Robert. They giggle when they are nervous as well as when they are happy."

"You seem to know their ways well."

She looked back at the lambs bounding through the sheepfold. "Working with the children was my greatest pleasure at Clarendon Abbey."

"I think you shall make a wondrous mother when you have babes of your own." He must not have noticed her flinch, for he continued, "Now you have both the children of your manor and your sheep."

"Yes." She did not dare to let her thoughts show, for Robert must not suspect the secret she kept within her. She made an effort to smile as he came to stand beside her. "Look, Robert! See how strong the lambs are. Even in this short time, the breeding has improved our flocks. A decade from now, Bredonmere wool will be the best at any market day."

His damp finger beneath her chin tipped her face toward his. "This is a side of you, milady, I have never seen."

"You thought I began this project as a lark?"

He shook his head. "I never questioned your fervor, only your expectations, but I see I was wrong to do that. You have pragmatic plans for this manor."

Pushing herself away from the fence, she said, "I must. Bredonmere depends on me now."

"I see that."

"Do you?" She gripped his arm. "Do you see, as well, Robert, why I wish no one to halt the work I have begun?"

"It gives you the great pleasure you found working with children in Clarendon Abbey?"

"Yes, that great pleasure."

"But," he said as he stepped closer to her, "is it the greatest pleasure you have found here?"

His fingers slipped along her arms before cupping her elbows and bringing her to him. As his mouth lowered toward hers, she whispered, "You know it is not."

Relinquishing herself to his masterful kiss, she pushed aside all her worries. Today, for this one moment, she wanted to grasp that sweetest pleasure. She knew, as her fingers stroked his soaked tunic, how fleeting it could be beneath the shadow of the joust to come, a joust she had found no way to stop.

*   *   *

The day of the challenge dawned cool and with only a suggestion of clouds hanging in the blue autumn sky. Audra stood at her window and searched the countryside, but no fog or rain offered the excuse to cancel the joust. Not that anyone within the manor house would heed her command. Robert was being as foolish as Gifford, and each time she walked through the keep's corridors, she heard the whispers of bets being taken. Guilty glances had met her furious glares, but nothing could stop the escalating excitement.

She opened the window and took a breath of the icy air that blew into the room. Her gaze went to the door of the church across the inner bailey. Could Father Jerome have obstructed this? Lord deWode would not heed the request of the brother of his enemy.

Nothing had changed in the past sevenday. Even though she had twice ridden with Robert to speak with the families on the southern tofts, no clue pointed to the false Lynx who had ordered Crandall's murder. She knew there was something they were failing to see, something right in front of them, but Robert was as blind to it as she was.

When Shirley came into the room, she reached past Audra and closed the window with a bang. "Milady, you will take a chill and sicken. That could be dangerous for—"

Audra squared her shoulders. Shirley had not mentioned her suspicions of Audra's pregnancy again, but Audra knew her body servant would not be dissuaded from the truth. Nor would Shirley speak of it to anyone else. For that, Audra was grateful.

She walked to the bench in front of the hearth and sat to stare at the roaring fire. If the crackling sound of the flames enveloped her, she might silence the recriminations in her heart. She should have found a way to put an end to this challenge.

She did not realize she had whispered as much until Shirley came to sit beside her. "Milady, you should not castigate yourself, for nothing you do shall prevent what must unfold this afternoon."

"There would be no need for them to ride the joust if I had chosen my husband."

"It is more than you, milady. It is more than Bredonmere that they contest."

Audra smiled sadly. "You are so wise, my friend."

"No wisdom is necessary, only eyes to see the truth and ears to take note of their words."

Rising, for the disquiet within her refused to let her sit still, she asked, "And what is to become of Bredonmere when the joust is complete and one is the victor? Do I surrender my birthright?"

"You must listen to your heart."

"So easy it is to say that, but the longings of my heart must be second to the needs of Bredonmere."

"Why?"

She turned to look at Shirley, who still sat on the bench. The glow of the fire had added color to the old woman's cheeks, but within her eyes, an even more intense fire blazed.

Shirley whispered, "Listen if you will, milady, to the counsel of a woman who has lived more years than you."

"Say what you wish."

"Save for you, I would vow that no one loves Bredonmere more than I. Yet my loyalty is to you as the last of the Travers family. Bredonmere is a wondrous thing, but it has no heart without you to give it one. If you betray your heart's longings, milady, you may betray the very thing you seek to preserve."

Audra nodded. "Shirley, please wait upon me in the great hall. I shall join you there. If all goes well, mayhap it will be to announce this afternoon's blood-sport is decided."

She hurried from the room before Shirley could respond. Climbing the stairs to the upper floor and the room that once had been her brother's, she did not stop except to close the upper chamber's door behind her.

The bedchamber was not as grand as her rooms below, but it did have the luxury of a bathing room. When she heard sounds from it, she turned in that direction. She had not gone two steps when her way was blocked by the blond lad she knew was Robert's squire and the one who had been Lynx's companion.

"Eatton, step aside. I wish to speak with Robert."

"Milady, if you will await him—"

"I wish to speak with him now."

A muted chuckle came from the bathing room, and Robert stepped into the narrow hall. Cloth was wrapped around his lean hips, and water sparkled across his chest. "Eatton, you would be wise to learn that Lady Audra will not be stopped when she wants something."

"Do you know that?" she asked, trying to ignore how her fingers tingled with the anticipation of touching the warm breadth of his naked chest.

"I have learned it, oft-times to my detriment."

She closed the distance between them. As her fingers wandered through the hair on his chest, she whispered, "Then let this time be for your welfare. I ask you to reconsider this horrible thing you are about to do."

He shook his head, spraying water onto the floor. "Do not ask the impossible of me, Audra."

"You called for this joust simply to give yourself time to find Crandall's murderer. We have found nothing. We may never know the truth. Let me send deWode away."

"That would call more trouble upon you. Do you think he will leave willingly now?"

"Do you think he will leave willingly if you best him?"

His laugh was ironic. "It is my misfortune to know deWode well. He never lingers where he has been shown to be the gutless fool he is."

"You could die in this joust. Then I would have no choice but to wed Lord deWode."

"You and I both know that you shall find a way to convince the king otherwise." He chuckled, then grew sober as he walked with her back into the bedchamber. "I have no intention of dying on the field today. You should have no doubts after the last meeting you witnessed between deWode and me."

"I have no doubts that he will prove to be a treacherous foe."

He motioned to his squire. Eatton still refused to meet Audra's eyes, but he came forward with the mail Robert would wear during the joust.

Audra sat on a bench and said nothing as Robert donned his gambeson. The thick undergarment was quilted to protect him from the roughness of his mail. Because it was to be a tournament with but a single event, he chose the older style links of metal instead of the armor made in plates to enclose the body. Sitting, he hooked the greaves around his shins. The armor would protect his legs from a chance strike by a lance ricocheting off a shield. His low boots were hidden beneath sollerets, which covered the top of his feet.

"Will you be able to ride in that?" she could not keep from asking when Eatton hefted Robert's hauberk. The heavy coat of mail was reinforced with metal plates on the elbows and must have weighed half of what she did.

"Well enough to prove to deWode that he is a fool." He turned to his man. "My surcoat, Eatton."

"Which one, milord?"

"Today I ride beneath the banner of the house of Exbridge."

"Aye, milord," Eatton said and handed the folded garment to him.

When Robert pulled it over his head, Audra stared, unable to halt herself. Across the scarlet surcoat rose a wild cat, its hind legs ready to propel it onto its victim. Claws were bared on all four feet, and the creature's mouth was open in a snarl.

"Lynx," she whispered.

He took his helmet from Eatton and smiled. "Although I did not come here to ride the night with my father's knowledge, I am his son. The lynx has guarded my family's heritage well as it has yours, milady."

When he picked up his mail gauntlets, he held out his hand to her. Her fingers trembled as they rose to settle on his. Her cuffs matched his crimson surcoat, she realized with horror. Lord deWode would see this as a token of her favor. Mayhap it was, although she was not willing to trust her own thoughts now.

"Is my birthright the only thing that matters to you when you ride today?" she asked.

"You know better than that." His mouth found

hers with the ease of the love beating in her heart. Lightly he held her, not pressing her to the lynx on his chest. "There is much we must speak of when this nonsense is completed."

"Yes," she whispered as she touched her stomach, "there is much we must speak of, if you survive this joust."

"Be brave, milady," Robert murmured as Eatton opened the door.

"I shall try."

He smiled. "You will succeed, for you can be no other way."

He led her from the room, and she tried to concentrate on his words, but whatever he said washed past her on the torrent of her fear. This day should never have dawned. She should have made her decision upon Lord deWode's arrival. It should have been so easy, for she abhorred deWode. Yet how could she love a man who had twice betrayed her and now had made no secret of his yearning to possess her birthright?

The great hall was filled with her men and Robert's and Lord deWode's. A hush smothered all voices as she entered the hall on Robert's arm. Stepping away from him, she went to where Fleming stood, an anxious expression lining his face.

"Is all as it should be?" she asked.

"Nothing is as it should be, milady," he blurted. His face flushed as he muttered, "I beg your pardon."

"Never apologize for speaking the truth, my friend."

He nodded. "Then I shall tell you that the field is prepared for the joust, but not a man among your men-at-arms is eager to swear loyalty to the victor."

·"Neither man?"

His hand stroked the hilt of his sword. "We shall follow you, milady. Your choice is our choice."

Audra looked across the hall to where Robert and Lord deWode were surrounded by their allies. "It is apparently my choice no longer."

"If you wish—"

"What I wish cannot be." She put her hand on his arm. "Urge every man to stay his hand this afternoon, no matter the outcome. I shall have no blood spilled needlessly."

"Any of us would die for you."

"Then let it be when we face the worst that is yet before us."

"This is not the worst?" he asked, fear creeping into his voice.

"I fear it shan't be."

Someone had thought of Lady Audra's comfort. When she arrived at the empty field beyond the manor house, she discovered a bench had been placed beneath an impromptu pavilion. The material wrapped around low walls and up over the top was whipped by the inconsistent wind. It would do no more than keep out the coldest air. She tightened her cloak around her.

"Do I have you to thank, Father?" she asked as she stepped into the pavilion.

"Fleming, milady."

She stared out onto the field. Rope had been strung to keep back the spectators, and the center was as empty as her heart.

Father Jerome said quietly, "Do not look so bleak. In a contest such as this, only honor should be injured."

"Honor! I have heard much of honor from Robert this sevenday, but what honor is there in dying pointlessly?"

"Do sit," Shirley urged, tugging on Audra's cloak.

She ignored both of them. Although she had never witnessed a tilt, even within the walls of the cloister, she had heard tales of men being maimed or killed while participating in what was supposed to be sport among friends. There would be no friends at this meeting.

A pair of flags flapped at opposite ends of the empty field. A rope hung between them through the heart of the field. She knew each rider must stay on his side of the rope. Father Jerome had tried to explain the intricate rules of the joust, but she had been too distraught to listen.

Fleming came to stand before her. Only her insistence had persuaded him to accept the position as the marshall of the field. He would have the dubious honor of directing the course of the joust and declaring the victor.

"They await your pleasure, milady, to take the field."

She glanced at Father Jerome. Could there be a way to suspend this at this final hour? When the priest put his hand beneath her elbow, she let him steer her toward the bench.

"Give Lord Wykemarch and Lord deWode my permission to enter the field," she said in a voice as hollow as Fleming's.

"Milady," murmured Shirley, "if you wish to depart—"

"Say no more!" she snapped. She would not let the idea of leaving tempt her.

Shouts and jeers rose into the bright sky above the splash of color from the trees. She glanced at Fleming, who was tensing at the sound that could signal more trouble.

"Prepare your men to be ready upon your command," she said softly.

"Prepare yourself as well," he replied. Looking back at the walls of Bredonmere, he added, "There is no dishonor in your seeking haven within the walls if our guests are unhappy with the results of this joust."

"I will not thwart you in the execution of your duties." She stared grimly across the field as Fleming went to deliver her command to the two contestants.

"He will be fine, milady," came Father Jerome's soothing voice from beside her.

She turned to meet his dark eyes. She had spent much time in his company in the last week as she sought the strength to face this ordeal. Not once had he coerced her to select his brother as her husband, although his loyalties were clear.

"Will he, Father?" she returned with pain in her voice.

"You give my brother little credit for skills you have seen him exhibit so seldom." He smiled as he sat beside her. "Never forget that he fights for something he wants desperately."

She could not halt the bitterness that crept into her voice. "I know he fights to gain Bredonmere."

"Are you certain that is all he fights to gain?"

Audra was prevented from answering by the arrival of two riders in full tournament armor riding across the brown grass. More cheers and insults were shouted across the field.

Audra leaned forward, gripping the low wall in front of her. Even from here, she could not mistake

Robert on the black steed he had ridden when he ranged across Bredonmere's lands as Lynx. The red plume danced atop his helmet. She looked at the other rider and tensed when Lord deWode suddenly urged his horse toward the pavilion.

Gifford deWode stopped only an arm's length from the bench where Lady Audra sat between her nagging body servant and the priest who would be vanquished along with his brother. Hearing other hoofbeats, he turned awkwardly.

Wykemarch was ever the fool! If he feared that Gifford was going to abduct Lady Audra, he had misjudged. He wanted Wykemarch's blood fertilizing this field. He wanted Wykemarch to gasp his final breath while deWode claimed the woman who would bring him more pleasure because Wykemarch had wanted her. He would have Audra and Bredonmere. Wykemarch would have only the unmarked grave he deserved beside the others who had halted Gifford from claiming what should have been his.

He smiled as he saw the fury in Father Jerome's eyes. The priest would be the second to die swiftly, followed by Fleming who was too loyal to the countess of Bredonmere. Father Jerome must know that his churchly raiment would not protect him.

Gifford's gaze went to Lady Audra, who was looking past him. That told him Wykemarch was nearing the pavilion. Good! Let his enemy hear what he had to say. "Milady, I beg a boon."

He faltered when she asked in a voice as empty of emotion as her face, "What do you wish, milord?"

"A token to wear into this joust."

"What?" Audra gasped, astonished that he would dare to make her choose so publicly between him and Robert.

Behind him, Robert slowly raised the visor on his basinet. His face was distorted with the fury he was fighting to control.

Regaining her poise, she said, "I think your request is most unwise."

"Milady, I only seek to show my esteem," Lord deWode said with the false smile that sent cramps of fear through her. "It is meet that you have a champion on the field of honor."

As she started to refuse, she saw Robert shake his head the merest bit. Instantly she understood. She could do nothing to send a spark into Lord deWode's men, who were waiting for any chance to secure their lord's hold on Bredonmere. She must follow all the traditions of the lists.

"A riband," whispered Shirley. "Give him one from your sleeve, milady."

Audra held out her arm and let her servant remove the white silk laced through her sleeve. When Shirley handed it to her, she held it out to Father Jerome. Triumph glowed in Lord deWode's eyes as the priest spoke a blessing over it. Hearing the Latin words she doubted the baron understood, she hid her smile. Father Jerome was asking only that the material not be ruined when Lord deWode was unseated.

Standing, she offered the riband to Lord deWode. He signaled for his page to take it. As the lad tied it to his master's left arm, Lord deWode smiled.

With a shout, he held up his arm. "I ride for the honor of the countess of Bredonmere! Hail me, Lady Audra Travers's champion."

Raucous cheers rang out from his men. Swords clanged against each other in a vicious cacophony.

"Later, Audra, I will show you my gratitude," he said more quietly.

She stiffened, and Shirley's arm went protectively around her shoulders. When she did not reply to the taunt, he lifted his sword in a salute to her. He flashed a victorious smile at Robert before snapping his visor in place. With a cloud of dust rising from the hard ground, he rode to his side of the rope.

Waving away the light brown cloud, Audra looked up to see Robert urging his horse closer to the pavilion. He chuckled as he said, "A posturing fool is still nothing more than a fool."

"You would do well to remember that even a fool can be lucky," answered his brother.

Instead of answering him, Robert turned to Audra. "Milady, it is unprecedented that two champions carry the same lady's token on the field, but then we have never followed traditional ways, have we?"

"Robert, there is no reason to antagonize him more." She tensed again as she heard a shout as Lord deWode entertained his men by slashing a pattern through the air with his broadsword.

"I ask that you honor me as well," he continued as if she had remained silent.

"Milady, this is not wise," Shirley interjected while Father Jerome asked her to consider any decision with utmost care.

"The choice is yours, milady," Robert said as his dark gaze caught hers.

How often had she looked into those enigmatic eyes, searching for something unknown and finding love? Robert Bourne had demanded nothing less from her than when he had ridden as Lynx: to give him only what her heart longed him to have. If he would offer her the same respect that she once had heard on his lips when he acknowledged her as the rightful holder of Bredonmere, she could forgive him the duplicity that had brought him into her life and her heart.

Robert Bourne . . . Gifford deWode. There could be but one choice if she were to safeguard her beloved fief, and she must delay making it no longer.

The autumn wind swept aside any noise as she stood again. Even Shirley's protests died when Audra held out her other sleeve. Murmuring a prayer, Shirley broke the few threads holding the riband in place. She unlaced it through the material and set it in Audra's hand.

When she let it fall through her fingers to the dirt in front of the pavilion, a rumble raced through the crowd. She did not lower her eyes from the unfettered fury in Robert's face at such an insult.

"Father?" she asked.

"Milady?" Anxiety strained his voice.

"If you would help me up onto the bench, I would be grateful."

Audra did not look at him or anyone but Robert as the priest assisted her. With her head brushing the fabric of the pavilion's roof, she held up her empty hands. Her voice was not raised, but in the quiet, it seemed as loud as a scream.

"You ask me to choose, Robert Bourne, Lord Wykemarch. That is only right, for King Edward has given me that honor. I have thought long on this."

Astonishment replaced the rage in Robert's eyes as she lifted her crucifix from her breast. Drawing it over her head, she held it out to Father Jerome. His prayer was silent, giving her no clue to what blessing he was imploring God to bring upon her action.

She motioned for Robert to come closer. When he turned his black steed so he was aligned with the front of the pavilion, she hooked the pendant around his neck. The gold clattered against the steel but caught the rays of the sun to shine gloriously.

"Milady, this lies over my heart," he said as he touched the cross. "It will be deWode's intention to aim his lance at this very spot. Your precious crucifix could be ruined."

"A gift given from the heart cannot be returned." She signaled for Father Jerome to hand her down. Looking up at the confusion in Robert's eyes, she could not help smiling. It was ironic that, at this point, when she was sure of herself as she had not been since leaving Clarendon Abbey, he was filled with the uncertainty that had plagued her.

Robert lowered his visor into place again and rode to his side of the field. When Shirley's hand settled on hers, Audra put her other one atop her maid's. She desperately needed the solace that could not be voiced. Her heart had spoken for all to hear. Now she must await the consequences of her decision.

Across the field, deWode swore vividly. Audra would pay for this! She had shamed him for the last time with her womanly wiles. When all her allies were dead, she would learn the price of begrudging him what should be his.

"My lance!" he snapped. When his squire did not respond instantly, he kicked him with an iron-covered boot. The lad groaned and leaped forward to grasp one of the wooden lances waiting on the ground.

"Milord?" he asked, holding it up.

"Not that one! The blue one!"

"But, milord, that—"

"None of your insolent lip! The blue one!"

Terror bleached the lad's face as he handed the lance to his master.

"Prepare yourself," deWode said with a smile.

"Milord?" he asked in confusion.

"Soon you shall be squire to the earl of Bredon-mere." He hefted the lance and looked toward his rival.

Robert ignored deWode as he accepted his lance from Eatton. He balanced the long pole against his thigh as he mused, "DeWode does not intend for me to escape unscathed."

"Aye, milord. Beware for treachery." Eatton shook his head gravely. "If I see anything amiss—"

Adjusting himself in the saddle, he lowered his visor in place as he said, "Wish me luck."

"You have the greater skill, milord."

"But I may need good fortune to meet his treachery and survive."

Audra leaned forward as she watched the opponents align themselves, parrying as they moved their horses into place, although half a field separated them. She stared at Fleming, who still stood at the side of the field.

He walked to a central point where both men could see him. He carried a sword with a brightly dyed cloth tied to it. He raised it high. Shouts filled the air as he dropped the blade. Instantly dust rose like a whirlwind's passing.

On the back of his horse, Robert's ears were full of the crowd's roar and the pounding of hoofbeats. DeWode was coming at him at full tilt. Gauging the angle of the other man's long lance, he raised his shield. He prepared to meet his strike. Suddenly, he heard a signal. The call to battle for the men of Exbridge. He shifted forward in the saddle to better absorb the coming attack and raised his shield higher.

DeWode's lance glanced off the shield, shattering it as if it were made of the finest glass. The concussion shot up Robert's arm. His fingers numbed. As he fought to bring his horse to a stop, he looked down. Nothing was left of his shield but the straps wrapped around his forearm. He bent his arm cautiously. It was not broken.

Turning, he saw deWode stop. His own blow must have been ineffectual. Sainted Mary, what had happened? He had watched deWode's inept practices. He should have been able to down deWode in a single run.

Eatton ran up to him with a lance. Only then did Robert realize his other lance was broken off not far from the hilt. A cold smile twisted his lips when he saw deWode shaking his arm. His strike must have been more effective than he guessed.

"Milord, are you unhurt? DeWode was riding with a battle lance."

"Is that so?" His eyes narrowed as he regarded his enemy, who clearly wanted his death more than he had guessed. As he dropped the broken lance to the ground, Audra's crucifix clattered against the metal rings on his hauberk. His smile returned as he settled the cross in the center of his surcoat. Taking the new lance from Eatton, he said, "DeWode will not dare such a trick again. This time we shall ride more evenly matched."

"Milord, you have no shield!"

"Don't you remember the day my father bested me with nothing more than a short dagger? I learned his lesson well that day." He smiled as he recalled practicing that trick on Audra. As he turned his horse to face his foe, he said, "I'm grateful for your warning. Without it, I might now be dead."

Eatton nodded and stepped aside.

Robert looked at Fleming. A tendril of thought

entered his mind as sweetly as Audra's hair on his bare skin, but he pushed it aside. He could not think of her until he had forced deWode out of her life.

As Fleming dropped the sword, Robert shouted. His horse leaped forward as if struck by a lightning bolt. He pulled the reins to the left. Protecting his unguarded side, he raised his lance. With a crash that resounded throughout his body, it struck deWode.

He gave it a sharp twist as he would a broadsword. DeWode's lance cracked. Both pieces flew into the air. One hit deWode. He toppled from his horse.

Robert reined in his mount and jumped to the ground. Cheers resounded in his ears, but he ignored them. He limped toward deWode. The dampness of blood dripped down his right leg above his sollerets. He guessed a splinter had struck him.

Flipping back the visor on his helmet, he stepped over the rope. He folded his arms over his surcoat as he watched deWode struggle to his feet.

"It is over," Robert announced. "Admit your defeat, deWode. Admit that this manor and all it possesses are mine."

"This is not over. I pledge that to you." He raised his voice so it could be heard at the far corners of the field. "I shall see you dead before I leave Bredonmere in your hands."

Robert laughed. "You have no honor even now, deWode. With your announcement, all see that you have broken this vow to settle our differences with a joust as you have reneged on every other pledge. Bredonmere is mine."

"You shall have neither Bredonmere nor Lady Audra. The king—"

"Will be pleased I alone hold this fief. I have won

what I came here for, deWode, and to you I grant safe passage while you leave my lands. This is all mine. No man will dare to gainsay me on these lands for as long as I live. The prize is mine."

"And that is all that matters to you?" His mailed fists opened and closed by his side. "Possessing Bredonmere?"

He chuckled, exulting in his victory. "What matters to me most is seeing you denied what you want. Now you can know how it feels to lose something you want desperately. It is a small price to pay for what you did to my sister." He took a step toward deWode and jabbed a finger at his blue surcoat. "I have my revenge on you by taking this fief out of your bloodied hands. That is all that matters to me."

A soft gasp made him whirl. On Audra's face, he saw the pain of betrayal once more. That anguish slashed through him more fiercely than deWode's lance. He reached out to her. "Audra, listen to me."

"I have no need to listen, milord Wykemarch. You have spoken the truth within your accursed heart most plainly." She gathered her skirts and fled across the field.

DeWode's mocking laugh rang in his ears as Robert stared after her. His rival was right to sneer. By defeating deWode, Robert might have lost more than he won.

20

The rain battering at the windows of the great hall with the sharp sound of sleet was ebbing, and within the great hall, the fire in the great central pit kept the dampness at bay. It should have been a relaxing evening, but it was not. A troupe of minstrels, which had sought shelter at Bredonmere, sang and played with a festivity that did not reach the household. Those who still sat around the tables as the afternoon darkened into night were restive and curt.

Robert was aware of every glance in his direction as he sat at the raised table where, when he had been the fief's armorer, he never would have been received as an equal. He disregarded them. Instead he watched Audra as she walked among her people. Did she reassure them that her loyalty to them would never diminish even when she was his wife? Sainted Mary, this was not how he had imagined this moment of triumph.

He should be reveling in his achievement of showing all of Bredonmere that he was its master while deWode crawled away like the beaten cur he was. Instead he could think only of the betrayal in Audra's eyes when he was congratulated as the new earl. He had tasted passion on her soft lips this afternoon, but he feared her heart was now closed to him.

"There remains but one thing for you to do, brother," Father Jerome said as he came to sit beside him.

"What is that?"

He smiled as he gestured toward Audra, who was now deep in conversation with Fleming at the far end of the room. "Lady Audra is yours as is this manor."

"The manor is mine, I concur. Lady Audra?" He shook his head.

"She loves you."

He laughed without humor. "She loves a night rider. What other man must fight for his lady's affections with a delusion that he created?"

"Bah! You won her heart once by giving her what she needed." Jerome gripped his brother's arm. "You offered her the belief that she could hold, and hold she has."

"And well."

"No man could have done better."

"I suspect you are correct. When I have ridden with her during the past week, I have learned how she has inspired her villeins, for they strive to gain more of her appreciation. I have listened to her questions and watched how she took heed of the answers given to her. Her knowledge of the tofts and what they need to be profitable is remarkable. Even when I was here as the armorer, I failed to take note of that."

Father Jerome arched a single brow. "You failed to take note of many things, brother. While you played your childish games, you were twisting her heart with lies that bring no honor to our family. Today you have cloaked yourself in the glory of defeating deWode, but when you wore the night as a cloak, you won something more valuable. Yet you cast her heart aside as heartlessly as deWode cast aside our sister."

Robert's voice was low and taut with fury when he replied, "If you were not a man of the church, brother, I would demand your life for those words."

"Then prove them wrong."

"Just that simply?"

"Why not? There is Lady Audra. Here you sit. I can join you in the wedding rite."

"If she will have me."

"She will, if you can prove to her that you offer her something as precious as Bredonmere."

Robert shook his head. "There is nothing more precious than Bredonmere."

"To her or to you? She will sacrifice anything to secure her birthright. What would you do for this fief? Would you marry its lady and give up your life as a night rider and the freedom to ride from our father's lands to the king's court? Would you assume the comparatively dull life of an earl?"

Robert almost snapped a retort, but then smiled. "I see you did not set aside your Bourne wiles when you joined the church, brother."

"So what do you say? Everything is in place for a wedding."

"Yes, it is," he said slowly. His gaze went to where Audra was laughing with Fleming. Everything about her urged an unexpected sense of protectiveness in him. Wanting to shield her from deWode's cruelty had led to the joust that left him more bruised than he wished to admit. DeWode was now defeated, and . . .

He rose and went down the steps from the raised table. He noted how conversation dimmed to silence as he passed and began again in his wake. This was the Bredonmere he had first entered, a manor house frightened nigh to death by the plague that had swept over it, smothering all hope. Then hope had been resurrected by one woman's belief that Bredonmere could regain its former glory and more.

One woman. One extraordinary woman who had dared the impossible to make it possible and had risked everything for love. Now that woman and her manor and her dreams could be his.

With a few long strides, he crossed the great hall to where Bredonmere's lady was giving orders to a kitchen maid. He grasped Audra by the shoulders and whirled her into his arms, interrupting her in midword. He ignored the maid's gasp as he stared down at Audra's startled face.

Too seldom he had seen her loveliness below him through the enchanting hours of the night. His body tightened with desire as he knew that once his brother named them man and wife, the pleasure of her soft body would be his to enjoy for the rest of his days.

He pulled her against him, giving her no time to react before his mouth captured hers. When she softened in his arms, he sought within her mouth for the pleasure he would never tire of, wanting her more than he had the first night he crept into her room. When he finally pulled away and released her, there was no sound in the great hall save for her fevered breath.

Audra stepped back, brushing her hands against her gown. "Milord, that was most unexpected." When her voice trembled, she knew she was fooling no one but herself by pretending to be unmoved by Robert's caresses. She might despise him for twisting her into believing that she was as important to him as Bredonmere, but she loved him when he was this gentle yet demanding lover.

"As unexpected as this?"

Her eyes widened as he dropped to one knee and took her hand. A collective gasp exploded from her retainers, then a hush spread out as if she had shouted for silence.

"Milord— "

"Heed what I wish to say to you, Audra." Pressing his lips to her hand, he held it between his broader ones. "I would *ask* you to consider giving me the honor of becoming your husband."

"Ask? You are asking me if I wish to wed you?"

"I have made that obvious by begging you to be mine in front of your household."

"But the joust— "

"I am *asking* you now, Audra. Will you give me your answer?"

"When?"

A grin twisted his lips. "Now would be the best time."

The pain that had held her heart in icy tentacles broke in the warmth of his gaze. Her fingers stroked the strong line of his face and combed through the silk of his hair. When his eyes closed so he could better savor her touch, she was suffused with a happiness she had feared she never would know again.

He had deceived her. He had infuriated her. He had taught her of love. She had treasured his friendship and wisdom when she knew him as Bourne. She had delighted in his passions when he came to her as Lynx. She owed him a lifelong debt for ridding her manor of the pestilence of Gifford deWode . . . twice.

And, mayhap most importantly, he was the father of her child, a child conceived in love who deserved the family she had been denied.

"Yes," she whispered, "I would marry you tonight if only it was possible."

"Then before the hour is out you shall be my wife." He leaped to his feet and pulled her into his arms. "You shall be *my* lady, Audra."

"Tonight?" She shook her head. "You heard Lord deWode's threats. He is not yet done with Bredonmere. If we wed now, he—"

Drawing her into his arms, he whispered, "It is time to think clearly instead of allowing deWode to clutter our brains. If you wed me, Audra, what do you risk? Bredonmere?" He shook his head. "King Edward wants you wed and the estate out of dissension. He wants me married, too."

"And Lord deWode?"

"What can he do when you and Bredonmere are mine?"

Audra looked away. *Bredonmere!* Robert was no different from Gifford. Both of them were eager to possess the fief. What a fool she had been to believe—again—that Robert loved her! When would she learn to be as callous as these men who tormented her heart? Since her arrival, she had pledged to do whatever she must to protect her family's lands. Marrying Robert would be the best way, even though she would have given almost anything had he come to her for love's sake only.

"You need not fear deWode's rage while I command Bredonmere's men-at-arms," he continued quietly. "And what else is there to fear?" He brushed aside her gorget and pressed his lips to her throat. When she sighed with involuntary delight, he murmured, "Do you fear the ecstasy we shall share for the rest of our lives?"

She could not answer as his mouth found her willing lips. As her arms encircled his back, she wondered why she always fought Robert when he offered her exactly what she wanted . . . except his heart.

"I shall marry you tonight or whenever you wish," she whispered. "I can delay no longer giving Bredonmere the lord everyone has told me it needs."

His face closed into an empty expression. She was baffled. What had she said to distress him? Or was he simply trying to hide his delight in stealing his enemy's prize at last?

"Come." He took her hand and led her to where Father Jerome was coming to his feet.

The priest signaled to Fleming, who hurried to his side. When the young man shook his head vehemently, Audra tensed. Behind them, she heard the mumble of disquiet.

"No," she said as Robert put his foot on the first riser to the raised table. "Let me speak with Fleming."

"He will obey you, Audra."

"I don't want his obedience alone."

Audra hurried up the steps and called softly to Fleming. When he came to her and dropped to one knee, she knew he would not make this easy for her. "Rise and speak the thoughts I see on your face, my friend."

He slowly came to his feet. Glancing at where Robert still stood on the lower floor, he said, "I cannot change my name or my place within Bredonmere, milady. I am as I always have been."

"For that I am more grateful than you can know."

"I suspected that," he said with a rare smile. It vanished as he added, "Know also, milady, that my loyalty to you will not waver under any circumstances."

"Even if I ask you to pledge that allegiance to another."

"If that is your wish, for although my heart might be reluctant, my vow of obedience to the will of the Travers family is never changing."

"Thank you," she said. When she put out her hands, he knelt again. She placed her hands on his shoulders. "I thank you more than you can know."

Fleming stood and stepped aside as Robert came to stand beside her. She waited for the two men to speak, but Fleming did no more than nod his head before walking away.

Robert's gaze followed the young man until Audra put her hand on his arm. He stroked her fingers and smiled. When Father Jerome walked toward them, Robert said, "You shall be a lovely bride, Audra, with the light from the hearth glowing on your hair."

"Here?" She shook her head. "This must be done correctly. If we are to wed, it must be at the door of the church."

"Audra—"

"It is the only place where my family can be with me, Robert."

The raw pain in her voice flailed him. He looked down into her eyes and saw the truth he had not wanted to accept. She held the manor not for her own personal glory and power. She struggled to keep Bredonmere from disaster to honor the family she had barely known.

Glancing at his younger brother, Robert tried to imagine losing everyone in his family. The death of one sister had ravaged his heart so much that he had launched himself on a quest for retaliation. To lose all of them . . . Mayhap he and Audra were even more alike than he had guessed. Stubborn, yes. Filled with glorious ambition, yes, but also loyal to those who shared a bond of blood.

"As you wish, milady," he said softly. "That will give time for me to send for one of my family who would not wish to miss hearing me speak my vows to you."

"Which of your family is here other than Father Jerome?"

He smiled at her puzzlement. "Ida."

"Ida? The old woman in the cottage beyond the walls? She is of your family?"

"Her tale of being a nursemaid to a knight who rode to serve his king was not far from the truth." He slapped his brother on the shoulder and grinned. "Ida had the unenviable task of governing all the Bourne children during their youngest years."

Father Jerome chuckled. "She has told me more than once, brother, that she doubted if you would ever have the good sense to see what you had here was what you have sought all these years."

Taking Audra's hand, he pressed it to his lips. "Bredonmere has brought me many joys I had not envisioned upon my arrival."

"May *Bredonmere* bring you many more," she replied, tugging her hand away. "If you will excuse me . . ."

She was gone before he could answer. Looking at his brother, he saw Jerome was frowning.

Shaking his head, his brother said, "I pray you know what you want when you stand before the door of the church this evening, Robert, for I fear even Lady Audra's generous heart can be broken only so many times."

"It is not my intention to break her heart."

"Is it your intention to give her yours in exchange for her father's lands? Or have you so hardened your heart in hate, brother, that you no longer know what love is?" He walked down the steps.

Robert slammed his fist onto the table and cursed when his brother's goblet crashed, spraying wine everywhere. He wiped the dampness from his tunic. This was not what he had thought his moment of victory would be.

Not at all.

Audra allowed no apprehension to be seen when she emerged from the keep. The stars were poking through the thinning clouds, and a cold, damp breeze tugged at her fur-lined cloak as she edged around the puddles. When she saw the torches brightening the inner bailey and the crowd of people holding them high, relief surged through her. Only her household and Robert's men were gathered here. All of Gifford's retainers were gone along with their lord.

Shirley matched her steps and toyed with the gorget on Audra's hair. "Are you certain of this?" she asked for the fourth time since they had left Audra's rooms.

"Like Fleming," Audra answered, "I cannot

change. I came to respect Robert when he was a part of Bredonmere before. My heart will not be transformed simply because he is not the man I thought he was."

"The king would have frowned on you taking an armorer for a husband."

Or a night rider, she thought, but said only, "This will please everyone."

"Save Lord deWode."

"He will have no further claim on Bredonmere."

Shirley rubbed her hands together as they neared the church. "I shall light a candle tonight and pray that the baron's shadow never darkens Bredonmere lands again." Her voice lightened as she whispered, "My plea was heard once."

"When Lord deWode left the first time?"

"No, when Lynx left."

Audra was glad she was saved from answering by Father Jerome coming forward to greet them at the chapel door with a cheek-splitting smile.

"Father, you have the appearance of a happy man," Audra said.

"That I must admit. From the moment I first saw you in the chapel and you spoke to me from the heart, I knew you would be the perfect match for Robert."

She smiled but turned away. When, even with the buzz of voices in the bailey, she heard Robert's assertive footfalls coming toward her, the leap of her heart told her what she should have known. She loved him, and she wanted to spend the rest of her life with him. Having Robert as her husband would be the best thing for Bredonmere and for her. If only he could love her in return, her life would be perfection.

Softly, she said, "I shall gladly become Robert's wife tonight."

Father Jerome spoke a swift blessing over her, then turned to his brother. Audra noticed that Shirley stayed beside her, but was shocked that Fleming was at Robert's elbow.

Fleming looked at her, and she put her hand out to him. He bowed over it, pressing her fingers to his forehead. As he straightened, he gave her a weak smile. No doubt, Fleming had come to the realization she had. For Bredonmere, this wedding must take place.

"Shall we begin?" asked Father Jerome.

When Robert's arm settled around her waist, his fingers brushing her in a clandestine caress, she fought not to melt at the pleasure he stirred within her. Not a sound could be heard other than the priest's voice as Father Jerome read the wedding service before leading them into the church for the mass. His full voice reached the top of the timbered roof and washed over the brass plates covering the Travers crypt.

Through the long service, Audra glanced at Robert again and again. His hooded eyes reminded her of the mask he had worn as Lynx, but that fearsome creature had vanished into the night. Not once did he look at her. Steadily, loud enough so no one could mishear him, he answered to the vows.

"You are wed in God's bliss for all time. Go forth in peace and joy," ended Father Jerome. As he folded their hands together, he grinned. "If you long to kiss your wife, brother, you need worry never again about any man halting you."

Taking her face between his broad hands,

Robert stared down at her. Audra heard the rustling of impatience when he did not kiss her. Caught by the fire in his midnight eyes, she slowly lifted her hands to rest on his forearms. At their light touch, he crushed her against him. His fierce kiss spoke vividly of the passion that had lured her into his arms.

A passion that she would treasure while she could, praying it would be enough when she longed to be in his heart.

Father Jerome led them from the chapel and shouted, "Behold, the lord and lady of Bredonmere!"

Audra watched as her household dropped to their knees. Her eyes widened when Fleming and his men stayed on their feet. Beside her, Robert frowned. He started to speak, but she put her hand on his arm. Angry words would solve nothing now.

Looking past Robert, she stared at Fleming. She saw the hurt and betrayal on his face. She understood his feelings deep within her heart. So hard they had fought to keep Bredonmere from defeat. Now the battle, only half-won, had been taken from their hands and passed to others. She hoped he would come to believe—as she must—that in losing tonight, they affirmed Bredonmere's future.

When she nodded at the question she knew he was thinking, he slowly lowered himself to one knee. His men-at-arms emulated his pose as they placed their weapons on the ground and their fingers to their forelocks.

Taking a deep breath, Audra sank to her knees as well. She was startled when Robert caught her elbow and brought her back to her feet.

"I want you by my side, Audra," he whispered,

"not at my feet." He smiled at her amazement before he raised his voice to take the pledge of fealty from each of her retainers, and she dared to believe that the future might be brighter than she had imagined.

Audra was pleased when Shirley left her alone in the grand chamber that now once more would shelter the earl of Bredonmere. Although the king would have to grant that title officially to Robert, it would be done before the winter snows vanished into spring.

Sitting on the sill, she hugged her robes tightly to her as she watched the lazy spiral of snowflakes on the other side of the glass. Winter was coming early, and plans must be made to protect the lambs and the pregnant ewes from the frigid weather that was sure to follow the unexpected snow. Some of the byres still needed repairs, and she wondered if atte Water's eldest son had settled onto the toft by the spring where Lord deWode had nearly killed Crandall. And there was . . .

Things that were no longer her concern. She looked at the ring of keys in the center of the table behind her. Bredonmere had a lord now to see to the lives of its villeins. Its lady needed to look no farther than the walls of the keep for her duties. Robert would govern her father's lands, and he had no obligation to ask her opinion on anything.

She silenced that perfidious thought. It would gain her nothing save more sorrow.

The door opened, and she started to slide down from the sill. Robert smiled and motioned for her to stay where she was.

"It is," he said as he leaned his hands on either

side of her, "different to have you waiting here when *I* come into this chamber. Each of those nights I came to you I hated having to climb back onto this sill to leave you."

"You never need leave again," she whispered. "This is your home, too, now."

"That is what I wish to speak to you about, Audra."

Her brow rutted in confusion. "You do not wish to make your home at Bredonmere? You wish to go elsewhere?" Dismay pierced her, for she never had considered that he might plan to return to his father's holdings. "You wish us to go elsewhere?"

"You know I cannot plan on staying here always. I am a warrior, Audra. My life has been aimed at answering the king's call to defend his lands on the other side of the Channel."

"That is to Bredonmere's benefit."

His fingers under her chin tilted her face toward him. "You are not heeding what I am saying."

"But I am. I know that Bredonmere needs a strong leader."

"That is true, but," he added as his hand uncurled along her cheek, "Bredonmere needs a strong leader to build the fief in this time of peace. It needs a leader who can inspire the villeins and dare them to believe in dreams of greater achievements. That leader is not me, milady."

She wondered if she had forgotten how to breathe, for her chest burned with the air trapped within it. "Robert, do you regret marrying me already?"

"Regret marrying you?" His laugh boomed over her. "My sweet lady, I cannot imagine the day when I would rue wedding the woman who should lead Bredonmere to the greatness it can obtain."

Audra regarded his smile in disbelief. "You wish *me* to lead Bredonmere?"

"I would be a poor lord for this manor if I did not recognize wisdom in others that I do not possess." His fingers combed up through her hair as he drew her mouth closer to his. "A man should give his wife a gift on their wedding night. I give you back, if you will do me the boon of accepting them, the tasks you have done so well to enrich the tofts. My chore will be to defend the wondrous things you shall create throughout Bredonmere. Say you wish this gift, milady."

Unable to speak past the lump clogging her throat, she pressed her hands over her mouth. Then she drew them away as she brought his mouth to hers. His smile tasted as sweet as summer honey. "Thank you, milord," she whispered. "I shall accept this gift with a joyous heart."

He lifted her from the sill and set her on the floor in front of him. As his finger traced an abstract pattern along her cheek and to the tip of her nose, he smiled. "It is a small gift when you have offered me your heart."

"I have another gift for you," she said as softly. Taking his hand, she drew it over her abdomen. "Our child grows here."

His eyes widened in astonishment, then pride curved a smile across his lips. "Why have you not told me?" His brows suddenly slashed downward as he gripped her arms. "You bear my child, but you considered marrying deWode and letting him claim my child as his own?"

She stared at him, aghast. How many times had

she dreamed of this moment? She had envisioned him speaking to her of love. Instead he was furious.

"It had to be a secret only I could be privy to," she replied, "while I decided Bredonmere's future."

"Because you were not sure which of us was the child's sire?"

She shoved past him. Before she could stamp away, he caught her arm and swung her back to him. She glowered at him, but he said, "Audra, I only wished to be certain that deWode did not force himself upon you as he did my sister."

"Is that all you wished?"

"No." He entwined his fingers with hers. Drawing her closer, he suddenly laughed and twirled her into his arms. Then he set her on her feet and kissed her with eager desire. His fingers brushed her face as he said, "I wished to tell you how this pleases me."

"Truly?"

"Truly." Sweeping his arm beneath her knees, he lifted her into his arms.

She leaned her head against his shoulder as he carried her to the bed. When he set her on it, she put her hands up to his cheeks, which were rough with the black shadow of a day's whiskers, and whispered, "Love me tonight, Robert, when I can see your face. Tonight I have waited for you as you have waited for me so often. Help me find again the perfection you have given me in your arms."

When she reached for the pin holding her flimsy robes together, he blocked her hand and shook his head.

"Robert, you do not want me?" she asked, shocked.

"Aye," he said in a ragged voice that banished

her trepidation, "I want you, my pretty one, but let me have the pleasure of undressing you. How many nights have I stood alone on some hill and imagined this moment when I could hold you without worrying about slipping away with the dawn? I do not want to think now when you are here to make my fantasies come true."

She answered him with her eager mouth on his. When he leaned her back into the pillows, drawing her legs up to wrap around his, she shivered with the longing she would never have to conceal again. Her bare toes stroked his firm legs, and he groaned against her mouth.

"Did you think I would refuse you?" he whispered against her ear before his tongue teased the whorls.

She closed her eyes and melted against his strength. As he withdrew the brooch holding her robes closed, the fabric fell from her shoulders. She moaned at the flicks of his tongue along her neck and across her breast. Her fingers clutched his brawny arms. When he released her hair from the pins, he drew the tip of her breast into his mouth to tease, to caress, to moisten with the heat of his craving for her.

Raising his head, he gazed down into her glazed eyes. She smiled when he did as her fingers hurried to release the sashes of his tunic. Although she could sense that he burned with the desire surging through her, he waited with rare patience until she loosened it and dropped it onto the floor. Her fingers swept over the firm muscles of his chest, touching, exploring, rediscovering the rough warmth of his skin. He tossed his tunic aside and kicked off the rest of his garments. When he pulled her against his chest, she learned as if for the first time how warm his hard body could be.

As he leaned over her in the nest of pillows, he smiled. "No curtains tonight, my love. I want to see your face as I share your body. There is no more need for darkness."

"No darkness," she whispered as she welcomed him into her arms. She gasped when his leg slipped between hers as he pulled her even closer to him. "Just pleasure."

"Always pleasure."

"Yes . . ." When his mouth covered hers, the single word became a heartfelt sigh. Her fingers moved along the smooth skin of his back to entangle in his hair, which was as black as the night that once had surrounded their loving.

He chuckled when her hand caressed his cheek, sweeping up to sift through the hair at his temple. "I never thought I would drive a woman mad with desire by keeping her from touching my face."

"To see you is wondrous."

His response was seared into her neck as his lips sought the pleasure they had been denied too long. Wrapping her arms around him, she surrendered to the yearning. She gasped when he took her hand and teased each fingertip with his tongue. She wanted that moist fire against her breast, flowing along her stomach, over every inch of her.

When she tried to draw her hand away, he teased the responsive skin on the underside of her wrist. She shivered, unprepared for the heat from such a light touch. The smoldering cauldrons of his eyes promised her that the rapture had only begun.

She leaned over him. Smoothing his thick hair

back from his face, she regarded him in silence. She
found it impossible to believe, even when she lay so
close to him, her bare skin alight with the burnishing
touch of his, that she had discovered her heart's
desire in a man who had been as elusive as a moon-
beam and as fiery as a ray of the sun.

As she lowered her mouth toward his, which
waited for her kiss, she did not close her eyes until
the last moment. She wanted to *see* the passion on
his face. She wanted to watch his eyes shut as the
shudders of pleasure rolled across him. She wanted
him. When his tongue slipped along her lips, sparks
burst through her, blinding her to everything but his
touch.

He drew her to lie atop him, so he could feel her
lithe body against his. With the experience of their
nights in the dark bower, he tantalized her, urging her
to give all of herself to the love she could not restrain.
Lifting her above him, his eager mouth sought along
her until she began to gasp with the unrestrained
hunger of passion. As if she had spoken of her yearn-
ings, he sampled the flavors of her breast before his
tongue slipped in an undulating path along her
abdomen.

Lower he sought, her breath exploding from her
as he tasted the fires deep within her. Her fingers
clenched on the covers. Writhing, needing to satisfy
the primitive beast within her, she arched toward
him to savor his lips upon her. She shuddered as the
rapture coursed through her blood, setting every
inch of her afire. When he drew her beneath him,
her trembling fingers gathered him to her.

She yearned to tell him how much she loved him,
but, as he brought them together, all words disappeared. Nothing existed, but the rapture increasing

with each motion. Her fingers clung to his shoulders, anchoring her amidst the tempest whirling about them. The sudden eruption of lightning-hot satisfaction blinded her to everything but his thundering gasps against her as together they found the ecstasy that would be forever theirs.

21

A frantic knock routed Audra from sleep. Drowsily, she put her hand out to Robert. She found nothing but his pillow. Opening her eyes, she stared into the shadows of the bed. He was gone!

She sat up, holding the blanket close to her. Why had he left her alone on their wedding night? He— The frenzied knocking sounded again.

Audra jumped from the bed and pulled her robes around her. As she shoved her arms into the sleeves, she noticed it was still dark outside. These were the hours when Lynx had been hers, but now Robert was her husband. Why would he leave her *now*? What was happening?

She ran across the room and bumped into something in the shadows by the door. Her gasp was swallowed by a soft chuckle.

"Robert!"

He put his arm around her waist and tugged her against his bare chest. His kiss was swift, but it roused the hunger in her once again. With a curse, he released her as he reached for the door.

She put her hand over his as the last webs of sleep fell away. "You should—"

"I am no longer Lynx, Audra. You need have no fears for me when I am within these walls."

With a smile, she opened the door and raised her arm to shield her eyes as a bright torch flared in the gloom.

"Milady, is milord within?" She recognized Eatton's voice.

Robert opened the door wider as he lashed his tunic around him. "Why do you come before dawn on our wedding night?"

"Milord, I—I—"

Audra screamed as the lad swayed. When Robert caught his squire and helped him to a bench, she saw drops of blood where Eatton had been standing. She ran into the outer room and shouted for Shirley. When her maid came rushing into the bedchamber, Audra sent her to find clean water and bandages.

Running to an ewer in the bathing room, Audra poured a cup of the tepid water. She brought it back and held it to Eatton's lips, but his hands came up to grasp it. He drank eagerly, and relief coursed through her. He was not hurt as badly as she first had thought. She blinked as Robert lit several candles and placed them on the table.

"Oh!" was all she could say when she saw how battered Eatton was. His face was crisscrossed with scratches, and bruises blackened both cheeks. The tip of his chin was raw with fresh blood.

"What mishap do you herald, Eatton?" Robert asked sharply.

The younger man squared his shoulders and

winced as he wiped his hand against the blood on his face. "Fires! The sheep byres are aflame on the north tofts."

"The sheep!" cried Audra. "Are the animals destroyed?"

"Not all of them. I spoke with Halstead for only a moment. He could spare no more time, and I wished to bring you the evil tidings without delay."

Robert went to the window and threw the glass open wide. Cold air careened through the chamber and danced wildly with the flames on the hearth. With it came the fearsome scent of smoke. "There?"

"If you are looking at Ludlow's and atte Water's tofts," Eatton answered.

"Ludlow's?" Audra dropped down on the steps by the bed. How proud he had been last week to display his breeding stock!

"That is a long ride," Robert said.

"I rode straight through the wood, to bring you word."

"Ludlow's," Audra whispered again.

Robert pulled his gaze from the bright pinpoint of light where there should be only darkness. Closing the window, he looked at his wife. His wife! Even now, that was an inconceivable thought.

He crossed the room and sank to his knees before her, looking up into her shattered face. His hand touched her cheek, and she gazed at him, an entreaty in her expressive eyes.

"We can rebuild as you have done before," he murmured.

"But will it all be devastated anew?"

Before he could answer, his squire's moan drew his attention back to Eatton. The lad's scratched face was covered with dried blood and distorted by the candle-lit shadows. "You are filthy, Eatton. What happened? Did you encounter the ones who dared to use my name? Can I hope they await my justice in the outer bailey?"

Eatton grinned wryly but winced when Audra rose and placed a damp cloth on his bleeding forehead. "I wish I could say that was so, milord. The truth is my horse refused to take that fence beyond Ludlow's toft. The one I told you we should take down long ago, Lynx."

Robert laughed at the use of that name but glanced toward the door. When Eatton nodded, understanding what he did not need to say, Robert said, "And now you wear the signs of my refusal to cause poor Ludlow more trouble."

"Aye, I went down, but fortunately not beneath my horse. The briars cradled my fall and left me ripped and bruised. My steed was not hurt and wiser than me, for there was a trench I had not seen on the far side of the fence. We found another way across and hurried here."

"How long?"

"Less than half an hour."

Robert stood. "Good. We might yet catch them with their hands holding the brands that set the fires." Motioning for Eatton to rise, he said, "We ride. Tell Fleming I want ten mounted men in the outer bailey before the watch calls the next hour. They are to be armed with bows and blades."

"Aye," Eatton said, then glanced at Audra. "I am sorry, milady."

"Thank you," she whispered, her arms wrapped around herself in a cocoon that could not keep out the horror.

Robert gathered his clothes and dressed with

speed. "Audra, I will leave Fleming here to safeguard the manor. We do not yet know the true intent of those who have chosen arson as their weapon. I will take my own men with me. They are more skilled at combat beyond the walls of a manor." A wry smile quirked his mouth as he lashed his tunic into place. "That was supposed to be the lads' next series of lessons."

"Be cautious. These men have killed before."

"Then they fought unarmed villeins. My men are better prepared to teach them that they endanger lives when they do such damage on milady's lands."

She smiled in spite of her fear. "I love you, Robert."

"And I shall return to love you . . . as soon as I can." He kissed her as swiftly as he had dressed, and then was gone before she could respond.

Minutes later, she heard the crash of hoofbeats across the drawbridge. She flung the window open. Fleming's shouts rang across the baileys. Dark forms raced to positions along the wall. Bredonmere had declared war on the false Lynx and his band.

When a hand touched her shoulder, she turned to see Ida. The old woman said, "Forgive me for intruding, milady, but it would ease my old heart tonight to be with someone else who loves Lord Wykemarch as I do."

Audra put her hand under Ida's arm and steered her to a chair. Closing the window, she called for Shirley to bring hot drinks for the old woman who shivered so hard Audra thought her brittle bones might crack.

She sat on a bench facing Ida and said, "Please tell me more about Robert."

"What do you wish to know?"

"All you wish to tell me."

"It could take a long time." Ida's face crinkled in a smile. "Lord Wykemarch was ever into adventures, even as a scrap of a lad. His sainted mother—may she rest in peace—would be aghast at his antics of late, although His Grace will be proud of his son who set aside all comfort to seek retribution from Lord deWode."

"Tell me all you can," she whispered. "We may have the rest of the night."

Audra realized how optimistic her hopes had been when Shirley woke her just before midday. Her maid shook her head before Audra could ask the question searing her tongue. Seeing Ida asleep in her chair, Audra tiptoed into her bathing chamber and dressed for the day.

She spent hours going through the keep and soothing the fears of her household. When word came to her that the villeins were at the walls, seeking shelter, she urged them to come within the manor house. No longer was she astonished at how the tale of trouble sped through Bredonmere. She considered sending a warning to Lord Norwell, but after being rebuffed when she had asked his assistance before, she doubted if she could depend on him now. She could imagine him sending back word that such a request must come from her husband.

Every fiber of her body listened for Robert. No one rode through the gate where the drawbridge connected Bredonmere to its lands. From the wall came no shouts of Robert's return. A peculiar silence settled on the manor house, aching within her like the vicious wind swirling through the baileys.

Food was made and brought to the great hall. Audra ate only when Shirley insisted and because she knew she must not chance hurting her unborn babe. When the minstrels made a half-hearted attempt at music, she left the great hall. She could not listen to their carefree melodies when her heart was heavy with fear.

The early night brushed the hills, leaving her blind as she opened the window of her bedchamber to stare out. Even the horrible smell from the fires had vanished.

"Where can they be?" she asked, more of herself than of Shirley who was sitting by the hearth, sewing. "It is so dark."

"Riding through the darkness is something milord should be well familiar with."

Audra turned and saw the truth on Shirley's face. "You know?"

"Yes, milady." She set her sewing on the steps. Rising, she closed the door to the outer chamber and lowered her voice. "I have long known that Lord Wykemarch once called himself Lynx."

"How?"

"Your door was barred night after night from the inside during a time when Lynx's pranks were at a lull. Then, when he vanished, the door was never barred." She lowered her gaze. "You quicken, milady, even though no one has seen a man enter your chambers. Who else but Lynx would be so bold as to seek another way into your rooms? I have told no one else what I know, milady."

"You may have saved Robert's life." She closed the window. "There are few within these walls who would welcome Lynx as their lord."

"They have been very frightened. Before Lynx vanished, I heard talk that he was no mortal man, that he was a shape changer who rode the night winds to prey on those who dared to halt him."

Audra stared out the window. "And what do you believe, Shirley?"

"I believe that any man you love must be a good man worthy of the title your father held."

"Your faith in me is amazing, especially when you knew all this." Her hands fisted on the stone. "I did not want to lie to you."

Shirley smiled. "I heard the truth in my heart, milady, and understood why you spoke as you did." Her face grew grim. "I have heard as well how Lord Wykemarch took a blood vow to repay Lord deWode for an insult to his family. Such a man is no beast, but a man of honor. I know why you love him."

"Where can they be?" Audra asked. "If they had captured the outlaws, they would have wasted no time returning to Bredonmere."

"Mayhap milord wished to spare you the sight of his justice."

Disgust quivered through her, but she shook her head. "Robert knows I understand the need for laws. Where can they be?"

"Stay brave, milady. Your lord will come back to you."

Audra wished she could be certain, but deep within her, a dark void warned her that disaster stalked the hills that Robert might be riding even now. The worst part, worse than not knowing, was that there was nothing she could do but wait.

The bedchamber door crashed open.

Audra leaped up from the steps by the hearth. "What is it, Shirley?"

"Fleming's men have sighted mounted men coming toward Bredonmere."

"Robert?"

"I don't know."

Throwing a cloak over her shoulders, Audra did not wait to ask more questions. She took the steps two at a time and pushed her way past the people crowding the great hall. When she reached the door to the inner bailey, she saw that the snow had changed to rain, which glistened on the stones. She did not slow. Taking a brand from the wall, she raced out into the storm.

Fleming rushed toward her as she came into the outer bailey. "Milady, you should wait within the keep. This night is not fit for you."

"Are the riders Robert and our men?"

"I cannot tell." He shook his head to push his wet hair from his eyes. "Do you wish me to raise the drawbridge?"

"That would be a sound idea. If—"

A scream severed the patter of the rain on the stones. Fleming grasped her arms and pulled her back against the wall. In horror, she saw a man topple backward from the top of the wall, the crossbow shaft through his body breaking as he hit the ground with a sickening thud. The others on the wall stared at the body as she wrapped her arms around herself and tried not to be sick in front of them.

Fleming shouted orders up to the wall. Men rushed through the bailey. "Milady, you must return to the safety of the keep," he said. His voice echoed off the walls as he bellowed, "Raise the drawbridge!"

"Too late," drawled another voice out of the darkness.

Audra whirled to face a bare blade. She pressed

against the wet stones of the outer wall as she stared across the length of the broadsword and into a stranger's satisfied smile. Beside her, Fleming cursed impotently. His broadsword was plucked from his hand, and the blade in front of Audra edged closer. Beyond them, a dozen men appeared out of the night.

Shouts sounded from the wall, but Fleming called, "Hold your weapons before Lady Audra is injured."

"Faithful to the end, Fleming?" taunted Gifford deWode as he rode from the shadows. "Too bad you have proven not to be as wise as you bragged. It seems Lord Wykemarch should have trained your men to be wary of a diversion that might distract them from an attack."

"You have been asked to leave Bredonmere twice now, milord," Audra said. "That request was mine, but my husband will be certain that you do not fail to comply when he asks you to leave a third time."

"You are, as always, a charming innocent." He swung down from the saddle. "Your husband will ask nothing of me. He is dead, Audra." DeWode swaggered toward her, pushing a pummeled form to fall at her feet. "Tell her, knave."

She moaned as she looked down at Eatton. His newly bruised face was so misshapen he had to struggle to say, "Milady, I fear Lord deWode speaks the truth."

"No!" she cried, shaking her head. "No! Robert cannot be dead!"

Lord deWode tossed a cloak at her feet. "Do you recognize this, milady?"

Bending, she gathered up the black wool that was heavier with the rain. Once Robert had worn this without a badge to identify it, but that had changed when he revealed the truth to her. Her fingers touched the tiny gold emblem on the shoulder. The lynx was as scratched as if the beast itself had run its claws across it . . . or as if a broadsword had struck it.

"I shall have you outlawed, milord," she whispered as she clutched the cloak to her breast. "You have no right to skulk through my lands and murder as you wish. The king will—"

"Give his blessing on our marriage."

"I shall never marry the man who murdered my husband!"

He snatched the cape from her hands and tossed it to one of his men, who dropped it to the cobbles and ground it beneath his foot. She choked in horror when she heard the brooch crack.

"I should have guessed you'd fail to understand, milady. It is simply more proof that you are incapable of overseeing this fief alone." Seizing her arm, he said, "I am the one who was attacked, Audra. Your husband, who granted me safe passage through these lands if you recall, attacked me and my men."

"That is a lie!"

"I have more than a dozen witnesses who will attest to that under oath."

"I have one who will cry the truth."

He released her and drew his knife. When he raised it toward Eatton, the lad closed his eyes in resignation.

Audra grasped deWode's arm. "No, do not kill him, too."

"There must be no question of the truth." He put the knife to the squire's throat.

She would not let Eatton die needlessly. Robert was dead. Eatton dying would do nothing but save Robert's honor.

"There will be no question of the truth," she whispered.

"No, milady!" cried Eatton. "Do not vow that! Let me die before you vow that!"

Raising her chin as rain splattered on her face, she said, "I vow to you, Lord deWode, that no voice within these walls will question the truth of tonight's incidents."

"Your husband attacked me like the heinous beast he is?"

"Milady," whispered Eatton, "please."

She closed her eyes, taking a deep breath. Then opening her eyes, she said, "Neither I nor no one within these walls will argue with that."

"No!" cried the lad as he collapsed to the ground.

Lord deWode laughed as he stepped over the sobbing lad and snatched her arm. "Then, come, milady, and entertain me."

"I must see to the injuries here."

He shook his head. "Let them tend to themselves."

"No," she said with quiet dignity. "I am the lady of Bredonmere. It is my duty to see that they are taken care of. I will not renounce my duty."

Pulling on her arm, he dragged her toward the gate to the inner bailey and the keep. She stiffened when he called for all the men-at-arms of Bredonmere to be gathered and put under guard.

"What will you do with them?" she asked as she saw Fleming's face tighten with fury.

"That is for you to decide, milady." He led her up the stairs to the great hall. As the door swung open, he shoved her into the hall ahead of him. He smiled as a screech of dismay came from one of the maids. Folding his arms over the mud-splattered surcoat on his chest, he stared at her.

Audra glanced around the huge chamber. Fear was as palpable as the heat off the fire. Heads were bowed in prayer, and many were weeping. When heavy footfalls sounded behind her, she looked back to see Lord deWode's men, their bloodstained blades in their hands.

Whispering her own wish that her family would forgive her and that Robert would understand, for she knew he would never forgive her for this, she lowered her stiff body to her knees. Moans of despair circled the room, but she watched as her household showed their fealty to Lord deWode as they had to Robert such a short time before.

Lord deWode did not command her to rise as he strode past her. Shouting for ale and food to be brought for him and his men, he climbed to the raised table. He called her name, and she looked at him.

He hoisted his hands over his head and shouted, "Bredonmere, hail your new earl!" His triumphant laughter resounded off the rafters as his men struck their blades together in a fearful dirge for Bredonmere.

Audra skulked through the darkness. The hour must not be far from dawn, the same hour when Lynx had slipped out of her arms to leave her to wake alone. She would not be alone in her bed again. Lord deWode had made that clear before he discovered that a few bottles of French wine waited in the Bredonmere cellars. His celebration had left him asleep in his chair at the raised table.

A shadow moved in front of her. She swallowed her scream, then rushed forward as she whispered, "Father Jerome! You must flee before Lord deWode realizes you still are here!"

"Do you think I shall leave you here to face deWode alone?"

"He will slay you as he slew Robert."

"You have only deWode's word Robert is dead."

His answer sounded so much like Robert's that she shivered with the emotions that boiled within her, bubbling ever closer to the surface. "No," she whispered. "He brought proof."

"Robert's body?"

She shook her head. Gesturing for him to follow, she led the way into the outer bailey. She took note of where deWode had posted men along the wall and rushed from one pool of shadows to another when the sentries turned away to scan the hills. The priest followed her.

"There," she whispered.

"It is—"

"Robert's cloak. The one he wore as Lynx."

"He would never willingly let deWode take that from him. It could have betrayed too much."

Her laugh was honed with hysteria. "What does it matter now? He is dead."

"Audra—"

She shook off his consoling hand. "He is dead, Father." She fell to the wet ground and grasped the cloak that had covered Robert's shoulders on the night she had given him her heart. Now his heart was silent. Holding the wool to her face, she sobbed. Everyone she had ever loved had died for Bredonmere. Her family, Crandall, now Robert. Through all the deaths she had remained strong, hiding her pain, soothing those who mourned, always being the brave lady of the manor.

No longer.

Next to her, Father Jerome dropped to his knees

and began to whisper a prayer for his brother's soul. When she saw tears streaming down his face, she offered him her hand. He clasped her fingers for a moment, then covered his face and wept.

She put her arms around his shoulders, unable to offer him solace when she had none to give. He leaned her head against his chest as she surrendered to the sobs that consumed her as the night grieved with them. The rain could wash away her tears, but never the pain. It would be with her always.

22

"You need to take more care, milady," whispered Shirley as she ran the jeweled comb through Audra's damp hair. "If you take ill from being out in that freezing rain, you may give Lord deWode exactly what he wishes. He then would be the closest kinsman to the Travers family."

"He is no kinsman of mine!" She spat out the words. She looked at her reflection. The scars of her sorrow were etched into her face, but as she put her hands over her stomach, she remembered the vow she had taken in the rain.

Robert's pledge to see Lord deWode defeated was now hers. Too late, she had come to comprehend Robert's obsession. Lord deWode had taken something incredibly precious from her. She would see him lose his dearest wish, although she was not sure how.

"Where is Fleming?" she asked.

"He is being held with the others in the stable."

"Can you find a way to bring him here?"

"It will not be easy." Shirley smiled. "But I shall bring him to you, milady, within the hour."

She stood and pushed her hair back from her face. "Take care. I need all my allies."

"Lord deWode and his men are not familiar with this manor. We can deceive them."

Audra plaited her hair as she had worn it while she was Sister Audra and went into the antechamber of her rooms. She could not remain in her bedchamber where the empty bed was a constant accusation of how Robert had died to safeguard Bredonmere. Blinking back tears, she squared her shoulders. She had vowed as well that Lord deWode would never see her weep. She would not give him that pleasure.

Opening the box that held her quill and ink, she drew out a piece of parchment and began to write. She did not worry about the words she chose. Any would serve. Lord deWode had ambushed the rightful earl of Bredonmere and illegally held the manor. With a smile, she waited for the ink to dry. She had pledged that no voice would speak of the night's events. No voice had, but her quill had told the story that would bring England's wrath down on Lord deWode.

The watch was calling the hour when the door from her audience room opened, and two cloaked women slipped in. When they flipped back the hoods on their cloaks, Audra breathed a sigh of relief.

"Fleming!" She squeezed Shirley's hand. "Thank you, dear friend. Will you—?"

"No one, not even Lord deWode himself, shall enter, milady." She opened the door and shut it behind her.

Audra said, "I never envisioned you as a bent old woman, Fleming."

He kicked at the thick cape he wore over his shoulders. "Neither did I, but Shirley's scheme was a good one. Ida and I will change places when I return to the stables."

"You will not be returning if you will do as I ask."

"Say what you need, milady."

"Fleming, I ask you to remember the vow you made to me the day you came to Clarendon Abbey."

"My arm and my life are yours," he said without hesitation.

"I must get a message to the king. There is no one I can trust to take it to him save you."

He held out his hand. "I shall take it with all due speed."

"It must be delivered into no hand but the king's."

"I understand."

She drew her father's signet ring from the box. "Give Edward this as a token to prove you come as my messenger."

"It shall be as you wish, milady."

As she handed him the small, folded page, she whispered, "Leaving Bredonmere will be the most dangerous part of this journey. Lord deWode has guards on every gate and postern."

"There is a way he would not know." He slipped the page and the ring into a pouch at his waist. "Crandall told me of a tunnel beneath the eastern tower that offers a last escape in times of disaster."

Astonished, she asked, "Why did I know nothing of this?"

"'Twas the way of the Travers family to have but one person possess knowledge of the tunnel."

"So you assumed I knew?"

He grinned. "Now you do, milady, for if I fail, the one you send to follow me must know the way."

"Go with speed and care, Fleming." She put her hands on his shoulders as he knelt in front of her. "I need you beside me to help me hold Bredonmere when Lord deWode has been outlawed."

He looked up at her. "Milady, I am so sorry—"

"Say nothing of that now." She brushed her hand against the corners of her eyes. "I can afford no more tears. Go, and do what you can to save Bredonmere."

"I shall."

She dropped to sit on the bench as he opened the door and rushed out of the room. Bredonmere's final hope rested on the shoulders of a man who had traveled but once beyond the fief's borders. If he was delayed even an hour in finding his way to the king's court, all might be lost.

Audra looked up in surprise as the door to her antechamber opened without a knock. "Milord!" she gasped as she came to her feet. Moving through the afternoon sunshine, she motioned for Shirley to stay where she was. She did not want Lord deWode to turn his wrath on her servants. "I had thought you would give me the courtesy of announcing yourself before you enter my rooms."

He sniffed. "You are chattering uselessly, for I have no interest in your complaints. Be silent." He rubbed his head, and she guessed it ached in the wake of his celebration last night.

"As you wish," she said a bit louder.

Glowering at her, he snarled, "Be silent." He sat at the table and said, "Open the door."

"What?"

"You heard me, woman! Do as you are told."

Not sure what he intended, Audra inched toward the door. She lifted the latch, praying she would not discover another example of his savagery on the other side. The door swung open.

"Lynx!" she gasped as she stared at the man whose face was swathed in black. She took a step forward, then froze. This was not Lynx. The man's chin was too narrow, and his hair was a brilliant red. "Shaw!"

Behind her, deWode guffawed as Shaw pushed past her into the room. The baron withdrew a knife and began trimming his nails. Shirley edged closer to Audra, but her servant would be no match for a honed warrior like Shaw.

Shaw closed the door behind him and dropped the bar into place. When she glanced from it to his smile, he unwrapped the material around his head. He walked closer, drawing the blade he wore in his belt. Her accusations vanished in her arid mouth as he raised the knife toward her.

When Shirley screamed, he ordered, "Be silent, or I shall let your lady watch me cut your tongue from your mouth."

Audra put her hand on Shirley's arm. Aware of Lord deWode watching, an amused smile on his face, she knew that Shaw would not attack without the baron's permission.

"Shirley," she said quietly, "please take your seat by the hearth."

"Milady—"

"Shirley, please!"

The old woman nodded and crept toward the hearth. She perched on the very edge as she stared in white-faced horror at the two men.

"Milord thought it wise that I speak to you, milady," Shaw said in the same pleased tone.

"Your lord?" She raised her chin. "Your rightful lord is my husband Lord Wykemarch."

"Who is dead as you could be."

Staring at him as he slashed the air in front of her, she did not move. She would not play a part in his twisted games. On his face she saw only jubilant evil. She must be cautious. His fingers were shaking on the knife, warning her that he was frightened. Of what? Gifford deWode? Her? Being outlawed? It did not matter, save that she must be wary. A scared man would dare anything.

"What do you wish?" she asked yet again.

Lord deWode motioned with his knife. "Ease her curiosity, Shaw. It is far from charming."

"I have no curiosity," Audra retorted, "when I see the truth in front of my eyes. Did you blacken your hair with the soot of the houses you burned when you pretended to be Lynx?"

"That is not what I wish to tell you, milady," he said, his smile widening, "although your guess is a good one."

"What other crimes have you committed?"

"Crimes? None, for I have done as milord commanded me. I wish you to know that I have not gone to all the trouble I have and risked my life only to fail because of you."

"Trouble? What trouble?"

He laughed. "You are a fool, Lady Audra."

"Shaw, you will pay for your words."

"Nay, I shall be rewarded for your folly." He rocked the knife in front of her face as Shirley murmured a fearful prayer. "Did you not think it odd that none of your siblings or their children survived?"

She whispered, "The Death—"

"Took but half of the tenants on the tofts. Even in the keep, only half died. Yet the earl and his family all perished in the plague. Lord deWode asked me to be sure of that."

"You killed *all* my family?" Audra whirled to face the baron, who was smiling as broadly as Shaw. She shuddered, overwhelmed by their malevolence. From the hearth, she heard Shirley's low moan.

Lord deWode smiled, a fiendish glint in his eyes. "Shaw thought he had. I offered him a generous reward for his help, so you can imagine my shock when he sent me word that that old ass Crandall asked him to ride to get the earl's youngest, who had been hidden away in a convent."

Shaw cursed. "All that work for nothing!"

She lifted her chin to avoid the sharp edge of his knife as he held it close to her. Dampening her lips with the tip of her tongue, she whispered, "So then you killed Crandall when he chanced upon your guise as the false Lynx?"

"He was troublesome, but he was wily. He had to be taken care of also." He chuckled. "As you should have been, milady. If I had been fortunate, you would never have emerged from the forest the night I abandoned you there. I had hoped some beast would find and finish you. Then milord would have had no one to contest his hold on Bredonmere."

"That night I had allies you could not guess."

"Damn Lynx!" He grasped her hair. When she groaned, she heard the bench scrape as Lord deWode came to his feet. Instantly Shaw released her. Fear obliterated his smile.

"Speak only," deWode ordered. "If you touch

this woman again, I shall cut your hand from your arm before I have you hanged."

"Forgive me, milord."

"Begone, Shaw, and do as I have ordered." Turning, he grabbed Audra's hand.

"What do you want?" she asked as he steered her toward the door of the antechamber.

"I thought you knew that by now." He laughed cruelly as he tilted his head in a parody of a court bow. "Lady Audra Travers, countess of Bredonmere, your presence is requested at our wedding."

"If you are reciting my titles, you have forgotten that I also am Lady Wykemarch," she retorted, vowing not to let him delight in her despair again.

With a sly smile, he said, "Soon everyone will forget that. You will be mine. You and Bredonmere and—"

"My child who is heir to both Bredonmere and the duke of Exbridge?"

"Child?" All color drained from his face. "What child?"

"My husband's child sleeps beneath my heart, milord."

"That is a lie. You had been wed only a day when—"

"That night was not the first I spent in my husband's arms. Do you think His Grace the duke of Exbridge will allow you to slay his heir's heir?" When she saw his smile fade, she pressed her small victory. "There are some things that even you in your basest treachery cannot change."

"Then let us change the ones we can." He twisted his fingers through her hair. When she moaned, his lips pounced on her mouth. She tried to wiggle free. He tightened his grip on her hair until she had no choice but to surrender. Raising his lips from hers, he murmured, "You learn very, very slowly, milady, but you will learn that I am and shall remain your master."

She spat. "Never!"

With a laugh, he dragged her into her bed-chamber.

Shirley rushed forward. "Milady—"

"Begone!" shouted deWode. He shoved Audra across the room.

She moaned as her head struck the wall. Ignoring the scarlet haze of pain, she lurched to the table in the middle of the room. DeWode's shout ached through her skull. She folded up to sit on a bench as she cradled her head in her hands.

She was not sure if an hour passed or a second before she heard a familiar voice say, "No, milord, that is not possible." She looked up to see Father Jerome's lips tight with fury. "I shall not wed milady without her permission."

DeWode's hand lashed out. Audra screamed as Father Jerome fell to the floor. She leaped to her feet when deWode pulled his knife from his belt.

"I have seen your brother's blood," he shouted. "Now I shall see yours!"

Audra fought her eyes which showed her three images. She groped to halt the baron from slashing into Father Jerome. She fell to the floor. Through the ringing in her ears, she heard another shout.

Not in deWode's voice. Not in Father Jerome's.

She flinched as someone threw the window open, crashing it into the wall. The voice came again from beyond the window.

Gentle hands aided her to her feet. "Are you hurt, milady?"

Forcing her eyes to focus on Father Jerome, she whispered, "I am only bumped. You?"

"I doubt if I will turn the other cheek to deWode."

His words strengthened her, and she smiled. Keeping her voice low, she asked, "What is happening?"

"I am not sure, but someone has been sighted from the wall."

DeWode snarled at them to be silent as he strode past them, nearly running her over. He shouted for a guard to stand at her door. The door slammed. Audra dropped the bar in place. It would offer little protection, but they might need the seconds it would give them.

Shirley gave a gasp as she looked out the window. "Milady! Come here!"

Audra ran to the window, nearly tripping on her wobbly feet. She looked past the walls to the road leading south into Bredonmere. A lone man stood there, raising his hand in a hail to the guards on the wall. Even though he stood the length of the manor from her, she could not mistake how the sun shone on his dark hair or the square set of his shoulders.

"Robert!" she whispered, pressing her hands over her heart.

23

Robert knew his hail would be answered. During the night while he had fought to hold on to consciousness long enough to reach Ludlow's toft, during the day while he lay on a hard pallet while Ludlow's wife tended to his wounds, during the hours it took for him to return to Bredonmere, he had known deWode would answer his hail.

Two men surged through the front gate of Bredonmere and pointed their broadswords at him. He held up his hands in surrender. When they looked at each other, as if unsure what to do when he offered no resistance, he hid his smile. DeWode's lackeys were as stupid as their master. If the situation had been reversed, he would have made certain deWode was dead before riding to claim Bredonmere.

And its lady. He clenched his hands, even though they remained over his head. That thought

had haunted him more than any other while he waited for enough strength to return so he could stumble
back here. He could not leave Audra to fight her
bastard cousin alone, not when deWode lusted after
her.

"Mayhap you would consider asking Lord
deWode what you should do with me," Robert suggested when the two knaves began to argue about
their orders.

"Silence!" snapped one, but then motioned
toward the gate with his sword. "If you try to escape,
you will die."

"I would not have come here," he muttered
under his breath, "if my first aim was to flee."

A quick scan of the outer bailey was reassuring.
Although rain could have washed away blood left by a
battle, he saw no signs of fire or broken weapons.
That confirmed his opinion that deWode was too
cowardly to fight openly even the small numbers of
men-at-arms within Bredonmere.

A furtive shadow near the wall caught his eye.
His plan might still succeed. With a motion too small
to be noticed by his guards, he gave Eatton the order
that might save them all or bring deWode the help he
needed to secure Bredonmere. It was a risk they must
take now.

As he entered the inner bailey, his gaze rose to
a single window in the keep. His toes could recall
every stone from the wall to that window, for he
had climbed that way often. When he saw there a
slender hand raised in a greeting, he smiled. Audra
was alive. Joy surged through him. He was not too
late.

DeWode strutted from the keep and looked
down his nose at Robert. "I did not guess you to be so

foolish as to return here so I might have the pleasure of killing you again."

Audra gasped as she heard the baron's malicious greeting. She rushed to the door and lifted the bar aside. When hands covered hers, she tried to shake them off. "Do not halt me, Father."

"No, milady, you must not interfere."

In shock, she turned to stare at Father Jerome. His bruised lips were tilted in a smile as savage as any Lynx had worn. "I must! Lord deWode will kill him."

"Give him the time his man needs to go for help." He drew her back to the window and nodded toward the drawbridge.

"Listen to him, milady," urged Shirley.

She saw a flash of gold. Eatton! He was sneaking toward the road. No one noticed, save for her, Shirley, and the priest, for all other eyes were riveted on Robert and deWode.

"Why didn't he go for help himself?" she asked with a moan.

"Do you need ask?"

She clutched her hands over her heart. "He wished to be sure we were safe. This is madness. Help may come too late."

"You must trust us, milady."

"Us?"

"My brother did not doubt that deWode would return. The only question was when. Like him, I did not suspect it would be so soon."

"What do you have planned?"

"Eatton is to seek help from Lord Norwell."

With another moan, she sat on the steps of the hearth. "Father, he is Lord deWode's ally."

"That is not certain."

"But Robert is risking his life on this uncertainty."

"It is all we have."

Audra shook her head. "No, it is not." She went to the door, threw aside the bar, and opened it before Father Jerome could halt her.

The two men guarding the door stepped forward. When she pushed past them, they fell back, shocked. She ran out of the room and down the stairs, ignoring their shouts. They would not dare to use their weapons without deWode's orders.

Rushing out into the cold sunshine, she called, "Halt!"

DeWode spun around, fury glittering in his eyes. "How did you get here?"

"It is my manor, milord. I go where I choose." She walked regally toward him as if there was nothing unusual about her husband standing between two swords held by his enemies. She longed to fling her arms around him and tend the wounds he must be hiding beneath his tunic.

"You hold nothing!" He drew his short blade and stabbed it through her long sleeve, pinning it to a crevice in the wall. He chuckled when she tried to pull away and the thick material would not tear. "I hold you, milady, but not as I shall when I finish with your soon-to-be late Lord Wykemarch."

"DeWode!" Robert took a step forward, then halted as the swords blocked his way. Sainted Mary, what was Audra doing here? He had expected deWode would have her securely imprisoned in her rooms. Could the bastard not even do that competently? "I would make you an offer that you shall find interesting."

"What do you have to offer that would interest me?"

"Bredonmere."

DeWode sneered. "You must have injured your head. I hold Bredonmere now."

"But not legally. You still risk being outlawed." Robert smiled and folded his arms across his chest, even though the motion sent a mind-numbing ache through him. He shot a frown at Audra, but she was watching deWode. If she would take her leave . . . "There is still a way you can have Bredonmere legally."

DeWode pulled his blade away from Audra and turned to face him. "How?"

"Two things stand between you and the possession of this manor, Audra and I, but that doesn't need to be."

He tilted the knife toward Audra again. "Do you suggest I kill your wife and child, Wykemarch?"

Robert was glad his hands were hidden so deWode could not see them clench in frustration. He had hoped Audra would keep his child a secret, but she must have had a reason for telling deWode the truth. It changed nothing. "Audra had retired from life to take the orders of Clarendon Abbey. Send her back."

"And you? Do you intend to become a priest like your brother?" He laughed viciously. "Your jests are not amusing."

"Send Audra to Clarendon Abbey, and you may have my life and a legal hold on Bredonmere."

Audra shook her head. "No, Robert! I do not want to go there. I do not want to go anywhere without you. I will not let you trade your life for mine."

"Listen to your lady, Wykemarch." DeWode grasped her arm and pushed her toward the door to the keep. "She will be *my* lady in the hour after your death. When your bastard is dead as well, she will bear me many sons to hold Bredonmere after me."

"DeWode—"

"Why should I bargain with you, Wykemarch, when you have nothing I want? I shall legally hold Bredonmere when Audra is my wife." He motioned toward the stable. "Put him with the others. Chain him well. They all will die at sunrise."

"No!" cried Audra.

"Be silent!"

"No matter how you pretend, Lord deWode, Robert is my husband. I shall not have him suffer in that stable when he has been sorely wounded. He should spend his last hours in the rooms that are rightfully his."

Robert silenced his groan. This was the worst time for her to start negotiating with deWode.

"To spend those hours with you?" The baron laughed again.

"I shall not set foot in there, if that is your wish."

Robert tried to catch her eye. He had to halt her before she ruined everything with her good intentions. Hell, he knew, was full of good intentions, and if he did not stop her, he would know that firsthand when deWode executed him and bedded Audra. He needed to get to the stable. With Fleming and the other men-at-arms, he would devise a way to overcome their captors.

"Audra, do not put yourself in debt to this cur," he said, hoping she would look at him.

She continued to stare at deWode. "Do you acknowledge me as the lady of Bredonmere, milord? If you intend to use my claim to ensure yours, it would behoove you to grant me this single act of kindness."

"Audra," Robert began again.

"Take him to the earl's rooms," deWode said

with a smile. "Milady, come with me. I wish to learn how you will repay me for this kindness."

"Audra! Do not go with him!"

Then pain exploded in Robert's head as he fell into darkness as black as deWode's soul.

Audra sat in the chair at the raised table in the great hall. Not the chair where she usually sat, but where her mother had. Beside her, Lord deWode was refilling her goblet.

"A final drink, milady, to us."

She searched her mind for another way to delay him from taking her to his bed. For the past hour, as the light from the setting sun coming through the windows at the peak of the hall had turned to twilight, she had devised excuses—from his need to check the walls personally to hers to confess to Father Jerome before she married again. Her confession had taken but a few minutes, for Father Jerome had understood what she could not say openly without fear of being overheard, for Lord deWode would not even grant her the privacy of the confessional.

She took a sip from her goblet and swallowed harshly, afraid she would sicken if she put any more wine into her empty stomach. She had not eaten all day.

Lord deWode grasped her around the waist and jerked her to him. "Let us show all your people that you are my very willing lady."

She almost gagged as his mouth covered hers. His arms tightened, holding her so close that she could not doubt his arousal. When he slid her from her chair and pressed her back toward the floor, she realized, in horror, that he intended to rape her in the great hall. His fingers reached for the front of her gown.

A shriek burst through the great hall. Not hers. A man's, she realized when deWode rolled away from her. He stood. Rising as far as her knees, she was stopped by his heavy hand on her shoulder. She peered over the table.

Shaw raced around the central hearth. "Milord, he has escaped!"

"He?"

"Lord Wykemarch!"

"Impossible!" cried deWode. "He could not escape from that room. You and three other men were guarding the only doors."

Shaw's mouth twisted. "He had help."

"Fleming! Send me Fleming! I shall cut his beating heart out with my own hands."

"Not Fleming!" Shaw exclaimed, saving Audra from having to devise some lie to hide that Fleming was on his way to the king in a desperate attempt to save Bredonmere.

"Then who?"

The red-haired man licked his lips and shuffled nervously.

"Speak up!" shouted deWode, banging his fists on the table. "Has a cat stolen your tongue?"

Audra laughed and stood. She fisted her hands on her hips, trying to hide her excitement. Could the suggestions she had passed to Father Jerome during her "confession" have come to fruition? With another laugh, she asked, "'Twas a cat, wasn't it, Shaw? 'Twas Lynx who rescued my husband, wasn't it?"

"Lynx!" choked deWode. His fear was mirrored on his men's faces and the sudden hope in the eyes of her household. "I thought the bastard vanished from Bredonmere."

"Mayhap his work here is not yet done."

A man raced into the hall. "Milord! Lynx is upon the outer wall."

"Capture him! Kill him!"

The man whirled to obey and crashed into another of deWode's men. The second man careened into the hall. He held up a handful of severed rope and gasped, "Lynx! He has freed the men in the stable."

Before deWode could answer, a third man came to the door and called, "We sighted Lynx on the road leading away from the manor!"

"How can he be three places at once?" the baron muttered. His gaze riveted on Shaw. "Mayhap there is more than one Lynx at work to help Wykemarch." He pulled his blade and smiled ruthlessly. "There shall be one less now."

"Milord, I—" Only a gurgle bubbled from Shaw as he stared down at the knife sunk haft-deep into his chest.

Audra moaned and turned away as he fell to the floor. This had not been part of what she had planned. How many more would deWode kill to satisfy his greed for power?

DeWode laughed. "Do not look so unsettled, milady. He deserves no more. A man who has foresworn his sword-sworn oath once can never be trusted." He grasped her shoulders and spun her to face him. "Shaw will help you and Wykemarch no more."

"He was not our ally."

"You lie. You—"

"Milord!" The second man who had come into the great hall ran up to the table. "Shall we give chase?"

"You will never catch them," Audra said.

"Do you wish to see how wrong you are?" He grabbed a length of rope from the man. "Send everyone but those on the wall to catch Wyke-march and that night rider." Twisting Audra's arms behind her back, he shouted for another man to hold her.

She tried to escape them, but they were too strong. DeWode lashed her hands behind her back and pinched her chin between his fingers. Demonic determination burned in his blue eyes. "Milady, you shall see your husband's death within the hour."

"Don't be a fool, milord. You cannot beat Robert *and* Lynx."

"That we shall see."

He dragged her through the great hall. Calling for his horse, he tossed her onto it. She struggled to keep from falling off, her fingers straining to hold the back of the saddle. As he was about to mount, a bloody man lurched into the outer bailey, his crossbow bouncing along the ground on every step.

DeWode gripped the horse's halter and tugged it with him toward the man. Audra's fingertips arched over the back of the saddle. She rocked forward, losing it, as he stopped when the man cried, "We have been betrayed, milord!"

"Betrayed?"

"Ambushed no more than a mile down the road."

"Ambushed by whom?"

"Those who value the law!" came a shout from the top of the wall.

"Lynx!" cried Audra as she slid to grasp the board behind her.

DeWode pulled the crossbow from his man's hands. Aiming it at the silhouette on the wall, he drew back on the string to fire it. "You will die, Lynx!"

"I will?"

Audra gasped. Another silhouette of a night rider stood on the opposite wall. Beside her, deWode swore. "Which one of you is the real Lynx?"

"Look behind you for the truth," came the deep voice that sent a thrill through Audra. Looking over her shoulder, she watched Robert emerge from the shadows. He carried his broadsword.

A pang of fear cut through her. She wondered if he could heft it with enough speed to battle deWode. If his right arm was injured, he would not have the strength.

"Wykemarch," sneered deWode, "I have suffered enough of your games."

"No game, deWode. You want Lynx. You see him before you."

"You?"

Robert laughed. "I have apologized to Audra for believing that she would have to surrender to you a Bredonmere that I had destroyed. I should have known better. She needed no help from me to prove that you are the bastard of your birth." Leaning on his broadsword, so its tip bit into the dirt, he said in a darker voice, "Surrender, deWode. Your hold on Bredonmere is at an end."

"I shall—"

"It is over, as I told you before. If you do not believe me, ask Lord Norwell."

Audra could not silence her gasp as her neighbor appeared from the shadows to stand next to Robert.

"Norwell!" snarled deWode. "You said you would stay out of this."

"My men have answered the call of the rightful lord of Bredonmere to protect his lands." He took a lurching step forward and looked at Audra. "I will support the one who can hold here."

She smiled. Even when he was her ally, Norwell would never admit it. Not that it mattered, for he had come on Robert's request.

"So, as you can see, deWode, it is over," Robert said quietly. "Release milady, and I shall postpone your sentence of death as long as you never enter Bredonmere's lands again."

"Release her?" He laughed. "I have Audra now. If you want her back alive, do as I say."

"DeWode, I shall not—"

"You shall do exactly as I say, Wykemarch!" He raised the crossbow to press the point against her chest. "I know you think little of my skills, but you must admit that even I cannot miss her heart from here."

"Robert!" Audra cried. "Do not—"

Her voice was swallowed by a man's scream. In horror, she stared at deWode. He choked something and lurched forward. Blood gushed from his mouth in the seconds before he fell, an arrow in his back. The bolt in his crossbow slashed through her skirt, striking the saddle as he fell.

The horse screeched as the tip cut into it. Rearing, it raced across the outer bailey and over the drawbridge. She shrieked as she grasped the back of the saddle with her bound hands. If she fell, she could be killed. Each bounce threatened to loosen her grip.

Shouts came in front of her. The horse fled off the road as other horses tried to cut it off. It ran into the woods. Branches struck at her, tearing at her hair.

The terrified horse raced directly for a stone wall. Her fingers held convulsively to the saddle. As the wind whipped her hair into her eyes, she closed them.

An arm snaked around her waist at the same time she heard a voice shout, "Let go!"

She obeyed. As she was swept out of the saddle, she cried, "Robert!"

"Hold tight! We are going over this time!"

She could not do as he ordered. Her bound hands found nothing to hold. She tensed as the horse gathered its feet beneath them.

Up, up, up they went.

Just when she was sure they would touch the sky, they dropped to the ground.

Hard.

So hard, her teeth jarred together until she feared they would break. Her head snapped against Robert's chest. His arm tightened around her, holding her across his lap. He gave the horse a low order and drew back on the reins. It trembled as he brought it to a stop.

Or, at least, Audra thought it trembled. Mayhap all the shivers came from her. When her chin was tilted upward, she welcomed Robert's lips in the second before sobs burst from her. She wept against his tunic as he loosened the rope on her wrists.

"Hush, Audra," he whispered. "There is no need for tears. You are safe. DeWode will harm you no more."

"He is dead?" she asked although she knew he must be.

"He should have known better than to stand

between you and Eatton's bow." He turned his horse
back toward the manor house. "I think I shall teach
you to jump. I tire of rescuing you from runaway
horses."

She smiled weakly. "I doubt if I ever will learn to
ride well with my hands bound behind my back. Eatton was on the wall?"

"And Jerome played the other Lynx, as you well
know." He chuckled, then winced. "It was not an easy
climb from your room when I am much battered by
deWode's attack."

"Father Jerome mentioned that you had had a
plan. I am sorry if—"

"Nothing as inspired as yours. DeWode never
guessed he had been tricked by nothing but an illusion."

"We of Bredonmere do not readily relinquish
what is ours."

"Even *your* illusions?"

"My illusions?" she asked, unsure what he
meant.

"Your illusion that, for Bredonmere, you must
sacrifice your happiness." His hand slipped along her
with the caresses she had feared she never would
know again. "Leave it behind, milady, with deWode's
corpse as I shall leave behind my *delusion* that my
heart should hold a yearning for revenge instead of
my yearning to love you."

"You love me?" she whispered.

"More than anything." His soft laugh swirled
through her with the heat of the summer night when
he first had come to her bed.

She smiled. "And would you swear to that, Lord
Wykemarch?"

"On my most precious vow, milady."

"Your vow to—"

He interrupted her as they crossed the drawbridge. Beneath the cheers of her men-at-arms, who were herding deWode's men into a corner of the outer bailey, he said, "On the love I would offer you for a lifetime if you will accept it."

Epilogue

Anxious eyes met Robert's as he opened the door from the bedchamber. Smiling, he said, "The babe is here. A girl as pretty as her mother. Both do well."

Father Jerome clapped him on the shoulder and chuckled. "Congratulations, brother."

"Yes, congratulations, milord," Fleming added with a grin so wide it strained his cheeks. Beside him, Eatton just beamed with so much pride Robert would have thought the child was his.

Robert's smile vanished as he added, "Jerome, we would ask that you baptize her with our sister's and Audra's mother's names."

The priest nodded. "I would be honored."

Turning to go back into the bedchamber where he could hear Shirley clucking about like a broody hen, he gave the men another smile. Without them, this day might never have come. All of them had accomplished more than they thought possible to secure the future of Bredonmere. When the cold winter nights surrounded the keep, they had sat next to a warm hearth with a tankard of ale and laughed about their misadventures that had saved the manor. Even Fleming's successful journey through the frozen countryside to gain the king's favor on his lady's request had become amusing as the months passed.

Shirley mumbled something about errands as she herded Ida out of the room to give Robert a few moments with his wife. He went to the wide bed where the curtains were not pulled closed even on the coldest winter night and leaned forward to give his beloved wife a kiss.

Audra raised one hand to his face. Her other arm cradled the small bundle at her breast. "You need to get some rest, my love," she whispered. "You look as haggard as if you had ridden across the fief."

"Let me be the anxious father." He smiled and sat next to her, gazing down at the baby. "She is beautiful, Audra." Again he laughed. "I suspect Chelsea Sabina Bourne shall try my patience as you have."

"She shall be as stubborn as you are."

He gently brought her mouth toward his. "And I shall love her as I love you, milady, forever and always."

"Always."

In the seconds before his lips touched hers, bringing her the joy a lynx had brought to a lady upon the sweet song of the night winds, he whispered, "Always, milady."

Winner Take All by Terri Herrington

Logan Brisco is the smoothest, slickest, handsomest man ever to grace the small town of Serenity, Texas. Carny Sullivan is the only one who sees the con man behind that winning smile, and she vows to save the town from his clutches. But saving herself from the man who steals her heart is going to be the greatest challenge of all.

The Honeymoon by Elizabeth Bevarly

Newlyweds Nick and Natalie Brannon are wildly in love, starry-eyed about the future...and in for a rude awakening. Suddenly relocated from their midwestern hometown to San Juan, Puerto Rico, where Nick is posted with the U.S. Coast Guard, Natalie hopes for the best. But can true love survive the trials and tribulations of a not-so-perfect paradise?

Ride the Night Wind by Jo Ann Ferguson

As the only surviving member of a powerful family, Lady Audra fought to hold on to her vast manor lands against ruthless warlords. But from the moonlit moment when she encountered the mysterious masked outlaw known as Lynx, she was plunged into an even more desperate battle for the fate of her heart.

To Dream Again by Laura Lee Guhrke

Beautiful widow Mara Elliot had little time for shining promises or impractical dreams. But when dashing inventor Nathaniel Chase became her unwanted business partner, Mara found his optimism and reckless determination igniting a passion in her that suddenly put everything she treasured at risk.

Reckless Angel by Susan Kay Law

Angelina Winchester's dream led her to a new city, a new life, and a reckless bargain with Jeremiah Johnston, owner of the most notorious saloon in San Francisco. Falling in love was never part of their deal. But soon they would discover that the last thing they ever wanted was exactly what they needed most.

A Slender Thread by Lee Scofield

Once the center of Philadelphia's worst scandal, Jennifer Hastings was determined to rebuild her life as a schoolteacher in Kansas. She was touched when handsome and aloof Gil Prescott entrusted her with the care of his newborn son while he went to fight in the Civil War. When Gil's return unleashed a passion they had ignored for too long, they thought they had found happiness—until a man from Jennifer's past threatened to destroy it.

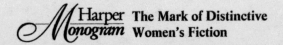